FORTUNE'S BRIDE

"Daevon?" Kayte commanded his attention with a whisper.

"Yes, sweet?"

"Am I a . . . harlot?"

Daevon threw back his head and laughed. "Kayte, do you know what a harlot is?"

"A woman who lives according to her own . . . physical desires. . . . She gives in to them."

"Do you want to give in to me?"

It was all she could do to nod.

"Then my love"—his mouth came teasingly close to hers—"you are just a healthy woman with natural desires. And exceptionally good taste in men!"

Avon Books are available at special quantity discounts for
bulk purchases for sales promotions, premiums, fund raising
or educational use. Special books, or book excerpts, can also
be created to fit specific needs.

For details write or telephone the office of the Director of
Special Markets, Avon Books, Dept. FP, 105 Madison Avenue,
New York, New York 10016, 212-481-5653.

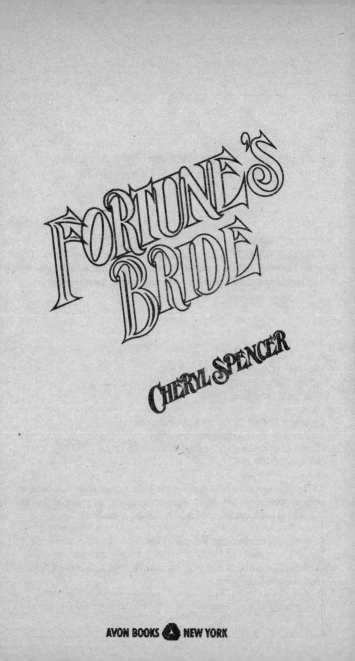

FORTUNE'S BRIDE

CHERYL SPENCER

AVON BOOKS ◆ NEW YORK

For my mother, Barbara Price Abraham,
who always knew I could do it.
I love you

AVON BOOKS
A division of
The Hearst Corporation
105 Madison Avenue
New York, New York 10016

Copyright © 1989 by Cheryl Lynn Purviance
Published by arrangement with the author
Library of Congress Catalog Card Number: 88-92113
ISBN: 0-380-75725-7

First Avon Books Printing: February 1989

AVON TRADEMARK REG. U.S. PAT. OFF. AND IN OTHER COUNTRIES, MARCA
REGISTRADA, HECHO EN U.S.A.

Printed in the U.S.A.

K-R   10   9   8   7   6   5   4   3   2   1

Chapter 1

The mist was receding. It had covered the ground through-out the early morning, disturbed by the arrival of mourners entering Newbury Cemetery. They had gathered about an open grave, the just-carved headstone ready to be set into place.

BELOVED FATHER. Beneath those carefully chiseled words was a name, JAMES EDWARD NEWELL, and the granite numerals which measured out the short span of his lifetime: 1763–1808. The long pile of earth next to the grave was freshly turned and black from the rain which had come across the sea before dawn. A scattering of late spring flowers adorned the casket, which had already been lowered into the ground. The group that huddled around the grave, weeping steadily, appeared in the strange morning mist as one body, shivering in the predawn cold.

Only one shrouded form seemed to have a life of its own. A young woman stood to one side of the headmarker, the delicate fingers of one white hand moving against the stone as if to send her warmth through it to the body lying in the plain wooden casket. Only her hand and the white-ness of her oval face showed from the black hooded cloak, a strand of dark hair tumbling onto her shoulder and curling over the swell of her breast. Her downcast eyes were red from crying, the lashes wet with tears, though now she was silent. She tried to focus on the slow, deep dirge of a voice which blessed her father's body and soul, and offered him up to heaven with a flurry of ornate and lengthy phrases.

Words, Kayte thought bitterly to herself. What good

will they do him now? Words can't free his soul of the
trouble that weighed heavily on him in life. She lifted her
head, trying to clear it by breathing in the chill air. It
seemed to help, and she peered about as if to savor the
comfort of others who shared her sorrow and grieved at the
passing of her father from their lives.

There was Adele, the spinster dressmaker, who had
once taken Kayte into her confidence and smiled slyly in
the hope she would one day marry James Newell. Kayte
wistfully recalled how many other young widows had
voiced that same hope. She could hardly fault them. James
Newell had been tall and dark-haired, with blue eyes that
sparkled and a smile that could melt a woman's heart.

Kayte returned her attention to those around her. Michael and Aileen had come with their daughter Amy, who
had brought flowers to James's sickbed. He had praised
her gifts like Midas enjoying a new golden toy. There
were Sean O'Connell and his cousin Daniel, the oddest
pair in the county. Sean was a short, scarlet-faced man of
property, his cousin Daniel a lean, gaunt man who sat
daily in his one black suit, working accounts in the front
office of the inn. They had been her father's favored
drinking companions. Kayte smiled, a rare thing for her
these past weeks, and recalled the nights that the three men
had spent singing drunken love songs under the bedroom
windows of several pretty widows in town. They had been
gentle, harmless men in their whiskey-soaked evenings,
drinking, singing . . . forgetting. She listened to the thud
of earth on her father's coffin and began to cry softly once
again.

The rays of the sun splintered against the gray dawn
sky, splaying soft color up into the horizon and over the
sea. Day came quickly then and dispersed the remaining
mist that lingered vainly about the mourners.

A black coach drove toward Newbury, barely slowing
its frantic pace over the rough roads. Inside, Daevon
Merrick, the earl of Merrick, folded his arms over his
chest and muttered several oaths. The coach was full of
dust and viciously uncomfortable, but he knew the business to come would be even more of an inconvenience.

He was going to Newbury to free himself of a bride.

The first order of business when he returned to London, he decided, would be to string up his solicitors one by one. Despite all the money he had lavished on them and all their collective degrees and supposed intelligence, they had not been able to break one simple betrothal contract.

That in itself was forgivable, but the fact that they had waited until two days ago to inform him of their failure was infuriating.

He had brought this trouble upon himself, he knew. He should have taken care of the business himself. But regrets were useless now.

Sinking back against the cushioned leather seat, Daevon Merrick tried to smooth out his thoughts.

At the age of thirteen he had been told that he was betrothed. At that age it seemed hardly a matter for serious thought and he nearly forgot about it before the year was out. As he attended the best English schools for young men and the most prestigious universities, he began to take control of the Merrick businesses. Through business he learned there wasn't a rival or a contract or even a heart that Daevon Merrick III couldn't break, either by sheer determination or by friendly persuasion. He assumed, naturally enough, that a betrothal would be no different. When the time came, he intended to turn the matter over to his solicitors, who would dispose of the burden quietly and efficiently. But since, as the years passed, no mention was made of it and no pressure was put upon him to fulfill the contract, he tended to forget it.

Then he fell in love with Monique. She was hardly more than a child at their first meeting, but soon grew into a young woman of remarkable beauty. He asked for her hand and promised her his name, his life. He presented Monique to his mother, Lady Anna Merrick, who took one sweeping look at the beautiful French girl and said simply to him, "But my dear, you are already betrothed. You can't possibly marry her."

Infuriated, he wrote to James Newell, the father of the girl to whom he was committed. With the impetuous fire of a young man in love, he pleaded for the contracts to be broken. He sent a hundred-pound note, promising more to come if his wishes were granted. The return letter said, simply, no.

Daevon asked Monique to wait until the contracts could be broken and she did, for two months. Then she married his business rival, Forrest Clay.

Daevon wanted only to escape. For the next year, he accompanied his shipping vessels to every imaginable port of trade, drank too heavily, bedded the most beautiful women, and refused to accept the idea that he might, indeed, be forced to marry some peasant girl he had never met. Knowing what he did of his deceased father, Daevon supposed that the contract had been made as reparation for some gambling debt or unpaid whorehouse bill, and he had no intention of making payment for vices in which he had not participated.

Instead of returning to DenMerrick House on the outskirts of London, Daevon settled in his own town house in Hounslow, where he could avoid reminders of the betrothal. To keep from seeing Monique he stopped attending London social functions. But he was not entirely idle.

With vicious determination, he set his solicitors to work. Then, for several years he threw himself into the business of compounding the Merrick holdings, all the while believing that the matter of the betrothal was being settled for him. It hardly seemed worth his attention.

Then, six months ago, he had been informed that the contracts were proving difficult to break. Still, Daevon saw the whole affair as nothing more than a bothersome thorn in his side. With time, he believed, any difficulty could be overcome. To speed the process, he sent his friend and assistant Henri Todd to Newbury for the purpose of finding some flaw in his intended, Kaytlene Newell—anything he could use as a basis for declaring her unfit.

Unfortunately for Daevon, Todd was as easily charmed as he was charming. Several weeks ago Daevon had returned home to find a pile of letters from Newbury. Henri had obviously been so besotted with women or whiskey that he tried to convince his friend and employer that Kaytlene Newell was a beauty—a tall, cat-eyed, witty angel.

Daevon imagined her in a very different light. She was a farm wench with callused hands, a grating voice, a rotund body, and very little brain. Her father had more than likely bested his own sire in some game of chance, and the contract promising Daevon to Kaytlene was payment. She and her father would hardly want to have the contract rescinded. God forbid that the marriage should take place, but as his wife, she would inherit a title, beautiful homes, and the promise of comfort and high social position for the remainder of her life.

Not to mention a husband who would hate her.

The carriage jolted, and Daevon realized how uncomfortable he had become. He shifted position, staring out at the approaching dawn.

This trip would have been unnecessary, he thought angrily, if his solicitors had done their job properly. Two days ago, while boarding his sloop, *Majestic*, he had been jabbed on the shoulder by a round, marble-eyed man in a stiff-necked suit who introduced himself as Jeffrey Marmel, solicitor. Stepping a little farther than arm's length away from Daevon, he had announced that James Newell was dying.

"And?" Daevon had replied angrily.

"I—" The man swallowed convulsively. "I regret to inform you, sir, that while we have put extensive time and money into this venture, we have"—another swallow—"failed to perform the task which you requested."

Daevon had had to clench his fists to keep from flattening the bastard onto the pier. While Mr. Marmel babbled on about legalities and codes of ethics, Daevon ordered his trunks removed from the sloop and hired a coach. He hadn't changed or bathed or slept since then and was eager to finish his business so that he could find an inn with hot baths, good brandy, and at least one willing kitchen wench. He was furious at having been inconvenienced like this, and those comforts would make up for it, at least somewhat.

The carriage slowed and stopped. Daevon, hearing the driver shout to someone at the side of the road, leaned forward to snap open his door.

"What is it, Burns?" he demanded. With cold disinterest he noted the peasant standing a few yards away.

The driver twisted in his seat. "Just askin' the way ta Newell's place, sir," he replied.

With a slight narrowing of his eyes, Daevon saw the few scattered dwellings ahead which marked the town of Newbury.

"And?"

"Well, sir," Burns answered slowly, scratching at the dark stubble on his chin, "I don't rightly know. Says James Newell won't be ta home."

Daevon finally looked at the young man who stood twisting a black cap in nervous hands. "Where will we find James Newell, then?" he demanded impatiently.

The boy swallowed and wiped dust and sweat from his forehead. "Well, sir, I . . . well they say he's . . . he's gone, sir."

"Gone?" Daevon raised a brow. "Gone where?"

The boy rolled his eyes heavenward.

Daevon frowned and glanced in the same direction. When he realized what the boy meant, he glared back. "Do you mean to say—"

"He's gone, sir. Last night, they say."

"He's dead?" Daevon shouted as if it were the boy's fault.

"They're buryin' him this morning."

"Burns!"

"Yes, sir?"

"Move this coach!"

The door snapped shut again, and as the thunderous sound of hooves resumed, Daevon spat out a string of vicious curses. Sweet Jesus, how could the man have died?

As the coach barrelled down the narrow roads of Newbury, the huge gray animals who pulled it tore at the ground as if they might consume it entirely. Speculative villagers peered from homes and shop windows to see the phantom-gray horses and their burden. As the carriage flew past, wheels spinning so quickly that the wooden spokes disappeared into a steady whir, the villagers whispered short prayers. Here was the devil, they said, come to fight for the soul of James Newell, gone only this past night.

The carriage slowed and stopped at the ancient gate of the cemetery, its hand-laid rock walls remaining solid against the intrusion of wind and storm-driven waves. The horses pawed nervously, eager to continue their run though their coats already glistened with foamy sweat.

Daevon Adam Merrick III stepped from the coach, angrily muttered orders to Burns, and strode toward the cemetery before the carriage pulled away at a saner pace. He pushed open the solid gates and entered the graveyard. He scowled, his gray eyes burning with anger.

Upon hearing the soft hymn, breathy and more than a little off key, that came through the trees from the gravesite, he slowed. Irony curled the tight line of his lips when he realized how long it had been since he had witnessed a religious service of any kind. He kept a good distance from the mourners, his figure blending into the dense trees beyond the clearing where James Newell was being laid to rest.

Silently Daevon cursed. A few hours, a few short hours more, and he could have spoken to Newell himself, reasoned with the man to free him of the contract. That damnable contract! Daevon's fist slammed against the ivy-crusted bark of a tree.

Now Newell was dead. And because Daevon had failed to take care of the contracts himself, there was no bargaining to be done. He was a Merrick and sworn to uphold the word of his family. Disgustedly, he decided that hanging would be much too easy a death for his solicitors. They should be drawn and quartered as well, and he should be shot for a fool.

The words of the letters Daevon had received from Henri Todd came back into his thoughts as he looked for Kaytlene Newell. He expected to find yet another large-breasted farm wench, a red-mouthed, wide-hipped girl whose experience with men was as extensive as her skill milking cows. That sort of "beauty" would easily catch Todd's eye.

Glancing over the faces of the mourners, searching for her, he picked out the young woman who stood by the grave receiving condolences with steady hands and dry

eyes. His thoughts scattered. His blood thundered. Dear
God, he thought, that couldn't possibly be . . .

Kaytlene had pushed back her hood and opened her
cape, throwing it over her shoulders. Beneath, she wore a
simple gown of black crepe that fastened from waist to
neck with tiny pearl buttons. The skirt fell softly over her
hips and flared over her stiff petticoats, flowing like water
around her at the slightest move.

Daevon was certain she was a vision churned up by his
exhausted mind after his hasty journey. But she refused to
disappear beneath the hard scrutiny of his glare. She was
real, this tall, slender young woman dressed all in black.
Her hair, which curled down her back, was brown and
satiny, gleaming in the brightening dawn light.

Daevon kept silent, unable to move. She was beautiful,
he would grant her that. But beautiful faces hid treacherous hearts. Greed and lust could be tucked into a beautiful
body, and venom was often spread by a smile as easily as
a bite. Her beauty did nothing to dispel his doubts.

As the sun and heat rose, Daevon thought Kaytlene
looked itchy and uncomfortable beneath her heavy woolen
cape. Time moved slow and dreamlike while the last of the
mourners pressed their hands to hers and muttered uneasy
condolences.

Daevon watched wordlessly while the black cloud of
mourners faded away. He tried to discern the finer details
of Kaytlene's face, but now her back was turned to him,
and he was left to stare appreciatively at the delicate curve
of her shoulders and hips. Now there were only two men
remaining, and the girl threw her arms around each of
them in turn, making a sound that contained both laughter
and tears.

"How are you, lass?" one of the men asked softly.

"I'll be fine, Daniel," she replied, "but I feel so . . .
alone."

"You're strong," he assured her. "Time will heal your
pain. And in the meanwhile, we'll be here for you."

Kayte smiled in an effort to keep from crying.

"Kaytlene," the short, round man said uneasily, "will
you come to the White Doe and honor us? We're having a
little wake of our own, you know."

She laughed, and her voice rained like icy fire over Daevon.

"He would have liked that, Sean," she replied softly, "but I want to be alone . . . with him. To say goodbye."

"Aye, lass." He sounded disappointed.

"But remember you promised to have me for supper." She lifted his now-smiling face with a fingertip under his chin. "I shall look forward to it."

"Oh, yes. So happy you accepted. There won't be . . . much time for us to spend together now. It's precious. Precious."

Kaytlene grasped the second man's hand and they stood for a moment in silence, unwilling to separate and comfortable together, even in sorrow.

Daevon lowered his eyes, feeling oddly that he had no right to intrude on this girl's life. As the men moved out of the clearing, he was content to watch her, momentarily forgetting why he had come. Her back still to him, she walked again to the grave and fell suddenly, unexpectedly to her knees, her head dropping forward as if all the exhaustion she had suffered she had saved for this moment of solitude. A tremor ran through her body and as she began to sob, Daevon's heart twisted with pain. Her body bent forward and her white fingers dug into the earth that covered her father's grave.

"Papa," she moaned, "Papa, why did you have to leave me?" As her body heaved with weeping, Daevon silently came out into the clearing, drawn by a powerful urge to pull her into his arms and kiss away her sorrow.

God, he thought, I must be losing my mind. He ran his hands through his unruly black hair and straightened his waistcoat. The crinkle of the stiff, folded documents in his pocket, which he had demanded from the solicitor, now recalled him to his purpose. He frowned, reminding himself that this trembling girl might be guilty of the same calculating greed as her father. He watched as she fell fully, breathlessly across the grave, her black skirts shifting to reveal the fine curves of her ankles and small, slippered feet.

*   *   *

Kaytlene finally allowed herself to release the depths of her anguish. She had tried to be strong. And brave. She had promised her father she would be both.

But now, alone with him, she let down the strong barriers she had built and let her heart speak. Tears came, choking her. She hadn't had much rest or food for the past days as her father lay dying. She really didn't care if she continued to live. Not now. Not with the knowledge that she was the property of a man she had never met.

His name she knew—it had been part of her life since her eighteenth birthday, when her father had first told her about her betrothal. Daevon Adam Merrick. For nearly four years she had feared him, hated him, wondered about him.

He had killed her father. Or, more plainly, the past had killed him. And somehow Daevon Merrick was a part of that past.

Long ago, her mother, Patrice Newell, had secretly slipped away from Newbury with her lover, leaving her husband, James, and their infant daughter. That act of cruelty had shattered James's heart and led him to drink.

He took to whiskey like a baby to milk, soothing his wounds and forgetting the treachery of the woman he loved. More's the pity, Kayte thought now, but James Newell had loved his wife until the day he died. When he drank, he talked. Though he never betrayed the details of his secrets, there were two names he spoke with vehement emotion.

The first was Daevon Merrick. James had cursed him, spat out the man's name as if it were refuse on his tongue. A breath later, he had been lost in the memory of Patrice. In most of his drunken moods he had recalled her fondly. Other times he had cursed her as harshly as he cursed Merrick.

In his lucid moments, James was as gentle and loving a man as any who lived. But whenever Kayte tried to glean more information about the relationship between her mother and Daevon Merrick, there was only silence followed by another drinking binge. By the time she was a young woman, she had learned that it was useless to ask. Even drunk, he would not reveal the truth.

On Kayte's eighteenth birthday, with the courage half a bottle of whiskey provided, James told his daughter that she was betrothed to Daevon Merrick, the name he had often spoken so harshly. Though she pleaded and sobbed and made every protest imaginable, James would say only that it was for the best, that she would be cared for and pampered and secure.

"Be strong, Kayte," he said. "There are reasons but I cannot explain them now. You will know someday, I promise."

Since then, he had been a recluse, so many years of whiskey finally taking their toll on his body and mind. He was weak and sickly a great deal of the time, and Kaytlene had spent the last two years nursing him, loving him, and watching him die. Two weeks before his death, James had given his daughter specific instructions on the preparations she should make for her approaching marriage. He had been seated in his favorite chair before the fire in their cottage, Kayte sitting on the floor at his feet. She listened, staring intently into the flames until he finished.

"He hurt you," she interjected suddenly. "Somehow he hurt you. He took my mother away, didn't he? Didn't he!" She knelt by her father, grasping one of his hands in hers, desperately wanting the truth. "I can't marry such a man," she pleaded.

"No, Kayte," James murmured. "He did nothing to me. Not this one. Believe me. I would not ask you . . . to marry someone who could do that."

"Then why? Won't you tell me, Papa? Please?"

He seemed to consider, then sighed. "I cannot, Kayte. I must give you . . . this chance to be happy. Trust me."

She curled herself at his feet, wondering if his mind was muddled after so many years of whiskey and sorrow. "I do trust you, Papa. I do."

"And you must promise me . . . promise me you will do as I've asked, Kayte."

She promised.

And now, in the bright light of early morning, her fists full of the black earth that finally separated father and daughter, she was terrified of that promise. Or more correctly, of the man the promise involved.

Kayte was certain that somehow the Merricks had hurt her father, and the betrothal was their way of making up for whatever damage they had done. It was the only explanation that made any sense. After all, she had nothing of value to offer in a marriage.

And she was not so naive as to believe her marriage could be a happy one. Aristocrats were well known for their infidelity. Newbury was full of young girls who made their wages by working in the summer homes of important lords along the coast. They were constantly chattering about lord so-and-so's latest lover, who lived in some London town house while his wife was banished to the country. Wives served their purposes as hostesses, mothers, showpieces. They were expected to be perfect models of propriety, and did it matter if they were neglected by husbands who took pleasure elsewhere? Yet Kayte had dreamed of having a husband who loved her as James Newell had loved her mother. That kind of affection could hardly come from an arranged marriage.

Remembering her promise to follow her father's wishes, Kayte tried to resign herself to such a marriage. She could make it bearable, she thought. After all, she could travel and read . . . and perhaps there would be a child to love . . .

No, she told herself sternly. She would marry, but there would be no child. She couldn't—

A faint rustle snagged her attention, and Kaytlene turned, incensed to find that her privacy had been violated. She rose to her feet, one hand on her father's headstone for support, and faced the most imposing figure of a man she had ever seen.

"How dare you!" she choked out, embarrassed because a stranger had been watching her.

He folded his arms across his chest, and his eyes narrowed. There was an odd intensity in the way he studied her.

He was well over six feet in height with black, windblown hair and tired eyes, gray like the sky in the throes of a storm. He had a darkly tanned face and wide, square shoulders. The first few buttons of his collar were unfastened, exposing hard, smooth dark flesh beneath the starched

ruffle. Her gaze trailed unwittingly downward. When he
politely cleared his throat, she realized she had been staring with impolite intensity at his thighs and the tight, flat
fit of his waistcoat.

She raised lashes of deep brown, drenched to black by
her tears, and met his eyes. She knew she was blushing—
the heat in her cheeks told her—but he acted as if he had
not noticed.

"I apologize for having disturbed your solitude," Daevon
said. He was upset by her obvious scrutiny, by the way her
gaze lingered lower than was seemly in a young lady of
good character. So she had been with a man, he decided
impulsively despite Henri Todd's belief that Kaytlene Newell was pure and untouched.

Kayte was more than a little angry at the man's cold
arrogance and lack of manners. "I accept your apology.
Now leave me at once."

"I wasn't aware that you had the right to order a man
from public property."

Disdainful, Kayte thought. Unfeeling. Bloody aristocrat! The thought nearly stopped her heart. Oh, God, no—

"It's God's ground, not mine, sir," she retorted.

Daevon nearly forgot his anger at having been so
inconvenienced by this girl and her father's untimely death.
Even the tired pallor of her skin and the swollen red flesh
beneath her eyes could not disguise her natural loveliness.

She shifted her eyes away from his. "I don't know you,
sir. And this is—"

"Your father's burial morning, I know. Please forgive
me, Miss Newell. You must think me quite the rogue."
He moved away, though he was unable to escape her eyes.
When he turned again, she was standing behind the gravestone, her expression weary and questioning. He saw her
bite her lower lip, and there was anxiety in her eyes. A
disturbed silence fell between them.

"Did you know my father, sir?" she asked finally.

She was exquisite, he thought, a strange and marvelous
discovery to make in such an insignificant village. He
wondered, with dismay, how many of the local farmboys
had taken their pleasure with her in some empty hayloft.
The thought angered him, tensing the muscles of his jaw

into a tight line. This girl was to be his wife. He tried with
little success to convince himself that it was the terms of
the betrothal that had aroused his righteous anger and not
an attraction to her.

"No," he replied at last. "I never met your father, Miss
Newell." He thought again of the documents in his breast
pocket.

"Then why are you here?"

"My business is with you."

"Me?" Her dark brows rose quizzically. "I have never
met you, sir. You are one of my father's old friends,
perhaps? I didn't know whom to contact when—" She was
pale, trembling. Her voice faltered, and she feared she
already knew who this stranger was. That fear, com-
pounded by her father's death, was unnerving her completely.

Daevon saw no reason to hesitate in telling her, but for a
moment he did. Finally, after taking a long breath, he
said, "Your servant, Miss Newell. I am Daevon Adam
Merrick, earl of Merrick."

Kaytlene stumbled back and the earl came forward,
thinking she was about to faint.

"Don't!" she screamed. Her huge amber eyes were
terrified, he realized. Tortured.

"How dare you?" she spat. "How dare you come to
destroy the sanctity of my father's grave with your coldhearted arrogance!" Here was a man who had not had the
decency to come to her until her father was dead. Until she
was weak, alone, helpless, and distraught.

Daevon knew her anger was justified, and the tears that
began to course down her pale face again made him feel a
fool. "Miss Newell—"

"Bastard! Come to claim your dutiful bride as she
weeps over the grave, still warm from his body!" A
tremor caught in her throat. Daevon's large hands caught
hers as she lunged at him, sobbing and murderous.

In that moment he believed she was capable of killing
him, for whatever her reasons. Had she been armed with a
pistol instead of just the pain, deep and unmistakable, in
her amber eyes, he would now be dead.

She struggled against him, her cloak falling free to
reveal the white flesh of her neck. Daevon pulled her

tightly against him, pinning her arms under his own and pulling her face up to look into his, one hand against the flat of her back and the other tangled in the thick mass of brown curls. She was silent as his eyes searched hers for some tangible explanation for her outburst. She was exhausted. And angry. And . . . afraid.

She struggled more weakly against the trap of his arms, her body pressed reluctantly against his. She hated the feel of his arms around her. But even more sharply, she felt the weight of weariness, hunger, and grief. Her body was like lead. She wanted to sleep . . .

She seemed to melt, her coppery eyes rolling back as the lids closed over them.

"Hate you," she whispered. "Hate you . . ."

The earl took his arm from around her waist and slid it down to her knees, pulling her up against him. She tossed her head toward his chest, murmuring something incoherent. Drops of sweat stood out on the pale flesh of her face, and Daevon regretted having chosen such a vulnerable time to approach her.

The tall black figure who strode from Newbury Cemetery with a woman in his arms gathered every eye to himself. The devil, the villagers whispered, brazen enough to walk into the street with an innocent girl in his vile arms. No one was willing to meet his steady gray eyes or challenge his boldness as he held the limp body of Kaytlene Newell to his chest.

His figure in the gaping doorway of the White Doe inn brought a quick end to the hum of gossip and the metallic clang of homemade instruments celebrating James Newell's return to his maker. Glasses raised in toasts to parched, rough lips paused in midmotion, lips lingering in the sweet, bitter doses of whiskey.

Daevon searched the crowd, his eyes hard against the patrons' questioning gazes.

"Innkeeper!" he shouted. The demand cut through their patrons' stupor and they gulped down their drinks in sudden apprehension. The earl continued inside, undaunted by the fact that he had interrupted their wake.

"Miss Newell requires a room," he bellowed, "and a physician, if you please. And quickly!"

The gaunt, ashen-faced man behind the wooden bar came to life. "Meg!" He motioned to a barmaid wiping glasses at the end of the counter. "Take Miss Newell to the empty room."

When the frail redhead refused to move, her eyes riveted fearfully on Merrick's dark figure, the barkeep slapped her behind and sent her flying off with a squeal like a suckling pig in search of a full belly.

Masculine laughter escaped from whiskey-burned throats, easing the tension. Daevon started up the stairs which twisted to his left, following the quick steps of the maid. The movement of her hips, he noted derisively, was an undisguised invitation. He wondered how many times she had already climbed these stairs, an eager young pup following behind with a leer of desire on his lips.

She scurried down the narrow hall, throwing open the door of the last room. As Merrick swung Kaytlene sidelong and entered the nearly unfurnished chamber, he barked at the maid to find water and a clean cloth, if those might be acquired in such a hellhole, and to come quickly with a doctor.

"Yes, sir." She gulped in trepidation at his dark fury and huge size, so near to her. She would have feared for the still figure he held as well, had she a split second in which to think clearly. Instead she was off and down the stairs at a rabbit's pace, to find the requested items under fear of her life.

Kaytlene stirred, her hand reaching up to find the indistinguishable form that hovered dark and frightening above her. It drew her out of the heavy sleeplike cloud that clutched at the very corners of her mind and twisted like a maniacal fire in her belly. She moaned when her fingers reached it, moaned Merrick's name like a plea or a damning oath, he couldn't tell which as her white fingers trembled against his lips.

The earl of Merrick stood staunch and straight next to the tiny bed. It was low to the floor and the crude bag of rushes upon it was clean but well trampled down. The cot was just large enough for two to lie in if they faced each other or were entwined in the throes of . . . He lowered his head, suddenly disturbed by a thought that would not have affected him an hour ago, before he'd held her in his arms.

When she groaned, as if to protest the tight, protective hold of her body against his, her eyes slid partly open, holding him in a half-lidded golden stare. She frowned, her brow wrinkling the well-shaped nose, the full pink mouth. When her fingers brushed lightly over the hard line of his lips, Daevon allowed an impulse to take control of him and drew her smallest finger into the hot, moist cavern of his mouth, his tongue tasting the sweetness of her for the first time. He would have preferred to be in his own bedchamber, in the dark solitude of his town house, so that the touch could continue to her palm, her throat, her flushed mouth. The desire for a woman had never risen so rapidly and so hot within him, unfurling like fire in his loins. At least she would fill that need in his life, he thought derisively. It was easy enough to give his body without endangering his heart.

He placed Kaytlene hesitantly upon the rushes as voices, low and speculative, moved toward the open doorway and three faces peered in. Merrick recognized two of the men as those who had lingered with Kaytlene near her father's gravesite, the two she had held and kissed so lovingly.

"What are you staring at like a pack of hungry children?" he demanded, his voice filling the room with an angry tremor. As it receded the group entered, their steps slow and measured, as if they feared crossing an invisible boundary that would heighten the anger of the dark aristocrat.

"What in the name of all that's holy are you waiting for?" Daevon bellowed at the physician, who stepped forward like a frightened virgin approaching her marriage bed.

"Yes, your lordship. Right away." The man knelt down to concentrate his attention on the patient. "Meg!" the doctor called to the serving girl who cowered in the hall, hoping for and dreading another glimpse of the devil whose eyes swept over her as she came in. "Get a blanket."

Before she could move, Daevon's icy voice stopped her with a word. With a press of his thumb he unclasped the intricately detailed collar of his cloak and drew it off his shoulders, then dropped to one knee and smothered

Kaytlene's body in the cloak's soft folds. The physician was holding his fingers against her inner wrist when she sucked in a sudden breath and began struggling to breathe. Without hesitation, Daevon's rough hands deftly loosed the tiny pearl buttons at her throat, pulling the stiff crepe away and pushing the smooth hair from her face.

Behind him, Sean wrung his puffy hands and cleared his throat, a sound that reminded Daevon of the peculiar call of a bird he often heard in the fields of his childhood home.

"Sir," Sean said firmly but with a tinge of fear.

Merrick stood and turned, aware of Sean's shocked, gaping mouth. Daniel showed no emotion, standing silent in the filmy yellow light emitted by a tiny, cloth-covered window.

"Yes?" Daevon replied cooly.

"You are a member of Miss Newell's family? A cousin, perhaps?"

"Neither relation nor friend, Mr. . . ."

"Sean O'Connell, sir. If you're neither friend nor family, then you show her a great deal of disrespect by taking liberties with her in such a condition."

Daevon savored the memory of Kaytlene's warm throat beneath his hands, the flutter of her breath against his palms.

"I have no intention of taking wrongful advantage of your young lady in any condition, sir." He bit hard on the last words, angered by the fleeting image of her pain and tears, both of which he had inspired with his presence.

"Then why are you here in Newbury? We heard downstairs from your driver that you came in quite a hurry. And why should your first attentions be paid to a lady whom you do not know?" O'Connell seemed to gain more confidence with each word, but only when he saw that the earl kept his place and showed no anger.

"I came to speak to James Newell after my courier brought me the news of his illness," said Daevon. "The contract that I needed to discuss with him also concerns his daughter, so I felt it was appropriate to speak to Miss Newell on the matter."

"You've chosen a poor time," the tall, slim man finally spoke up.

Daevon was growing bored with their attempts to recognize social niceties. "You knew her father?" he demanded.

"Aye." Sean O'Connell nodded. "My Elizabeth helped Kaytlene into this world." His tone turned sad. "And she was nigh to a mother to the child after—"

"After?" Daevon's brows rose. The two men seemed uncomfortable with his desire to know.

"Kaytlene's mother left James when Kayte was hardly a year old," said Sean.

"I see. And when was she born?"

"In 1786."

"The month?"

"October, your lordship. All Hallow's Eve."

"And her parents? They were wed in the spring of 1783, were they not? In Newbury?"

"Just so, my lord."

Daevon nodded. This matter of dates and places confirmed what he had already been told. He had hoped to find some error in one set of facts or the other, thinking that perhaps in some disparity he would see the true reason for the contractual bond that held him to the daughter of James Newell.

"Just so," he repeated. "Did you know that your Kayte was betrothed?"

The expressions on their faces told him yes, they had.

"To me? The earl of Merrick?"

"No, your lordship. That, at least, comes as quite a shock."

"Miss Newell is my bride-to-be. Knowing of her love for her father, I had no great desire to separate them. I hastened to reach her, to be a comfort to her during her father's last hours. I was, as you see, too late. She was distraught when I found her."

Sean O'Connell scanned Daevon's face. "It seems an odd circumstance," he finally said hesitantly.

"I have been away a great deal over the past few years. I was not aware that James was ill until two days ago. I left immediately, but didn't reach Newbury until after the burial."

"And is it her will to agree to the betrothal?"

Daevon stiffened at the suggestion Sean O'Connell was making. As a woman, Kaytlene Newell had little choice but to conform to the contract her father had signed. But it was obvious that the O'Connell clan had no intention of allowing her to be dragged off unwillingly.

"I would certainly not contrive to take Miss Newell if it is not her wish. I see you don't trust my word." Daevon reached into the inner pocket of his coat and drew out a well-worn parcel of documents. He turned them over to Sean.

"Please read over these. I won't make enemies of Miss Newell's friends. You seem to care about her and I'm sure that if you are satisfied as to my intentions, she will be also." He bowed his head slightly to them both, then turned back toward the bed.

"She rests easy, my lord," the physician informed him. "It has been difficult for her, these past weeks."

"That I can see in her face," Daevon answered softly.

"And through it all, she has been the brightest angel in our little village." Sean's tone was as gentle as his voice.

"That, also," Merrick said softly, "I can see."

"You can be sure you've chosen a wife beyond price." Sean O'Connell peered appreciatively at her sleeping form, his voice full of the emotion of memories. "Hers is the sweetest voice, the softest step, the loveliest face in our lives."

Daevon wondered idly whether Miss Newell had grown accustomed to hearing men extol her virtues. "Take care of her," he said at last. "She's alone now and if any harm comes to her, the one who offends her will answer to me."

Sean O'Connell nodded to his cousin and they shared a look of approval at Daevon's declaration of responsibility for their Kayte.

"Will you see her to better lodging, Mr. O'Connell?" Daevon turned to see the man stepping toward him, one hand outstretched.

"Sean, sir, and I'll see her to my home when she's able."

Daevon clasped Sean's hand in his own. "I'm in your

debt, Sean. I should like to see Miss Newell once she's had a chance to recover."

"Share supper with us, then."

Daevon considered, his brow darkening. "I have important matters to see to at home." He wasn't eager to get on with this business, though he knew it was necessary.

"Please, your lordship, don't deprive us of one last evening with our Kayte."

When Daevon was still not wholly convinced, Sean O'Connell made a more direct attempt to sway him. "It would allow Kayte to get accustomed to her new . . . life. And to make arrangements. Surely in her state we should not rush her into a hasty decision."

Daevon turned back toward the girl. She breathed so lightly that it was nearly no breath at all. Her face had regained most of its natural color now, and it was obvious that she preferred sunshine to sitting in a corner with some needlework, as young ladies were expected to do. Her hands now grasped the edge of his dark cloak, her fingers pale against the black. Unconsciously, he allowed a deep sigh to escape his throat.

"We shall do it your way, Sean," he said. "For her sake."

Chapter 2

A long, dry afternoon passed in Newbury, sucking the moisture left by the night's rain from the ground, leaving only dust behind. There was little activity since it was Sunday, and Daevon Merrick went about his business with little interruption and much speculation.

He had gone reluctantly from the dank little chamber where Kaytlene Newell lay sleeping, his mind full of unanswered—and perhaps unanswerable—questions.

It was possible that Kaytlene Newell was an innocent victim in this confused tangle of oaths and contracts—or was she? If her father had kept as isolated as Daevon suspected, then she had been Newell's only real influence. Daevon's solicitors had written James Newell countless queries, threats, and even offers of small fortunes in order to have this betrothal dissolved. All had been refused. Had the man kept them a secret from his only child as well, or had she been his willing accomplice, urging her father to keep strong in his resolve to assure her a well-padded future? Daevon could almost see her bright golden eyes brimming with tears as she begged her father to keep the contract so that she might not be destitute after his death. Her hair softly gleaming, her hands trembling—how could any man refuse her, least of all her own father?

"Damnation!" Daevon swore. How could he have allowed those lovely eyes to dig beneath his skin and begin slicing at his own resolve? If she was as guilty as he believed her to be, he would discover it before they were forced to marry. He began to wonder if it had been wise to come to Newbury at all.

His mother would have scolded him soundly for that thought.

"No more of your spies," she would have said. "I won't have you sending off Henri Todd to do your work for you. Kaytlene Newell is betrothed to the earl of Merrick, and it would be an insult if he did not go to her himself. I won't have you disgracing the girl."

And she would have been right, he thought. He was here because the responsibility of Kaytlene Newell's care now fell to him. He would do the right thing, out of loyalty to his family's name and to appease his mother's social sensibilities.

Daevon's angry stomping down the steps into the inn's pub once again drew a bevy of wide-eyed stares, though the activity did not cease. Most of the patrons had been liberally partaking of the open flasks and jugs before them and cared little for the devil and his doings. Daevon stood on the last wooden rise, his shoulders well defined by his black coat, the hard muscles tensed as he searched the faces. At the doorway to the kitchen he noticed with grim amusement that the barmaid still regarded him with a mixture of dread and desire that he had seen many times before. A smile of masculine arrogance passed quickly over his lips, and she fled to the kitchen.

Daevon found his driver seated against the wall beneath the stairway. The man's shirt was loosened, and the dust from the streets had mixed with sweat to run black and grimy along the folds of his neck.

"Have you any intention of honoring your agreement with me, Mr. Burns?" he demanded. "I hired you with the stipulation that you remain sober enough to drive. Shall I return to your employer with no silver in payment and no sign of you?"

Michael Burns stood, bowing shakily toward the earl. His eyes were watery and red-rimmed, as though he had been consuming fire instead of whiskey. "Yes . . . sir . . . your lordship." His voice was slurred.

"Have you seen to some lodging?"

"There's nothin' in the village but this inn." Burns made a sweeping gesture that threw him off balance toward Daevon, who forced him back against the wall.

Burns reacted to the motion with a drunken grin.

"Then we shall fend for ourselves this evening," said the earl. "I shall expect you at Newell's at daybreak for the trip back to London. And get a bath and some proper clothes by that time. I won't have you before my lady looking like the drunken sot you are."

Daevon was out of the inn before Burns was able to summon a coherent reply.

"My lady." Daevon heard himself say the words and wondered whether he was losing his grip on reality. Women, God curse them, were not worthy of that title of respect. Their eyes smiled while their mouths spoke pretty half truths to trip a man into his own grave. They were sweet-smelling, soft-bodied demons, the best of whom clutched as violently at a man's reason as they did his flesh once they had seduced him into their treachery-lined beds.

Daevon muttered a string of expletives as he made his way through the dust-bathed street to the stable where his favorite pair of grays were enjoying a hot mash. Upon sighting their lord and master, they snorted into their dinner pails but kept their noses buried in the food.

"Greedy sots," Daevon said softly. "You're more concerned with a full belly than anything else I might offer you."

The larger of the two animals stiffened its velvety ears, pulled away from the mash, and threw its head over the half door, searching along Daevon's coat with its nose. Daevon laughed.

"So, changed your mind, have you?" He pulled two sticky lumps of sugar from his pocket and offered one to each animal.

"Can I help you, sir?" A young man's voice caused Daevon to glance around. He was surprised to find a blond boy of about thirteen pushing a lock of hair behind his ear. At Daevon's fierce frown, the boy stepped back.

"Did I frighten you, my lad?" Daevon attempted to befriend the boy with an easy smile.

"You're . . . you're his lordship, the . . . earl."

"Yes? And?"

"They call you . . . are you truly the devil, sir?"

"Do you think it proper that the devil should appear on a Sunday?"

"I think, sir, that if you truly are the devil, you wouldn't give a care to the day."

Daevon suppressed a laugh that rumbled deep in his chest. "You're clever, my lad. Are you the blacksmith's son?"

"Apprentice, my lord." The boy bowed. "And a good one, if you have need." His pale, freckled nose crinkled as he smiled.

"I won't forget. Now, will you get me a horse? I must ride a little this afternoon, on business."

"Yes, your lordship. Choose yourself." The boy led Daevon farther down the rows of stalls, pausing at the last ones. Several animals, all tall and bright-eyed, stamped and pawed in their places.

"You keep fine animals, lad," Daevon said, and the boy beamed.

"Justin," he replied proudly, offering his hand to the tall stranger, who accepted his show of friendship.

"A very fine stable, Justin." His eye was caught by a muscular, wild-eyed bay. "I shall take this one out, I think."

"That's Cyclops, sir. He needs a heavy hand, but can ride for a week without rest or water."

"I shall need him just for the day."

"You can wait out in the yard, sir, while I get him ready."

Daevon nodded and watched the boy eagerly attack his job. Once in the bright light outside the stables, Daevon removed his jacket and waistcoat and checked the gold timepiece in his pocket. He had ample hours in which to complete his business and perhaps bathe and change clothes before he was expected at Sean O'Connell's house.

He wandered to a fence corner, propping one elbow on a post, and admired the gait of a white mare a few lengths away. Her mane and tail were a silvery gray, her eyes large and brown.

"That's Circe," Justin called as he led Cyclops into the close-cropped grass yard. Daevon took the reins and swung up onto the horse's back with a squeak of freshly oiled leather.

"Circe? The sorceress?"

"Yes, my lord. Kayte named her. She's fond of the Greek legends."

"Oh?" Daevon tossed his coat to the boy.

"Do you know Kayte?" Justin asked.

Daevon looked again at the white animal. Circe. The spell-weaver. How appropriate a name for Kayte herself. "I met her this morning," he replied. "You know her well?"

"Yes, sir. She comes here in the afternoon after her lessons. We ride together."

Daevon grimly recalled the hundred-pound note he had sent to James Newell so long ago. Newell must have used the money to hire a teacher for his daughter to prepare her for life in London society. Very generous of him.

"Oh? Is she being tutored?"

"No. She teaches the children in the village farms, my lord. After the school in Newbury closes. She's easy to look at, but a hard taskmaster," he said with a sheepish grin.

Daevon raised a surprised brow. "How much did she pay for the animal?" He nodded toward Circe.

"Five pounds, my lord," Justin replied. "As a filly."

"And she pays for board and stall?"

"Oh, no, my lord. She works here for it. If I do say, she's almost as strong as I."

Daevon laughed again.

"A gentleman pays for the feed and stall now, sir."

"Oh?" That was an interesting arrangement. Had Kaytlene Newell decided that mucking out stalls was too harsh for her delicate sensibilities and traded it for—

"She recently sold Circe."

"Sold?"

"Yes, sir. To Mr. Harkins in the village."

"But why?"

"Now her father's gone, sir, she's going off to get married."

"I see. And if she loves the animal, why would she sell it? Does her new husband have no money or compassion?"

"She's said nothing of him to me, sir, except that she wants him to carry no debts of her making."

"Very noble. What debts has she?"

"She used the money she got from the sale of Circe to pay for her gowns and the gravestone. The money to buy Circe had been a gift from her father. She said she wanted to give him something in return."

"Gowns?"

"Promised her father she wouldn't disgrace her husband looking like a village girl. And she had no proper mourning gown. Personally, I couldn't care a lick whether she does disgrace the man. She says he's probably a black-hearted, fat old man who spends his evenings with a mistress and a pipe."

Daevon laughed and wheeled Cyclops toward the path that led inland. "Let us hope she fares better than that!"

The ride to Henri Todd's cottage was a short one, but Daevon lengthened it by slowing Cyclops to a walk. The animal was obviously incensed by the slow gait and strained against the reins, but at length he gave up his attempts to run. Daevon wanted time to think.

Every villager who spoke of Kaytlene Newell had only praise to sing for her. But, although her beauty was obvious to any man with blood still moving in his veins, her purity of heart and mind were not so easily discerned. Was she ignorant of James Newell's reasons for arranging the marriage? And if she was, would she truly hate Daevon as she had sworn over her father's grave?

Daevon realized he had been sitting a little too rigidly in the saddle and relaxed, moving more smoothly with Cyclops.

You can be sure you've chosen a wife beyond price, Sean O'Connell had said. Daevon had been confounded by the idea that Kaytlene Newell was a beauty and might be a good match for him. He had been so certain she was guilty of greed and subterfuge that he had not wanted to consider her innocent. Yet she had certainly not appeared eager to marry him.

It was difficult to thrust the questions from his mind. And the memories. He had loved Monique with the hot breathlessness of youth and, with the mantle of family responsibility already on his shoulders, had been ready to make her Lady Merrick. But James Newell had stubbornly refused to break the betrothal. Barely two months had passed after Newell's negative response before Monique was wed to Forrest Clay, his business rival, and barely ten months after that she gave birth to her husband's child.

The bitter taste of hatred once again rose in Daevon's throat. Lying, sweet bitches! No, he would not give Miss Newell the benefit of the doubt. She was a woman, and like all women, untrustworthy.

Daevon's heels bit angrily into Cyclops's flanks, and the horse's hooves tore up the earth as it galloped across the countryside.

A thin curl of smoke wound up from the chimney of the farmer's cottage that Daevon himself had leased for the past six months. A chestnut-brown mare was tethered at the far corner of the small barn.

Henri Todd had taken up residence in Newbury with instructions to find out as much about Kaytlene Newell and her father as he was able. He had come willingly enough, with the prospect of fresh females to amuse him in bed.

Daevon had chosen Todd for his ability to attract women—a quality that Daevon himself was never quite able to understand. Henri wasn't terribly attractive, had a tendency to wager too much of his income at the drop of a hat, and had been known to drink a bit too heavily. It seemed to be the very childishness of his behavior that drew women to him like bees to honey. His easy humor, masterful flattery, and sentimental nature seemed to be what women wanted.

But of course they wanted such infantile qualities in a man! They made him weak, easy to control. Easy to manipulate until a man found himself on his knees at a woman's feet, doing her bidding, sniveling like a child at her slightest hint of discontent.

Henri had the advantage in this case, however. He had met Kaytlene Newell as a stranger and gleaned bits of information about her which he reported back to Daevon. There were frustratingly few facts, however. Henri had written that the girl had a sharp wit, a flash of temper, an exceptional mastery of academics, and the most incredibly beautiful eyes he had even seen. He had even gone so far as to describe one afternoon when his attraction to Kaytlene had led him to attempt stealing a kiss.

"Kaytlene Newell is as beautiful as any woman I've seen," he'd written. "But she's skittish as a colt if a man gets too close. She tells me in the sweetest little voice that she treasures my friendship, but she does not love me and she must stay pure. Pure! Good God, Daevon! Virgins are hard to come by, but it seems you've got one. Lucky bastard. If this angel doesn't bleed for you on your wedding night, I'm a braying jackass!"

Daevon hadn't read the remainder of that particular letter. Henri's description didn't fit Daevon's image of Kaytlene Newell and so he threw the letter away. It would hardly be so easy, however, to dismiss the woman herself.

Daevon dismounted with ease and tied Cyclops's reins to a convenient post. He rapped quick and hard against the crude wooden door. From inside he heard a giggle, and then a soft, masculine whisper which was unmistakably Henri Todd. A short silence followed. When at last the door opened, Todd himself stood there in a pair of brown doeskin breeches and a white shirt. His boots had been removed, his shirt was completely undone, and his hair was in a state of dishevelment, the likes of which Daevon had seen on Todd a thousand times before.

"I should have known it was you, Daevon Merrick," Henri said. Daevon could not miss the glint of surprise in his friend's eyes. Henri's hair, a flash of dull red which for some reason women found attractive, curled against his nape. He had grown a stubble of beard to accompany his mustache, and his blue eyes sparkled.

"You always seem to be putting pleasure before business, my friend," Daevon said with a smile, giving the man a firm handshake as he was ushered in. "Where is she?"

"Dressing."

"Of course."

"As for pleasure before business, I wasn't expecting you."

Daevon nodded. "James Newell's illness brought me here sooner than I expected."

"Ah, and have you met Miss Newell?"

"This morning."

"And?" Todd's eyebrows rose hopefully.

"And . . . she fell into my arms."

"So! The Merrick charm has not been forgotten after all!"

"She fainted."

"I see. Is she ill?"

Before Daevon could respond, a thin girl with pink cheeks emerged from a doorway off the tiny kitchen. Her loose hair fell to her waist. She smiled, lowered her eyes, and blushed at seeing Henri's friend.

"Daevon, this is Lettie. Lettie, his grace, the earl of Merrick."

She tried a little curtsy which was stiff and awkward. "How do you do, your lordship?"

Daevon acknowledged her with a quick nod and a disdainful gaze under which she shifted. "I think it would be better for us to have some privacy, Henri," he said sternly. The girl was at least intelligent enough to take his words to heart, he decided as she kissed Henri lightly on the cheek and mumbled a hasty farewell.

Henri rubbed one hand over his rough cheek as if the kiss had embarrassed him. "You were saying, Daevon? About Miss Newell?"

"Newell?" Daevon murmured absentmindedly, his thoughts still fixed on the memory of her golden eyes.

"Good Lord, man! You've already fallen hard, haven't you? I thought I'd never see it in my lifetime!"

Daevon turned on him with a dark scowl that was more like the earl Henri knew. And knew well—every gesture, every tightening of the muscles across his square jaw, every show of emotion, however small. And now something new passed across his friend's gray eyes—some emotion that Henri had seen only once, and then it hadn't been so wild. Daevon had been twenty-three then, and that same desire had burned in his eyes each time Monique Lisle was nearby.

"I thought you knew me better, Henri," Daevon said with a smile. "I'm not stupid enough to allow that again."

"So you've said," Henri replied, though he doubted Daevon Merrick could resist Miss Newell for very long, despite his resolve.

They proceeded into a long discussion of matters at DenMerrick House, including Lady Merrick's recent heart illness and the state of the Merrick shipping holdings. Despite Henri Todd's often infuriating weaknesses—mainly women—he did have a keen business sense, which he had inherited from his father.

Six years before, on Henri's twenty-first birthday, Geoffrey Todd, an affluent and influential magistrate, had calmly announced to a roomful of celebrating guests that his younger son, Roger, was to be named sole heir to the Todd holdings. Amid shocked gasps and horrified murmurs, Geoffrey stated plainly that, after he had harbored suspicions regarding Henri's paternity for some time, his wife had admitted to having committed adultery twenty-two years before. Henri, he announced, was the result of that indiscretion and therefore was ineligible to inherit.

Daevon had not been able to resist a glance at the Todd matriarch. Henri's mother sat beside her husband, ashen-faced and unwilling to come to the defense of the son she adored. The son who was the exact, younger image of his father.

Daevon recalled that announcement with bitterness. He had been standing next to Henri at the time. Henri's fiancée, Rae, had been toasting her true love's health and happiness, and Daevon added his own glass with a clink of crystal.

Rae nearly choked on the expensive champagne. Henri's face was a calm, unreadable mask in the instant before he turned to Daevon, smiled brightly, and lifted his glass again.

"To Roger!" he shouted to his guests in a toast. "A long and happy life!"

The glittering crowd gaily joined in with cheers and applause. Draining his glass, Henri passed the empty crystal to Daevon and divested Rae of hers as well before leading her to join the dancing.

Daevon stood watching, amazed that his friend could behave so nonchalantly at the proclamation that had denied him his inheritance. True, Henri was known for his irresponsible behavior, and Geoffrey had never approved of his rebellious older son. But to leave milk-faced Roger in charge . . .

An abrupt movement on the dance floor caught Daevon's attention. He saw Rae pull stiffly from Henri's close hold. She said something to him in angry whispers and jerked the diamond engagement ring from her finger. With the expensive piece of jewelry clutched in her hand, she wheeled about and slipped through the crowd to Roger, whose attention she sought.

Three months later, she married the heir to Geoffrey's money. Rae, wearing the engagement ring Henri had given her, had simply had his first initial rubbed out and replaced with an *R*.

Daevon glanced up at his friend now and noted with satisfaction the maturity and wisdom such hardships had stamped on his face. Instead of becoming an embittered, pessimistic young man, Henri had learned from the past. And, wisely, he had used his knowledge to avoid emotionally entangling romances.

Swallowing the remainder of the brandy that Henri had served in liberal doses, Daevon focused on what the younger man was saying.

"So tell me, Daevon," he began cautiously, "what are your plans now, with James Newell gone?"

"I've got to return to London. Mother isn't well."

Sympathy shadowed Henri's expression.

"You love her, Daevon. I'm sorry."

"She's been the only faithful and loving woman in my life."

"But you haven't known so many women."

Daevon smiled. "How many women would you say I've known, Henri?"

He grinned like a cat finishing off its prey. "If you mean known in the biblical sense, I must admit I've had my suspicions that your bed sees more use than my own. And that isn't an easy thing for me to accept."

"I think you overestimate. You never were very good at mathematics."

Henri Todd's normally jovial countenance darkened and the tiny laugh lines around his eyes deepened. "I know there have been many, Daevon. And none of them worthy of you. I don't mean worthy of your high position in society or your wealth. I mean a woman deserving of the title Lady Merrick. Someone like Kaytlene Newell."

Daevon turned furious gray eyes on his friend, but said nothing as Henri continued. "You saw it too, Daevon. The pure beauty in her face, the innocence in her eyes. And, I think, enough fire in her spirit to keep even you satisfied. The perfection of heaven, the temptation of hell."

"I don't believe she wants to marry the earl of Merrick, Henri."

"What makes you say so?"

"She said she hates me," he said coldly. "Before she fainted."

"I see. And when she woke?"

"I haven't seen her since then."

"Well, then. You haven't had a chance to change her mind, have you?"

"Henri, what makes you think I'd want to? She is honor bound to marry me. If she doesn't, it's her disgrace. I won't force her."

"I am not speaking of force, Daevon, but love."

Daevon could hardly mask the surprise that Henri, a man so badly hurt by a woman, could still see the beauty and benefit of love. His thoughts went back to the past.

After living with Roger and his new bride had become too much for Henri, he had taken what little money was his own and left London. When he returned—drunk, filthy, and drowning in depression—Daevon had taken him in and watched over his recovery.

It had taken Daevon nearly six weeks to convince Henri to work for him, and Henri had agreed only after Daevon promised to give him assignments that would keep him as far from London as possible. Could a man who had suffered so much at a woman's hands ever believe in love again?

Henri laughed at Daevon's expression. "Yes," he admitted, "there are faithless women. I can't deny that. But the faithful ones . . . oh, God, what treasures!"

"A man can't love a woman in an instant," said Daevon. "A woman can't earn his love in so short a time."

Henri shook his head. "When will you learn, my rock-headed friend, that if love must be earned, then a man must earn it as well as a woman?"

Daevon began to feel angry. "What have I done to Kaytlene Newell to be unworthy of any . . . feeling she might have for me?"

"You have doubted, old friend. Since you were told of the betrothal, you have doubted her, refused to come and meet her. You made every attempt to cut her out of your life without first giving her a chance. And you're still doubting."

Daevon shook his head. "I can't trust so easily," he said with a groan.

"Do you trust me?"

The question surprised Daevon. "You know I do."

"And there have been a few times when you trusted my friendship and good judgment enough to take my advice."

"There have been more than a few times."

"Then listen to this advice even if it makes you deaf to anything else I ever say. You need Kaytlene Newell, Daevon, and she needs you."

Chapter 3

Kaytlene was roused from velvety black sleep by a cold cloth dumped unceremoniously onto her forehead. Her amber eyes flew open, shocked and wide, and her thoughts raced to recall where she was and how she'd gotten there.

"My Lord a' heaven, miss!" Meg Tillman, who had administered the cloth, said quickly. "You mighta given a girl some warning afore coming back from the dead."

Kaytlene tried to fight off the dazed numbness that seemed to grind her few coherent thoughts into tiny shards. After a moment she could see the sparse, dirty furnishings of the tiny room where she lay. From the strength and angle of the sunlight that filtered through the window, she guessed it was late afternoon. All her memories of the past months flew back into her head in a rush of sensation. She sat up, pushing away the heavy cloth that covered her.

"What am I doing here?" she asked shakily.

"Fainted, Miss Newell," Meg explained as she helped her to her feet. "That handsome gent brought you here."

Meg picked up the rumpled black cloak from the bed, and Kaytlene stared at the heavy silver clasps which somehow looked familiar. She searched her recollection. Vaguely she remembered a man with black hair and eyes like the silver-gray foam that bubbled when waves dashed along the cliffs. He was not only a man, but *the* man whom she had dreaded meeting ever since she had been told he would be her husband.

Your servant, my lady, he had said so nonchalantly, *Daevon Adam Merrick, earl of Merrick,* as though it were the most natural thing in the world for him to shock her with his sudden and unexpected intrusion.

Meg disappeared for a moment, returning with a chipped white china basin and pitcher. She placed the bowl on a dressing table, poured a little of the steaming water from the pitcher into it, and set out a dish of soap and a clean cloth.

"Mr. O'Connell is expecting you for supper within the hour, Miss Newell."

"Supper? Oh, yes. And what of his lordship?"

"Ooh, you mean the earl?" Meg's brows rose in obvious appreciation of the man. "He'll be joinin' you. Quite a piece of manly flesh, he is—"

"Meg!" Kaytlene's voice was sharp. "I'm in no mood to hear your evaluation of my betrothed. I'm a woman and have eyes of my own." The outburst was irrational, she knew, but it silenced Meg's lustful description of Daevon Merrick.

"Now get me a hairbrush. And a tin of powder."

Meg was off in a flurry. In her absence, Kayte sat glumly at the ancient dressing table and stared at her reflection. She was pale, her eyes slightly swollen and pink, and her hair nothing short of wild. Her gown was wrinkled and dusty, and a smudge of dirt marked her neck. She winced at her reflection, recalling that the earl had seen her like this. After her rash behavior in the cemetery, he must think her a spoiled, disobedient child.

But then . . . what was wrong with that? What did it matter if his lordship found her unattractive and undesirable, as long as he left her alone? She had made every preparation her father had requested, had even had three gowns made so that she would not embarrass his lordship by looking like a serving wench. She had been forced to sell her beloved Circe in order to fulfill that promise, using the remainder of the money to buy her father's headstone.

By the time Meg returned with the requested articles, Kayte had solidified her thoughts into a simple plan.

"Thank you, Meg. Leave me alone now, will you?"

The girl bobbed a quick curtsy and returned to the pub.

"And now," Kayte said to her disheveled reflection, "I must prepare for my evening engagement."

She put aside the tin of cheap powder Meg had provided, wiped the dirt from her neck, and brushed out her hair. That, she decided, was enough. She had never promised her father that she would make herself beautiful for his lordship. She had never said that she would wear the lovely gowns Adele had made or dress her hair or even speak graciously to her betrothed.

Kayte's reflection smiled smugly back at her. If Daevon Adam Merrick found her too spoiled, hotheaded, and unattractive to take as a wife, that would be entirely his decision.

Sean O'Connell's cottage was a white, two-room building situated on the flat peak of a rocky knoll. It faced the sea cliffs and could only be approached from the rear, since two sides were cut off by sheer rocks that ran down to the beach. A third side was wild with brush and occasional jutting rocks, and it was there that Kaytlene had spent many hot afternoons picking fat, black mulberries and licking the juice from her sticky fingers.

She and Elizabeth O'Connell would then spend hours baking pies and making jam. Occasionally Elizabeth would make her famous mulberry wine, using the recipe she had passed on to Kaytlene, since she and Sean had no children of their own. They had longed for a family, but a miscarriage early in the marriage and the fever that had raged in Elizabeth's body afterward had left her barren.

The only clear road to the O'Connell's house was the footpath through Mr. Harkins's fields, which swept out into a wide arc of green grass and wildflowers, then was broken into two rolling strips. The left rose gently up to the O'Connells'; the right led downward to a strip of white sand along the shore.

As the sun set, wrapping the house in red and gray, Kaytlene laid out the table settings, one soft lip drawn between her teeth as she worked. The soft rustle of her skirts and an occasional clatter of china were the only sounds in the house.

Elizabeth O'Connell hummed busily in her tiny kitchen, a starched white apron tied over her dark blue cotton skirt and white blouse. She took a loaf of hot bread from the

oven and arranged thick slices on a warm platter. She
turned to speak to Kaytlene, stopping when she found the
younger woman fussing over the exact arrangement of a
platter and a wineglass.

"Here, Kayte," Elizabeth said softly, "you put out the
bread while I get some wine."

They busied themselves filling glasses, then Kaytlene
went to the cellar for a small china bowl holding a lump of
fresh butter.

"We should have some flowers, Beth," Kayte said with
feigned solicitude. "I'm sure his lordship is accustomed to
huge silver bowls of roses at his table."

"I think perhaps his lordship won't mind tonight. He
has something far prettier to look at." Elizabeth lay a hand
over Katylene's. "Won't you say what's troubling you,
dear?"

"Beth, I don't want to marry anyone, least of all a man
who contracted to purchase me with a piece of parchment
and a promise of financial security. You taught me that
there are more important things. Love, for example."

"Yes." Elizabeth drew Kaytlene to a pair of fat gold
wingback chairs facing the bright orange glow of the fire.
"I also taught you that love is not just a flighty emotional
fancy. It is a strength that comes of faith, complete com-
mitment of yourself to another."

"But I don't know him. How can I devote myself to a
man I don't know?" She folded her hands in her lap, then
twisted them until her knuckles showed white against the
black of her dress.

Elizabeth was the wellspring of advice and understanding that Kaytlene had drawn on for many years, but now
she knew the decision was her own to make.

The sound of hooves thudded up the knoll toward the
house.

Elizabeth leaned over, squeezing Kaytlene's hand. "All
I can tell you is to give him a chance. Let him answer your
questions before you make a decision. You've spent a long
time making guesses. Now see the truth and judge wisely."

Laughter rang out just beyond the door. Footsteps
sounded. Kaytlene trembled at the deep voice that had
spoken so gently to her that morning.

The door swung inward. Sean O'Connell strode in first,
eyes dancing. He went directly to Elizabeth as if no other
person existed in the world.

As Elizabeth rose to greet her husband, Kaytlene stood
and turned toward the door. Daevon Merrick entered quietly, closing the door behind him and waiting.

"Ah, Beth, let me introduce you to his lordship, Daevon
Merrick, earl of Merrick."

Elizabeth made a perfect, sweeping curtsy. "I am very
pleased to meet you, your lordship."

Daevon strode forward, taking Elizabeth's hand and
pressing it to his lips.

"My wife, Elizabeth, your lordship."

"You lied to me, Sean. She isn't only lovely, she's
exquisite."

His voice moved across Kaytlene like a cool breeze
from the sea. Elizabeth *was* lovely, with her light brown
hair piled neatly atop the crown of her head, her blue eyes
like crystals, her face flushed from her baking.

"Thank you, your lordship," said Elizabeth.

Daevon hardly heard Elizabeth's words, for his attention
was focused altogether on Kaytlene. He straightened, clasp-
ing his hands behind his back.

"And you know Kayte, Daevon," said Sean.

"Good evening, Miss Newell."

"Your lordship." Kaytlene curtsied just slightly, but
her knees were so weak she nearly fell at his feet. His
hand came down to take hers and brought her up to stand
before him. Not able to meet his eyes, Kayte sought out
Elizabeth but, to her dismay, the O'Connells had moved to
the kitchen, drawing closed a dark curtain that separated
the two living areas.

At Kaytlene's surprised expression, Daevon looked toward
the kitchen and faced her again with a smile. "I think I'll
like your friends," he said pleasantly and stepped toward
the fire.

For the first time, Kaytlene dared to defy the fear in her
heart and looked at him. He had bathed and shaved and
changed into a black coat and breeches, with a black silk
waistcoat and white linen shirt that gathered into a starched
ruffle at the cuffs and open neck. A gold chain was clipped

to one of the buttons of his waistcoat and disappeared into a small, silk-lined pocket just over his ribs. His face was illuminated by the firelight, the shadows deepening his already strongly contoured face. He was awe-inspiring, beautiful, and . . . frightening.

"Miss Newell?"

Color rose hot in her face when Kaytlene realized that he had once again caught her staring at him. She stammered an apology, hardly hearing her own voice.

"I should help Elizabeth." She started toward the kitchen, taking in a quick breath when his hand closed firmly but gently on her wrist.

"Please." His voice was tentative, questioning. "Don't go."

She looked up into his gray eyes. They were clear now, searching hers for something she felt powerless to give. His hand moved away from her arm, the knuckles running along her soft, tapered sleeve.

A shudder ran through her at his touch.

"I am . . . sorry for your father's passing. And for my intrusion this morning. It was unforgivable."

"Yes," she replied. "It was."

Daevon studied her uneasy expression until she finally turned away.

He had spent a restless afternoon considering Henri's advice. Even after two days and nights with little sleep he hadn't been able to enjoy a nap because his thoughts had been sucked into a vortex of golden eyes. He had tossed on the wide bed, his body pulsing with heat at the thought of the scent of her sweet skin, the touch of her lips pressed against his own.

He looked at her now, her face bathed in the fire's glow, and could not have imagined a more lovely picture. How odd this was, her being such perfection in the flesh. He had expected . . .

Kaytlene knew that her behavior warranted an apology, but she had no intention of making one. It would only help her purpose if he thought her a poorly mannered hoyden.

After a moment, Daevon spoke again. "Perhaps we should pretend that this morning never happened," he

suggested. Under the spell cast by her eyes, he decided she
was at least worth taking one chance.

Kayte considered his proposal. Let him answer all your
questions, Elizabeth had said. Meeting his penetrating gaze,
Kayte wanted to do just that.

Daevon watched a hint of a smile begin on her mouth,
but she stifled it quickly, as if she were barely tolerating
his presence. Still, he interpreted it as an affirmation. He
took her hands in his and brought them to his lips. "I'm
glad, Kayte." He released her at once when Sean pulled
back the edge of the drapery.

"You'll be having a cold supper if you don't get along
soon," Sean said, sounding pleased with the position in
which he found his guests.

For Kayte, dinner was unnerving. Though she hardly
spoke to her betrothed, he seemed very much at home in
the little cottage, exchanging wit and wisdom with the
O'Connells as if they were lifelong friends. He spoke
frequently to Kayte as well, he was generous with his
smiles, and over dessert he lifted her hand from where it
rested on the base of her wineglass and pressed a kiss to it.
To Sean's inquiry of what he thought of their little Kayte,
Daevon smiled warmly and said simply, "I'm stunned."

Bewitched would have been a better description, Kayte
thought with a frown. That morning he had acted as
though she were beneath his consideration. Now, despite
her efforts to be unpleasant, he was looking at her like a
besotted swain.

Kaytlene gritted her teeth, smiled woodenly, and pretended to tolerate his thorough perusal. Why would her
father have promised her to such a man? Her father . . .

She looked past the others and out into the dark, cloudless sky. The moon was already a full, glowing orb.

"Miss Newell?" Daevon's hand was on hers. He and
Sean were staring intently at her, and Elizabeth was hurry-
ing from the kitchen, carrying a cool cloth in one hand
which she pressed to Kaytlene's forehead.

"I'm all right." Kayte pushed the cloth away. "Why
are you staring at me like that?" Her eyes were fixed on
Daevon's.

"You left us for a moment, darling," Elizabeth said quietly. "We feared you were in some sort of shock."

"I was thinking about Father." Kaytlene lowered her eyes, but lifted them again when Daevon's reassuring hand closed around hers. His fingers squeezed once, gently, and his thumb traced a soft arc back and forth over her knuckles.

"Perhaps Miss Newell should retire. I've enjoyed her company selfishly."

"I *would* like to go home, please."

"But it will be so lonely for you with James gone," Elizabeth objected. "I thought you might stay with us."

Katylene knew it would be lonely in the little cottage that was so full of the past.

Glancing up at Daevon, she suddenly realized that he would not mind an unattractive wife. After all, he would have his mistresses, wouldn't he? But if she guessed correctly, there was one thing that a man of his position would *not* tolerate in a wife. Another plan formed in her head and Kayte acted on it immediately—before she could change her mind.

"Will you see me home, Lord Merrick?" she asked demurely.

He smiled. "As you wish."

Once they were out in the chill night air, the salty scent of the ocean cleared Kaytlene's head. She intended to send his lordship home without his bride, and she knew exactly how to accomplish it.

Sean led two horses from their places at the corner of the cottage, one which Kayte recognized as his own Challenger, and the other one of Justin's stable mounts.

"Hello, Cyclops," she said, rubbing the stallion's sleek muzzle.

"He seems to know you," Daevon said behind her.

"He should. I've given this beast so many lumps of sugar that he should melt in a heavy rain."

"Here, Kayte," said Sean. "You take old Challenger here. I'll give you a lift up."

"Oh no, Sean," she said coolly. "You have business in town tomorrow, don't you? And I won't be blamed for the inflammation in your leg acting up again because you have to walk. If Cyclops doesn't mind, I shall ride with his lordship.'' She paused to see the earl frown questioningly. Apparently more intrigued than suspicious, he took her hand and, bowing over it, brought it to his lips.

"Cyclops would be honored to carry such a lovely burden.''

Sean appeared shocked by Kaytlene's forward suggestion, but Elizabeth's knowing smile and her hand on his arm kept him silent.

"Will you help me up?'' Kaytlene placed caressing fingers on Daevon's arm.

"With pleasure.'' He fixed his hands on her small, flat waist, lifting her to Cyclops's back with easy grace. His arm flexed and relaxed under her hand, sending a current of sensual power into her body. In another instant he was behind her, and she pressed back against his wide, hard chest.

"Good night, and thank you again,'' Daevon said, nodding to their hosts.

Sean and Elizabeth said their goodbyes only after they had the earl's promise that he would visit them again just before he returned to London.

As his fingers guided the reins, turning Cyclops toward the village, Daevon wondered at the exquisite, golden-eyed witch who had cursed him that morning and was now leaning provocatively against him. Her warmth began to stir his blood.

She said nothing. The night wind blew her hair around his face, and when she leaned back with a sigh, her cheek rested against his shoulder, the pale pink shimmer of her lips tantalizingly near.

"Are you not feeling well, Miss Newell?'' he asked.

"I'm quite well, thank you.''

He looked down into her face and for a fleeting instant thought to kiss her.

"And you, sir?'' she asked, pleased to see surprise and warmth in his eyes. He almost seemed too confused by her actions to speak. It seemed her plan would work.

When Cyclops stopped at the flat rock formation at the base of the knoll, Kaytlene sat up and slid her hands over Daevon's.

"May I?'' she asked softly.

He relinquished the reins to her smaller, gentle hands and slid his own hands to her waist. She turned Cyclops to the left and leaned forward. "Go, Cyclops!" she whispered into the velvet ear. Immediately the animal bolted, down and left toward the sea.

Daevon was so taken by surprise that he automatically tightened his grip on Kayte's waist to keep them both from being unseated. Not that he minded holding her so close, but she confounded him.

The horse's hooves dug with soft thuds into the white sand and threw showers of seawater onto Deavon's legs and Kaytlene's skirts. When at last the ride ended, she released the reins and slipped away from Daevon to slide down onto the sand.

Daevon dismounted, too, and Cyclops moved slowly away to gnaw on a tuft of grass. Unable to think of a better alternative, Daevon sank down to sit beside Kayte on the beach.

She was on her knees, the sand sticking to her gown where the spray had moistened it, her hair falling over one shoulder.

"It's been a couple of days since I've ridden," she said. "Forgive me, but I suddenly wanted to feel again how wonderful it is to run with the wind." She looked at Daevon, her amber eyes glowing under the moon.

Daevon felt as if he was falling under her spell.

"You're so beautiful," he murmured, unable to stop from taking a lock of her hair between his fingers. He straightened the curl, then watched as it sprang back into a perfect brown spiral.

"Thank you, my lord." For a moment she wavered between telling Daevon of her fears and continuing in her effort to change his mind.

"We must discuss our . . . arrangements," he finally said.

"Yes, your lordship."

"My name is Daevon."

"Day-ven." The word sounded strange and sweet on her tongue.

"May I call you Kayte?"

"Would it matter if I refused? You seem to be the kind of man who takes what he wants, regardless of one's wishes."

Daevon pulled back his hand. "I am sorry you feel that way."

Kaytlene rose abruptly, moving angrily toward the sea, almost as if she wanted to escape into it.

"How should I feel, sir, in these circumstances?" She turned to face him, ignoring the water that lapped at the hem of her gown, turning it a deeper black.

"You have come to take home a bride who has been contracted and paid for. But I am not a piece of property purchased at auction, sir. I am a woman!"

Daevon brushed the sand from his clothes and stood, closing the space between them with slow, measured steps. "That fact, at least, is obvious." His eyes swept downward over her.

"Why do you want to marry me? Why?"

He looked incredulously down at her. Did she truly not know? Had his doubts about her been misplaced after all?

"If my father owed you money, I will repay every shilling, I swear." She reached out and grabbed the lapels of his coat to accentuate her plea. Her eyes were liquid, pleading. Her mouth was much too close. He moved away.

"Do you think me so callous that I would accept a woman in payment of a debt?" he demanded angrily.

"You drew up the contract. You tell me."

"Lady, I did not draw up the contract. I hardly know myself why our parents agreed to the betrothal."

"You tell me you don't know the details of a contract signed almost four years ago?"

"Four years? Is that how long you've known?"

"Since my eighteenth birthday," she replied. "I assumed then that the contracts had just been drawn up."

Daevon laughed sarcastically, hardly able to believe such a thing.

"Don't laugh at me!"

He stopped abruptly, taking in her perfect face, her wind-whipped hair, her extraordinary eyes.

"We have been betrothed for over twenty years," he

said icily, seeing the disbelief in her expression. "It seems that neither of us had much say in the matter."

"But why?"

"I don't know."

They stood close in the shallow water, both contemplating their own thoughts.

Daevon wondered whether this girl was truly as innocent as she seemed. He was angry at his own helplessness; he could not disprove her claim one way or another.

"All this time," she whispered blankly, "I thought—"

"You thought that I was a fat old man with a mistress and a pipe."

Her eyes widened in surprise at his astuteness. "Yes," she admitted.

After a long silence she asked, "Will you still marry me?"

Daevon turned away from his contemplation of the yellow-white moon. "What?"

Kayte swallowed convulsively and steeled her wavering determination, then went slowly toward him.

"I asked if you still plan to marry me, Daevon."

She paused at the edge of the sand, a few steps from his dark figure. Her eyes locked with his.

"Do you?" she asked again. It was a whisper buffered by the slow, steady swish of water and sand.

"I hadn't quite decided that," he answered stiffly.

She closed the remaining space between them, pressing her body close to his. Her hands slid beneath the lapels of his coat and went to his shoulders.

With the barest hint of a smile, he pulled her tight against him.

"Don't you want me, Daevon?"

Her question snapped his control. He grabbed her wrists and jerked her body a scant inch away from his. "You would like me to, wouldn't you, Kaytlene?" With one arm secure around her waist he plunged his free hand into her hair and forced her head back.

"I—" She sucked in her breath at his abrupt change in mood. This wasn't what she had meant to happen! She had only meant to convince him that she was not the sort of woman he would want as his wife, yet now he was taking advantage of the situation, hurting her with his fierce hold, his eyes burning like gray fire.

"You want to be a lady?" he mocked. "And wear jewels and have a bed of silk, with lovers to play in it with you? Is that what you want, Miss Newell?"

She stared, shocked, at the pain she saw in his eyes. So he had expected her to be a greedy little tramp? She would have laughed if there had been air in her lungs. It would be so easy to rid herself of Daevon Merrick. All she had to do was act the part he expected her to act.

"Did you think I would prefer this homely little village to your many estates?" she mocked tartly.

His eyes flared with anger. "You little whore!" he accused.

Kayte's eyes widened as he forced her back a step. She prepared herself for the stinging blow that she expected, easy payment for her freedom. But it never came.

Instead he was hauling her roughly against his hard frame, forcing her head back and her mouth down to his.

She groaned and clutched at his jacket, her nails grazing the bronzed flesh of his neck. Her hands balled into fists and pushed against the solid, immovable form that held her in submission. When his tongue forced her mouth open, she moaned.

God, this couldn't be happening!

He pulled back. If Kaytlene Newell wanted to buy him with her body, then he was going to extract every shilling's worth she offered.

"Let's see if you bleed, shall we, lady?" he whispered harshly. "I'll wager Henri Todd's wrong about that as well."

He pushed her and she landed with a dull thump on the sand.

"You're mad!" she cried.

He fell beside her, one hand on her throat, pressing her into the sand. Her hand flew up from the grainy bed and slapped him viciously.

He smiled. "Let's see, shall we?"

Her body sank further down under the weight of him sprawled across her, his leg pinning hers. Ignoring her savage kicking and the water lapping at their feet, he

lowered his mouth to hers once again, hungry and demanding. He held her wrists in his hands, on either side of
her head. The uneven rhythm of her body as it struggled
against his only fed his anger . . . and his desire.

He pressed her lips apart, thrust his tongue into her
mouth, and let her feel the hard pressure of his arousal
against her thigh. He heard her whimper and by slow
measures softened the kiss.

It was several minutes later when he realized that he had
released her wrists and that her hands were lying motion-
less in the sand. She was not struggling.

Daevon lifted his head and studied her. Her eyes fluttered open and she peered back at him with the same
startled, questioning gaze. When he kissed her again, it
was with a nearly forgotten gentleness, to which he felt her
slowly respond. Her hands left the sand and slid up his
arms, leaving wet grains on his coat.

Her mouth moved inexpertly with his, and from her
throat there still issued soft groans of protest, but she was
weakening against his practiced seduction. And he wasn't
altogether certain he wanted to stop.

Kayte couldn't fight. The dizzy sensations he was creating with his mouth dammed up her thoughts and turned her
mind numb. The cool breeze off the ocean flowed over
their bodies, lying intertwined on the beach. She felt herself slipping dangerously close to something that was wrong
. . . and right. Something warm and gentle and compelling.

Until her conscience drove like a dagger between them.
She had spent so long dreading this man's arrival . . . and
now she was spread out on the ground for him like some
common doxy. She was a whore, just as he had accused
her. A base, selfish woman of pleasure who offered herself
to the first man who—

She pushed at him until he broke the kiss.

"Oh . . . please." She was gasping for breath, pushing
herself away from his hold.

"Don't!" She crawled several yards from him before
collapsing in a sandy, wet black lump against the earth
wall that lined the beach. Guilt and shame and tears assaulted her, and she buried her face in her hands to allow
her emotions to escape.

"I can't," she cried. "I can't!"

Daevon stood and watched her silently. If she was acting, he finally decided with a sigh, then she rivaled the best actresses that London had ever produced. She was as tortured and tormented now as he had been for the last few years. Guilt took the place of desire in his heart as he knelt beside her in the sand.

"I'm sorry," he said simply.

She didn't pause in her sobbing to respond. Daevon looked back out over the beach, watching as the waves lapped higher to smooth out the indentation their bodies had made together. He wondered how long it had been since anyone had heard an apology from the earl of Merrick. A very, very long time, he guessed. And now that he'd lowered himself to ask for a woman's forgiveness, she was too engrossed in tears to hear him. He supposed he deserved that irony.

"Miss Newell?"

She finally peered up, her eyes still overflowing with tears.

"I . . . can't marry you." She hiccupped softly.

Daevon smiled and shook his hand. Was she real?

"I can't!" she insisted, collapsing again. "I can't." The last words were muffled by sand, copper-brown hair, and black crepe.

"I know," he said, bending over to scoop her into his arms. He stood with her, still wondering, and she looked into his face with a grave, red-eyed directness that twisted his gut.

"I . . . don't want to marry you." She sighed, finally allowing herself to relax against him as he carried her. Her words came slowly, slurred by her subsiding sobs and the exhaustion that darkly engulfed her. "I hope you won't be too . . . disappointed."

"No," he said softly, honestly. "I'm not in the least disappointed."

Chapter 4

DenMerrick House had been quiet for hours, its palatial facade darkened by twilight's shadows. Only one lamp burned on the lower floor, and a tall figure paced before it, casting distorted shadows onto the book-lined walls. There was no sound as the pacing steps sank down into the thick burgundy carpeting, though an occasional, impatient grunt vibrated through the silence.

Tristan Merrick scanned the opulent furnishings with bitterness.

This would be Daevon's house. Daevon's desk. His books. His rugs. And it would be Daevon's money that supported and sustained it all. Daevon Adam Merrick, the heir and his father's favorite son.

As a boy Daevon had been like a splinter of wood pushed under Tristan's flesh, a wound left to fester for some twenty-odd years. Now it was a canker, oozing hate like blood and pus, poisoning its victim until he became nothing more than the determination to destroy the object of his hate.

Yes, Tristan thought pleasantly, Daevon Merrick's rich mantle of wealth and responsibility would fit very well on his own shoulders. He ached to wear it.

The elegant monster of a fireplace lay cold and empty, though it was the only fire that normally burned throughout the night. The deep blues and browns of the furnishings seemed to meld slowly to black.

A nearly silent knock on the double library doors stopped Tristan's pacing and, without the courtesy of waiting for a reply, a black figure stepped inside.

"I don't like this business," said the man, pulling a cap from his face, revealing a pair of glittering black eyes.

"It's necessary, Regice. The money my brother so graciously allows me is insignificant for my needs. And if you wish to continue lining your pockets with my generous portion, you'll do whatever I think is necessary to keep my coffers overflowing."

The smaller man moved about the vast room, examining a pair of silver candlesticks, a vase, and several ivory carvings on the ornately sculpted French mantelpiece.

"What should I take?" He pulled a long, thin black bag from his belt and spread it open.

"You're an extremely poor thief," Tristan Merrick replied. "Take everything."

Regice began stuffing the bag with the small items that he thought might bring a high price. After several minutes the bag was three-quarters full, and Tristan had lost his patience.

"Enough!" His brown eyes sparkled with malice in the vague light. He took an ivory carving from the thief's hand. "I'll hold this, I think. How did you get in?"

"I cut the lock off the old cellar door. Then through the pantry to the kitchen. I'm afraid I had to rope one of your pretty pantry maids to a chair. She was having a snack."

Tristan laughed. "Darby, I'm sure. Since my compassionate brother brought her into the house, she can't seem to get a full belly. I think she's afraid we'll throw her out and she wants to fatten up first." He gave his counterpart a sly grin. "Perhaps if I personally see to her rescue, she'll show some eager appreciation toward me."

"I think perhaps she just might." With a loud clatter, Regice placed the bag he carried on a chair.

"Quiet, idiot!" Tristan whispered. They both stood silent for several moments, but there was no answering sound or movement in the house.

"Now the proof," Tristan finally said, his voice low and pointed as he poured himself a glass of brandy.

The second man parted the front of his patched black coat and extracted a parcel from where it had nestled against his shirt. A smile turned up Tristan's lips as he took the bundle.

"So you were successful after all."

"Isn't that what you pay me for?"

Tristan nodded, already perusing the documents that
Regice had stolen from Daevon's office safe. Though no
official records were kept of the Merrick smuggling operations, Daevon had carefully recorded requests from America, notes on the availability of illegal goods, contacts,
shipping lanes, and deliveries made. Regice was a poor
solicitor, but with his underworld contacts, he had had the
records stolen and copies forged, then the originals returned to Daevon's safe, leaving none the wiser. Except
Tristan, of course. And he planned to make good use of
the flawless documents.

"May I?" Regice indicated the liquor and picked up a
clean glass.

"Don't be stupid. What would I tell the authorities
when they found two empty glasses here? That I invited
the thief in for a drink?"

Regice replaced the snifter and waited in silence as
Tristan settled into a long leather couch to begin reading.
He finished one page, set it aside, and read a second, then
a third. A grim smile crossed his lips several times. When
he finally unfolded the last long, meticulously written
parchment, he took a deep, apprehensive breath.

"Have you read this, Regice?"

"No, but Erickson gave me a fairly thorough overview."

"This document is dated October 1789."

"Yes?"

"Do you mean to tell me she's made no changes since
then?"

"None that I'm aware of."

"Very well." Tristan began reading the last will and
testament of Lady Anna Merrick. Halfway through, his
hand crushed the paper.

"Damn her!" He rose and crossed the room in a few
strides.

"I told you it wouldn't please you."

"All right, Regice, you're the goddamned solicitor.
How do I fight this?"

"I don't think you should."

"Are you mad?"

"Listen, Tristan, if you try to fight it, you'll have to prove that your mother was not in her right mind when the will was drawn up. You know how Daevon will feel about that. As executor of the estate, he'll have enough money to fight you indefinitely."

Tristan paced. He crumbled the copy of the will and thoughtfully rubbed the side of his chin.

"What other choice do I have, Regice?"

"Let Daevon contest the will after she dies."

"You're mad as a rabid dog, my dear man."

"If he loves you as much as you say, he won't be satisfied with your lot. With Lady Merrick gone, he may take steps to have the assets divided more fairly."

Tristan saw the truth in that idea and absorbed it for a moment. "Yes, you may be right. It would be just like my noble brother to feel that I'd been cheated."

"And with the ten percent of the cash assets already allotted to you, you would have enough to set yourself up comfortably until he made the new arrangements."

Seating himself once again, Tristan finished off the last of his brandy, his reddish brows pulled into a frown. He knew the limits to which Daevon Merrick could be pushed and he wasn't certain but what he might be pushing too far with this scheme.

"What if Daevon is more suspicious than we think?"

Regice leaned back and smiled.

"Then those forgeries should provide you with the means toward a comfortable nest egg. With the information I've brought you," Regice said, reminding Tristan who had been responsible for their collection, "you can blackmail your dear Daevon until his coffers run dry."

"True enough. Well, my friend." Tristan placed his hands on his knees and rose. He was careful to fold the documents and place them inside Regice's bag of stolen articles. "Keep these safe. I hope I won't be needing them, but as a last recourse I'll spare nothing—not even the life of my rebel brother—to take what is mine."

"Are we ready, then?" Regice pulled an ivory-handled pistol from his pocket.

Tristan waved a cautioning hand. "There's one other matter that I think will greatly aid our purposes."

"Something else I can do?"

"Yes. Contact Delamane."

"What do you want with that weasel, Tristan?"

"You saw the will. Daevon has to marry that Newell girl to inherit. Eliminating her will get us closer to our goal."

"Do you really think that's necessary? Daevon's been fighting this betrothal for years, and he won't know about the stipulations of the will until it's too late."

"*I* know about them, don't I? Who's to say *he* doesn't? Now, contact Delamane. I want it seen to before Daevon returns to London."

"This wasn't part of our plan," whined Regice.

"Consider it a revised plan. Now, do you understand me, or do I have to find another greedy solicitor to collect your fee instead?"

"Very well." To Regice, it was a small price to pay: one girl's life for one man's lifetime of pleasure.

"Now," Tristan said cheerfully, "we're ready." He picked up an ivory statuette, tossing it up and catching it as he walked toward the French windows. He opened one window and exchanged a knowing glance with Regice.

"I want Delamane contacted right away."

"I'll see to it." And with that, Regice raised the butt of his pistol, bringing it viciously down against Tristan's nape. With one short, painful groan, he crumpled, his torso lying on the cold stone of the terrace, his legs bent at a slight angle on the library carpeting. The ivory statuette was still clutched in his hand.

Regice thrust the bag of goods over his shoulder. He gave a long, shrill whistle, made his way over the low terrace, and escaped through the side garden to a waiting carriage.

Regice drove his team directly to Fetter Lane and turned into a fetid alley. This was an area void of light and gentle society, a melting pot of thieves, cutthroats, and castoffs. The heavy scents of refuse and decay seemed to linger around the rows of poorly built dwellings, and even the strong white glow of the full moon seemed turned to ash gray.

Several years before, the infamous Mrs. Brownrigg and her son were arrested here and quickly became the most notorious pair of criminals. Her son was never prosecuted, but Mrs. Brownrigg was named the chief culprit in the abuse of three of her female apprentices. After subjecting them to stripping and scourging, she starved and continually beat them. One finally died, another escaped, and the third turned over enough evidence to have her tormentor tried and hanged.

Since the publicity of those events, the inhabitants of Fetter Lane had kept their activities more clandestine, but murderers could still be hired here, and that was Regice's intention.

His carriage stopped at one particularly hideous facade, a house that was as battle-worn as its occupants. Always alert of the fastest means of escape, Regice did not climb down from the driver's seat. A boy of fifteen sat on the badly chipped front steps.

"Wot's the job, Mr. Regice?" he asked.

"It's Daevon Merrick's woman, Toby. Kaytlene Newell. Right away."

The boy paused in tossing pebbles into the street. "Where?"

"Village of Newbury, or somewhere on the road between there and here."

"An' wot's the price, Mr. Regice? It'll cost ya."

Regice had no desire to tussle with the lad over money, for he knew the boy spoke for his father and was the best haggler in London.

"Hundred pounds," Regice said with a hiss. He knew he could double that easily, but it was a good offer and the boy nodded quickly.

"See to it, then. Half in advance in the usual spot?"

"Yeah."

"And, Toby, tell him that nothing is to happen to Merrick or there will be no final payment. Understood?"

The black-haired boy smiled and nodded.

Regice urged the horses on, pleased with himself. He would tell Tristan that Delamane had demanded two hundred pounds and keep the extra for himself. The exchange was so simple: a problem solved, profit made. He congratulated himself on his good business sense.

Kaytlene woke, shivering. For a moment she thought Daevon had left her alone on the beach, but the cool air cleared her head, and she focused on the furnishings of her cottage. The grate was cold, and the windows were still open, offering a place for the chilling fog to settle.

She moved to slide her feet to the floor and realized that she was in Daevon's arms. He must have carried her into the cottage after she had fallen asleep and had sunk down with her into the chair before the fireplace. He must have been as exhausted as she was. Even now he slept soundly, despite the cold and her movements.

The shock of waking to find herself in his lap startled her like a wave of icy water. Even so, she thought after staring at him in the semidarkness, he seemed harmless. She studied his rugged, dreaming expression, his head leaning against the chair back, lips slightly parted. How beautiful he was. And then some new emotion rose in her chest and curled tightly around her heart. It seemed to draw her to him, as though she must touch him to complete her own existence. She swallowed hard, balled her hands into fists, and allowed her conscience to overrule her emotions.

With stealth, she managed to slip out of Daevon's hold and find a candle, which she lit. She went first to the two tiny windows at the front of the house, securing the shutters, then set the candle into a scarred tin holder on the fireplace mantel and looked once more at the man who slept where her father had so often dozed. With a sigh she went through the kitchen to fetch a blanket.

When Kayte returned with a warm quilt in her arms, Daevon woke. Before his eyes opened, he felt the cold air against him where she had laid her head and knew it was her absence that had stirred him.

A sudden noise from behind startled him, but he recognized Kayte's soft expletives in the dark and smiled, shifting more comfortably in the chair. That cursing, he thought, was a disgraceful habit that he would ensure she broke.

Assuming she was going to her own bed he pulled his

cloak tightly about him, finding its warmth no substitute
for the heat of her body next to his. Her footsteps were
barely audible as she paused, as if making some serious
decision. Daevon kept his eyes closed, straining to hear
the slow, measured steps when they began again. They
stopped next to his chair and, carefully, Kayte bent to
cover him gently with a quilt. He could feel the angel-soft
brush of her hair against his cheek, but her uneven breathing was inaudible compared to the heavy, tortured thud of
his heart.

Kayte's hand shook as she allowed herself the freedom
to touch him. She found the warm spot of exposed flesh at
his neck and felt the gentle, even hum of his breathing
beneath her fingers. At the feel of the sleep-leashed strength
there, she drew in her own breath, snatched her hand
away, and went quickly to her own room.

"And a good night to you, Kayte," Daevon whispered
with a smile.

Kaytlene's sleep spun out long and free of dreams, and
when she woke again she expected to find the late morning
sun coming through her single window. Instead, she saw
only the slate-gray sky of predawn. She was in her own
bed, curled in the black crepe of her mourning gown and
her favorite quilt.

She snuggled deeply into the nest, her bare feet nearly
hanging over the side of the bed, her skirt twisted up to
leave her calves bare beneath the blanket. She wondered
where Daevon was. She knew by instinct that he was
somewhere near, though his presence hardly filled the void
left by her father's absence.

Perhaps, she thought sadly, God meant Daevon to be a
substitute, a new caretaker to see to her happiness as
James Newell had done. Then a fleeting memory of the
earl's kiss came to her. No, he had no intention of acting
like a father.

"Kaytlene?" He spoke her name with incredible gentleness, and she looked up to see him, his jacket removed,
waistcoat undone, the sleeves of his white shirt rolled to
the elbows. Kayte scuttled into a corner with the coverlet
tightly about her. Daevon's smile was warm and mysteri-

ous and difficult to ignore, though she managed not to let it affect her.

"A man should see his betrothed first thing at least one morning before he says his vows," he said.

"And does my sorry appearance change your mind, my lord?" she replied.

"On the contrary, Miss Newell." His voice was a rough caress as he sat on the edge of her small bed and took her hands in his. His eyes seemed to absorb her in a quick sweep. "Any man who had the pleasure of waking beside you every morning would be a fool to give it up."

Kaytlene's golden eyes reflected the spark of dawn coming through her window, and Daevon, reaching to take her face in his hands, wanted to ignite that flame in her.

Kaytlene could not take her eyes from his face, from the black hair where the light danced over its thick waves, or from the wide, muscular shoulders. When his hands cupped her face and his lips came gently down on hers, she offered no resistance. But she was afraid of the demonic power he held over her when she gave herself to him, the burning core swirling like a vortex in her breasts. It was as terrifying as it was compelling. It rose again now, intensifying as the protective quilt fell from her and he pressed her to him, an answering groan coming from his throat.

Daevon's mouth on hers seem to question her, and he received a shy and tentative yes in reply. His hands moved down to the curved sweep of perfumed white shoulders, tangling in the black velvet bows that came easily loose under his touch.

Kaytlene was mesmerized under the growing insistence of his kiss, unable to protest as he loosened her gown and it began slipping down. He bent his head to her neck, his tongue drawing a line to the pounding pulse that raced against his mouth in the hollow of her throat.

"Daevon," she murmured, her fingers unable to decide whether to push him away or to grasp hold and not let go until the longing in her body was fulfilled. She made a harsh, sudden sound as Daevon's hand brushed the silky chemise that covered her breast and her hands made their decision. She pushed him roughly away.

She was too shaken to speak. Daevon leaned back, his

left hand on his knee, the other massaging one temple. He was not sure what he should think. Kaytlene's eyes were liquid with fear or desire—perhaps both. She pulled the quilt back up to her chin, making herself all the more innocently appealing.

"Have you . . . ever been kissed by a man before, Kayte?"

She didn't know how to tell him the truth.

"I . . . yes, but—"

From the stricken look on her face as she turned away from him, Daevon assumed the worst.

"Did someone hurt you?"

"No. They were just kisses. They didn't make me . . ."

"Make you what, Kayte?"

"Want," she answered simply.

Daevon smiled, realizing that he had not merely imagined her naivete after all. He smoothed a tousled curl against her throat.

"And what is it that you want?"

She was surprised to hear the reply that came from her own lips. "More," she whispered.

A long silence passed before Daevon spoke again.

"I've been looking for answers for a long time," he said. "Answers about this betrothal. I tried to force you out of my life before you ever had a chance to enter it. Someone told me yesterday that I need you. He was right, Kaytlene, though I couldn't admit it to myself until last night."

He seemed so sad, Kaytlene thought, so alone. It was an act of trust, this opening of himself to her, and she loosened her hold on the quilt to reach out and touch his face. He took her hand quickly, as if she might otherwise draw it away at any moment, and pressed it to his lips.

"My life is full of shadows, Kaytlene," he went on. "I have been only a name to you for years, but now I'm flesh and blood. If you marry me, you'll live with me in the shadows."

"What is it?" she asked gently. "What is it that haunts you?"

"A past I cannot remember, a present full of secrets, Kaytlene . . . and hatred."

"I've been haunting you all this time as well, haven't I?"

"Yes." He kissed her hand again. "But it doesn't matter. I thought at first that you and your father had somehow blackmailed my father into signing the betrothal contract." He searched her sleepy features for a show of anger, but saw only a tentative smile.

"How odd," she replied. "I thought the same of you."

"Does it matter now, Kaytlene? If our fathers had some feud between them, let's not make it ours as well. Perhaps their scheming did some good."

"Good?" Kayte asked, astonished he could think such a thing.

He smiled. "Will you come to London with me, Kayte?" he murmured. "Perhaps we both owe each other one chance."

"Do you mean that?" she asked solemnly.

"Yes."

"I have no reason to say yes."

"I know."

"And a thousand reasons to refuse."

He nodded. "Yes," he answered. "I know."

"I'm in mourning."

"I'll give you time to mourn. I'll see to it that you are happy and well cared for, and that no restrictions are placed on you. You may come and go as you please."

"Wouldn't it be easier to leave without me?"

He smiled, admitting the logic in that.

"A marriage of convenience. Is that what you're offering?" she asked.

"I suppose I am."

She studied him again, seeing nothing in his eyes that would give her cause to doubt the sincerity of his offer.

She considered the promises she had made to her father. Why had he trusted Daevon Merrick? He had never done anything but watch out for her good, and he wouldn't have promised her to a man who would make her unhappy. But had someone forced him to sign the contracts? She had been only a baby when the agreement was made. Why? She wanted to know. Who was this man and why was his life so intricately tangled up with hers? The offer he made would allow her to search out the truth and still maintain a distance from him. If the Merricks were guilty of hurting her father in some way, she would run from them and live her life in Newbury.

"I—" She turned questioning eyes up to his and stopped. She was trying to say yes, but her brain could not force the word off her tongue.

"I don't know," she said and sighed.

If Daevon Merrick truly meant her no harm, she thought, then . . . could she love him?

"Very well," she said at last. "I'll go."

Chapter 5

Not since she had been a year old had Kaytlene Newell's life known such abrupt upheaval. Many times the
unnerving shock of it threatened to send her reeling, but at
those moments she found Daevon beside her, offering a
strengthening hand on her elbow or a gently spoken word
of confidence in her ear.

They paused only for tea that he boiled for them and a
breakfast of biscuits and fresh apples. He explained that he
had originally planned to ride straight to London, but now
he did not wish to add to her trouble by pushing her so
ruthlessly.

Kaytlene nibbled on a crisp biscuit. "You planned to
return without a common village girl in tow to hinder your
progress," she said dryly.

"Yes," he replied truthfully, "I did. But I won't mind
the delay. It will give me that much more time to hoard
your attentions to myself." The smile that he gave her
released something untamed and warm in Kayte.

"You should have told me, my lord, that you were
given over to such fits of selfish whim."

"I shall be careful to warn you of my bad habits in the
future." With that, he took a deep swallow of his tea and
choked on the taste of it.

Kaytlene looked down into her own cup and again at
Daevon as his coughing became a rumbling laughter.

"I shall give you fair warning too, my dear, if I am ever
again taken by the urge to prepare tea for you."

Kaytlene took a cautious sip from the cup she held
pressed between her palms. The tea ran like acid along her

tongue and she was barely able to force the bitter stuff down her throat.

"It is a poor attempt, my lord," she said, her voice raw, "but perhaps you will improve with patient practice."

They laughed together, and Kaytlene thought the sound warm and strong against the walls of her little house. Her father's laughter had been like that as he lifted his tiny daughter into his muscular arms, swinging her around the tiny kitchen with unabashed adoration. Then, free of his loving grasp, she ran into the friendly shadows of the house, giggling softly as he attempted to find her in her obvious hiding place.

Daevon cocked his head to one side and a deep cleft formed between his brows at the thoughtful expression that had come over Kaytlene's face. If it were not for the faintest curl of a smile at the corners of her mouth, he would have thought she was ill.

"Kayte?"

Her eyes closed. Her shoulders drooped forward. The memory that had felt so like reality was now sucked away from her by a deep sense of loss.

"Kaytlene?"

A tear slid from beneath her lids, revealing pain in her amber eyes. Daevon desperately wanted to take the pain onto himself. His lips parted as if he were about to speak.

Kayte held up a hand to stop him. "Please . . . leave me," she said softly. "I need . . . to be . . . alone," she pleaded, her tone softened by a long sigh. Without waiting for Daevon's reply or meeting his eyes, she slipped out of the kitchen and into the tiny room where her father had died. The door closed behind her with a soft click.

Daevon stood staring into the empty hall where she had disappeared. Despite the walls between them, he could hear her sobs. With a pang, he realized that, despite all his money and all his influence he could not erase her private anguish. Kayte was suffering a pain and loneliness that even he could not soothe. Reluctantly, he set down his half-empty cup of tea and went out to saddle Cyclops.

Unable to control the sobs that strained her lungs and scratched her throat raw, Kaytlene lay partly on the little

cot where her father had slept and dreamed and died.
Nearly an hour passed before the numbness in her legs
forced her to move, and she rose shakily to take a better
position on the hand-woven seat of a willow rocker. The
bed, the rocker, and a large black trunk took up all the
space there was. Three pieces of furniture and memories.

This was where she had read to her father for endless
hours by the light of a single candle. This was where she
had knelt when she swore to fulfill her father's wish by
marrying Daevon Merrick.

"Be happy, my Kayte," he had whispered with weakening breaths.

She had held tightly to his hand. "Yes. Yes, Father."
And his hand had slid from hers as his soul escaped his
failing body.

Now her father had been gone for little more than a day
and she had already behaved like a harlot in an effort to
free herself from the promises she had made. She had
allowed Daevon such awful liberties, letting him kiss her
as if she were a whore.

She sighed and rocked the chair. It was shameful to
behave so. It was shame that sent her, weeping like a
child, away from Daevon Merrick.

The comfortable little chair and its familiar, singsong
creaking were comforting and she leaned back, exhausted
from weeping. Sometime later, she was jarred awake when
she realized that footsteps were sounding outside in the
narrow hall. A quick rap on the closed door urged no
response from her. She peered out the crude window. It
was barely past dawn. Another knock sounded.

"Come in, your lordship."

The door swung open, and Daevon took a tentative step
toward her.

"Are you ill?" he queried softly, concerned that she
looked so pale.

"No, my lord."

He wondered at the lack of emotion in her face as she
sat with her hands folded primly in her lap.

"I'm sorry if my behavior earlier disturbed you," he
said. "It was thoughtless of me."

She did not respond to his apology. He watched as she

sighed, then began rocking the chair, her eyes lowered. He had been more than thoughtless, he thought. Selfish, arrogant, cold—those were more apt terms. She was hurting and he had been concerned about being inconvenienced. God, he thought suddenly, how could I have let myself become such a bastard?

"Forgive me, Kayte?" he said gently.

"It was my actions that shame me, my lord." She stared down, afraid that meeting his eyes would cause her to throw herself into his arms for comfort.

Daevon could barely comprehend this lovely girl's vacillating moods. What did she mean, her actions shamed her? Was she a part of her father's plot after all, and beginning to regret it? The doubts crept in, unwanted.

"I've been to see a friend, Kaytlene," he said. "He'll see to your house and whatever you leave here."

"I'll not have it sold," she said with surprising vehemence.

"I never mentioned selling. This house is yours, to do with as you wish. But someone must be sure that the fresh air gets in and that the weeds don't take over the garden." He attempted to pull a response from her with a smile, but she squeezed her hands together and her eyes stayed lowered.

She knew he was trying to ease her mind, to convince her to come away with him.

"Have you changed your mind, Kayte?"

She thought he sounded as though he hoped she hadn't. She found no air in her lungs to force out an answer.

"We must go now. Burns is here with the coach. Do you want to take anything? This trunk perhaps?"

"Don't touch that!" Kaytlene's hand stopped his before it settled on the heavy leather straps.

"Why, Kaytlene?" His voice was suddenly frigid with the ominous, unavoidable questions that had been frozen in his heart since he was thirteen years old.

"What secrets are you keeping from me, Kaytlene Newell, when you know I have too many of my own?"

"Daevon," she replied in an equally cold tone, "if the contents of that trunk are a secret, then they are a secret to both of us, for I've never looked under the lid."

"It was your father's?"

"Yes."

"And what were you to do with it once he was gone?"

"Burn it, my lord."

"Without looking inside?"

She nodded, knowing how incredible it must sound to a man who claimed his life was wrapped in secrets.

"And why would you do that?"

"Because I promised."

Daevon tried to make reasonable thoughts of the notions that came quickly to his mind. He had never before believed that a love could be so true and simple that one could promise to do entirely as the other bade and fulfill that promise with neither question nor curiosity. All his experience, all his reason, told him it could not be so. And the contents of this trunk could provide the means to prove her true or false. It would be best to know now, before he received her hand in marriage and richly adorned it with the gold ring that would be hers as his wife.

"You may keep your promise, Kaytlene," he said, "but I have taken no such oath. And if I find what is lying beneath this lid to my dislike, then I will fulfill your promise to burn its contents. And then I shall decide what to do with you."

Kaytlene leaned back in the chair. He thought her false, she realized. Exactly what he suspected her of she could not be certain, except that the doubts which he had so eloquently expressed yesterday were as much a part of him as the hard pain swelling in her own breast.

"You do not trust easily," she murmured.

"Trust is to be earned," he replied.

"And how long will it take for me to earn yours?"

Daevon sighed as he watched tears forming in her eyes. She did not allow them to fall. She's a stubborn one, he thought derisively. Proud, willful. They were a great deal alike, he realized.

"I am sorry," he began. "I'm accustomed to giving orders. I have no right to open the trunk—it belongs to you."

Kayte's mouth opened slightly in surprise. He was backing down! She was certain that it was something he was not in the habit of doing. She could see in his eyes that he wanted to open the trunk, but he was restraining himself out of consideration for her. As her betrothed, he had every right to claim her possessions as his own.

He was trusting her. That in itself was amazing, and it made her want to throw herself into his arms and thank him. She chose instead to stand slowly and walk to him. Resting her hands on his shoulders and reaching up on tiptoe, she shyly pressed her mouth to his.

"Thank you," she murmured.

He reciprocated by sliding his arms around her waist and kissing her thoroughly. When he released her, she was breathless.

"What do you think you might find there?" she asked softly.

"Answers," he replied. "About the betrothal. An opportunity to learn the truth."

Kaytlene considered his words for a long moment. She allowed him to hold her, thinking how pleasant it was to be in his arms, and realizing that she wanted his trust just as much. She wanted nothing to come between them. The trunk might contain something that would help him find his answers, and she would always feel responsible if she withheld it from him now.

"I want to give you something," she murmured. "Because you didn't force me to break my promise, I want to do something for you in return."

Daevon looked down questioningly. "What are you saying?"

"I want you to have the trunk."

"You want me to—"

"Open it," she whispered. "I want you to have your answers, if any are there. But I don't want to break my promise to my father. I will not open it myself."

"Why?" he whispered, grateful for her gift.

"Because," she returned, "you've struggled with questions about me for too long. Our fathers wouldn't give us any answers. Now, perhaps, I have the power to unlock the secrets you've waited so long to discover."

She paused as her determination grew beneath his approving gaze.

"You've been unhappy because of me," she went on.

"Now that we are to be married, I would rather your
doubts be laid to rest. I won't have a husband who calls
me 'love' yet distrusts me. Look there and see if you can
put both our minds to rest."

Daevon bent to kiss her again, this time more gently.
"Now I must thank you," he murmured against her mouth.

She stepped away from his arms. "If you will excuse
me, sir, I'll leave you in private."

"I shall excuse you, Kaytlene, only because I know I
will have the pleasure of your company again soon."

She was gone with a smile.

Daevon stepped into the pale light of a rose-colored
dawn and bade a fine morning to his favored pair of grays,
which were pulling his carriage. Mr. Burns, red-eyed but
alert, sat atop the driver's seat. After Daevon instructed
him to see to the bags which had already been packed and
arranged neatly in a corner of the entry, Daevon returned
to the trunk.

With the door behind him securely fastened, though he
knew it was unnecessary to do so, he lifted the lid of the
trunk and removed a gown that had been folded neatly on
top. A wedding gown. He laid it carefully aside, its beauty
unable to keep him from what might be beneath it.

He removed books—French, geography, history—a tiny
white dress—an infant's baptismal gown, he guessed—and
dried flowers that turned to dust under even his gentlest
touch. Underneath were legal documents of births, mar-
riages, deaths.

Daevon removed family relics such as any man might
hold dear, but nothing provided the answers he sought.

Daevon sat back hard on the roughly hewn floor. Why
would it be necessary for Kaytlene to destroy such things?
Surely her father must have realized she might like to pass
them on to her own children.

As he pondered these thoughts, his gaze roved over the
trunk. Gradually he realized it looked larger from the
outside than . . . In an instant Daevon was up again,
tearing at the false bottom of the box, which came up after
only a short struggle.

A hundred letters lay yellow and dry beneath his fingertips. He pulled up stacks of them, recognizing the hand of Jameson Ferris, one of his London solicitors, among others. The letters had never been opened. The lumps of sealing wax were crumbling at their edges but holding firm. James Newell had never even opened them!

All but one.

At the center of the hole Daevon had burrowed was a letter penned in his own hand, in the flamboyant scrawl of an eager young lover. The rough edges parted easily as he thrust a finger and thumb inside to retrieve the contents. He unfolded the letter, which he knew well despite the long passage of time, and something fluttered to his lap. As the paper came open fully, pound notes of all sizes fell to the floor about his knees. He knew before counting them that there were ninety-five pounds. His tabulation confirmed the thought.

How much did she pay for the animal? he had asked Justin.

Five pounds, my lord. As a filly, the boy had replied, and later he had said the money had been a gift from her father . . .

Kaytlene closed the door of her narrow room. After all that had passed between herself and Daevon she felt good. She had done what she felt was necessary to ensure that her marriage had a better chance of succeeding.

Though she tried her best to keep her mind on the requirements of mourning, each glance from his warm gray eyes sent her thoughts reeling. Each gentle smile that softened the hard angles of his face made her more willing to accept the marriage, and more curious about the kind of life she would lead as his wife.

Kaytlene knew nothing of what passed between a man and his wife in the sanctity of their bedchamber, except for the joy and passion that she had so often gleaned from the pages of the heavy Bible in her father's room—the Song of Songs.

"I am my beloved's and he is mine." Kaytlene slipped off her wrinkled black dress and stepped into a simple midnight-blue muslin gown. The rounded neckline and full, tapered sleeves were edged with white lace, but otherwise it was as unadorned a gown as any she owned. It was flattering, though, with its snug-fitting bodice and slightly flared skirt. She wondered with a small frown if it would please Daevon.

If the thrill of his touch and the hot stirrings he aroused deep in her body with his kisses were any indication of what pleasure was to come, she knew she could grow to love her husband. If he earned her trust. He had already made a good start. His knock sounded on her door as she began to fasten the back of the dress.

"Kayte?"

"Yes, my lord. Come in."

As he entered, she studied his expression, but could read nothing there.

"Did you find your answers?" she whispered.

"Not entirely," he replied. As he took in her new gown with an appreciative glance, she knew that he was, indeed, pleased.

He grasped her gently by the shoulders and tilted her face up to his. "Your father never opened the letters from my solicitors. And he didn't spend the money I sent to convince him to break the contracts. But there was nothing there that gave me any information about the reason for our betrothal. I'm sorry. I don't have any answers for either of us."

"We'll find them eventually," Kayte answered.

He smiled in reply. "Perhaps. But for now, may I escort you to your carriage?"

Kaytlene gave him a deep, formal curtsy in acceptance, and the breath escaped her lungs in a gasp as she was pulled up against his chest, his face above hers, his arms wrapped tightly around her. A second sensation sent a flush into her cheeks.

Daevon laughed softly after his initial surprise, but he did not take his hands from the bare flesh of her back. "It seems, my lady, that I shall have to appoint you a maid to help with your dressing. I can't have a wife who appears at her engagements half dressed. I'm afraid I would be given over to serious fits of jealousy."

"Would you truly, my lord?" she replied breathlessly.

"You no doubt have spent your life in the company of women who are beautiful and well bred."

"And they pale in the light of your pretty golden eyes, Kayte."

As he moved down to press her mouth to his, Kaytlene pulled away abruptly. "I think, my lord, that it would be very unseemly for you to be found kissing me in my bedchamber."

"Ah, just so," he agreed, bowing in an exaggerated show of chivalry. "Please allow me, my lady Kayte."

When she hesitated, he turned her, allowing him access to the back of her dress. He pushed her hair over one shoulder, his fingers playing in its silky texture.

"Lovely," he murmured, his mouth so near her nape that she felt the soft vibration of his words on her skin.

His kiss was an offering placed at the base of her neck. His fingers ran along the open V of muslin, barely skimming the light chemise that kept their bodies separate.

At his touch Kaytlene wondered how it must be for a man and a woman to become "one flesh." When a stranger's very smile beckoned such a raw response from her that she could hardly stay on her feet, how could she accept more of his exquisite torture without begging shamelessly for all of him? The ways of the flesh were, indeed, a great mystery to her. One which, she reminded herself sternly, she might have to deny herself the pleasure of revealing—if she meant to be his wife in name only.

"Your lordship!" An unshaven, wild-eyed face peered into Kayte's room from the doorway, so surprising her that she sprawled backward against Daevon's chest. He laid his hands protectively on her shoulders.

"What is it, Burns?" His voice was little more than a growl.

The man removed his tall black hat and bowed apologetically. "Beg pardon, mum. Will there be anything else ta load?"

"Kaytlene?" Daevon asked.

"No. I'll bring the rest of my things."

"Wait for us at the carriage, Burns."

"Yes, sir." With another bow, the man scurried off.

"I'm sorry," Daevon whispered with a half smile against

her ear. "I hope you don't feel I've compromised you, Miss Newell."

"If I've been compromised, Lord Merrick," she answered with renewed anxiety, "it is only because of the position in which I've placed myself."

Daevon smiled, turning her back to face him, and kissed her forehead lightly. He laughed gently. "You're a prize, Kayte," he said against her skin.

"Your laughter is wonderful," she replied before thinking.

"I've neglected it for a long time. But I have a feeling you will bring it back to me."

"I shall try, my lord."

"Call me Daevon. Please, Kayte?"

"Daevon," she answered shyly, peering hesitantly up at him.

He answered with a soft groan and bent to kiss the still-exposed side of her throat, then her earlobe. The sensations he evoked silenced her.

"Daevon," she said finally, "the morning wastes away."

"I would hardly call this a waste," he declared with a final kiss at her temple. "Perhaps soon I can convince *you* of that as well."

"I have no doubt you can, my lord," she whispered back.

Chapter 6

The trip to London began later than Daevon had hoped, though it was his own purposefully slow fingers that had delayed them. Normally his hands were quite adept with the fastenings of women's clothing, but he played the clumsy novice just to keep Kaytlene near him, to smell her lilac-scented hair and feel the warm smoothness of her back beneath her chemise. If it were not for the urgency of his mother's illness, he would not have regretted it in the least.

Keeping his promise to Sean O'Connell, he instructed Burns to drive the carriage first to the inn for Kaytlene to bid her final farewell to her friends while he spent a few moments conferring with Henri Todd. He had several last-minute arrangements for his friend to see to, and Todd was equally anxious to finish the business so that he, too, could leave Newbury.

Just past midmorning they were riding toward London, following a road that twisted first along the rocky coast. It was a lovely ride, Kaytlene thought, though a bit monotonous. After nearly two hours she could still look out the small carriage window at the neverending sea.

As Daevon reached to take her hand in his, she met his eyes for the first time since the little cottages of Newbury had disappeared from sight.

"You miss them already?"

"I've known only a life in Newbury, my lord. It shall be difficult to accustom myself to a wider world."

"You will have to come back often. To keep Justin

abreast of his lessons. And to see to Sean's inflammation, I suppose.'' Daevon smiled faintly.

Grateful relief colored Kaytlene's cheeks. "Thank you."

"And you must invite them to DenMerrick House."

That was a pleasing idea which had not previously occurred to her. As Lady Merrick, the responsibility of inviting and entertaining guests would naturally fall to her. It was an exciting prospect. But, sadly, she knew that her social graces had never been tested in such a vital matter.

"Thank you again, my lord," she said wistfully, "but I would not think to impose on your mother's place in your household."

"Do you not wish to act as my hostess, Kayte?"

She saw a flash of disappointment in his eyes. *My hostess*, he had said.

"My mother is hardly able to see guests now," he continued, "so you will be relieving her of a great strain if you assume the burdens of entertaining which society expects of a man in my position."

"Then of course, for your mother's sake, I shall be glad to do so."

Daevon squeezed her hand in acknowledgment.

"I know the overnight stay we intend to make along the way is only for my benefit," she pointed out softly. "With your mother taken ill, you won't rest easy until you're home. Perhaps we should ride straight through until we reach DenMerrick House."

The earl had been content to be near her, to have her hand in his, and he was studying the countryside when her suggestion brought his eyes back to her. She sat waiting for his reply, her golden eyes aglow with the light of morning that poured into the carriage. For a moment he was too stunned to reply. Most of the women in his life were always so concerned for their own comforts that they failed to acknowledge the needs of others. He had blindly assumed Kaytlene would be that way as well. In her situation he would expect her to be in such a state because of the loss of her father and the sudden turn of events in her life that she would wish to ease gradually into her new life, taking an extra day or two to prepare. But now she was thinking only of him.

"It's a long way to be confined in this box of a carriage," he said. "There's no comfortable place to sleep, and the dust can be a nuisance."

"Will you mind it?"

"I've done it before," he replied, "and survived, but I'll never admit to liking it."

They exchanged comfortable smiles.

"I don't find the coach so confining," she said at last. "I don't mind a little dust and . . ." She looked at the bag that lay at her feet, which turned out to be lumpier than she had imagined. "Well, this would make a good pillow."

Kaytlene expected either a shake of his head or a nod, and, although the reply she received was completely unexpected, it was exquisite in its own way.

With Kayte's right hand in his left, Daevon pulled her to him with a sudden jerk. The lurching of the carriage conveniently aided in landing her on his lap with one steel-muscled arm supporting her back and the other tightly around her waist.

"Daevon!" she protested, shocked.

"Don't worry, love. There's no one to interrupt us here. We have hours before Burns will stop."

Before giving her an opportunity to protest, he put his mouth on hers with a fervency that surprised them both.

Kaytlene struggled, pushing against the hard flesh of Daevon's chest, feeling the smooth white linen of his shirt. But her strength was feeble beneath his and her body fought and won a battle with her mind as he claimed her lips.

His initial fierceness became a melting heat—slow, deliberate, wanting. His mouth urged hers open and searched inside, exquisitely aware of the sensations he built in her. When he had stolen all the breath her lungs held and filled her brain with blinding, dizzying color, he sealed her mouth and its protests with a teasing fire from his tongue. He traced the line of her lower lip, then slid the arm that braced her back down, watching her head fall back and a mass of dark hair shower down to touch the tight cloth covering his thigh.

He watched her breathing, her hands now clutched white-knuckled on his shirt, and felt her spine moving, arching, offering.

His kiss went to the center of her throat, down to her shoulder, and further, his tongue lapping teasingly at the flesh just below the lace of her bodice.

Kaytlene prepared herself for the next assault of pleasure, and now even her mind screamed for him to continue, to caress her breasts as expertly as he had her mouth. When he nuzzled the vulnerable hollow just above her collarbone, a groan of disappointment caused Daevon's brows to rise.

He supported her head with his palm, massaging her scalp with his outstretched fingers. Her eyes were half closed, and a thick purr of pleasure came from her throat.

"It's . . . lovely," she murmured, "but . . ."

"Do you not enjoy my attentions, Kaytlene? I would be so disappointed if you said no." In a swift, smooth move he rested her head in the crook of his arm and loosened his hold.

"I've acted so . . ." She strained for the right word.

"Perfectly." Daevon's smile melted her so that she feared she would become a permanent part of his flesh.

"So shamefully," she managed to return, her cheeks flaming.

Daevon leaned back against the thickly padded seat and took a long breath. The contracting of his muscular chest pressed her breasts to him, caressing the aching tips. He was unaware of the touch and its effect on her until she moaned his name and stiffened her spine.

He had felt the response so many times that it startled him. The half-closed eyes, the parted lips through which came quick, shallow breaths, the hard tips of breasts pressed invitingly against the cloth of a bodice. She wanted him, but with an uncertain, trembling innocence that Daevon had never known. All the sexual affairs into which he had thrown himself in the past had been with expensive ladies of society. Though their pretty manners feigned innocence, part of the whore's games, he had never had a virgin in his bed. Even his beloved Monique had admitted, when it finally had become impossible for her to do otherwise, that she had once been with a man.

"Daevon?" Kayte commanded his attention with a whisper.

"Yes, sweet?" His fingers traced the line of her jaw, her skin hot to his touch.

"Am I a . . . harlot?"

Daevon stared, amazed at her intent, questioning gaze.

"A what?"

She was sure she had used the word in its proper context. "A harlot," she stammered.

The earl threw back his head and laughed, then held a little tighter to his betrothed when the carriage jolted and threatened to slide her from his lap.

"Now, where did you pick up such an unladylike word?"

Unladylike. He thought her a common girl.

"I read it."

Daevon's brows slanted downward in a frown. "What sort of literature have you spent your afternoons absorbing, Miss Newell? I'm quite certain that you did not learn that from your geography text."

"Shakespeare," she replied. "And the Bible."

"Ah, I see. Then perhaps I should tell you to 'get thee to a nunnery,' for you sorely tempt my limitations."

Kaytlene recognized his reference and frowned. "Then I *am* a harlot?"

Her voice was sinking into a tone of near despair, and immediately Daevon wanted to relieve her mind. "Kayte, do you know what a harlot is?"

"My father said a harlot is a woman who lives according to her own . . . physical desires. She gives in to them."

"Do you want to give in to me?"

It was all she could do to nod.

"Then, my love"—his mouth came teasingly close to hers—"you are a woman. Just a healthy woman, with a healthy woman's natural desires. And exceptionally good taste in men."

Daevon's lingering kiss was gentle but left Kaytlene's flesh tingling nevertheless. It intensified, lengthened, threatened to consume her. Heat stirred and whirled through her body, leaving her with a single, rushing emotion—need.

"You see, my Kayte," Daevon said, pressing his lips

against her ear, "this is the natural progression of things. It is all quite normal."

"Then if you say it is so, my lord, it must be." She reached up and pulled him down once more. In a spurt of irrational boldness she parted her lips and laid them against his, and a more willing invitation Daevon had never had.

His tongue slid between the perfect milky teeth into the small, hot cavern in which he lost himself, touching, caressing, teasing. When his tongue moved along the edge of hers, she moved with him in the play.

The pleased rumble in Daevon's chest reassured her, and she engaged in the kiss more enthusiastically. For long, lovely, aching moments they kissed, her hands on his neck and his hands moving slowly in her hair.

Kayte fought to accept her feelings. They were natural, he had told her. She was only a healthy woman with natural desires. And it was so much more pleasant to lie in his arms kissing him than to fight her feelings. Victory against them, however moral, was hollow. It was surrender that gave the most pleasure.

"You see, lovely girl"—Daevon's voice seemed to echo in the little carriage—"giving in is not so difficult."

"Are you so certain that I have, my lord?"

He smiled down into her eyes, knowing that he must kiss her again or lose his sanity. "I know the taste of surrender," he said gently, "and I taste it on your lips."

She was heat and water all at once. Burning. Melting. Moving under his caress.

Daevon took her mouth again. Never had he spent so much time just kissing a woman. The pleasure of it seemed always to wear off with a few kisses, its simpler passion overshadowed by his need for coupling and physical release. And that, he realized, was where the difference lay. He had never been so concerned with what the woman felt when he made love to her.

Kaytlene was different, though why was not quite clear to him. When one made love to a whore, she was expected to moan at the correct moment, say the right words, stroke the flesh just so, and it was accepted, played out, and paid for. In contrast, Kaytlene's sigh, her tentative kiss and

touch, were pure response, unadulterated by endless nights
of rehearsal with nameless suitors.

Kaytlene was startled by his brusque end to their gentle
kiss. When he pulled her against him as if to strangle her
in his arms, his eyes seemed to glow with an angry flame.

"You are mine," he whispered, his voice hoarse. "And
if ever you play me false, I shall kill you myself, pretty
Kayte."

He regretted his threat as soon as her eyes widened in
shock, but the thought of being betrayed again was devastating to him.

"Mine," he said much more gently. "Do you understand?"

And when his mouth fell hungrily on hers once again,
Kaytlene knew she did.

Monique Clay paced the marble floor in a state of
frenzy. Her full, daffodil-yellow silk skirts rustled each
time she stopped, turned, and started back down the long,
wide hall. Fifteen minutes earlier she had shed her shoes
and now stepped more lightly, nursing a blister that had
formed on her right heel. Stopping midway in the hall, she
sent a glare of hatred at the pendulum clock her husband
had imported from Switzerland for her birthday a few
weeks ago.

"Stupid louse," she muttered, "cuckolded under his
very nose! In his own house!" The damned idiot was now
not a hundred feet away while his own wife awaited the
carriage of her lover.

She looked again at the clock face and spat a curse at it.
Fool for a husband and the epitome of arrogance for a
lover.

When the familiar rattle of wheels and horses' hooves
sounded, Monique ran toward the door, prepared to scratch
her lover's eyes out with her own hands. Then she changed
her mind.

"Meta!" she called down the hall. A slight girl with
curly, shoulder-length brown hair came running out in her
nightclothes and robe, her blue eyes drooping with sleep.

"Yes, my lady?"

"See him to my room," she said with cold calculation.

"Yes, my lady." Meta watched her mistress, seductive

hips swaying, hurry down the hall and into the corridor to the right. She didn't see any reason to have gotten out of bed just to escort Lady Clay's lover to the bedchamber he already knew so well.

A bold knock shook Meta out of her thoughts and she unbolted the ornately carved front door, pulling it inward as he entered. The sight of him never failed to impress Meta. His dark eyes flashed over every detail of the house, noting any changes since his last visit nearly three weeks ago. His roughly textured brown cape swirled around his steellike thighs and calves, the color reflecting the reddish hues of his deep brown hair. He turned to Meta with a melting smile and a gleam in his coppery brown eyes.

"Good evening, sir," she managed to squeak out. "Her ladyship asked me to see you to her room."

His brows rose. "And his lordship?"

Meta's eyes glanced toward the stairway at the end of the hallway. "Upstairs. Asleep, sir."

"Ah, good girl, Meta." He laughed, tossing his cloak to her. His white shirt had full sleeves, and he looked as if he had just gotten up from his own bed and tucked it hastily into his black breeches. He crossed his arms over his half-bared chest and gave Meta another smile. "Well," he said smugly, "lead on."

She knocked hesitantly at her mistress's door.

"You may come in, Meta," rang the silvery voice.

Monique had removed her gown and tossed it across her velvet-draped bed. She sat at her dressing table, unwrapping the long black braid that had been wound into a knot at the nape of her neck. Her lover's smile reflected in the mirror and she showed no outward reaction, though her blood began to pound madly in her ears.

"Tristan?"

He gave her a deep, mocking bow. "You were expecting me, were you not?"

"You were expected at eleven, sir. It is nearly twelve-thirty now. As you can see, I had given up on you and decided to retire." Her fingers deftly unbraided the black hair which, loosened, covered her back.

Tristan Merrick took in her hair and figure greedily. He had had a few common wenches writhing under his expert

FORTUNE'S BRIDE

thrusts during the past few weeks, but through each moment he had relished the idea of returning to Monique's bed.

"Ah, too bad." He feigned disappointment. "Then perhaps I shall have to find my pleasure elsewhere." Turning to Meta, he caught the girl in his arms and tilted her face upward. "Little Meta with your pretty curls and virgin's blue eyes, would you like some company to keep you warm tonight?"

Meta forced her eyes down, flushing with terrible embarrassment at being used as a pawn in this lovers' game. Yet his offer was too tempting for her conscience to rest easy.

"My Meta is a good girl," Monique said, her dulcet voice tinged with anger. "She keeps her mouth closed. Her legs as well, my dear." Her eyes bore down on the serving girl with a silent message that left no room for misinterpretation. "For if she doesn't, she might be forced to beg in the streets. Now let her get back to her lonely bed, Tristan. She's exhausted."

As soon as she was released, Meta bolted for the door.

Monique laid aside her hairbrush and stood, turning to the man for whom she had been so impatiently waiting.

"Welcome home, Tristan darling." In a moment, she was in his hard embrace, their mouths devouring. They said nothing as passion consumed their bodies. Tristan's hands forced away her chemise, baring her aching breasts to his searching, and he pulled her against his length, his palms hot on her white thighs.

"I've missed you, Monique." He pulled away to strip off his shirt and she knelt before him, one perfectly manicured finger tracing the throbbing outline of his hardness through the skintight breeches.

"Get them off," he ordered urgently. "For God's sake, get them off!"

Under her practiced hand, the breeches slid down and off.

"*C'est magnifique.*" Monique's hands ran up the length of his hard brown legs and she kissed the smooth indentation of his navel as passionately as she had his mouth.

Tristan held on to one of the bedposts with one hand and

took her ebony hair in the other. "Don't tease me, sweet French bitch," he said roughly. "I've missed this."

She peered up at him with a crisp smile. "Oh, my lord is so rude. Impatient little boy. *C'est un enfant terrible.*"

"Please, Monique." His voice softened.

"Ah, so much better." Monique's hands circled his shaft and teased with a light stroke along its length. His response was an animal growl from the back of his throat. She encouraged his moans with her hands and finally her mouth, whispering in French as she gave him what she knew he wanted. When his muscles tensed and quivered under her touch she rose, walking to the bed and settling in its center, her hands roaming provocatively over her own now naked flesh.

"Come, my love. I will have my pleasure, too."

"And I will see that you do." Tristan lay next to her, his hands running along the white thighs, his mouth hard on one breast.

"Yes, *mon cher.*" She groaned. She seemed to thrive on Tristan's speed, his punishing fierceness. In her mind was a memory of gentle hands, of slow, deep kisses and loving adoration glowing in storm-gray eyes. Of Daevon's hair, Daevon's eyes, Daevon's lovemaking, so gentle that her eyes misted with tears at the wonder of it.

When Tristan's body entered hers, he recognized the familiar look in Monique's eyes. She was thinking of his brother. Fierce and wild he thrust, punishing her.

"I'll get him out, French bitch," he whispered, pleased at her every whimper of desire and pain. "I'll get him out of your mind."

It was a little past three when Monique rolled from atop Tristan and onto her back, her body glistening with sweat. It was tiring, pleasing him, for he seemed to have no thought of time or weariness when he made love. All that mattered was the climb, the release, and now she was near exhaustion while he lay unsated, smiling like a demon. His fingers were laced behind his head, the lean, tall body stretched out on its back.

"Tired so soon, my love?" He chuckled.

"You will kill me, *mon cher,* if I continue."

"How regrettable," he said sarcastically. Monique knew

that her love for Daevon made her an easy target for Tristan's anger.

"As you can see, my dear, I still have not been fully satisfied."

Monique did not have to look at him to know that he was still stiff, pulsing . . . and waiting.

"Go home and get a whore, if you wish. I have already done the work of three women, *mon ami,* and will do no more."

Tristan rolled onto her, pinning her arms against the bed and entering her savagely to finish his pleasure.

"If I were your beloved Daevon, then you would do the work of ten women to please him. Yes, my jewel?"

Angry at his behavior, Monique spoke without thinking. "Yes!" she cried.

His slap was more of a fisted blow, and he was spent and lying on the other side of the bed before she could think or see clearly again.

"Bastard!" she muttered when the ringing in her ears had ceased. She went to her wardrobe for a wrap.

"Don't hate me, my pet. A man has his pride."

"Your pride has given me a terrible bruise, I think," she said, studying her jaw in the dressing table mirror.

She did not hear him slip across the room until he was just behind her, his hands at her throat. A silver and jade necklace fell from his fingers to lie against her white skin.

"For you, my love." He smiled. "But only if I am forgiven."

Monique's Achilles' heel had been shot cleanly through. She gave him a little pout before accepting his bargain and accompanying him back to bed.

"So tell me, how fares our little creation?" Tristan patted her flat abdomen.

"I did as you said, of course."

"And no complications?"

"*Mon Dieu!*" she exclaimed. "That doctor of yours gave me some terrible potion to drink!"

"And it worked?"

"*Oui.* I miscarried naturally, they say. And bled for a week."

"Poor darling. But better to keep your lovely figure and keep the earl of Merrick breathless at your elbow, eh?"

"And when does he return, *mon cher*?"

"My spy says he is returning with the Newell girl. He swore the two behave like first lovers." Tristan enjoyed the flame of anger that burned in Monique's face.

"You promised to get rid of the common little bitch." She pouted again

"Not to fret, my love. I am seeing to it."

"While lying here in my bed?"

"I cannot do both at once, my dear, and I thought it better to hire someone to see to her rather than to replace me here."

"Selfish brute. When?"

"The man was unable to locate Daevon's coach last evening, but now he is on the road to London. She shall be dead soon." He spoke the words as easily as he might bid a friend good morning. Noting the small question in Monique's eyes, he went on. "And yes, my dear, your adoring Daevon shall be free at last."

"And what of Forrest? *Mon Dieu*, I cannot be Lady Merrick and Lady Clay at once."

"Indeed. That would be a real sin, would it not?" He gave her an amused, sidelong glance. "I think perhaps our sweet little Meta should do the cruel deed for us."

Monique smiled. "You are too clever, Tristan. And then off to boarding school for my poor little fatherless children, *non*?"

"Yes," he replied emphatically. "Your designs on my brother the earl will move much more smoothly without the little cretins running about underfoot."

Monique settled back against the fat satin pillows, content with the arrangements.

She had met Tristan's brother at her cousin Yvette's first formal party. She had hung behind the heavy blue draperies of the ballroom at Quenell Manor, watching. He was incredibly tall and dark, even a bit standoffish, but with an unavoidable wit and handsomeness that no woman could deny. Several times Daevon spotted her watching him, and the faintest of smiles seemed to lighten his countenance.

Tristan's low snores disturbed Monique's reverie, and she turned to see him sprawled on the bed, the coverlets half off his flawless back. She sighed. How long ago had it been since Daevon had first pulled her onto the dance floor as a shy, trembling girl of fifteen and sent his delicious fingers down her spine? He had only danced with her to be a gentleman, she knew, but it had convinced her that someday she must be his.

Two years later, she had seen him again, in London, and he had seemed more than a bit shocked and pleasantly surprised at her transformation to a slim, buxom young lady who fawned on his every move and speech. She took great pride in the fact that he spent his free time in her company, a privilege never before bestowed on a mere woman.

In early November of 1801, Daevon asked for her hand in marriage and she accepted. But when he presented her at DenMerrick House, Lady Merrick reminded him of his earlier betrothal and simply walked away.

Monique was devastated, but Daevon's proud, determined declaration of love for her gave her some courage.

"I could have accepted the betrothal," he said, her hands held in his, "but now I have you." And he wrote a letter to James Newell, explaining his love for Monique and his desire to break the contract. Monique went home to wait. She received a letter from Daevon shortly afterward.

29 November 1801

My dearest Monique,

It is with the heaviest heart and slowest hand that I write this note. James Newell refuses to break the betrothal contract, even after I have offered him everything which is mine to give. My only hope is to wait until his daughter reaches her twenty-first birthday and convince her then that the match would be wrong for both of us. The time will pass quickly, my love, so do not despair. I am determined to have you as my own.

Yours,
Daevon

Monique rose from the bed and took the letter from her jewel box, caressing it lovingly. She had been a young woman and very much in love with Daevon, so she had accepted his belief that all would be well.

For the next several weeks they were nearly always together, and on Christmas Eve, Daevon made love to her for the first time. By the New Year's arrival, it was clear that her father, Philippe Lisle, and his previously lucrative shipping business were deteriorating together. A bleak winter brought his death and word of payments due to creditors who were determined to split apart Lisle's belongings to pay his accounts.

After half of the dogs had been thrown their chunks of meat, there was nothing left, and Monique, as the only living child of her father and long-dead mother, was forced to accept the debts as her own—without a wealthy husband or benefactor to pay them.

She turned, of course, to Daevon, who was distraught over her situation. He paced the green and white hallway in DenMerrick House, a solid figure as she sat, weeping, on a straight-backed chair in a corner. She screamed and cried, begged and threatened and sobbed at his feet, but Daevon would not go to Newbury to speak to Newell himself and have the contracts broken so that he could marry her.

Monique knew, somehow, that his mother encouraged his stubborn refusal. Daevon offered to clear the debts and set her in a comfortable place as his mistress, but she wanted more. That same night she promised her hand in marriage to his rival in business, and having her revenge, she vowed vengeance upon Kaytlene Newell as well.

Her life was now nothing but dull social functions. Forrest Clay was gentle and truly cared for her pleasure, but it was Daevon's hands she wanted, his words she craved. Ten months after her hasty marriage, she gave birth to a daughter, premature but strong, and began to regret her decision to marry Clay.

Tristan came into her life—and her bed—nearly as soon as she recovered from childbirth. Their affair cooled only once, when she gave birth to twins a year later. Her third pregnancy had ended just weeks ago.

The miscarriage had been Tristan's idea, accomplished by the use of a bitter mixture given her to drink by a physician he had hired. Monique had lain upon her bed like death for nearly a fortnight, with Forrest pacing in the hall. The poor, stupid fool, she thought, and for a moment allowed herself to feel genuine pity for him. He would not survive this plan of Tristan's and neither would the little Newell bitch. And she, at the center of this treacherous ploy, would be reunited with the man who had loved her and, she was sure, still secretly yearned for her in his heart.

"Yes, Daevon," she whispered as she smoothed the letter back into its hiding place. "You will have me again, and I will finally be your lady. No matter what it takes."

Chapter 7

Kaytlene woke with the heat of the sun in her eyes and a terrible pain crawling up her left leg. She reached out to relieve the cramp and groaned.

"Easy, love," came Daevon's soothing voice. His hand went smoothly down her skirts to the stiff calf and massaged the pain easily away.

"Burns could surely use a little rest. Perhaps we should allow him to stop and stretch."

"I'm sure he would enjoy that, my lord."

Daevon rapped once on the front wall of the carriage, which slowed and stopped at his command. He reached to snap open the door. Kaytlene came down into his arms and wavered uneasily against him, her knees so stiff that they nearly buckled.

"What time is it?" she asked and yawned, raising her hands high over her head to take the aching numbness from even her fingertips.

Daevon enjoyed the tautness of her waist as the skin stretched beneath his hands, but pulled away to take a deep breath and check his timepiece.

"Late," he declared. "We're late."

"To reach the inn?"

"To have dinner. Burns, get down that basket." As the driver reached for the parcels on the top of the coach, Kaytlene was surprised to see that they had lost sight of the sea cliffs and were now in the midst of a rolling green plain with a wooded glen to the right and a small pond on the left.

Daevon was reaching into the open carriage for his

cloak and then up to the driver's seat for the large hamper.

"Your lordship," said Burns, "I'll be gettin' the pair down ta the pond for a drink and have my dinner there."

"Fine. Kaytlene, does your offer still stand to ride through without a night's rest?"

"Of course."

"Put the horses on picket lines, Burns. We'll rest here for an hour."

Burns nodded and turned the horses toward a shady spot near the water.

Daevon put down the hamper and spread his cloak with a flourish. "Please, my lady." He waved to the makeshift tablecloth and she took a seat at its edge, settling her skirts about her in a wide arc. The fabric was scratchy and her white stockings were clinging to her legs with tickling sweat.

When Daevon turned away to open the hamper and unpack its contents, she took advantage of his inattention. Quickly and silently she slipped off her shoes, tucking them under her skirts to hide them. Taking the edge of her hem in her hand, she lifted it to allow a cool breeze to skim beneath the blue muslin.

"Quite a pretty sight," Daevon observed. Kaytlene dropped her skirts with a gasp and pulled her feet up under the fabric. He laughed and caught her hand for a quick kiss, and she relaxed as he returned to the unpacking.

"My lord," she said, "if you always behave so, you must have a horrible reputation in London."

Daevon finished arranging the vast array of food and opened a small tin of oysters.

"Oh, no," he replied, his voice full of humor, "in all of Europe."

"I should have guessed." Kaytlene imagined him taking his pleasure with another woman. She frowned, not seeing that his eyes were still intent upon her. She wondered how many there had been. What an innocent little fool she was! When all this time she had begun to believe this man might care for her, it was probably all just an amusing game of seduction for him. Why should he care for someone he had just met? Her hands folded tensely in her lap, she realized how well she had played into his hands. Flowery speeches and the fact that they were betrothed—and alone—would not get her into his bed.

His hand crept into her lap to grasp hers. "Kaytlene, tell me what makes you so sad. You were happy a moment ago."

She looked hesitantly at him, afraid she would be lost again once she met his disarming gray eyes. She was right, for as soon as their gazes locked, her determination began to waver.

"I . . . I was wondering, my lord," she was able to say.

Daevon frowned and Kaytlene thought how dark and foreboding he looked.

"You were wondering. About me?"

She nodded.

"And you were changing your mind about wedding me," he said with finality. He released her hand and rolled back onto the grass, rubbing his temple as if to produce some thought to sway her. He had seen the change in her smile and eyes and believed that she had thought better of accepting his marriage proposal.

"No, my lord. My decision hasn't changed." The words drew him up, and he leaned on one elbow, interested in her expression.

"I was wondering," she began again, "what sort of man you are."

Daevon raised his brows. "You may not like what you find."

"Have you a mistress, my lord?"

He fell backward again onto the soft mound of grass and laughed until his voice rang across the maze of trees beyond.

"It hardly seems a question to find amusing, sir. I have a right to know whether you are keeping a woman."

He sat up, near enough so that she was immediately under his expert spell once more. His lips curled up into a half smile. "And if I do?"

Kaytlene tried to mask the horror in her expression. "Then I shall not marry you."

Daevon seemed to consider her declaration as he reached for a pear and cut it into small pieces. He took a wedge between his fingers and offered it to Kaytlene, but when she reached for it, he pulled away his hand.

"Do you intend to starve me, my lord?"

Again the heat from his smile poured into her. He shook his head and offered the fruit once more, sliding his free hand over both of hers. She finally realized his intention and parted her lips. She was unable to move her eyes from his as she took small bites. When she had finished, he took pleasure in licking the sticky juice from his fingers.

"I have no mistress, Kaytlene."

She wondered why her sigh sounded so much like relief.

"I have met a woman, though, whom I hope to seduce. I first thought to ask her to be my mistress, but that would be impossible now."

Kaytlene's jaw went slack and quivered as though he had slapped her. "How dare you! You arrogant bastard!" She raised her own hand to strike him, but he caught it by the wrist. Her fingers curled to sink her nails into his hand.

"Don't put out your claws with me, sweet Kayte. If you choose to fight me, I should warn you—I won't lose."

He took her other wrist and used his hold to push her back onto the ground. Kayte was determined to escape and twisted away from him, kicking at him with her bare feet.

"I hate you, Daevon Merrick! And nothing in this world could force me to marry you. Not even your damnable contracts! You will get no pleasure from seducing me, I can assure you."

The weight of Daevon's chest pressed against her, stilling her vain attempts to push him away and firing her desire all over again. She was angry at herself for her unabashed reaction and turned the anger on him.

"Go home to your pretty lover, Lord Merrick. I would not be accused of having spoiled your enjoyment."

"I can't go home to her. She isn't there."

"Left you already? How awful for you. At least she showed some good sense."

Kaytlene found a hand clamped securely over her mouth.

"I want her," he said tensely. "I want her by my side day and night. I want her heart and soul and body." He bent to her neck and buried his mouth in the sweet fra-

grance of her flesh. "I don't know what it is that makes
me want to possess her."

"You bastard!" Kaytlene's voice was nearly a sob as
she tried to fight the arousal that sent jolts of pleasure
through her body. "Why must you torture me? I told you
you didn't have to marry me!"

She felt his heart drumming against the soft space between her breasts. Breathing was impossible. He was glaring fiercely into her eyes, but Kaytlene thought for an
instant that it was passion's smoke there and not anger.

"I cannot make her my mistress," he finished, "because
she has consented to be my wife."

Kaytlene's body melted under the pressure of his and
the realization that he had been talking about her all the
time. And then his lips were against hers, drawing fire
from her soul. She gave up her struggle and her hands
clenched at his shoulders, feeling the hard cords of muscle
tighten in response to the kiss. His groan melted down into
her mouth.

He released her slowly, then pulled her up so that she
was sitting again and he did the same, running fingers
through his hair.

"I'm sorry for teasing you, Kayte. Forgive me."

Her heart seemed to fall as quickly as her eyes. "You
didn't mean any of it, did you?"

He took her face between his hands. "Yes, Kayte. I
meant every word. But I upset you. I had no right." His
hands dropped away. "Truth to tell, I don't fully understand my own behavior."

But Kayte was beginning to, in some small way. She
smiled and picked up the pieces of pear he had tossed onto
the center of his cloak, selecting one slice carefully and
offering it as he had done to her.

"Do you think it possible, my lord, that a man could
feel the same way toward his wife as he might toward a
mistress?"

Daevon allowed himself to smile in spite of his tangled
web of emotions. How could he feel so deeply for this girl
so quickly? As he ate the food she held to his lips, he took
in her disheveled golden-brown hair, her shy, perfect smile,
her eyes which had turned liquid and dark gold. He took

her hand again and his tongue chased a drop of juice as it trickled down her knuckles.

"I would never have believed it before today," he replied, "but now I think it might be a very definite possibility."

They spent the remainder of the hour sharing the large feast, taking food from each other's hands and drinking mulberry wine, a bottle of which Elizabeth O'Connell had tucked into the corner of the large hamper. Though they sat side by side, Daevon made no attempt to kiss Kayte again, partly due to his sheer enjoyment of her company, and partly because he knew his resistance was wearing thin. Once Burns returned with the coach, they packed the remaining food and took another long, luxurious stretch before continuing the journey.

When the sun hovered just over the horizon, daylight faded and Kaytlene settled into a corner, pulling a book from her bag. Swift's *Gulliver's Travels* had been a parting gift from Sean and Elizabeth and she was eager to begin reading.

Daevon settled in the opposite corner facing her, not as much for comfort as to have a good vantage point from which to study the lovely girl who was to be his wife. A square of light slanted onto her from the window, illuminating the delicate fingers that held the volume she read and her face, framed in a soft lace of hair.

The past two days had begun to change his attitudes about life, though how he wasn't quite sure. Since his father's death, when the Merrick holdings had fallen to him, he had spent his time fulfilling responsiblities to his family, to his business, and to society. Every day since he was thirteen had passed with a terrible foreboding of his unavoidable marriage. Only once had he allowed himself to feel what he thought was love for a woman. But had it truly been love? It was so different from what he had begun to feel for Kaytlene Newell. This purer emotion was much more intoxicating.

For the first time in the last rage-filled months, he was able to stretch out and relax both his body and his mind. He explained to Kayte that they would be stopping in a few hours to rest the horses and have supper, and that he

would be meeting with one of his employees there. He had
sent word to his aide, Lyle Miller, the previous afternoon,
and needed to spend time with the young man to clear up
some business that he had been able to finish before
leaving London. Then he allowed the slow, rhythmic movement of the coach to lull him to sleep. And slowly, slowly,
Kayte turned the pages of her book.

A soft snap sounded in the black carriage as Kayte
grudgingly closed the volume she had been enjoying. She
laid it aside and leaned her head back, rolling the tense
ache from her neck. She had become so involved in the
story that she had forgotten to stretch or change her position for the past few hours, and now she was reaping the
consequences of her immobility. Her eyes were bleary
from reading in the light, which had grown so faint that
now there was only a pale pink-gray glow in the sky.

She turned her attention toward the dark sleeping figure
across from her. Daevon's long, muscular legs were stretched
out and his feet rested on the seat beside her, one crossed
comfortably over the other at the ankles. His arms were
folded over his chest, and there was a serene expression
smoothing his finely chiseled features.

As if her fond attention had drawn Daevon back from
his sleep, he stirred. His eyes opened and he smiled as she
continued to peer at him through the dim light.

"I thought you really were a dream," he said quietly,
"but I'm glad to see you're still here."

"It would be difficult to depart from you, my lord. At
least while we are moving."

Daevon smiled more broadly, causing a heated blush to
rise in her cheeks.

"I hope I can teach you more important reasons for not
leaving me."

"I have no doubt you will, my lord."

She peered up at him, hoping her eyes did not betray the
emotion she could feel spinning through her. Daevon reached
across for her, but she evaded him.

"It seems we have arrived, my lord. Please do not
embarrass me publicly."

Daevon leaned back, planting his feet on the coach floor
and fastening one shirt cuff as they stopped for the second

time in over twelve hours. Before leaving the coach, he bent forward and found the irresistible sweetness of Kaytlene's mouth, as though it were a beacon of light in his darkness.

"I shouldn't dream of embarrassing you," he said deeply in the quiet. "Not publicly, at least."

He ushered Kaytlene out of the coach, and she took a moment to survey the quiet street. The inn lay opposite a wide market, which now was empty except for a few obviously drunken barterers. Two tall boys exchanged barbs regarding each other's latest love interests while they lit the lamps at the front of the inn.

Daevon offered his arm to Kaytlene and led her inside. Her first impression was an incredibly rotten odor which seemed to radiate from the kitchens. As sour as the air was, the noisy patrons seemed not to mind.

"The drink must numb their noses," Kaytlene whispered.

Daevon chuckled softly and pointed out the rows of lights that illuminated the hall.

"The smell comes from those Scottish cruzie lamps," he explained.

"And what do they burn? Fish oil?"

"Yes," Daevon answered plainly, "they do." He pushed her toward the steps where an old woman waited with yet another of the foul-smelling lamps. In spite of her appearance, her voice was soft and her movements graceful.

"This way, my lady."

Kaytlene followed her up the stairway to a door in the middle of the hallway. Inside she found no relief from the stifling air. She had not thought to ask of Daevon before the woman hurried silently away, leaving a single lamp burning on a side table. To her dismay, Kaytlene saw no windows and could not bear the idea of breathing that awful, acrid smoke for long. As she bent to blow out the sputtering flame, the door opened again and a girl ran in, out of breath and flustered.

"Oh, no, my lady! This way!" Kaytlene followed again, out into the hallway and farther down to a corner room.

The girl pulled a long, skeletal key from a huge apron pocket and pushed the door open to wait for her entry.

Kaytlene's nostrils drew in fresh air. The new room was

large and clean, with two windows, one facing south and the other east. A large fireplace with a polished steel grate had already been laid with wood for a fire, and the marble chimneypiece was adorned with tall tallow candles in silver holders.

When the door snapped shut behind her, Kaytlene felt she was in another world. A soft golden carpet rolled out to the corners beneath her feet and on the last wall was arranged a huge bed, swathed in dark curtains and coverlets with gold sewn at their edges.

The girl turned back the bedclothes and opened the door again to see that a table carried up by two houseboys was placed neatly before the fireplace. In another moment the table was laden with food and wine.

"His lordship asked us to see to your every comfort while he receives news from his courier, my lady." She bowed and departed.

Kaytlene looked about her. "Thank heavens for these tallow candles," she said aloud. "And thank you, Lord Merrick."

She was not surprised to find a clean washbasin, cloth, and pitcher of steaming water on an ornately carved table near the east window, and made good use of them. When she parted the heavy curtains, evening lay calm and cool below her.

With great interest, Patrick Delamane watched the womanly figure silhouetted against the candlelit window. After a few moments he let out a deep sigh of disappointment. Even with only a shady outline, watching her undress would have been a pleasure. Well, he would have his chance with the lady wench soon enough. A black scowl darkened his face. If the girl was in Merrick's room now, perhaps his lordship had ideas about having her stay. Not that he would blame the man, of course. She was as pretty a wench as God's hand ever created. Nervously, Delamane fingered his dagger. As pretty as God had ever made, or he had ever killed.

The powerful mount beneath him stamped with impatience, but Delamane whispered soothingly and waited.

*   *   *

Daevon knocked once, lightly, and received no reply. He repeated his request for entrance. Again no answer. Taking the key that had been placed in his keeping, he slid it into the lock, only to find that the door was not bolted. A low, angry growl rose to the back of his throat when he entered to find his betrothed lying atop the bed, one hand palm up on the coverlets, the other flat against her waist. He slammed the door.

Kaytlene let out a frightened squeak and sat up, only to fall back down against the pillows when she saw who had roused her. Hands against her heart, she said raggedly, "My lord, you frightened me awfully."

"Good," he answered. "If there had been someone else behind that door, you could have been robbed . . . or worse, before I could get to you. See that you keep your damned doors locked, Miss Newell!"

"I'm sorry, Lord Merrick." She slid up until her back was against the wall behind the bed and tried to smooth her skirts down over her bare ankles.

Daevon looked once at the prim figure lying where he had slept days before. She tried to put on a show of calm decorum, but every few seconds her amber eyes glanced toward him as if he planned to pounce upon her at any moment. Giving up his anger with a deep sigh, he sat on the edge of the bed beside her and took her face in his hands.

"I didn't mean to frighten you." He spoke with a gentleness that relieved her fear, but his touch sent her heart racing.

"I don't want anything to happen to you before—"

"Before you have to marry me?" she said with strains of weariness in her voice.

Daevon smiled and pulled her to his chest, his arms a strong haven in which her doubts once again began to ebb away.

"Before I have a chance to discover what my life might be with you." He kissed her forehead tenderly. "And, of course, before I have a chance to seduce you," he added teasingly.

She didn't see the humor in that. "I'll be careful," she said quietly.

"Very well." Easing away from her, he relaxed, his
eyes now more silver-blue than gray.

"I've decided we'll stay overnight after all, Kayte. My
courier tells me that Mother is doing very well these past
few days."

"I'm glad."

"I had arranged to have this room for myself on the trip
home." Daevon paused and looked a little sheepishly at
Kaytlene. He was, in his silent way, apologizing for having wanted to return without her and was finally rewarded
with the small, shy smile that he had been trying to draw
out of her.

"You'll be taking the room instead," he finished.

"I don't wish to put you out," Kayte objected.

"I'll be in the room across from this one. If you need
me."

Their eyes met as the full impact of what he had said
became clear. He wanted her to come to him. And . . .
She blushed and swallowed hard. He was allowing her the
choice.

"I shall remember, my lord," she whispered. She bit
her lip. "But . . . I've no need of anything, thank you."

If there was disappointment in his eyes, it was hidden by
icy calmness.

"Then good night, Miss Newell. I wish you very pleasant dreams." He left the room as abruptly as he had
entered.

Kaytlene slipped out of bed to lock the door as she had
promised, but as her hand rested on the handle, a knock
interrupted her. It was Burns, lagging under the weight of
her largest trunk and mumbling an explanation for his
lateness in carrying out his lordship's orders.

The trunk was settled at the base of the bed and once
Burns was out and the door secured, Kaytlene raised the
trunk lid and searched through the piles of modest dresses
and nightgowns. The only new nightdress was a peach-
colored muslin that fell in a thick ruffle at her feet. Egg-
shell lace edged the long, tapered sleeves and rounded
neckline, which showed only a little of the upper curve of
her breasts. It would have to do, though it was a bit more
suggestive than she would have liked, and she wished

Adele hadn't insisted upon making it for her to replace the high-collared gowns she had worn at home.

The array of food on the small table caused her stomach to churn, and Kayte took two small cakes, spread them evenly with red currant jelly, and found her copy of *Gulliver's Travels*. She took her small bundles to the bed and plumped a fat pillow to sit up against as she read. The candles in her room consumed themselves as she turned the pages.

Hours later, she opened her eyes to darkness. The little volume in which she had been so absorbed had fallen carelessly to the floor, waking her with a dull thump. Though she had finished the delicious flour cakes, a scattering of crumbs on the bed was causing her to itch. She brushed them to the floor and was searching the cool, thick carpeting for the book when the door swung inward. Her fingers froze.

She waited breathlessly until a tall, shadowed figure became outlined against the yellow light from the hall.

"You frightened me again," she whispered into the blackness as the door closed behind him. Frightened her, yes, but with a thrill that shot through her veins. She straightened and leaned back against the pillow, her hair curled in disarray about her face. To her amazement, Daevon stayed still in the blackened room. The waiting was doing terrible things to her nerves. She knew it was wrong, but her body had little regard for the whims of conscience.

"Daevon," she asked softly, "what . . . do you want?"

The figure came forward and knelt by the bed, its face hidden in deep shadows. He came only a little nearer, not close enough for her to discern the features there, but it was enough to bring a strange, faint odor to her nostrils. It was the scent of leather, of horseflesh and pine. Her hands clenched at the edge of her coverlets and touched the fabric of his coat, which was rough against her knuckles.

Kayte's gasp was stifled as a callused hand came down over her mouth. The face was so close that their breath came together. His black hair and eyes were demonlike as he hovered over her. His lips parted in a cruel smile, revealing a line of straight, yellowed teeth.

Her heart pounding in terror, Kayte struggled to free herself, only to find an arm securing her to the bed like a timber fallen over her waist.

"So, can't wait, can ya?" The voice was as abusive as the hands on her flesh. "Well now, me darlin', I'll give ya what ya want." He pulled a kerchief from his pocket and forced it into her mouth, then bound her hands with a short length of rope. She fought, vainly trying to scream or kick or scratch as he lifted her from the bed and carried her toward the doorway.

Daevon! Kaytlene's mind screamed as they quickly passed the stairway leading down to the now-riotous drinkers in the pub. Somewhere down there Daevon was discussing business with his courier . . . or perhaps—no, she told herself quickly. He would not have hired this man to kidnap her. She tried vainly to wipe away an image of Daevon Merrick laughing downstairs with one of the pretty whores clinging lewdly to him. No, she tried to believe, he would kill this bastard in an instant!

To Kaytlene's dismay, the hall was empty. Her abductor continued to the far end of the corridor, through a door, and down a flight of steps which creaked under their weight. Once he stopped his descent, another door opened into the kitchen. How could he ever hope to escape with her through such an obvious route?

Kayte saw only the sputtering lamps along the walls, the shelves of dishes and two windows that had already been shuttered for the night. She tried to throw her head backward to see more and caught a glimpse of the cook and her shaking assistant, both of whom sat bound and gagged near the rear door. And then she was in darkness again, out in the courtyard behind the inn. She was lifted easily onto a waiting horse and her abductor swung up heavily behind her.

Chapter 8

Daevon sat across from Lyle Miller, a young man who had been working for him for the last year, but who showed great promise. His blond head was bent over the last of the documents which required a signature from his employer's hand.

Finally, Lyle finished his scrutiny of the contract and passed it along to Daevon with a single word of explanation. "Freemont."

Daevon nodded and flattened the paper in front of him. Freemont was the estate he had recently purchased from Henry Montclaire. It was a generous piece of land to the south, but an oddity. To Daevon, it represented an injustice.

Henry Montclaire was the twenty-six-year-old heir to a family fortune. Two years before, his father was killed in an accident that some said Henry had arranged. Henry immediately began indulging himself in every conceivable whim—travel, women, homes, land . . . and slaves. He was particularly fond of the idea of owning another human. After reading extensively regarding the rich American plantations, Henry decided he wanted to duplicate that way of life for himself. He commissioned the building of Freemont, an estate to rival any of those in the southern states of America. And he bought slaves to work the land. He had them in his fields, but refused to allow them into the estate house, with the exception of the female slaves whose job it was to please him in bed. Henry quickly gained a reputation for cruelty and drunkenness and was actually considered insane by many who met him. Daevon had been approached by the man himself a year ago.

With the abolition of slave trade finally accomplished in England in 1807, Henry was unable to supply himself with the slaves he needed. Men died quickly at Freemont and were replaced just as quickly, but with the movement against slavery and the fact that it had been outlawed, Montclaire was in a rage. Drunk—or perhaps just crazy—he had come to Merrick shipping to hire vessels in which to smuggle slaves for his personal use. He offered a great deal of profit, but Daevon turned him down. Daevon also offered to buy Freemont and its remaining slaves. Montclaire departed, furious, but returned a week later when all his attempts to convince other shipping merchants to carry his illegal cargoes had failed. He sold Freemont for one-tenth its original cost, and rambled on about his latest notion of becoming the benefactor of a particularly poor girls' school in Stanhope.

Daevon turned his attention to the deed which gave the estate house to Joseph Lancaster. Though he had never met Lancaster, Daevon admired the Quaker's ideas of free schools and wanted to put the elaborate house to some good use. The remainder of the land he had had fairly divided among those who had worked for Montclaire and who wanted to stay on the land. Daevon provided them with the materials to build adequate homes and plant their first crops, without demanding a percentage. If a man remained on the land for two full years, he would own it, free and clear. With such an incentive, most stayed, but those who left were given enough money to begin life elsewhere.

Daevon affixed his name to the deed to the Freemont estate house and waited, as the ink slowly dried. "See that this is dispatched to Lancaster as soon as possible, will you, Lyle?"

"Of course. Anything else, sir?"

Daevon rose and stretched his legs, one hand lingering on his glass of Madeira. "Yes. Get some sleep, will you? You look like the devil." It was said pleasantly, but Daevon noticed that his young assistant was dismayed that he should find anything wrong with him.

"I will, sir. I—"

"I know you've been working hard to impress me,

Lyle. I'm impressed. Now deliver these and then get some sleep.''

Lyle smiled gratefully. "Yes, sir. Thank you.''

Daevon finished his drink and gave the lad a firm handshake. But his thoughts were on the dark-haired beauty who was probably asleep on the bed upstairs. The time-piece in his waistcoat pocket told him that two hours had passed since he had left her room.

He went toward the stairs, remembering how Kayte had felt in his arms, the eager, untutored passion of her kisses. And, too, he reminded himself of the loss she was experiencing. He wanted to ease her pain, and promised himself that he would give her only what she needed now—comfort, patience, and companionship.

A scream from the kitchen froze the thoughts in his head.

"Help! Dear God—oh, someone help!'' A girl ran hysterically past him, but Daevon discovered the cook and her assistant before the girl returned with a large number of drunken, openmouthed spectators. Daevon knelt and began to untie the expert knots that bound the cook's puffy wrists. Once she was loose and the gag fell away, Daevon helped her to her feet and she began to babble, almost incoherently.

"Oh, dear God! The roast burned and . . . that man! That awful man. My wrists!'' She rubbed furiously at the chafed flesh as she went to where a thin curl of smoke seeped from the edges of the stone oven. The younger kitchen maid seemed more levelheaded, but she was clearly distraught.

"The lady, your lordship! He took the lady!''

An uncontrolled panic rushed through Daevon. He had not even considered that Kaytlene might be in danger.

"Tell me what happened,'' he said with as much control as he could command. His hands covered hers reassuringly. "Easy now, and tell me the whole story.''

The girl related the events of the evening. She and the cook had been cleaning up and preparing rolls for the next day's breakfast when the cook sent her out for a pail of fresh water. She had been grabbed from behind and tied up, and a rag had been stuffed into her mouth. Then she had been pushed back into the kitchen. The cook was next, accosted as she tended the roast. He had grabbed the cook's chain of keys and gone upstairs. When he returned, he was carrying Kaytlene.

"She fought him like a cat, your lordship. He had somethin' stuffed in her mouth and she couldn't scream."

Daevon could not hold back the shudder that coursed through him like freezing water. Another man holding Kaytlene—a filthy bastard who would kidnap an innocent girl and . . . Kidnapper? Or rapist? Dear God, how could he have left her alone?

"How did they leave?"

"Horse, my lord. Only one, I think."

"How long ago?"

"Quarter of an hour, maybe. And they didn't go north."

"How do you know that?"

"We had rain last night, my lord. The whole north yard is full of water, and I didn't hear their horse go through it."

"Good girl."

A man's hand rested on Daevon's arm and he turned to see Lyle Miller. "The horses are ready, your lordship. We should go now or they'll have a greater lead on us."

Daevon rode eastward and sent Miller south, to cover the two most likely routes of escape. Though Daevon prided himself on having the natural instincts of a tracker, the late hour and overabundance of Madeira he'd consumed during his meeting with Lyle slowed him just enough to frustrate him to the point of anger. His thoughts were moving quickly, however. The idea of Kayte's innocent softness forced into violent submission by some horrid act inflamed his fury. It was something from which she might not recover.

Damn! He had wanted her from the first moment he'd gazed into those golden eyes. Not only her body beneath his, but her beauty, her strength, her love. By some amusing quirk of chance his betrothed was the one woman he had ever met who made his blood and senses flame with a a mere touch.

He must get her back . . .

*   *   *

Kaytlene woke on a crude bed of pine boughs, a thin coverlet spread over her. Had she fallen asleep? She tried to rise but found that her hands were bound and the side of her head stung with a pain that sent her back down onto the fresh pine, colors dancing before her eyes.

Then she remembered. They had seemed to ride endlessly. When her captor had found a tiny cave near a spring, he'd grunted thankfully and dismounted. Kaytlene had tried to kick his chest as he reached for her, but the attempt had only brought her down atop him. He'd thrown her sideways, slamming her head against a flat rock. She had been unconscious ever since.

Now a small fire burned just inside the cave's mouth, and Kayte could make out the imposing figure sitting cross-legged before it. He started when her attempt at rising drew his attention and he stooped down to where she lay.

"Awake now, are we? Good."

Kaytlene wanted to scream when he pulled a long, glinting knife from his belt and held it up for her to see. She could only gasp in terror and close her eyes against the sight of him. He was obviously enjoying his game of cat and mouse.

"What do you want?" Kayte found the courage to ask.

"I shouldn't tell ya, missy, but seein' as how you'll soon be dead, I don't guess you kin tell no tales. Truth is, someone done hired me to see ya dead. Ya wouldn't hold a grudge against a man earnin' his wage, would ya?"

"Kill me then. Get it over with."

The man raised the knife and brought it down. Kaytlene closed her eyes to prepare for the shock of its penetration into her flesh, but it never came. Instead the silver blade sheathed itself in the ground. Her abductor's low laughter rang in the tiny cave.

Kayte's eyes flew open as he tossed aside the thin fabric that covered her and slid one hand from her waist to the peak of her breast,

"I have to kill ya, missy, but I intend to have a little fun while yer still livin'."

"You filthy bastard!" Kaytlene tried to lash at him with her hands, but in one motion he forced her arms over her

head, securing them to his saddlebags. The pain in her head
quickly subsided as she realized that he fully intended to
take her there, then slit her throat as casually as you
please. Panic filled her with energy and boldness.

"I would rather you killed me first," she spat.

Only a faint chuckle came from his throat in reply. His
hands covered her breasts and ripped at the fabric until one
side split from shoulder to waist. Kaytlene screamed in
horror and struggled beneath his hands, her heels digging
into the sandy floor. He stuffed a piece of cloth into her
mouth again to stifle her screams, and the obvious desire
in his eyes made her shudder uncontrollably.

"Just relax and ya might even have a good time, lady."

The heavy weight of his leg over hers kept her from
kicking as his hands went inside the torn gown to squeeze
her nipples painfully. Tears ran down Kaytlene's temples,
but she could make no more sound than a pleading whimper.

As his mouth came down to her throat, nearly collapsing
her windpipe with its fierceness, she closed her eyes and
screamed inwardly.

"Wot pretty flesh," the black-haired man whispered
hoarsely into her hair. "I'm surprised his lordship didn't
want ya for hisself first."

Her mind flew back to Daevon. Where was he now?
Perhaps he had even arranged this assault. Putting on a
pretty show in front of everyone and then, when she was
kidnapped and killed, he would have their sympathy and
not their suspicion. Could she have been wrong about
him? So wrong that she had even considered giving herself
to him . . .

The shock of her abductor's rum-warmed mouth on her
breast brought a fresh wave of horror and a new courage to
try to struggle, but to no avail. She screamed until the
back of her throat was raw, and though only muffled pleas
emerged, her head was filled with the echo of her cries.

Then, unexpectedly, the weight of his body fell heavily,
limply on her, his mouth and tongue obscenely slack
against her breast. She could hear nothing. He did not
move and, it seemed to Kayte, did not breathe either. She
could see only the dark line of his shoulder and a patch of

night sky beyond until his body was lifted and pushed away.

Daevon! her mind screamed once more, joyfully, as his knife split the ropes at her wrists and he tore the cloth from her mouth.

"Daevon!" she cried out in agony and joy.

He pulled her into his arms, sinking back against the cave wall to support them both as he stroked her hair.

"Kayte, I was so afraid—" His voice choked with a relief that she felt through to her heart. She lifted her head, taking in the loving gray light in his eyes, and knew that her doubts about him were all false. Smiling, she snuggled against his shoulder, her tears forgotten as his hands smoothed away her fears.

Daevon cradled her against his chest. The sickening scene he had just witnessed was emblazoned into his memory—Kaytlene's struggle against her captor, her moans of pain, the terror in her golden eyes. She had nearly lost both her innocence and her life in one violent stroke. The two hours he had searched for her had been the bleakest of his life. All the while he'd imagined what terrible acts had befallen her, and his worst fears had seemed confirmed when he had found the cave.

But now she was breathing lightly against his chest, her eyes dry, and a joyful relief purged his terror. She was alive, badly shaken but intact, and looking to him for comfort and help. He felt like a knight rescuing his lady from a dragon. The thought amused him, and he smiled. How odd that this lovely girl could make him smile in the midst of such an awful scene.

"Kayte?" he whispered. She looked up and, for the first time, he was aware of the soft bare flesh of her breast pressed to his chest. An unavoidable heat of desire seeped through him as he reached for something to wrap around her shoulders.

Kaytlene lowered her eyes and blushed as he covered her.

"Let's get you away from here, sweet." Daevon lifted her against him and stood, his head and shoulders bent to accommodate his tall frame beneath the low rock ceiling. Kaytlene caught a glimspe of her captor's body crumpled unnaturally in a corner, a dagger placed neatly between his shoulder blades.

"It seems you have many talents," she said shakily as they emerged into silver moonlight outside the cave.

"So I have. And I have just added another to that long list—saving innocent maidens." He smiled down at her, making the past hours seem like nothing more than a bad dream. She could not resist the urge to turn her face and press her lips to his in thanks for saving her life. Daevon groaned.

"Don't tempt me so," he murmured, "or you won't be so innocent by the time this night is over."

She raked her eyes up to his, laying one palm against his cheek. "I wouldn't mind so much," she whispered tentatively, "if it were . . . someone I . . . loved." And she began to cry.

Daevon's lips moved gently on hers in a gesture of comfort. He raised his head, kissed her forehead, and lifted her onto the saddle of his waiting gray.

"Easy, Demon." He settled Kayte and patted the silky neck beneath the horse's mane.

To Kayte he said only, "Stay still," then disappeared into the mouth of the cave, reappearing after a moment to stamp out the fire in its circle of stones.

"Who was he?" Kayte asked. "And why did he want to kill me?"

"I don't know." Daevon had no desire to tell her that he well recognized the man's face. Delamane, one of the most ruthless men who resided in Fetter Lane. He had been hired to kill Kaytlene—the fifty pounds stuffed into the man's pocket told Daevon that much. But why? Daevon's eyes rose to take in the picture of his betrothed sitting straight on the back of his favorite mount. Why would anyone want to harm her?

Her pale peach nightgown had crawled up her legs, exposing the lovely curve of her calves and ankles. Her bare feet were brown with dust. Her hair framed the pale oval face, an appealing disarray of moonlit brown, and her amber eyes were still wide and liquid, reflecting the terrible ordeal she had just survived.

Daevon realized suddenly that who the man was or who

had hired him were of no importance compared to the young woman who had entrusted herself to his care. Her comfort must come first.

The flames extinguished beneath his ash-covered boots, Daevon thought only to be near Kaytlene, to protect her. He swung up behind her and urged Demon forward, catching the reins of Delamane's gelding as they passed and leading it behind. The body would remain until he had time to contact the local authorities.

Kaytlene could not resist sleeping in the secure hold of Daevon's arms. As he held the reins loosely in his left hand, she cradled her head against the curve of his right shoulder and fell asleep.

Daevon gave his gray free rein and spent the better portion of their ride staring down at her. The dark brown blanket he had wrapped around her shoulders loosened as she slept fitfully.

Daevon pulled it farther away from her neck as drops of sweat began to form on her brow. He scowled at the darkening bruise on the right side of her throat. The bastard! He wished now that he had used a more painful means to kill Delamane. A nightmare-induced groan came from the bundle in his arms and he soothed her until she was quiet again.

Kayte slept until men's voices roused her from the pleasant blackness. She opened her eyes to see Daevon in the open doorway of a bedchamber at the inn. A tall blond gentleman stood with him, nodding occasionally. She had been nestled into the huge bed and covered to the neck, the bedcurtains closed on three sides.

As the blond man went out into the hall, Daevon closed and locked the door, returning to the chair next to her as Kaytlene's eyes came fully open.

"How are you feeling, my love?" He took her hand in his, placing several small kisses along her fingertips. In the short hours he had spent with her she had become so precious to him. He desperately wanted to make love to her. For now it was impossible—she had endured too much and trusted him too little. But she needed him. Henri Todd had been right about that.

"I feel better now, I think," she murmured sleepily. She stretched under the coverlets and yawned. *My love*, he had called her. It made her feel safe and . . . warm . . .

She turned toward him and winced. Daevon was on his knees by the bed, smoothing the tender flesh of her throat with his fingers.

"Be still, Kayte. You have a nasty bruise."

Her head lowered, and her tears began again. "You must think me quite ugly after . . . after everything."

In answer, he enclosed her in his arms and kissed her hair, her temples, the white bridge of her nose.

"No, Kayte. Never that. I want you to rest now." He coaxed her gently back onto the pillows.

"I can't sleep in this gown," she whispered. "It's dirty and . . . he . . ." She choked down a sob.

Daevon's finger slipped over her lips to banish the memory. "I'll get a girl to help you."

But he couldn't leave the bed. Her hands were locked on the open folds of his shirt, and her eyes pleaded with him for the compassion and closeness she needed desperately now. The walls dividing right and wrong disappeared. Kayte was shaking, crying softly, needing protection and warmth and strength. He could give those things to her . . .

"Don't leave me, Daevon. Please?"

"I won't ever leave you, sweet. Not ever."

Kaytlene pulled herself up and toward him until his hands rested on the laces that closed the gown at her back.

"Then you'll stay with me, won't you, Daevon?"

"Kaytlene, you're tempting me again."

"I know," she whispered.

His fingers untied the laces and loosened the bodice, slipping his hands beneath the silky fabric to touch the flesh beneath. His breathing became hard and ragged in her ear.

"You've been hurt so much, love."

"But you couldn't hurt me," she said softly, innocently. "Could you, Daevon?"

"No, dearest. No." His mouth caught hers as she looked up at him and burned lingering and sweet, with a desire only to give . . . to please and comfort and shelter.

His hands came to her shoulders, and she tentatively traced her fingers over the silken hardness of his chest. His groan reverberated into her fingertips. The warmth of him was healing the icy fear that lingered inside her.

"Daevon, I was so frightened," she murmured.

"I won't let anyone hurt you. Or take you away from me ever again."

Kayte lay back, the nightdress slipping down to bare her shoulders and the soft rise of her breasts beneath their torn covering.

"Stay with me," she pleaded again, tears drying on her pale cheeks.

Daevon wasn't sure how to reply. He had made love to many women in his life, and never had he felt this odd reluctance to sleep with one. This girl was to be his wife. Didn't that give him every right to do as he pleased? He didn't think he could control the desire for her all through the night.

"I . . . don't think that is a good idea, Kayte." He rose with a great effort and sat heavily in the chair, running one hand through his dense black hair. He couldn't bear to look at the hurt expression in her eyes.

"I'll stay here until morning," he tried to say calmly. "You need to rest."

"I can't sleep in this gown," Kayte exclaimed angrily, throwing back the covers to get out of bed. She brushed the dust from the sheets with one hand, holding together the ragged edge of the gown with the other. Ignoring Daevon's offer to call a serving girl, she went to the side of the bed opposite him and stripped off her clothes. The sheer curtains that separated her from his gaze created a dark silhouette of her body.

When Daevon finally looked up, her shapely, dark form destroyed his last bit of resistance. The smooth, deep curve of her waist and rounded peaks of her breasts as she turned was more temptation than the stoutest saint could have withstood.

"Kaytlene, I'm sorry. You don't have to torture me like this," he said, his voice stricken with desire or amusement, he wasn't certain which.

"Torture *you*? You foolish man!" She took a wet cloth

and began rubbing the dust from her face and hands and feet, but even that didn't wipe away the emotional filth left by her captor. She pulled a white sheet from the wardrobe and wound it under her arms, dragging it behind her as she went to the fire to rid herself of an unyielding chill.

"Torture you?" she cried. "How dare you! I've been through a dozen kinds of hell and all you can think of is your animal lusts! You're no better than that . . . that . . ." She couldn't finish the thought. Her body collapsed on the deep, soft carpet before the fire, her head buried in her hands.

Daevon was kneeling beside her before she could release a single, harsh sob, holding her against his chest and rocking her like a child. She fought him weakly, then finally collapsed against his chest and poured out her anguish.

Daevon held her, saying nothing, knowing that her father's death, his own abrupt arrival, and his reprehensible behavior toward her had all conspired to shred her life, her security, to ragged strips. It made the attempt on her life all the more terrifying. And the attempt at rape—God, she was devastated! Her body shook with involuntary tremors. Her hands were now clutching his shirtfront, afraid to let go and be alone in all her fear and pain.

When her sobs quieted a little and his shirt was wet with tears, Daevon silently offered her the handkerchief from his pocket. He shifted his position, sinking down with his back against the heavy settee, and coaxed her into his lap. She curled against him like a newborn kitten, dabbing at her eyes and making soft, infrequent sniffs.

"I miss Father," she said timidly. Now the tears were done and she wanted to talk.

"Yes," Daevon answered, his voice hushed, "I know. You loved him."

She nodded and he found he liked the feel of her silky hair against his chest where his shirt lay open.

"I'll be lonely."

He was forced to wait until her fresh sobs stopped before answering.

"You have me now," he reminded her.

"No. You don't love me. You don't even want me, not really."

He drew her face up and had to pause before he said anything, for the aching loneliness he saw there nearly unseated his reason.

"I do want you to come with me."

"But you don't love me," she repeated sadly. Her eyes closed and a single silvery tear slipped down her cheek. He kissed it away.

"I'm afraid of love," he said gruffly against her satin skin.

Now she was studying him closely, watching his eyes. "You mustn't be," she whispered, childlike. "You mustn't be afraid to love someone. It nourishes you. It keeps you alive."

"Then I've been dead for a very long time."

"I'm sorry for her."

"For who?"

"The girl you love."

Daevon smiled, but it was weak and pain-filled. "Don't be sorry for her, Kayte. She has a fine husband, all the silk and jewels she can wear, and lovers aplenty."

"But she doesn't have you."

"No," he whispered back, melting in the fiery gold of her eyes. "And for the first time I think I'm glad she doesn't."

"It's very hard to lose someone you love." Kayte leaned her head down onto his shoulder and sighed. "Hold me, Daevon. Please?"

His arms closed around her, keeping her warm and safe in their comforting circle.

"He knew I would need you," she murmured after a long silence.

"Who?"

"Father. He knew I would need someone strong. Someone to protect me, to hold me." She looked up at him again and found him watching her, his mouth hardly an inch from hers.

"To love me," she finished brokenly.

His eyes narrowed. They were like quicksilver in the room's pale light.

"Though I can't imagine why he chose you." Kayte attempted a smile, but it died suddenly. He was eating her alive with his eyes.

"Can you . . . will you . . . love me, Daevon?"

The question was like a physical jolt. Was she asking him to feel affection for her or—?

"Are you afraid of me?" she whispered.

He smiled, but his eyes said yes, he was afraid. Very much afraid.

"Will you love me if I promise not to hurt you?" she asked.

"Love and promises don't mix well, little girl."

"We need each other, don't we?"

It was the truth. She needed a protector, someone to cling to and drive away her loneliness. He needed someone to teach him how to trust again.

But did he want to learn?

"Yes," he answered softly, brushing his lips across hers and back again, lightly, watching her eyes flutter closed. "Yes, we need each other."

Was that what this betrothal was about? he wondered. Two fathers knowing that their children would need someone else one day? Was that all there was to it?

The light teasing of his kiss was gone, replaced by the firm pressure of his mouth against hers. He tasted the faint flavors of red currant jelly and salt tears on her lips.

"I knew you would come for me, Daevon," she said finally, weakly, after his kiss had drained her of all remaining strength. "I knew you wouldn't let him hurt me."

"God, Kayte . . . I'm sorry." He took her mouth again, quickly. "I have enemies. Perhaps you shouldn't have come."

"You need me," she reminded him gently.

"Yes, I suppose I do." He touched her temple with his finger, drawing it down across her jaw to trace the pale rose lips that were beckoning him again.

"Kaytlene Newell, will you marry me?"

"I . . . might be agreeable to that," she murmured, "if—"

Daevon wanted no restrictions. His mouth stopped hers from listing them and elicited a melting groan. In sweet desperation his hands clutched at the folds of crisp white linen at her back. He wanted to be gentle, but the hunger she was building in him was toppling his restraint. He was being pushed too far by her body's close heat. He could almost hear the straining pulse of her heartbeat through the sheet that molded to her curves and hollows as his hands wanted so much to do.

He took her to the floor with him, her body relaxing against the thick carpeting, accepting whatever he chose to offer. The fire just beyond them cast demonic shadows onto her hair as it fell away from her face. Never had such a furious need been kindled in him and now he sought its release, its maddening pleasure in this girl who promised so much of what he needed.

His lips moved on hers with an abandonment of all his senses, of time, space, and reality. Her lips parted to accept the deep exploration of his tongue. He knew that, though her kisses were a taste of heaven, they would never be enough.

"Daevon," she started to say, but the words were lost as his hand moved from her waist to the soft fullness of her breast. He cupped it in his palm, his thumb running in excruciating circles over its tightening peak. She groaned softly and tangled her fingers in his hair.

"I want you, love. I want to show you how much pleasure there can be. To take away your pain." He pulled her possessively to him, his hands finally satisfying their desire to roam unrestrained over her soft curves.

The touch sent sparks through her, and she moaned his name.

"I want to take away the feel of his hands on you, Kayte. To make you forget. To make you mine."

Daevon Merrick had said a great many things to women in the heat of passion, but for the first time he was allowing a vulnerable truth to spill from the crack that Kaytlene Newell had made in his hard shell. She was his . . . It made him want to love her, protect her. Loving her might be maddeningly sweet, he thought suddenly, and he wanted to try.

Kayte gasped when Daevon's mouth kissed her skin just above the sheet that covered her. When his fingers touched hers where they clutched the edges, she kept her eyes on his, afraid yet trusting. She allowed him to part the make-shift gown and expose her body to his eyes. He bent his head to kiss her mouth softly.

"You are beautiful, Kayte," he whispered. With that assurance, her body unclenched its tense muscles beneath his hand, which traced the line of her leg to her waist and along her rib cage to her breasts.

Her eyes closed. Daevon's caresses forced eager sounds from her throat. He stroked her skin, his fingers lightly brushing over the hardened pink tip of each breast, and watched pleasure glow on her face. He had never imagined that a touch he had performed so perfunctorily so many times before could give such obvious pleasure.

Kaytlene's body arched tensely as his mouth touched her breast and his tongue teased the rosy center into aching hardness. His lips trailed down to the valley between her breasts and to the other peak, massaging with his tongue and sucking gently until her moans came urgently.

"Daevon . . ." She pulled her mouth to hers. "Teach me," she pleaded softly. "Love me."

"Kayte . . ." His head lifted away from her and he stood, removing his shirt in a haste of desire that was new, even to him. As his hands loosened the ties of his breeches, Kayte turned her head, nibbling fearfully on her lower lip. Before she could rethink her decision he was beside her again, his tall, lean frame pressed to hers, his mouth and hands rebuilding the intensity of heat that melted her to him.

"Kayte. Kayte, you are exquisite." His fingers pulled her right thigh toward him, allowing him access to the silky folds of moist heat between her legs. His fingers moved expertly, drawing her up into a maddening pulse of sensation that soaked through her flesh.

Kaytlene lost all ability to think as her body strained to capture some terrible ecstasy she could not yet name.

And then Daevon's body was hard and warm atop hers, his whispered adorations adding to the music in her head. She arched her body to his as his hips pressed into hers. A soft cry of pleasure and pain tore open the silence that had enfolded them so gently.

"It's all right, love. The pleasure will be so much greater than the pain, I swear it. Trust me, Kayte."

A moment of sanity cleared her head enough for her to see the silvery eyes delving into hers, asking for trust.

"Yes," she murmured, feeling as though her body and mind had been detached. While her body was experiencing the pleasure of the fierce and gentle fusion that led her into her new life, her mind, with all its fear and doubts, was floating away.

The wave of pain that tore open Kayte's innocence was spent in an instant and ebbed away in a flash of pleasure. Her body seemed to understand the rhythmic dance to which she surrendered, even when she felt only its thrilling sensuality, heard only the words Daevon whispered and the sound of his deep, guttural moans. He spoke to her gently, soothingly, wrapping her in a passion that went far beyond the joining of flesh to flesh. Slowly he moved, stopping once to take her face into his hands and they stared at each other for long moments, his body still a part of her own. His eyes told her a myriad of things he would never have thought to say. Finally he abandoned himself to wanting her and gave up trying to comprehend what had happened to make him so vulnerable to emotions he'd thought long since dead.

With a groan he buried his face in her fragrant hair and claimed her again, deeply. She gasped, her breasts heaving with hot, quick breaths. He took her quickly to the edge of a release that she knew would be the culmination of their passion, leaving her hanging over the edge as he thrust slowly, hard and knowing.

"I'm . . . I am yours now," she murmured as she held tightly to his shoulders. She wanted desperately to hear him say the same, to claim her with his words as he had already done with his body. She wanted to belong to him.

"Yes, little girl," he answered almost fiercely, "now I've made you mine. You belong to me. Always."

He slid his hands under her back, to her buttocks. He lifted her hips, sliding further into her until she threw back her head and her fingers dug into the flesh of his shoulders.

"Daevon!" Her hands scratched at the nape of his neck,

taking a handful of hair into each fist as she stopped climbing with him and began to fall.

"Sweet Kayte," Daevon breathed into her ear, "don't fight it so. Let it take you."

Her grip stayed firm, but her body relaxed to accept his movements and she went upward again. She reached the pinnacle, the core of emotion shattering within her into brilliant, fiery light. The sinewy cords of muscle beneath her hands tightened as she pressed her palms against Daevon's back. Tightened, shuddered, relaxed. And her conscious mind heard only one sweet note in the lovely song that played in her head. Her name. Daevon was saying her name, again and again. And that one lovely sound lulled her to sleep.

Chapter 9

Daevon woke just before dawn. Even with Kayte holding close to him in sleep, the floor was uncomfortable and the fire had dwindled to glowing embers.

Careful not to wake her, Daevon lifted Kayte up into his arms and laid her gently in the center of the huge bed, covering her cool flesh to the neck. He dressed leisurely, watching her as she curled in the coverlets, unconsciously searching for the heat that his body had supplied for her.

Daevon coaxed the embers back into a small, warming blaze and picked up the white sheet from the floor. A smear of blood had stained it and he threw it into the fire. There was no doubt that Kaytlene Newell had been a virgin. She'd given him a precious gift, especially considering the events of the past night. When he thought of how cruel Delamane would have been to her, his hands clenched into fists. He would kill the bastard who had hired him.

His first thought was that one of his business rivals had hired Delamane. But there were easier means to steal profits—by dropping prices or destroying vessels. Besides, he had never considered a business rival an enemy and had never given any of them reason to hate him so much.

The English crown had the most reason to want to hurt him, though he hoped no one in the government knew it. For the last few years, Daevon had been smuggling goods to American ports which were off limits to English vessels and buying illegal American goods.

He meant no ill toward the English, and no disrespect of the crown, but, unlike many others, he could not stand by and watch the former colonists lose the fruits of the precious land they had just secured from Britain. He could not prosper without guilt, knowing that other men who deserved the same chance to trade freely were watching their own products rot.

Some would call him a smuggler or a privateer, though he hardly felt he deserved either title. To himself he was, simply, a man giving aid to other men. If he were forced to conduct business under similar restrictions as the Americans, he could only imagine what sort of destruction it would bring down on the Merrick holdings. Though he exported few perishable goods, even the china and silver and crystal in his warehouses would go to waste and lose him more money than he cared to consider. Without the right to free trade, his men would not be paid. His ships would sit empty in their ports, enticing targets for disgruntled dockhands who could easily burn them for an evening's entertainment. The warehouses would be raided, their bounties of silks flying like banners over the water or used to wrap the sailor's favorite whores in makeshift gowns. China, crystal, and japanned wood pieces would simply be thrown to the relentless sea or carted off to adorn the slums of London's poorest. What a waste of men and money.

Responsiblity for the present situation fell on the head of one man—Thomas Jefferson.

Achieving their independence from Great Britain had not freed the Americans from conflicts with their motherland. First the French Revolution had sent the states clashing once more with England. Though Washington and his cabinet issued a proclamation announcing that a neutral stance would be taken by their country in regard to European affairs, the overly zealous French minister, Genêt, had proceeded to insinuate himself and his ideas among the people of Philadelphia. There he was able to secure crews for privateering ships which settled in American ports, giving the appearance that the free states were French allies. Several British vessels were captured—enough to raise the attention and ire of Great Britain. The ''French Philadelphians,'' as they were called, took up Genêt's cause with frenzied enthusiasm, even to the point of calling one another "citizen," flying the tricolor, and forming imitations of the French Jacobin clubs. The frenzy was short-lived, however. When Washington reprimanded Genêt and the Frenchman tried to turn the people against their president, the Americans immediately sobered.

As the war progressed, English ships seized American merchant vessels, declared that the provisions and foodstuffs they carried were illegal contraband, and took the liberty of emptying the holds of American ships and paying for the seized goods as they saw fit. The Americans, their trade crippled, were resentful.

The years during the term of John Adams were fraught with tension. Then, on March 4, 1801, Thomas Jefferson came into the power of the American presidency. His successful dealings with the pirates of Tripoli, one of the North African Barbary States, and the purchase of the Louisiana Territory made him a much-applauded leader. Now, in his second term, however, his economic policies were doing much harm and little good, it seemed.

In June 1807, an American frigate, the *Chesapeake*, was sunk by the English *Leopard* while cruising to the Mediterranean. Enraged, the Americans were ready to force English reparation or go to war. Four months after the incident, Jefferson supported the Embargo Act, an effort to punish the English by refusing to trade with them. But Jefferson did not achieve his desired goal. On the contrary, while the British easily survived without American trade, the free states suffered. In one year their exports dropped from $111,000,000 to $22,000,000. Wheat prices collapsed. Worst affected were the shipping interests of New England and the tobacco barons of Virginia. Smuggling became a way of life.

That was where Daevon Merrick involved himself. He supposed with reluctant admiration that he had inherited his father's devious nature, for he went about his treasonous business with confidence and stealth.

Daevon leaned heavily against the mantel and sighed. Once this struggle was over, his merchant ships could return to business as usual, instead of providing illegal supplies and information to America. In all the time he had been smuggling, not one man had been killed and only two injured, neither seriously. He hoped his favor with God would continue.

He stood quietly for several moments as his body warmed with the growing heat from the fireplace. The light flickered gold and red along the carpeting, and his eyes rested on the rumpled nightgown that Kayte had stripped off so carelessly. A smile softened his features. He looked forward to sharing his vows with Kayte. Even in his boldest dreams he had never imagined that she might be beautiful and intelligent and desirable. Even more amazing to him after all that she had suffered was her desire to trust and love. The reaction of her body to his lovemaking had shown him that she would be excellent company in his bed as well as in his home. He looked forward to showing her off.

He retrieved her torn nightdress and fed it to the fire. He wanted nothing to remind her of the horror she had experienced at Delamane's hand.

"Daevon?" Kaytlene sat up suddenly, clutching the coverlets against her. Her normally dulcet voice was interlaced with fear that made her words quiver. She had awakened to find herself alone in the monstrous bed, the shadow of a man's tall form at the fireplace. Echoes of her own screams passed through her memory.

"Yes, love. It's me."

She allowed her breath to escape with a heavy sigh as she fell back into her pillow. "I thought—"

"Don't, Kayte. Don't remind yourself of that. I promised to take care of you. You have me, now. Remember?"

He bent to kiss her lingeringly, reminding her of other kinds of need. She pulled shyly away.

"Regretting, love?" Daevon asked softly.

She shook her head. "No, I—" She paused, looking sleepily into his face. "Daevon, you really do have to marry me now, don't you?"

He laughed. "Yes, Kayte, I suppose I do at that."

"I'm sorry."

Daevon stretched out on the bed beside her, still dressed, and cradled her against his body. He would rather have done without the coverlets tucked so demurely around her, but he didn't want to frighten her away, so he simply settled her head on his shoulder and kissed her forehead tenderly.

"Do you really think it will be so unpleasant to marry me, Kayte?" he teased.

She turned solemn amber eyes up to his and considered the question. Would it be so unpleasant? Or would it be as honest and beautiful as their lovemaking last night?

"No," she admitted, settling back into the warmth and strength of his arms. "No, I don't think it will be unpleasant at all."

At dawn Daevon woke again. When he slipped from bed, Kayte woke as well.

"Daevon," she murmured sleepily, "must we leave? Can't we stay here forever?"

"No, love, not forever." Stretching the sleep from his limbs, he attempted to straighten the wrinkles in his clothes. "I'd better change," he said finally, abandoning the attempt to salvage his rumpled shirt and breeches.

"I . . . should get dressed," Kayte replied, embarrassed.

Daevon's smile only deepened the blush on her cheeks. "I'll get some breakfast and then we can start early. Can you be ready?"

She nodded, still thinking how her skin was burning, and not altogether from shame. It was the way he looked at her . . .

Once he had gone, Kayte padded over to the chest that contained her clothes. The air was cool on her bare flesh and she slipped on a chemise. It did little to dispel the memory of his warm hands against her hot skin. Taking a deep breath, she chided herself for thinking so wantonly and searched the bottom of her trunk for a fresh pair of leather slippers.

She chewed on her lower lip as she contemplated what to wear. Her three new gowns were the only clothes she owned that were suitable for meeting Daevon's family. Two were in no condition to be worn. Both her black crepe and blue muslin were rumpled beyond a quick repair.

The third gown was of black and rose silk with a
brocade bodice and overskirt. Should she wear it to
DenMerrick House or choose one of her simpler, homespun gowns which would be more comfortable on the
remainder of the trip? She chose the latter.

When Daevon returned with a tray of oysters and tea,
cheese and bread and butter, Kayte was seated at a dressing table, brushing the tangles from her brown hair. She
had decided on a pale gown of linsey-woolsey which had
been dyed in a huge boiling pot in the yard behind her
father's cottage to a perfect shade of spring green. It was
tied at the waist with a wide braid of darker green, and a
stiff, dark green ruffled petticoat peeked below the hem.
The sleeves were full to the elbows, then tied off with
double satin ribbons, the neckline rounded with a slim
crescent of lace at its edge. She pulled back her hair and
tied it with another ribbon to keep it off her neck as the
day became warmer.

"Are you ready for breakfast, or shall I devour it all?"
Daevon asked, placing the tray of food on the hearth and
sitting against the wall, his long legs stretched out on the
carpet.

As his gaze flowed over her face and breasts and hips,
Kaytlene was attacked by a sudden flush of embarrassment. She felt as if there were nothing at all between his
searching gray eyes and her flesh.

"Are you ill, Kaytlene? Perhaps you should rest longer
before we start out."

"No. I won't keep you from your family any longer."
She looked up apprehensively. "Do you think they'll ap-
prove of me, Daevon?"

He laughed in relief. For a moment he had thought she
had been thinking of some way to be rid of him.

"They will be as pleasantly surprised as I was, Kayte.
And they will love you."

But will you? her mind whispered hopefully to him.

As midday approached, Kaytlene was glad she had decided on her simple dress. The heat was nearly unbearable
in the small coach, and the large linen handkerchief with

which she wiped rivulets of sweat from her face and neck
was soaked through. Reading had exhausted her and now
she rested fitfully, dreaming of a man in the dark, a hand
over her mouth. When she woke, the closed carriage
seemed more like a small, threatening cavern, and she sat
up with a sob.

"Kayte?" Daevon's reassuring hold was not enough.
Still half asleep, Kaytlene struggled against him. "Let me
out! Please I . . . I can't breathe. It's dark! Daevon, help
me!"

He struck the ceiling of the cab, and the coach came to a
quick stop. Holding Kaytlene against one shoulder, he
unlatched the door with his free hand and climbed out,
dragging her with him. Her arms struck out at him, sending them both to the ground.

The impact snapped Kaytlene back into the brilliant sun
and cool breeze of the afternoon.

"Daevon?"

"You were dreaming, little girl."

"No," she corrected. "Remembering."

He brushed unruly strands of hair from her face and
helped her to her feet. "It's all over now, love. Shall
we?" He started back toward the coach, Kaytlene's hand
in his, but she bolted backward.

"Please, Daevon—don't make me get in."

"What would you have me do, my lady? Strap you to
the top of the carriage like a hunting trophy?" He frowned
when his attempt at humor failed.

"Very well, Miss Newell. If you insist." He swept her
up into his arms and nearly threw her up onto the seat next
to Mr. Burns.

"Daevon!" she protested, but the seat was too high for
her to descend on her own. She shared a stunned glance
with Burns as Daevon went to Dancer's head and spoke to
the animal.

"Mr. Burns, will you hand Miss Newell the reins?"

"The . . . reins, my lord? She's—" He brought his
voice to a whisper as if to prevent Kayte from hearing.
"She's a lady, your lordship!"

"I'll have you know, sir, that I've driven many times in

my life," she protested. "I'm perfectly capable!" Kayte took the reins from his reluctantly outstretched hands.

"Step down, Burns. Make yourself comfortable in the coach. There's a bottle of rum under the front seat if I'm not mistaken." Daevon watched the driver disappear through the coach door and rubbed the horses' noses as they sensed some odd hand at their reins.

"Slow, Demon. Easy, Dancer. She's a qualified expert, didn't you hear?" He looked up with pride and amusement at the young woman who confidently held the reins.

Kaytlene loved the feel of sun and the fresh, cool breeze tousling her hair. "Shall we go, my lord?"

The ride was exceedingly pleasant, though after a few moments at the reins it was evident that Kaytlene did not know as much about driving a pair of spirited animals as she had boasted. Most of her experience had been driving gentle old Petronella with the stable cart.

After leading Daevon's pair astray three times, twice off the right edge of the road and once to the left, over a little rise and through an ankle-deep deposit of sticky black mud, she was completely frustrated and unable to meet the eyes of the man who sat beside her.

Finally she had to admit her ignorance and pulled back on the reins. "Whoa," she said softly, for the animals' sensitive ears. The pressure of her small hands against the reins was a poor attempt at even slowing them and they pranced sidelong, off the dirt path on which she had so desperately attempted to keep them.

"Whoa, I said!" she shouted. They went left and forward.

Unable to control her temper, Kaytlene stood and stamped her foot.

"I said stop, blast you!" Unthinking, she pulled her fists to her waist and jerked the reins with a snap. Before she realized her mistake, the horses bolted, sending her flying backward onto the seat. Daevon grabbed up the reins that she dropped in an attempt to stay in the lurching seat. With a firm hand and calm words, he soon had the grays trotting at a brisk pace and, to Kaytlene's great relief, keeping on the narrow road.

"So, you have a mastery of driving, do you?" he asked dryly.

"Yes!" Kayte replied defiantly, irked at his teasing tone.

"Tell me, Miss Newell, was your experience driving horses?" He caught her glance and held it, allowing the grays to continue at their own pace. She began to wish she had remained in the dark interior. Her face felt as red and hot as a glowing ember.

"Horse," she corrected.

"One of your own?"

She looked down at her slippered feet and twisted her fingers into a hard knot. She had owned only one horse in her lifetime—beautiful, spirited Circe. She missed her terribly.

"I drove one of the stable's brood mares. We called her Petronella."

Daevon laughed, only partly because of her remark. Being in her company, the beauty of the afternoon, and her lovely smile made him feel like a boy again, living life with a true prospect for happiness.

He turned to see her lips set in a tight, thin line. "She was quite obstinate at times!"

Daevon made an effort to control his amusement and became quite serious, with only the faintest trace of a grin lingering on his lips. "Oh, yes. I see."

As they both turned to look speculatively at the other, neither could resist laughing.

Daevon spent the better part of an hour instructing Kaytlene in the proper way to hold the reins and the subtle, almost indistinguishable twists and pulls which would lead the animals in any direction or speed one desired. After she tired of the lessons, they sat talking of London and the Merrick businesses there. The horses slowed to a walk.

Daevon was almost sorry to speak of it, but finally he admitted, "We're almost home."

Kaytlene swallowed a lump of fear in her throat. "Is DenMerrick House on the coast?" she asked. She was already homesick for her little village near the sea and hoped that her new home would be like it in at least one respect.

"No," he replied, reading her silent thoughts, "but DenMerrick is. Perhaps I shall take you there someday."

"I don't understand, Daevon."

He paused before answering to take in the sight of her. Perhaps with a wife like Kayte . . . No. He would never live at DenMerrick again.

"You see, Kayte," he began, "the house of Merrick was estabished late in the twelfth century. According to family tradition, Robert Merrick was the bastard son of King Richard the Lion-Hearted. His mother was Ellen Merrick, wife of one of the Cornish peasants who enlisted to fight with Richard in the Holy Crusades. When she learned that her husband had been slain in battle, she became obsessed with taking revenge on her liege and king, and she attempted to murder him once he had returned to England and the treaties of peace had been signed."

Kayte drew in a sharp breath, absorbed in the story of Daevon Merrick's forebears. "And she failed?"

"Yes."

"But what happened to her? Was she executed?" Kayte shuddered at the thought.

"No. The story relates that on the night of a great celebration at the castle she dressed herself all in black. Richard had returned to England with a new bride, the princess from Navarre."

"Berengaria," Kayte murmured absentmindedly.

Daevon peered at her, appreciative of the obvious education she had received. He nodded. "By early morning most of the people in the castle were asleep or drunk. Ellen found Richard alone in his bedchamber and stood by the bed, her dagger raised."

"And?"

"He woke, wrestled her to the floor, and threw aside the blade."

Kaytlene sighed in relief. "And he forgave her?"

"He made love to her."

"Good Lord! On the floor?"

Daevon cast an amused glance at her and knew from the lowering of her eyes that she had not forgotten their own lovely entanglement on the soft carpeting of the bedchamber floor the night before.

"It is said," he added softly, "that once their eyes fell upon each other, they loved." *How similar our stories are,* he thought.

"And she became his mistress?"

"He saw her only once more. Though he professed to love her, he couldn't marry her and she refused to be a man's mistress, even if that man was the king of England. When she found she was carrying his child, she went to French relations."

"And he never knew?"

"He discovered the truth quite by accident years later, shortly before his death in battle. He willed a rather meager portion of land to Robert, never acknowledging that the boy was his own, however. It wasn't until John Lackland had been crowned and Richard buried that Ellen and her son returned to England. On Robert's sixteenth birthday his mother succumbed to a fever, leaving him alone to make his fortune. His grandson, Geoffrey Merrick, built DenMerrick."

Kaytlene sensed that this mysterious place DenMerrick was a sore wound in Daevon's past, one of the secrets he had spoken of, perhaps. Whatever the source of the pain, she realized that this summation of his family history was difficult for him to speak of. He had leaned forward in the seat, resting his forearms on his knees, the reins held loosely in his long, tanned fingers.

Kayte touched his shoulder, making a little circle with her palm. He turned his head and could not help but smile at her tender gesture.

"You see, Kaytlene, DenMerrick is the Merrick estate on the coast. It was built on the original piece of land willed to Robert by the king. DenMerrick House is the family home on the outskirts of London that we have kept since . . . my father's death."

Kaytlene found no dark secrets in what he revealed. DenMerrick had been his childhood home, a place of love and security. Once his father had passed away, it had become too difficult for him to live in the shadows of a past happiness. As the earl of Merrick, he had decided to move his family to a new home near London. What was so difficult to understand?

"I see," she said simply. It was a relief to know the truth, but his voice cut through the serenity of her newfound knowledge before it could take root.

"No, Kayte, you don't see. Not yet, at least." He looked straight ahead, over the heads of the grays who had quickened their pace, and tried to focus on an imaginary point on the horizon of the cloudless sky.

"I pray God you don't change your mind about me when you learn all there is to know about my history." He faced her again, his eyes aflame with a torture that seemed deep and strong and securely fastened to his soul, like a leech sucking away life's blood.

"Daevon, could you ever do me ill?" Kayte peered up at him with a searing, trusting glance.

His eyes widened in surprise at the question, but a twisted half smile curled his lips. She was doubting him. Did she believe that perhaps he might be a drunkard or a wife beater? His reply was painfully honest.

"I would sheath a dagger in my own heart before I would do you harm, Kayte. I need laughter and beauty in my life. I need you, Kayte. Or don't you remember that?"

Kaytlene glowed under the scrutiny of his eyes. If he hadn't needed both hands to steer the horses left, he would have pulled her onto his lap and covered her mouth with kisses. Well, perhaps later, when the house and its inhabitants were asleep. The idea pleased him immensely.

"I remember, Daevon," she replied.

"And you won't forget again, will you Kayte?"

"No. And I won't let you forget, either."

He smiled, but she hardly noticed that.

Kaytlene did not see anything but his eyes. The two-story white house with its stately columns and huge, sparkling windows came closer as the steady clip-clop of hoofbeats continued, slowly and more slowly as the reins dropped slack in Daevon's hands. He, too, could see only the woman beside him, her hair like polished brass in the sunlight, her lips as pink and perfect as a first rose of spring. Her scent, the faintest lilac, burned into his senses and became as necessary for life as the breath that carried it to him.

"Daevon?" Her half-whispered question was like a prayer breathed to some revered, omnipotent god whose power it was to deny or grant her deepest wish.

His right hand slipped from the reins and encircled her slim waist, pulling her against him. An indistinguishable sound of pleasure rose from Kayte's throat when his mouth sought out her lips and found a willing response.

The pair of grays, now on grounds familiar to them, continued forward without Daevon's urging.

Chapter 10

Lady Anna Merrick peered at her reflection in a gilt-edged cheval glass and tucked several strands of gray-white hair away from her face. She knew that the healthy color on her normally pale cheeks would please Daevon. Her elder son was continually worrying over her, and even though he had taken up residence in his town house in Hounslow for the past few years, he had continued to see to her every need. When he was not at sea with one of his trading vessels, he came each Sunday to spend the day with her. The only condition made on his weekly visit was that she was not to bring up the topic of his betrothal to Kaytlene Newell.

Now he was coming home to live, and bringing Kaytlene with him.

Since Lyle Miller had called early that morning to announce Daevon's imminent arrival, DenMerrick House had been in an uproar. Hasty preparations were being made for a celebration dinner, a room was being readied for Miss Newell, and the entire house was being straightened, swept, and polished.

Lady Merrick smiled at her reflection. She had spent the morning preparing herself for the homecoming as well. Though the past week had been difficult for her, she had been recovering nicely and gotten out of bed as soon as Lyle Miller had departed. Even Darby, who had been saddled with the task of looking after her in Daevon's absence, could not keep Anna Merrick tucked away in her bedchamber when there was so much to be done. For the past few days she had allowed Darby to pamper her, but enough was enough.

Anna Merrick had a chronic heart condition. Her heart was beating irregularly, Dr. Ashton said. When she became too excited or overtaxed she felt weak and dizzy, and she had just recently begun to suffer fainting spells. But Anna Merrick was too stubborn to allow such frailties to keep her completely immobile.

"Today," she had told Darby, "my heart be damned. I'm getting out of this bed." And she had.

Now, bathed, dressed, and ready to meet her son's wife-to-be, she felt uneasy doubts begin to creep into her thoughts. Was Daevon ready to accept marriage to a young woman whom he had only just met? Had she been wrong to uphold the betrothal to Kaytlene Newell for so long, even after he had learned to distrust and hate women?

Lady Merrick feared that, unless Kaytlene was an angel blessed with enough determination to break through Daevon's defenses, there would not be a wedding. Through the choices he had made and the disappointments he had suffered, Daevon had learned to harden his heart toward women, and because of it there was no joy in his life.

As a child, he knew of his father's dalliances with pantry maids, village girls, and whores. The elder Merrick was usually drunk during his amorous games and took no care to be discreet. When Daevon was six, his father fell in love with one of his paramours and brought her to live at DenMerrick. Daevon was badly scarred by that year-long arrangement, even though Lady Merrick and her son were sent away to live with relatives in the north. But her husband quarreled with his mistress after one year, and Anna and her son returned. The affair resumed years later when the paramour returned again, and Lady Merrick was banished by her husband to the servant's quarters. She was forced to relinquish her gowns, jewels, and authority to her husband's mistress, and stayed to endure such atrocities only because Merrick refused to allow her to take their sons and she could not give them up. If she had, Daevon might have become more like his father, and she could not have borne that.

When the elder Merrick began to quarrel with his lover

once again, life became unbearable. But it did not last long. One night during one of their violent arguments the sound of shots echoed through the house. Merrick and his mistress were both killed but Anna had blocked the memory of that terrible night from her mind. All she could recall was the sight of her elder son lying unconscious on the master's bed at the feet of his father and his father's dead whore, the dueling pistols used to kill them only inches from his body. Blood had seeped through the bedclothes and Daevon had been stained with it.

He had been badly hurt by the incident and its repercussions of scandal and social rejection. Lady Merrick had felt it wise to move her sons to London, where they could all put the past away and the boys would be educated. Daevon had dubbed the London estate DenMerrick House.

Lady Merrick sighed and left her looking glass to peer out the open windows of her second-story bedchamber. After leaving her husband's family estate, she had considered trying to break Daevon's betrothal contract.

James Newell had come to London with his infant daughter to discuss the matter. With two sons who were not of age, Lady Merrick would be taking charge of the Merrick affairs and he wanted to know her intentions regarding the betrothal.

Kaytlene was a toddler—a happy, curly-headed little girl who instantly won Anna's heart. Clearly, she would be a beautiful woman. And James was earnest in explaining that he intended the betrothal to ensure only his daughter's future. He did not want to benefit personally from the arrangement in any way.

Lady Merrick found James Newell to her liking. He was well read—especially considering his lack of formal schooling—levelheaded, and sensitive. A child growing under his tutelage would more than likely develop those same qualities. A young woman who lacked the whimpering vanity of so many of the young ladies of highborn families would make her son a good wife.

Anna and James had parted in agreement. Both promised to raise their children as best they could and uphold the betrothal.

Lady Merrick wondered now whether she had kept her

part of the bargain. Her Daevon was roguishly handsome, well educated, and heir to a sizable fortune. He was intelligent, sensible, and sought after by all manner of eligible young ladies. But he was fiercely opposed to marriage.

A tender heart was the one thing that Anna could not teach her son. Instead, experience had been his tutor where women were concerned, and its lessons had been harsh. When Monique Lisle had opened a vulnerable place in his heart, Daevon had seemed all the better for it, though Anna considered her not worth his time or attention. When he presented Monique at DenMerrick House and informed his mother that he had asked for her hand, Lady Merrick had calmly reminded him of his betrothal. He had been furious.

When Monique, who was desperate for a wealthy caretaker, accepted the proposal of one of Daevon's business rivals, he became inconsolable. He either isolated himself in the town house in Hounslow or accompanied his shipping vessels to various ports of trade. He poured all his restless energy into the Merrick businesses. Since he could not give his heart and soul to a woman, he gave them to his work.

The next years saw an increase of incredible proportions in the Merrick holdings. Daevon himself helped to rebuild the warehouses along the piers that had been destroyed by fire six years before. He inspected each of the merchant ships in the Merrick fleet, had them manned, repaired, stocked. They were now running export routes to the Orient and India for ivory, jewels, silks, tea, and spices, all valuable commodities in war-sickened England.

Of course, there had been women in his life. Expensive ones on whom he spent too much money, very little time, and the precious seed that would someday, Anna hoped, produce a Merrick heir. His women provided a release of physical need, he admitted, but what he never confessed was his intense need for companionship, affection, trust, and love. Unconsciously he was both searching for it and rebelling against it.

Outside of the brothels, he would see no women. There was a rumor that Lord Patrick's daughter Josephine had set about to ruin her life by becoming a harlot in order to get

Daevon's attention, and she was immediately whisked away by her father to a Swiss boarding school.

No word of the betrothal was spoken in the house, and Lady Merrick suspected her son of plotting with his solicitors to find some loose thread in the contracts that would unravel them altogether. There were none, she knew, but she now wondered if perhaps she had made a mistake in her determination to have him wed Kaytlene Newell. In all these years she had never explained the betrothal, nor the dark secret that had made it necessary.

"Please, God," she prayed fervently, "bestow some special gift on Kaytlene Newell that she might give my son the joy he has not yet known in life."

"Lady Merrick?" A soft, Irish voice from the doorway interrupted the older woman's dreams of a gentle girl who would love Daevon Merrick on sight. Lord, let it be so, she prayed silently again.

"Lady Merrick?" Darby's brown curls and pale green eyes peeked around the open door.

"Yes, Darby. I'm ready."

"Fine, ma'am." Darby's soft footfalls went down the padded blue carpeting toward the servants' stairs and were closed off in silence as she descended.

Lady Merrick went back to her mirror again and touched the string of pearls she wore. One more of Daevon's gifts to her, she thought with pride. He was constantly showering her with clothes, jewels. He knew of her fondness for pearls and Chinese teas and was ever instructing his vessel, the *Odyssey*, to return from its Orient run with its holds full of both precious items for his lady, or not to return at all.

Some commotion below her balcony drew Lady Merrick toward her window. Daevon's carriage! Though her eyesight was not the best she had no trouble recognizing her handsome son at the reins. To her delight and disbelief, his favorite pair of grays were slowly trotting with absolutely no guidance from Daevon. One of his hands had dropped a rein carelessly and was wrapped tightly around the waist of a dark-haired girl in a mint-colored dress. From the way the girl's body was pressed to Daevon's and her arms were thrown about his neck, it could only mean that the kiss was as eagerly accepted as it was given. And was the girl Kaytlene Newell?

The hair color was the same burnished brown, the figure more petite but much prettier than her mother's full-breasted, full-hipped form. Yes, it was Kaytlene; no doubt lingered in Lady Merrick's mind. Even from this distance she knew that the girl would also have her mother's huge, melting eyes. Seductive eyes. And Daevon was obviously taken with her.

"Thank you, God. Thank you!" she cried aloud, stepping back into the room.

Tristan Merrick witnessed the same scene from the window of the library on the ground floor. He stood as rigid as the green marble dragon that spewed sculpted fire in the corner of the entry hall, its jeweled red eyes glittering as if to mock him.

Under his breath he spewed an endless string of expletives that would have embarrassed the most experienced sailor. It was obvious that he had been betrayed, either by Regice or Delamane, perhaps by both. The two hundred pounds Regice had supposedly paid Delamane for the murder might have been split between them. If that was the case, Tristan could expect Regice to come crawling to the house any day now, carrying some unbelievable story about the plan's failure.

He left the window to aid his brother with his bride-to-be.

Kaytlene had been lost so completely in Daevon's kiss that the external world seemed to disappear altogether. It wasn't until the horses stopped that she saw the gleaming white columns of a huge house from the corner of her eye.

Daevon slowly ended his magical kiss. "Welcome home, my dear," he said.

Kaytlene wheeled around in the seat, Daevon's right hand still securely around her waist.

"Welcome to DenMerrick House, Kayte." His lips pressed into her hair and then he was gone, rounding the front of the carriage and greeting the man who held Dancer's harness. Kayte had not even noticed the figure standing quietly with a sneering grin on his face.

"Hello, Tristan."

"Welcome home, Daevon. Quite a pretty parcel you've got there."

Daevon seemed not to hear the comment as he lifted his arms to Kayte. She slid down to him like an obedient child, eager to be held.

Damn, Tristan thought, if I had known this girl was so lovely, I'd have done the job myself and had a little fun before slitting her ivory throat. He knew that Delamane would not have had the slightest regret in doing the same. The thought of her innocence being lost to that yellow-eyed wolf turned him cold.

"Miss Newell, may I present my brother, Tristan?" Daevon's introduction was a little stiff.

"Ah, Miss Newell. We have all been so anxious." Tristan bent over her hand, pressing it delicately to his lips.

"Please call me Kayte," she replied. His hand did not leave her wrist as he straightened.

"Kayte," he whispered appreciatively. "How lovely."

His gaze made her more than a bit uncomfortable. "Anxious, my lord?" She asked for an explanation of his greeting.

"You must call me Tristan, my dear. My brother will no doubt prove to you that there is only one lord in DenMerrick House." He smiled with an expression that wavered between amusement and hatred. Daevon stiffened, his left palm still against the small of her back. "We have been anxious," Tristan explained, "to see whether Daevon would return without you. It seems that my elder brother has been trapped by a woman after all."

Daevon was ready to reply with a lash of temper at his brother's insult when Kaytlene's pleasant laughter stopped him. She turned to him, her hand leaving Tristan's to slide up the open folds of Daevon's shirt.

"If ever you find yourself trapped, my lord," she said, smiling, "then I shall be happy to release you."

Daevon could only grin at her generous response to Tristan's rude behavior. "That seems fair enough, wouldn't you say, Tristan? A man surely cannot be trapped when he becomes a willing captive." He sealed himself to her with a gentle kiss.

"I see." Tristan seemed to growl. "And where is your driver?"

Daevon led Kayte to the wide arc of white stone steps that led up to the front entrance. "In the carriage, drunk probably. He's had quite a ride this afternoon."

"It wasn't so bad," Kayte replied as she entered the huge foyer with Daevon. "It was . . . wonderful." The last word was meant for the house's pale green and white entry hall. The floors were green marble, the walls painted white and adorned with plants and works of jade and ivory. As she stepped over the threshold, she saw two statues, one on either side of the doorway. On the left was an ornately jeweled jade dragon and on the right an ivory bird, long-legged and with a thin, pointed beak.

A dome rose thirty feet above her head, the center made of hundreds of small panes of glass, and a crystal chandelier seemed to be suspended in air from the middle, dangling with tiny jade and silver beads.

"Are you an earl or a prince?" Kaytlene's whisper seemed to echo.

Daevon laughed, the sound ringing through the silvery glass dome, and pulled Kayte into his arms, swinging her through the motions of an exaggerated waltz. When he finally ended the dance, she was flushed and breathless.

"For you I am a prince. If that's what you want me to be."

"Daevon Merrick, that's quite enough foolishness! You'll have the girl thinking we're all quite mad."

Daevon turned at the reprimanding tone and smiled broadly toward the figure on the staircase. "Mother!" But at once the joy in his features turned to the hardness of stone. "What are you doing? The doctor told you—"

"Pooh! Some men say things they do not mean. Isn't that so, my son?"

Kaytlene could only peer up apprehensively toward the figure on the staircase. She was floating in yards of ivory lace, a delicate double strand of perfectly matched pearls about her neck. Despite her long, silvery gray hair and considerably wrinkled face Kayte saw signs of extraordinary beauty. High cheekbones, straight nose, eyes as gray as her son's. And the two of them looked on each other with a love that Kaytlene hoped would someday be hers as well.

In a startling instant Kaytlene was left alone in the center of the green marble floor to watch Daevon rush up the stairway. Before the startled gasp came from Lady Merrick's lips, he had her in his arms, relieving her of the strain of completing the descent on foot.

"Daevon Adam Merrick," Lady Merrick whispered to him, "I have lost all my dignity today."

Daevon only smiled. At the base of the staircase he released her gently, taking her arm into his once she stood beside him. Kaytlene swallowed her fear as they came to her.

"Mother," Daevon said gently, "may I present Miss Kaytlene Newell of Newbury? Kaytlene, my mother, Lady Anna Merrick."

It wasn't until Kaytlene had given her best curtsy that she was able to look fully into the face of the mother of the man she was to marry.

"I am so pleased." Lady Merrick stopped suddenly as her gaze fully met Kaytlene's. "My dear," she said after a moment, "your eyes are extraordinary. Gold, are they? Lovely."

"Thank you, Lady Merrick."

Yes, Anna Merrick thought at once, this child has her father's gentle temperament. Thank the Lord! She is more than I could have wished for. She reached out and took one of Kaytlene's hands in her own.

"Come, my dear, and sit with me in the drawing room. Daevon, see to Miss Newell's things. She shall have the corner room overlooking the garden, I think. Yes, that will do very nicely."

Daevon hesitated, glancing toward Kaytlene, but his mother's voice softly scolded again. "I shall take good care of her, dear. And you may have her back once I've finished. Get on, now."

Daevon kissed his mother lightly. "I have missed you too, Mother," he said, and then he was gone to do her bidding.

Kaytlene accepted the thickly padded chair that Anna Merrick offered and sank down, realizing only now how

stiff the driver's seat of the carriage had left her. The
drawing room and library were on opposite sides of the
front entry. Though the library doors were open, Kaytlene
had only noticed the dark, rich slashes of color as she was
ushered into the drawing room, which was decorated in
tones of cheerful yellow, with accents in white and green
to reflect the foyer colors. Most of the furniture was
arranged around the huge fireplace which faced the doorway, soft, overstuffed pieces in pale green and yellow.

"It's lovely," Kayte stated at once.

"Do you think so, my dear? I have only my two boys to
decorate for and men's tastes can be so odd, don't you
agree? It will be so nice to have another woman's opinion."

The two chairs the women occupied were nearest the
front windows, and Kaytlene felt suddenly quite sleepy
with the sunshine glaring in her face. A shrill chirping
brought her fully alert.

"Hush, Perdie!" Lady Merrick pointed a pale finger at
the golden bird who had begun to flutter about in its
delicate bamboo cage. At the sound of the familiar voice,
Perdie broke out into a long, sweet song.

"One of my little pets," Lady Merrick explained. "Quite
a noisemaker, but it's lovely to hear his song in the dead
of winter."

"I should imagine," Kaytlene replied, fascinated by the
downy yellow throat that produced such pure music.

"We are so pleased you've come, Miss Newell. It is—I
hope—a permanent visit, is it not?"

"Mother!" Daevon entered the room and crossed it
quickly to toss Perdie a bit of crust. "Hello Perdie," he
said affectionately. "You see my mother is playing the
inquisitor today."

"I only wished to know what sort of arrangements are
to be expected. Whether I should introduce Miss Newell—"

"Call me Kayte, please."

The old woman smiled. "Kayte, then. Perhaps Kayte
would like to meet some of our eligible young men." She
was goading Daevon and he was well aware of it.

Kayte responded before either of them had a chance to
say more. "His lordship and I have decided to disregard
the betrothal contracts." She was inwardly pleased by

Daevon's shocked expression. "However," she finished softly, "Daevon has asked for my hand and I have accepted."

The entire room seemed to shiver with Lady Merrick's relief as she leaned back. Daevon came to Kayte's chair and laid a grateful hand on her shoulder.

"I shall wish for your blessing of course, Mother," he said seriously.

"And I am happy to give it."

"Thank you, Lady Merrick," Kayte said softly. "I hope that I shall make your son a good wife."

Lady Merrick searched her son's face and saw a softness, a tenderness never before evident. "I have no doubt you shall, my dear."

After several minutes of discussion on household matters, Daevon noticed his betrothed's eyes battling fiercely to stay open. "Mother," he said, "Kayte has been too long without decent rest or comfort. Perhaps we should give her leave to rest before dinner."

And so Kayte was swept off to the upper floors of the house with Daevon's arm to guide her to her own bedchamber.

He pushed open the door and, when Kayte froze in her place, it took a little push from his hand at the small of her back to get her into the room.

"But this is . . . this must be a room for special guests," she protested.

"You're right, my dear. And you are more special than any of the others who have ever slept here. For now it is yours, to do with as you wish. You may burn it down and begin fresh if you so desire. Whatever you require will be at your disposal."

"I can't," she said, touching with a trembling finger the tall white posts of the canopied bed. "It can't be truly mine."

"You may require some time to grow accustomed to the idea, I see. Very well. Here are all your things." He waved a hand to indicate that her possessions had been moved into the huge white bedchamber. "I have arranged a bath for you and—oh, damnation!" Suddenly annoyed with himself for having forgotten to see to all her needs,

Daevon stepped back into the hallway. "Darby!" he shouted with a fury that shook the house. "Darby!"

When he returned, a wide-eyed girl nearly Kayte's own age greeted her with a shy smile and a curtsy.

"This is Darby. She'll be attending to you."

"But your lordship—" Kayte began.

"I'll not have another word, Miss Newell." His roar was like a tame lion's. "You are under my roof now and I shall lay down the laws according to my own will. No lady of mine will be drawing her own bath or turning down her own bed. Am I understood in this matter?"

Kaytlene smiled, knowing that this show of authority was meant for Darby's sake. It would undermine Daevon's authority in the household for the servants to see him as a henpecked husband.

"Yes, my lord." She curtsied prettily. "I'm sorry."

"Very well," he declared. "Darby?"

"Yes, your lordship?" The brown curls bounced as the girl bid her employer a hasty curtsy.

"See to your lady's bath."

"Yes, your lordship. Right away."

The full extent of Kaytlene's exhaustion became evident some minutes later as she slipped into the long, deep brass tub filled with steaming water. Darby had laced the water with a generous handful of dried flowers and a touch of spice. It was heavenly, this bathing ritual that, as Darby explained, was the usual custom for ladies of Kaytlene's newly acquired standing. The petite Irish girl bowed and scraped until Kayte found her quite annoying.

"Darby," Kayte murmured, drowsy in the fragrant tub.

"Yes?" She gave another short curtsy.

"Must you bow every time I open my mouth?"

"My lady?"

"How old are you, Darby?"

"Nearly eighteen, my lady."

"You're only a few years younger than I am. Couldn't we be friends? I don't like the idea of having a servant."

Darby failed to stifle a giggle.

"What's so funny?"

"It's just that—why, you've a hundred servants, at

least, my lady. Cooks and stableboys and pantry maids
and—''

Kaytlene sat up stiffly. "What?"

Darby rocked back as if she had been slapped. She
twisted her hands nervously in the starched white apron
over her simple black dress. "Why, you're the lady of the
house. Or will be. Isn't that so?"

Kaytlene settled back into the water, considering the
truth of the girl's words. Darby waited for a reply, hoping
for an affirmation of what was being whispered in the
kitchen.

"Yes, I will, Darby. Please forgive me. I'm awfully
tired and it will be difficult for me to get accustomed to
my new status." Her eyes fluttered closed. "I may be
tempted to run back to my tin washboard and candle
dipping any day now," she said drowsily.

"You . . . you made candles, my lady? Did you have
no servants?"

"I lived with my father in a small cottage in Newbury.
My home would fit in the hall downstairs with room to
spare. I miss it already."

"I know just how you must feel."

Kayte half opened her eyes to watch her newly found
accomplice in this adventure of living. The girl was sitting
a bit slumped, hands folded meekly in her lap.

"I miss my home, too," Darby said sadly.

"Have you not been with the Merricks very long?"

"Oh, no. My father was one of Lord Merrick's men. A
captain on the *Lady Ariel* that ran the trade to America
before it was outlawed." Darby's green eyes became misty
with recollections. "My father—oh, what a lovely sight he
was in his uniform as he waved goodbye to us from the deck
when they left port! Or in his battered rags and several
weeks' worth of beard when they returned at last."

"We?" Kaytlene queried, lathering her wet hair with
the soft cake of scented soap Darby had offered.

"My sister Evelyn. She was a year older than I, but
frail, with such lovely white skin and our mother's blue
eyes. My mother died a long time ago, you see. But Papa
told us how lovely she was, with her black hair and
sky-blue eyes."

"What happened to Evelyn?" Kayte asked as Darby complied with Kaytlene's request to rinse her long hair with clear, cold water.

"Evelyn fell in love with a young American who was a friend of Lord Merrick's. She sailed to America with Michael to develop a piece of land his lordship gave them as a wedding gift. On the trip home my father died in a storm that nearly drowned Lord Merrick as well."

"I'm sorry, Darby. Why did you not go to America to be with your sister? Do you have other family here?"

"To tell you the truth, I'm too afraid of those creaking boats."

"And so Lord Merrick gave you a position in his household?" Kayte now felt quite refreshed, and she was afraid to linger in the bath too long lest her skin take on wrinkles. She stood, wrapping a huge towel about her head, drying her body with another as she stepped from the tub.

"Oh, no. His lordship offered me the little cottage on the outskirts of the DenMerrick House property and a fine position in one of the shops in London that sells the trade from his ships. I wanted to come and work in his house."

"But why?"

"His lordship and my father were as close as brothers. Lord Merrick owes me nothing, but I owe him a great deal. He was generous with his gifts when my father was ill, and his friendship gave my father the strength to go on living after my mother passed away. Lord Merrick gave him a position and a devotion that brought him back to the truly living. For that I will always be grateful. And he's a good man, fair and honest."

Kaytlene seated herself at the dressing table, having been dusted in a thin layer of lilac-scented powder and dressed in a plain chemise. She watched as Darby patiently drew a thin-toothed comb through her wet hair.

"It seems that your lord and master is the ideal man," she mused. It was not hard to imagine this generous Daevon Merrick of whom Darby spoke so fondly.

"Aye, my lady. But a hot temper he has, like a flash of lightning. And though he's generous to those he loves, his enemies might as well be dead already for the hatred he shows them."

Kaytlene smiled, unable to fathom such a man. The Daevon she knew was happy, even jubilant. His voice was nearly as soft as the touch that had taken her body so easily beneath his. His kiss was a gentle lightning that sparked a storm beneath her flesh.

"My lady?" Kaytlene had not noticed that Darby had nearly finished drying her hair. "You'll be expected for dinner. Better dress now."

Kaytlene was glad she hadn't worn her last new gown for the trip to DenMerrick House. She smoothed the black silk underskirt and the rose brocade bodice, wondering if the gown was fine enough for the Merricks. As she stood at the top balustrade of the stairway and began her descent, she had her answer.

Daevon appeared from the library and leaned in the doorway, arms crossed over his chest, savoring the sight of the woman who ignited his senses whenever she neared him.

She had worn her hair down with only a black ribbon to hold it away from her face. Darby had tied it into a tiny bow at her right temple, since her mistress lacked any jewels or other adornments. Her hair seemed more like copper now and floated softly into curls that fell to the center of her back.

She stole Daevon's breath away and restored it to him all in an instant. The black and rose dress was simple but stylish, with a bodice that, Daevon was pleased to note, fit more snugly than her others and betrayed the soft upper curve of her breasts.

He stood at the bottom of the staircase as she came to him.

"I cannot be so blessed," he whispered to her, "for you are an angel and I am but a weak man of flesh."

Kaytlene touched his smoothly shaven jaw, her fingers fluttering briefly over his lips. "Weak enough," she replied, "to succumb to an angel's seduction if she should choose to so honor you?"

Daevon took her hand and pulled her tightly to him. "If you should care to honor me, sweet angel, then I shall offer myself as a most willing sacrifice."

Kaytlene, on a step above him, tilted her face downward

as his mouth reaffirmed his offer. She nearly drowned in the sweetness of his insistent kiss, her body pulled to his as if he were attempting to absorb her into his desire.

"Were my mother not waiting for us in the dining hall, I would take you into my own chambers and love you as I did last evening."

"Would your mother not understand if we asked that dinner be held for an hour?"

Daevon laughed and swept Kayte into the hall without letting her feet touch the last few steps.

"I would gladly starve in favor of making love to you, Kayte, but my mother would not understand. Now, take that lovely gleam out of those golden eyes and save it for me . . . for later."

He placed a chaste kiss on her forehead before they entered what Daevon had referred to as the dining hall. It did, indeed, resemble a hall, thought Kayte, since it was more rectangular than square. She had envisioned a huge banquet table, reminiscent of the provisions which ancient castles made for their own inhabitants as well as to accommodate visiting troupes of actors or knights traveling on horseback. The Merrick table seated only ten, and was made of purest mahogany with a twisting vein of leaves carved onto its edge, as well as on the backs of its ten chairs. Double French doors led onto a stone balcony at the far end of the room. The table filled the center of the room, with a wall of cabinets to the right. The hand-carved wood was an unusual reddish gold and slightly fragrant as Kayte passed. Along the opposite wall was a tall china cupboard with glass doors and an elaborate buffet. Between them, another door led to the kitchen.

"Good evening, Kayte," Lady Merrick greeted her from the end of the table. She seemed small and frail in the dim light coming from the French doors behind her.

"Good evening, Lady Merrick. Tristan."

Daevon's brother rose from his seat at the center of the left side of the table, but he responded with only a courteous nod. For some reason that Kayte couldn't fathom, he seemed to be regarding her with cold disdain. She was determined to charm him into liking her.

Tristan resumed his seat in the straight-backed chair. As

soon as he took over the Merrick estates, he thought, his first official act would be to see that all of Daevon's precious treasures were tossed out and that more comfortable, modern furnishings were substituted.

His brother seated Kaytlene directly across from him and he nearly choked on a sip of a dry Spanish wine. God, she was exquisite! He smiled, imagining what magical events had occurred to turn his brother from a snarling wolf into a breathless swain in a few short days. She was much too delicate for his own tastes, but enticing nevertheless. He wondered what sort of woman she became in Daevon's bed

"My brother has excellent taste in food and wine, as you will see, my dear," Tristan said, and smiled at Kayte. "Almost as fine as he has in women."

Daevon looked up from settling Kayte at her seat directly opposite Tristan, a deep furrow between his dark brows. He glanced down to the china place setting that had been laid for him at the head of the table and smiled.

"My lady mother," he said, "would you mind if I left my place at the head of the table this evening?"

Anna Merrick was amused by her son's request. She motioned for a serving girl to move the master's place to a seat between herself and Kayte.

Daevon glanced at his brother and saw blatant interest in Tristan's eyes. Feeling an overwhelming urge to protect Kayte, he covered her hand with his own.

"I shall stay close, my dear. I fear my brother has ideas of his own where you are concerned."

Kayte could not help but sense the tension between the two men. Though they spoke in polite tones, she suspected they did so for Lady Merrick's sake. If she and their mother were not present, she feared they would show no restraint in expressing their animosity. But why was there such dislike between them?

"It would seem, brother," said Tristan, "that you have a knack for choosing women who attract other men."

Daevon gave him a shadow of a smile and bit into a roll, using that as an excuse to grind his teeth together, knowing the remark was an obvious reference to Monique.

"Until now," he replied finally, "I have been foolish

enough to let them go. I shall not make that mistake again.'' He smiled warmly at Kayte, who was now regarding him with a look of distaste. Damn! He knew what she must be thinking.

Kaytlene regarded both men through half-closed eyes. Other women? She felt a pang of . . . what? Jealousy? Yes, damn them! She was jealous, and why not? This man was going to marry her, give her his name . . . his children.

There are no other women in my life, he had said. Perhaps not now, but would she be forced to contend with his past lovers?

"Monique lost her child, you know." Tristan continued to eat as though his words meant little. "Natural miscarriage, they say. Messy business, childbearing. I'm glad God had the wisdom to let it fall to the women. She bled till she was nearly dead.''

Daevon stared with outrage at Tristan. Before he could find the words to respond, Kaytlene touched a rich red napkin to her lips and replied sweetly, "As one of the . . . less fortunate sex''—she looked directly into Tristan's eyes, which registered his surprise—''I should say that I've always believed that a woman's love for her child tempers whatever pain might be involved in childbearing.''

Daevon turned his attention from Tristan to settle upon her, as if her voice were some siren's song that drew and soothed him. The soup plates were being cleared as she continued. "And if, as you say, God showed some wisdom in meting out that singular ability to women, I agree. It is said in Newbury that a man who faces war and famine without so much as a second thought would lose his natural color and faint dead away if faced with the necessity of bearing a child.''

Tristan stared, silent. Daevon grinned proudly. And Kaytlene considered them. She did not know what conflicts pulled these two men apart, but it was certain whose camp she belonged in. If there had been any doubt—in the Merricks or their servants—she had just banished it. Kaytlene took the last roll and held it out to Daevon.

"Would you like another, my lord?''

His boyish grin became fraught with the promise of how he would thank her once they were alone. He bit off half the bread and watched with amused delight as she ate the other half, chewing with seductive slowness.

Lady Merrick's laughter brought the three of them out of their self-absorption as the next course was served.

"It seems she's got the best of you, Tristan my dear," she said, pleased. "Do forgive them, Kayte. They were speaking of Lady Clay, an old . . . acquaintance of Daevon's."

"Lover," Tristan corrected. "It would hardly seem logical that Daevon would want to marry an acquaintance."

"Whatever the details, it was quite a long time ago. Monique Lisle married and had children, so put your questions to rest, my dear Kayte. The woman has just lost a child and is in mourning, as is her husband."

Mourning? Tristan thought with cold amusement. She wore no black when she writhed under my body, Mother. Outwardly he smiled sweetly. "Do forgive me, Kayte." He started tearing at a slice of spiced beef with a knife and fork. "I meant no disrespect to women. Especially when we have two such lovely ones here in our midst. And, of course, Daevon's relationship with Monique will have no bearing on our family's eagerness to celebrate your own wedding."

The past, Kayte thought, now had a name—Monique. Tristan had said, *Daevon's relationship with Monique*. Was it still a love affair? Or did Daevon plan to end his old affair now that he had another willing companion for his bed? She caught Daevon's eyes. He looked a bit worried, like a little boy wondering whether he would be punished for his poor behavior. One thing was certain. Daevon Merrick had a great deal of explaining to do.

"I'm sorry to hear of your friend's loss of her child," Kayte told him softly. "Perhaps you should arrange for flowers to be sent in condolence."

Daevon nodded. Tristan had just slapped her in the face with Monique and not only hadn't Kayte so much as raised an eyebrow, but now she was suggesting he send flowers! God, but she was a wonder, even if decorum was shielding her true feelings. She was entering Merrick life with the grace and charm that he knew Monique would never possess.

Lady Merrick's suggestion that coffee be taken in the

library was met with eager assent. Tristan stood to help his mother from her chair, tucking her arm into his while Daevon took Kayte's.

The tension Kayte had felt at dinner faded while she was led to the library and given a comfortable seat by the fire. Coffee and cordials were served, and Lady Merrick, seated across from her, took up knitting—something that looked suspiciously like an infant's gown. Daevon, leaning against the mantel, grinned.

"Planning ahead, are you, mother?"

"One can never be too farsighted," was the reply, made without a break in the sound of needles clicking.

Kayte glanced up at Lady Merrick, then at Daevon. When he winked suggestively at her, she flushed a bright pink, and he laughed. Bending to kiss Kayte's cheek, he whispered, "Perhaps we should work on it this evening. We wouldn't want to disappoint her, would we?"

"Daevon!" she gasped, none too softly. The sound of his laughter was warm and soothing. He kissed her cheek, his lips grazing the soft corner of her mouth. Closing her eyes to savor the scent and feel of him, Kayte wanted to turn her head to offer her mouth. When he straightened, she found herself looking up into his face, saying yes with her eyes. Her expression made Daevon take a long, deep breath.

Lady Merrick was thrilled at the glance that passed between her son and his betrothed. Tristan suppressed a yawn.

"I'd say you've got at least fifty good years left for lovemaking," Tristan pointed out to his brother. "How about a game of chess to amuse you in the meanwhile?"

While the two men retired to the corner for a long, involved game, Kayte allowed herself to be amused by Lady Merrick's stories of Daevon as a child. She could hardly imagine the tall, assured gentleman as a boy, trying to saddle one of the family dogs or splitting his pants climbing a tree.

"Mother," Daevon finally interjected in the midst of moving his bishop, "must you spread such vicious lies about me?"

"It's all true," Tristan added with a grin at Kayte.

"Except that she neglected to mention the time Daevon saved little Molly Quaid from drowning and demanded a kiss for his trouble."

Daevon coughed. "It isn't true," he objected.

"And how old were you?" Kayte asked.

"Eight."

"Did she kiss you for your trouble?"

"She slapped him," Tristan explained. "You see, Miss Quaid was an excellent swimmer. And she was fourteen."

The remainder of the evening passed pleasantly. Kayte had her first knitting lesson, Lady Merrick got acquainted with her future daughter-in-law, and Daevon and Tristan played three games of chess. Tristan won two of the three, but Daevon claimed that he was distracted by Kayte's presence.

"Stop looking at her, then," Tristan offered jovially, "and maybe you'll win a few."

As Daevon and Tristan played their fourth game, Kayte was lulled to sleep by their laughter, the sound of a fire crackling in the hearth, and Lady Merrick's sweet humming as she knit. It was all so pleasant . . .

"Bored?" Daevon's voice was at her ear, and she opened her eyes to see him leaning over the back of the chair, holding her book. "Perhaps this will help keep you awake, love."

"Thank you."

He bent to kiss her lightly, then returned to his discussion with Tristan. After several minutes he glanced at Kayte again to find her roaming about the room as if to study its every detail. He stepped up behind her as she stood at a long marble sideboard. Before he could bend to speak quietly to her, he noticed something out of place.

"Tristan, where are the silver pieces? The Spanish silver?"

"Didn't you tell him, Tristan?" Lady Merrick's soft voice came from the fireplace chair.

"Tell me what?" Daevon asked.

Tristan rubbed the back of his neck. "I didn't want to trouble you with it, Daevon." His voice and eyes were apologetic. "We were robbed. The library, at least."

"Robbed? When? Where were the dogs?"

"The night after you left for Newbury. I was in here, with the doors closed. Evidently the thief tried to come in through the cellar. Darby was tied to a chair in the pantry when we found her. The dogs must have caught on to him and he went out and came in through the library doors there." He indicated the glass doors that led onto the stone patio. "We struggled, I got the worst of it and went down."

"But he saved the ivory, Daevon," said Lady Merrick. "Must have taken it right out of the man's hands. He was clutching it like death when we found him lying there, unconscious."

Tristan looked a little sheepish as his heroics were divulged. Daevon saw his collection of ivory statuettes complete on the mantel and smiled broadly at his brother.

"You should have taken more care for yourself, Tristan," he said, "but you know I'm grateful." The men shook hands Daevon placing his left hand on Tristan's forearm. They looked like real brothers now, Kaytlene thought, thoroughly confused.

"Quite a pair, aren't they?" Lady Merrick asked Kayte. The men were still discussing the outcome of the burglary.

"Love and hate," Kaytlene replied. "It's certainly bewildering."

"Daevon loves his brother dearly."

Why didn't she say, "And Tristan loves Daevon as well"? Didn't he?

"I could not imagine him doing otherwise."

"Ah, Daevon has shown you his better side. Good. Good." Lady Merrick seemed pleased with herself as she leaned back and closed her eyes. "It has all worked out so much better than I had hoped."

What did she mean by that? Kaytlene wondered as she rose, collecting her book and starting toward the door. There was so much in this house that confused her, and she needed time to think. And sleep.

She was halfway down the hall before Daevon softly called her name. She stopped as if pulled by a chain, but did not turn to face him.

"Forgive me, Kayte. I gave no thought to your comfort.

You're tired.'' His hands were on her shoulders as he spoke gently in her ear.

"Yes,'' she replied curtly. "I'm going to bed.''

He turned her to face him and was surprised when she failed to respond to his tender kiss.

"Alone,'' she said harshly.

"You're angry with me?''

Her anger faded as she stared into his ice-silver eyes. "There is so much here I don't understand. And yes, I'm exhausted.''

"Then to bed.''

"Daevon?''

"Yes, dearest?''

"Tomorrow we talk.''

He kissed her lightly, this time feeling her move beneath his lips. "Tomorrow,'' he repeated to confirm the agreement. "Good dreams, Kayte.''

Of me, he added silently as she hurried up the stairs, a handful of skirt in either hand.

Chapter 11

Kayte quickly entered her room. Darby was kneeling next to an open trunk, pulling out the black mourning gown and coughing as dust choked her.

"I'm afraid my wardrobe is not as extensive or as well kept as a lady's should be," Kayte said apologetically.

Darby laid the second garment aside in a wrinkled mass of blue muslin and scrambled up to help her mistress undress.

"Don't worry, my lady," she said, smoothing the black and rose gown onto a chair near the bed. "His lordship has given me strict orders that you be ready for shopping right after breakfast."

"Shopping?" Kayte said with surprise as she pulled on a cool nightdress and slipped into bed. The huge white mattress was filled with down. She snuggled gratefully into the softness.

"Yes, miss. For your wardrobe. Gowns, hats, shoes and . . . the trousseau."

"I see." Kayte smiled, her eyes already nearly closed. "Whatever his lordship desires, then. Good night."

"Good night, Miss Kayte." Darby extinguished all the candles and noticed with satisfaction that her mistress was asleep before the last had been darkened.

Sleep came with a harsh wave of dreams that forced Kayte to relive the horrors of days past. Dreams of her father's cold body lying in its bed of earth on the salt-soaked coastal grave; and of herself, falling into a shallow grave beside him, clawing to free herself of its stench. A knife slashed at her throat, glinting silver-gray, and she looked up at the black-shrouded devil who wielded it.

"Daevon!" she cried out in her sleep, tossing restlessly. His touch brought her from the imagined world to the reality of her dark bedchamber.

She saw a tall figure bent slightly over her.

"No, Miss Newell, I am not your beloved Daevon."

She kept back her startled gasp and sat up, pulling the coverlet to her neck as Tristan sat down heavily in a chair next to the bed. His face was clearly illuminated by the moonlight that fell through the unshaded windows. His soft brown jacket had been removed, as had the silk cravat he had worn at dinner. His fawn-colored shirt was loosened at the throat.

"Please don't be alarmed, Miss Newell. I only wished to speak with you. Privately."

"Your business had better be of life or death importance or I'll throw you out on your ear!"

Tristan smiled inwardly. What a tiger, he thought. But he could sense the fear beneath her strength. He forced a serious tone to match his expression.

"Please hear me out, Miss Newell. I am only here because . . . I fear for your life."

The concern in his voice seemed genuine, as did the trembling in his hand as he reached to take hers.

"You must leave here, Kayte. Quickly." His voice was low and harsh.

"But why?"

"You don't understand our family, Kayte. Or my brother. He may appear willing to go along with your betrothal, but . . . forgive me if I falter, Kayte. I loathe having to tell you this." He hung his head and took a deep breath.

"Go on," she urged gently. He didn't hate Daevon, she realized. He was *afraid* of his brother!

Tristan looked up. "For years my brother has hated your father for forcing him into an unwanted marriage. He . . . has sworn these many years past to be rid of you, even if he had to bring you here and do the deed himself."

"Dear God." Kayte sank back against the pillows. Had all Daevon's attentions and sweet words been a screen for his true intentions? Tristan's words were not enough to make her believe it.

"How can you be certain Daevon means me harm?"

He hesitated again. "Did he tell you about DenMerrick, our family estate?"

"Yes."

He seemed surprised by that. "And did he tell you why we left the estate to live here?"

"Your father's death. I thought the memories in that place were too much for him to live with."

"That much is true. But it wasn't good memories that pushed him away, but . . . evil ones."

"What do you mean, Tristan?"

He looked up to meet her eyes. "Daevon murdered our father."

Kayte sucked in a breath. The thought of Daevon killing his father flashed through her mind and was physically revolting. Could he—? She wished she were still asleep, but the reality of Tristan's claim shook her. She knew she was not asleep. No, she thought, Daevon wasn't capable of committing patricide. But if he were provoked . . .

"Our father was a good man but a weak one," Tristan went on, pleased with her horrified reaction. "He was quite handsome. Tall and dark, like Daevon. And he was loving and generous, but weak when it came to women. Daevon seems to have inherited all those qualities. After Father had an argument with his lover, Daevon found them together. He shot them."

"You think Daevon brought me here to kill me?"

"I'm sorry, Kayte." He rose and she numbly allowed him to pull her into his arms.

"I can't believe it, Tristan. He's protected me. He . . . kept me from being . . . from . . ." She took a deep breath, trying to control the trembling in her body. "I was nearly raped last night. Daevon . . . saved me." She broke free of Tristan's grasp and moved nervously away from him. "He . . . the man said that he had been hired to kill me."

"Did he hurt you, Kayte? By God, if—"

"Last night at the inn," Kayte went on, "Daevon was downstairs, and . . . a man got into my room. He took me to a cave. He was going to—"

"Don't, Kayte." Tristan walked to the window facing the rear gardens.

"Daevon killed him. Why? Why would he hire some-one to kill me and then save my life?"

"To win your trust, I suppose. I don't know. But, by God, I'll have his head if he harms you!"

Kayte thought bitterly that there might be another rea-son. Maybe he had wanted her for himself. She trembled violently when she recalled how wantonly she had fallen under his spell. Still . . .

Kayte looked squarely at Tristan, a hard determination in her eyes. "I'll stay with Daevon," she said suddenly, "and let him answer your accusations."

Tristan only clenched his fist against the pane of glass. "Jesus!" he exclaimed harshly, his attention focused on some-thing occurring beyond the window, outside in the darkness.

He turned quickly away. Kayte, her curiosity aroused, slipped out of bed and stepped toward the window, but he grabbed her before she was halfway there. "Kayte, don't. Don't!"

She struggled, but he held fast to her. "Please, Kayte. It will only hurt you more."

She stopped, looked intensely into his eyes, and felt fear. But she had to look.

"Let me go, Tristan."

He did, but only after gritting his teeth. He kept his back to her as she went to the window and gave a shocked gasp.

Kayte's hand flew to her mouth to hold back an an-guished scream. Below the window was a circular clearing of lawn surrounded by honeysuckle and roses. There, a woman lay in the grass, her long blond hair spilling over bare white shoulders and breasts, the bodice of her dress pushed down around her waist and the skirts pulled up to the middle of bare thighs. Her legs were parted, one knee pulled up slightly, her arms spread lazily over her head. The smile on her face spoke brazenly of sated desire.

Daevon was standing at the woman's feet, wearing only a pair of soft doeskin breeches, his hands on his hips. The woman laughed, rose daintily to her feet, and reached up to kiss him. She stepped back and began to rearrange her clothing. Daevon turned his back on her and walked out of the clearing. Grabbing up her shoes, the woman disap-peared in the opposite direction.

Numb with shock, Kaytlene backed into the room. She was stopped by Tristan's hands on her shoulders. She gasped in several hard breaths before she could manage to think coherently.

"I must go home," she said at last.

Tristan did not hesitate to reply. "I'll have a horse waiting for you at the rear of the house. Ride east until you ford a wide stream. On the other side there's a wood on the right with a small hunter's cabin hidden there. You'll find food and a bed. I'll arrange for someone to meet you there tomorrow morning and see you back to Newbury."

"Thank you," she whispered. Her golden eyes glistened with her tears as she clutched Tristan's hand with a grateful sigh.

"I'll be waiting," he said, and then he was gone.

Kayte knew she would faint if she didn't move. Hastily she pulled on a dark brown peasant gown and fastened her hair back with a kerchief of the same color. She found a black shawl and laid it flat on the bed. In its center she placed a clean chemise, a thin blue cotton dress, her book, hairbrush, soap, and the tiny box that contained her most valued possessions, including her mother's emerald ring. She opened the box and touched the slim gold band to assure herself that it was still there. For some reason she still didn't understand her father had not wanted her to have it, but he'd been unable to ignore her pleading tears. He had given in and she had the only keepsake she had ever owned of her mother's.

She jumped with fright when she heard the echo of the huge entry doors slamming in the hallway below, then the heavy thud of footsteps coming up the stairs. Eight steps, nine, ten. Then they stopped, as if the person was considering the noise he was making and the people sleeping above. The climb continued, more silently, though Kayte was still aware of how far the steps progressed down the hallway. She knew the exact moment when his softened footfalls ceased outside her doorway. She was hardly aware that her knuckles had drained to ash white where her fists were clenched between her breasts, but she felt the hard thump-thump of her heart against them and held her breath.

There was a soft sound against the door, as if a piece of

cloth, or a hand, had moved across its surface. Then it was gone, and Kayte didn't know how long it was before she let out her breath again.

She quickly tied up her bundle, carrying it at her side as she slipped out into the corridor. The house was dark and silent. As she crept along the hall and down the stairway, she prayed that Daevon would not hear her steps as she had his. She had no idea which room was his.

"Kayte?" a voice whispered from the lower hall, causing hot fear to run down her spine. "It's Tristan. Hurry."

Relieved, she sped down the remaining steps and found her hand caught up in his. He led her past the dining hall and into the kitchen, then out into the cold night air where Dancer, saddled and ready, was pacing nervously.

Tristan lifted Kayte into the saddle and raised his eyebrows when she threw one leg over the pommel, pulling her skirts up to bare her calves.

"It will be faster this way," she explained, enjoying the feel of the animal's solid muscles beneath her thighs. "Thank you, Tristan. I . . ." Tears stung her cheeks.

"Don't worry, Kayte. I'll see you get safely home. Do you have friends in Newbury?"

She nodded.

"I'll take you to them. I'll see that he doesn't follow you."

"But he . . ."

Tristan's hand grasped hers as she held the reins too tightly.

"He's mad," he said quietly. "He'll kill you if you stay—one way or another. I couldn't bear to see you hurt, Kayte."

"I can never repay you, Tristan."

"Your life will be thanks enough."

She reached down and laid her palm flat against his cheek. He turned to press a kiss into it.

"Go now."

Kayte watched him reenter the house and stuffed her small bundle into one side of Dancer's saddlebags. A cool breeze whipped her hair away from her face. She raised her face to the moon, feeling suddenly as if she were being watched.

The magnificent gray pranced sideways, rearing with its front hooves and landing heavily. Kayte's eyes searched in the darkness, easily finding Daevon's figure in an upstairs window. The silver moonlight gave an eerie sheen to the trees about the house. He was standing in a darkened room, staring at her, his hands in fists on either side of the window. He ran one hand through his hair and disappeared.

He was coming after her!

Kayte turned Dancer east and dug her slippered heels into his sides. Once the animal was galloping, she had difficulty taking in breath because of his speed. The gray moved like a blast of storm wind along an empty valley, and Kayte felt more like a vengeful goddess than a frightened young woman running from the man she was supposed to marry. The man she had briefly loved.

While Dancer's body galloped beneath her, Kayte's thoughts raced just as quickly. Could Daevon have murdered his father? He had admitted that his past was full of secrets. Was murder one of those secrets? There were too many unanswered questions and coincidences to let her mind rest. Why would someone have tried to kill her on their trip from Newbury? Daevon had said he had enemies, but if he had come to Newbury at the very last moment, as he had told Sean, who would have known where to find him? And how had her captor known she was alone in the room at the inn?

Daevon had said there was no room for other women in his life, but he had obviously had time for the voluptuous blonde in the garden. Why had he lied? And why had she been so blind? How could a man who resisted a betrothal for so long suddenly decide he wanted to spend his life with a woman he had known for only a few short hours?

With the cold night wind in her face, Kayte's tears were whipped instantly away. Daevon had been leading her along, she decided finally, playing with her emotions, drawing her into his passionate scheme until she believed he might actually love her.

It was unholy, she knew, the intense power Daevon had over her. In a few days he had become a part of her breath, her blood, her senses. In nights to come she would lie awake remembering their one time together . . . and hating herself for still wanting him, for still believing in him—though he had proved himself to be everything Tristan had claimed, an angry, selfish man with an eye for beautiful women. Bastard! Bastard! she thought angrily, knowing that to him, she had meant just another night of amusement.

What was it he had said on the ride to DenMerrick House? *I pray God you don't change your mind about me when you learn all there is to know . . .*

Kayte was hardly aware of the hooves pounding as madly as her heart, of the growing darkness as the moon became veiled in clouds, or the distant rumble of thunder. All that consumed her was the reality of her fear. Fear of Daevon. Fear of leaving him.

After nearly twenty minutes of hard riding Kayte knew she had moved far enough from the house to have lost Daevon, and she slowed Dancer to a trot. The first drops of rain had begun to pelt down and she wished she had remembered to bring her dark, hooded cloak. As the storm picked up momentum, her hair and clothing dripped rain-water onto Dancer's steaming sides. A flash of lightning lit the heavy underbrush, and a jagged streak seemed to fall into the trees to the left of horse and rider.

Dancer lurched forward again. The growing intensity of wind and rain was a challenge to which the animal eagerly responded. Another crash of lightning lit the sky, and thunder followed immediately, frightening Kayte. It was as if the sound were mixed with the angry neigh of a warrior's destrier, a sound full of the promise of violent death. She shuddered and forced the thought from her mind.

Tristan Merrick returned to the library for a brandy, chuckling to himself as he poured the liquor and replaced the decanter's delicate crystal stopper. Yes, he would do as he promised and send someone for darling Kayte tomorrow. Himself. Once Daevon had discovered her obvious treachery, he would return to the old, vengeful man Tristan knew he could deal with. He had seen to it that several pieces of his mother's favorite and most expensive jewelry were missing and that the old woman had been given a strong sedative with her bedtime tea.

Almost immediately after he had returned to the house he had heard Darby's shrill voice upstairs, screeching in

her Irish brogue, which became thick when she was flustered, that the burglars had returned and would surely kill
them all. She beat on Daevon's door until he emerged, still
in breeches and a shirt that lay completely open against his
chest. Darby explained in a rush of hardly understandable
words that her ladyship's jewels had been taken and she
could not rouse Daevon's mother, though she was breathing normally. After hearing Daevon's expletives, Tristan
had taken shelter in the library, careful to close both doors
silently behind him. Nevertheless, he heard the door of
Lady Merrick's chambers slam shut.

Tristan smiled at the two trained black hounds lying on
the hearth, sleeping, their mouths still half full of the
sedative-laced meat chunks he had fed them. He poured a
little of the medication into his own glass, threw the empty
vial into the fire, and added a generous splash of brandy to
his glass before returning to the leather couch and taking
another deep draught, nearly finishing the liquor. The
remainder of the tainted brandy spilled over the edge of the
couch and onto the floor as Tristan fell into a drugged sleep.

Damn! Daevon slammed out of his mother's room. She
had been drugged. And Kaytlene was out riding one of his
horses in the middle of the night. What in heaven's name
was going on?

Tristan!

Daevon went first to his brother's room. Finding it
vacant, he rushed downstairs, giving a low, long whistle.
Where in hell were the dogs?

He pushed open the library doors.

"Tristan! What the hell—?" Striding barefoot to the
couch, Daevon took the glass from his brother's hand and
sniffed the sticky yellowish film that clung to it. Sedatives.
He looked at the sleeping dogs. Kayte must have fed them
a little drugged raw meat from the kitchen. She must have
asked the cook for a few scraps and, while the old woman
was collecting them, she had poured a little of her sleeping
potion into his mother's tea.

Damnable bitch! She wouldn't get away with it! Daevon
went out into the rain and, without benefit of donning
boots or closing his shirt, ran to the stable to throw on

Demon's halter and ride bareback off the grounds. He headed east.

Dancer crashed through briars and thorns and broke headlong into a downward slope, heading toward the river-bed. The animal showed no fear of the water and plunged in, eagerly fighting the strong current.

The cold water felt almost warm on Kayte's chilled skin. The rain and wind had nearly succeeded in freezing her. She had become numb hours ago and looked forward to finding the cabin that Tristan had promised was well stocked and secure.

Near the opposite bank, Dancer secured his front hooves on the gravel and tried to lurch upward with a hard grunt. Kayte leaned toward the straining neck, a tuft of soaking mane held in each hand. Dancer snorted and tried to get onto the bank again, unsuccessfully.

"You can do it, Dancer. Easy, boy. Easy." Kayte laid her cheek against her hands. From upstream she saw a huge branch roll toward Dancer's left flank and screamed as it struck the gray flesh. The animal neighed harshly in protest, shaking his massive head as he stumbled to his knees, throwing Kaytlene over his shoulder to the ground. She looked up in time to see Dancer succumb to the growing surge of water and be swept downstream until she lost sight of him in the black water and sky. When he emerged on the opposite bank she was relieved that he had survived at all. But when he turned away and ran off in the direc-tion from which they had just come, the pulse in Kayte's chest slowed and she was nearly overwhelmed by tears.

She clawed angrily at the soft, muddy sod and refused to cry. Damn Daevon Merrick! He had turned her into a fool, but he would not reduce her to a sniveling idiot when he wasn't even near. She looked up through the wet veil of her hair toward the pine wood where the cabin should be. Thoughts of a dry bed, warm fire, and something to fill her grumbling belly were all that kept her moving across the open field and into the wood, which provided some shelter from the merciless rain. She picked her way through the outermost ring of trees until she found a clearing. And her storm shelter.

Once inside, Kayte collapsed onto the plain plank floor. She was shivering, her limbs nearly gray with cold. She threw off her mud-filled slippers, slinging them toward an empty corner. A stick and daub fireplace faced her, next to it a neatly stacked pile of dry wood. Lacking the strength to stand up again, she crawled to the hearth and found a cone of kindling already laid beneath several larger pieces of wood. Half a tin of sulphur matches lay on the hearth and she used them to start the kindling aflame.

As she became a little warmer, Kayte glanced around the cabin. Simple rush mattresses lay on two small wood and rope frame beds on either side of the fireplace. Rough brown blankets covered the two small windows, and several more blankets of varying colors lay piled at the head of each bed. A sink, complete with pump, and a table with four crude chairs filled the right side of the room. There were two small cupboards which Kaytlene hoped to find stocked with enough food to last her until morning. A door between the fireplace and the right corner was securely latched.

Soon she was able to stand, but her clothes were soaked. Having ridden hundreds of times in the rain she knew well that if she wasn't out of them soon, she would be sick with fever before morning.

Stripping off her sodden gown and undergarments, she used one of the scratchy blankets to dry herself and rub some circulation into her flesh. Arranging her clothes on two of the hand-hewn chairs, she pulled them nearer the fire to dry and wrapped a soft red flannel blanket about her, securing it under her arms. At the sink she threw her hair over a small iron basin and pumped out enough water to rinse the spatters of mud and twigs from her tangled tresses. The water was nearly as cold as she was, but she lathered and rinsed her hair quickly, then used the towel-blanket to soak the extra water from it.

The cupboards were as well stocked as Tristan had promised. In addition to pans, salt, candles, and small burlap sacks of wheat, flour, and cornmeal, there were packages of dried beef and sealed glass jars filled with jelly, tea, coffee, and fruit. A long tin of crackers and a pot for brewing completed the array.

Kayte took down a heavy skillet and dumped a handful of dried beef into it. She added two large cakes which she fashioned from cornmeal, water, and salt. Taking her crude meal to the fire, she raked a pile of red coals onto the hearth and, lacking any sort of stove, laid the pan directly on them. The meat needed water to soften it and Kayte filled the pot with water for tea, pouring a little onto the beef. She had to rip off a piece of linen from her chemise to fashion a small bag for the loose tea leaves, but it produced a satisfying brew—better than Daevon's, she recalled with a smile. There was no sugar, but she was grateful to have the tea at all.

Setting the hot brew aside to steep in the pot, she brought out a jar of peaches and a crude knife and fork, setting them out on one of the chairs across which her clothes lay. She tugged at one of the mattresses until it came free from the bed and dragged it to a spot near the fire. A rolled blanket became her pillow, and she wrapped another snugly about her shoulders as she sat before the fire. She used the corner of one blanket to pull the hot pan from its bed of coals.

She ate with great appreciation. The meat had turned soft and melting, and the corncakes stuck to the pan but were crisp and golden. She was warm now, with food and hot tea to give her strength. Her hair was nearly dry and she pushed it behind her ears as she ate.

She had finished off most of the peaches in their sweet syrup when the fire began to die. She piled on more wood and was finally sated when it roared up again. Not bothering to wash the dishes, Kayte covered the skillet with the brown kerchief she had worn, knowing that she would welcome the remaining meat and cake by the time she woke.

She loosened the red blanket from its tight hold around her and, covering the mattress with another, lay nude beneath it. Her limbs were finally free of the shivering cold that had plagued them.

Filled with nourishment and growing fatigue, Kayte listened to the slow fall of rain on the shingled roof. Another storm began, with wind that slapped ruthlessly at the windows, but the relentless torrent of water and thunder could not keep her awake. She sank into dreams of the man she feared, tears slipping from beneath her closed lids to moisten her rough pillow.

Daevon had searched for hours. He was freezing and cursing himself for having left the house without boots or his heavy cloak. He had expected only a light, early summer storm, not the tempest that had raged for so long. Now the storm was intensifying, and if he didn't find shelter soon the cold would kill him. Having lost any hope of finding Kaytlene's tracks in the continuous downpour, he had gone east, knowing that she would not head for London, nor back to Newbury. Or at least not by the same route on which they had traveled that day.

Now he was beyond caring. Exhaustion tore at his flesh, while an even greater pain seared his heart, so recently opened to the woman who now evaded him.

He turned back, following the hunter's trail that Tristan often used during the autumn months. The stream would be much too dangerous to cross now. It had proven nearly fatal when Demon had first forded it two hours ago. Since that time he had seemed to move in aimless circles, hoping to find some clear hoofprint, or perhaps a torn shred of Kayte's clothing. But she was gone. Gone. She'd swept into his life after so many years of doubt, and swept out after a mere few days—days that had given him so much hope. He didn't care if she was a thief. He wanted her.

He was nearly unconscious when he came upon the cabin. The wind had turned bitterly cold, and his skin was grayish blue under its sting, his feet nearly numb. He walked Demon into the lean-to stable and shook himself from a near-death sleep, slipping off onto the straw beneath the stallion's hooves. It was all he could manage to pull the halter off the gray's stately head. He grabbed three heavy woolen blankets from the rail that ran along the wall at his back, one for himself and two for Demon.

Savoring the small warmth which the cover provided, Daevon thrust his feet into the straw, wriggling his toes to get the blood flowing again. Several minutes later he was able to hobble toward the back door of the cabin.

"Damn!" The door failed to open. With painful determi-

nation, he made his way through the lean-to and back out
into the freezing air.

The front door of the cabin swung inward with a loud
scrape, and Daevon fell to his knees in exhausted surprise. Whether his surprise came from finding a warm
blaze in the hearth or from seeing the woman who lay
before him, he wasn't sure.

"Kayte," he whispered, ignoring the tingling pain in
his joints. "Kayte . . ."

Waking abruptly, she nearly screamed when she recognized the man who had once again invaded her sanctuary.
At first she thought he would kill her, the look in his eyes
was so intense, but when he fell to the floor in an exhausted heap, murmuring her name, she could only go to
him. He was nearly frozen and fell unconscious almost
immediately.

With the blanket tucked securely about her once more,
Kayte slammed the front door shut against the wind and
threw down the long wooden bar that secured it. When she
turned to Daevon, a painful sob caught in her throat.

"My God, Daevon, you're mad!" She saw his feet,
nearly frozen from having worn no boots, his flesh as pale
as her own had been. He hadn't even worn a cloak.
Quickly she stripped off his shirt and wrapped his chest in
a dry blanket. She threw another piece of split lumber on
the fire, then pulled the second mattress next to hers on the
floor.

"Daevon?" Shaking his shoulders roughly, she managed to rouse him.

"Kayte? I've been searching . . ."

"I know. You must get up, Daevon. I have a warm bed
waiting for you. Come with me."

Half crawling, they managed to move to the mattress
nearer the fire. Kayte pushed Daevon back onto the rough
ticking, not hesitating as she loosed the pale breeches and
pulled them from his cold skin. She had not watched him
undress the night they made love and was unprepared for
the beauty of his naked body. His skin was bronzed beneath the cold tinge, his chest hard with muscle, tapering
down to a slim waist and flat stomach. His calves and
thighs were cords of sinew, gold in the firelight. Vainly

she tried not to stare at the juncture of his thighs, at the flesh that could be an instrument of unbelievable pleasure, soft flesh nestled in a bed of black hair. She drew a blanket over him.

Pouring a cup of hot tea, Kayte cradled Daevon's head in her left hand, tipping the cup to his lips with the other. "Drink this. It will help." He slept soundly in spite of her attempts and finally she gave up, admitting that nature knew more than she and sleep must be the better remedy.

Why had he rushed out after her so unprepared? He had no weapon, but Kayte knew perfectly well that he could crush her with his bare hands if he so chose. He hadn't known she was here—the startled expression on his face when he stumbled through the door told her that much. Tristan hadn't betrayed her. Had Daevon seen them together in the yard?

Daevon shifted suddenly, a harsh sound coming from his throat, and began to shake mercilessly. He was warming but not quickly enough.

Kayte loosened her own blanket and stretched out beside him. His flesh was icy next to hers, but she knew he would need her warmth to avoid catching a fever. He turned instinctively to her, wrapping her in his arms, his body drawing heat from their touching. She slipped her arms about his neck, pressing his head between her breasts, his chest to her abdomen. Their legs entangled and he groaned, as if he felt her touch even in his fitful dream.

"Oh, Daevon," she murmured into his now dry hair. "I don't care if you are mad. I don't care about any of your secrets. Please come back to me. Tell me that everything that happened tonight was just a horrible dream." She ran her fingers through his hair, gently placing a kiss on his forehead. She sighed, a sad, questioning sound that he did not answer, and fell asleep.

Much later, Daevon awoke. His eyes flew open at the feel of soft limbs entwined with his.

"Kayte?" Dear God, she was asleep against him, and his head lay against the soft rise of her breast. Had this all been a dream? Lifting his head, he peered about the cabin. No, not a dream. He could barely remember stumbling into the room and seeing her there . . .

He pulled slightly away, resting her head in the cradle of his arm, looking down at her dreamlike beauty as she murmured in her sleep. He touched the soft curve of her jaw, traced the lips that had lied to him. But God help him, it didn't matter. For good or ill, the spell she cast was securely fixed over his heart. After having felt his heart and soul bleed when he thought she had been lost to him, he had no desire to be torn away from her again.

She stirred, her hands resting against his chest, and tried to draw him to her again. He would not move.

"Daevon," she whispered, "it doesn't matter." She pressed herself to him, her cheek against the warmth of his chest. Warmth? She raised her head and found herself staring at Daevon. He was staring back.

"Daevon, you're . . . you're warm."

"Thank you, my lady witch. Or should I say my lady thief?"

Kayte stiffened in his arms. "What are you talking about, Daevon? Why do you call me that?"

"Which word disturbed you? Witch or thief?"

She pulled the red blanket around her and sat up, pushing his hands away. "How can you accuse me of being a thief?"

Daevon propped himself up on one elbow. "My mother's jewels were stolen. Isn't that why you ran away from me? Isn't that why you're hiding?"

She made no attempt to conceal the hurt and anger in her eyes. "You bastard! You *are* mad!"

She turned and started to rise, but quickly found herself thrown onto her back amid the tangled blankets, Daevon's steel grip on her arms. His eyes were tortured with pain, but she saw only anger.

"What did you say?" he demanded harshly.

"Don't! Please don't hurt me. I'll stay . . . or go . . . whatever you want. But don't kill me, please . . . ." Her voice was a soft plea, tears spilling from her eyes.

Daevon stopped. Even his breath seemed to pause in the midst of a sharp intake. Kayte was obviously terrified of him. Did she really believe he intended to kill her for what she had done? His grip loosened and she slid away, out of bed and into a corner, dragging her makeshift garment behind her.

He stood, grabbed his breeches, and pulled them on. He paced for a long moment, running a hand through his thick hair. He wasn't certain what to say.

"Why did you call me that?" he asked at last. "What makes you think I'm mad?"

Kayte's voice trembled as much as her body did. "Tristan said—"

"Ah, of course. Tristan, my beloved brother." Daevon sat down at the table, resting his head in his hands. After a long consideration, he turned back to face the woman who still cowered in the corner.

"Do you think I'm mad, Kayte?"

She studied him quietly for several moments. The man she saw was gentle and sad; but not insane. Worried, tired, lonely perhaps, but not mad. She shook her head.

"Why did you run?"

"I thought . . . you were trying to kill me."

Daevon laughed, a sarcastic sound that scraped against Kayte's ears.

"You thought I would kill you over a few pieces of jewelry?"

"I don't know what you're talking about. I don't have any jewelry!" she cried. "I saw you! I saw you with her in the garden! With that . . . whore!" Tears choked her. "Why don't you search for your precious jewels if you don't believe me!"

"I believe you, Kayte." He groaned, only then realizing that the girl in the garden had been sent purposely, that Kayte had been meant to see them together. But why?

"Kayte," he said more gently, "it isn't what you think."

"I don't know much about these things," she replied with as much dignity as she could muster between sniffles, "but isn't that a rather shoddy excuse? She was practically . . . naked, for heaven's sake! And you were nearly undressed."

"I had just finished taking a bath, my dear, when Darby came to tell me some poor girl was in hysterics downstairs. I thought it would be best not to bother with cufflinks and cravats. I had no idea—"

"Darby?" Her sniffing subsided.

Daevon sighed wearily and rubbed his temple with one hand as if to smooth out his thoughts.

"She came to tell me that a young woman had come to the house demanding to see me. Darby tried to get rid of her, but she said the girl was nearly hysterical. She was waiting for me in the garden."

"Yes, I saw that much."

"Her name is Josephine Patrick. She's used some pretty farfetched schemes to get me into her bed before, but nothing like this. She was lying there . . . well, you saw her. She was half dressed. She said that if I didn't perform to her satisfaction, she'd run to her father and claim I'd raped her. Her father will have her married off within the week after Darby tells him how she behaved."

"You sent Darby to—"

"Yes," he said softly. "I didn't want any scandal. Not with you in the middle. I stopped outside your door when I came upstairs. I wanted to tell you before you heard it from the servants' gossip, but your room was quiet and I knew you needed to rest, so I decided to wait until morning."

Kayte bit her lower lip gently. She knew Darby wouldn't lie if she asked the Irish girl about the events, so Daevon couldn't be making up that. And she had heard him stop outside her door, just as he claimed.

Daevon watched her make the slow, painful decision to trust him.

"Come here, Kayte," he ordered softly.

She was drawn to him, inescapably, and stood, wiping the traces of tears from her cheeks. She walked to him, the red blanket slipping unheeded from her shoulders. Her hands reached for him, wanting, despite whatever else might happen, to be in his arms. He groaned in relief at her gesture and took her roughly by the waist, pulling her against him, burying his face between her breasts.

"Now," he said gruffly, "I want to know why you were afraid of me. I thought you trusted me."

"I . . ." Kayte sniffed and Daevon settled her comfortably on his lap, brushing away her tears with the pad of his thumb.

"Why?" he prompted.

"Tristan said you hated my father for forcing you into a marriage you didn't want. He said you swore you'd be rid of me, even if you had to do it yourself. He said you were weak when it came to beautiful women.''

"When you saw me with Josephine, you assumed he was right. About the women, at least.''

Kayte nodded.

"And he told you I had hired Delamane to kidnap you?''

"No," she said, "he didn't say who it was. You knew that man?''

"I knew his reputation, Kayte. He was one of the more notorious hired killers in London. But I didn't hire him. I had no idea that we'd be returning to London together, or that we'd be staying all night at the inn. There wasn't enough time for me to get a message to someone in London and have him kidnap you, all within a few hours.''

Kayte, watching his expression carefully, sighed.

"Listen to me, Kayte. If I wanted to be rid of you, I could marry you and send you to some country estate for the rest of your life. As your husband, I could have you put away and you'd be as good as dead to me. Do you understand? I have no reason to kill you. My family is just as responsible for the betrothal as yours, so it would be ridiculous to blame your father for it. And you were just a baby. It would be even worse to blame you for the contract.''

"Would you?" Kayte whispered. "Put me away, I mean?" She looked up into Daevon's eyes. To be his wife and denied the pleasure of being with him would be worse than death.

"No," he murmured, bending to kiss her softly. "Never.''

Kayte began to cry again, with the gentle heat of his mouth on hers.

"Don't ever leave me again, Kaytlene. Please," he whispered.

"I'm sorry, Daevon. I'm sorry. I didn't want to go, even after Tristan said—''

"You mean you were willing to stay, even after you thought I might be a murderer?" The idea of her trusting him so deeply was even more satisfying than holding her in his arms. When she nodded, he looked down into her tear-streaked face and kissed her roughly.

"What else did Tristan tell you?" he asked, but he was afraid he already knew the answer.

"He said . . . you murdered your father. And his lover."

Daevon groaned, pulling her more tightly to him so that she could not see the anguish in his eyes.

"You didn't do it, did you, Daevon?" she asked quietly.

"God, Kayte, I don't remember. I can't remember what happened that night, but the circumstances led everyone to believe I did it."

It was her turn to comfort him then, smoothing the lines on his brow, kissing his jaw and chin and throat with an angel's touch.

"Kaytlene, I can't let you become a part of my life . . . of my secrets. You would die in my world. I've been selfish. I should take you back to Newbury and leave you in peace."

"But you need me," she murmured, knowing from the pain in his voice that he could never send her away. Nor would she let him. "Tell me, Daevon. Tell me your secrets. Then I can share them with you." She brushed her lips against his and he moaned softly, pulling her head back in a long, demanding kiss.

"You don't know what you're asking."

"Tell me. Please, Daevon."

He stood, gathering her into his arms, and carried her to the mattress. He let her down gently, tucked her coverlets modestly about her, and began pacing again. The story he told entranced her.

"My father was a satyr, a whoremonger. That surprises you. I suppose Tristan painted him as a saint."

"More or less. He told me your father was a good man who had weaknesses."

Daevon nodded. "Weaknesses. Expensive brandy, cigars, and women. All women. Any women. But one . . . was special to him. He was possessed by her. My father met her while on business in Cornwall. She and her husband were on their honeymoon."

"She was married?"

"Yes, but I don't even know what the woman's name was. After he met her, Father sent my mother and me away for over a year."

"Dear God," Kayte whispered, unable to fathom the cruelty of such a man.

"Once we returned—Tristan was just a baby then—Father quarreled with his mistress and she went away for a long time. That's when father began to drink. He became . . . violent." Daevon smiled at Kayte's stunned expression. "Don't be sorry for me, Kayte. I was glad for anything that took the place of his mistress, even drink. But it lasted only six months or so. He began traveling to see her again. When I was ten, his mistress moved back into DenMerrick."

Kaytlene could find no words to describe her disgust. And she had innocently believed that unpleasant memories kept Daevon from his family seaside estate.

"My father hardly knew Tristan was alive. And mother was banished to the servant's quarters. Father gave his mistress my mother's gowns, her jewels, her apartments. All the power and wealth of the Merrick estates was at her disposal. Two weeks after she came, she and my father were shot in his bedchamber."

Having already anticipated the outcome of his story, Kayte made no outward show of emotion.

"Then why would Tristan accuse you?"

"I heard them arguing. I went to see . . . I don't remember what I found. I woke up half lying on their bed. There was blood all over me. A pistol was an inch from my hand." He shook his head as if to clear it. "I must have done it. I hated them enough."

"I don't believe it, Daevon." Kayte sat up and rocked back on her heels. "I shouldn't have doubted you. You're so gentle, Daevon, so loving. I don't believe you would ever murder your father."

He smiled down at her and for the first time since coming to the cabin he saw the woman who had made him want her so desperately.

"Do you remember what I told you about Ellen Merrick?"

She nodded.

"I neglected to tell you about her curse."

"Curse?"

"She became very bitter, growing to old age with a bastard son and being deprived of marrying his father and living in luxury. So she cursed Robert Merrick and all his descendants. 'May your sons and their sons throughout time know the curse of loving a woman who will never be yours. May you become a race of whoremongers and murderers, slaves and thieves. And may you never know peace in all your lives.' ''

"It seems your father fulfilled the curse," Kaytlene whispered.

"Yes. And I thought I had also, until you came to me. I may be a murderer," he said soberly, "and I thought I loved a woman—"

"Who will never be yours? Monique?"

"There is nothing between us now, Kayte. Monique is a married woman, and regardless of what delusions Tristan may have, I am not like my father in most respects."

"If I believed you were, I could not marry you, Daevon."

"And do you still intend to be my wife, Kayte? If you do, you'll break the curse. You'll be mine."

"The curse will only be broken . . . if you love me," she said softly.

He went to his knees beside her, touching her bare shoulder lightly. "You would be easy to love, little girl."

"Then I think the curse is already broken, my lord, for I was yours the first moment we met."

Kaytlene curled against his chest as he pulled her to him. They lay down together, her hair splayed over his chest and arms, a soft teasing touch on his inflamed skin.

"Ah, Kayte . . . will you marry me?"

She giggled in reply. "You asked me already, my lord."

"I'd like to hear you say yes once more."

"Yes," she said.

"Today?" he asked hopefully.

She pretended to consider the offer. "Tomorrow," she answered, bending to kiss his mouth softly. "Today," she said, "I would like to spend deciding whether we are compatible."

Daevon rolled Kayte onto her back, jerking the red flannel from her body with one deft movement of his wrist. He took in her perfection with an appreciative sigh.

"Compatible . . ." he murmured as his lips fell on hers.

He had begun to teach her of tenderness. Now he taught

her body the pleasure of demand, of intense yearning. His
hands touched her with a driving need that became her
own; he rolled onto his back, pulling her with him, demanding and receiving a response from her lips, her hands.
She took agonizing moments to untie his breeches, finally
slipping them off only after he had begun to complain
about her slowness.

Dawn was far away, as far away as the rest of the
world. In the moments she spent with Daevon, all other
life ceased to exist. The wind and the rain paused breathlessly. Time slowed as Kayte once again took in the lean
hardness of Daevon's body, the evidence of his need
stretched to its fullest and lying flat against his abdomen.

"Kaytlene," he murmured sensually, mistaking the widening of her eyes. "Don't be afraid. Not of me, Kayte."

She raked her gaze up his body. "I'm not afraid, Daevon.
I never realized how . . . beautiful a man can be. How
perfect."

His hands found hers and pulled her down. She lay
against his chest, fire pulsing between her thighs as his
hardness grazed the silky triangle of her hair.

"Daevon, I want—" She was uncertain about making
such a request.

"What is it that you want, Kayte?"

She slipped down to nestle comfortably against his side.
"I want to . . . touch you, Daevon."

He wanted desperately to smile, but knew that if he did,
she might think he was laughing at her. She wanted to
know him as he knew her, to explore the secrets of his
body and her power over it. Daevon kissed her palm and
laid it flat against his chest.

"Anything," he whispered as he closed his eyes in
anticipation. "Anything you want."

Kaytlene was eager to discover the hard, muscled flesh
lying beneath her hand, but she was relieved that Daevon
had the patience to allow her this exploration, and the
sensitivity to know that she would be mortified with embarrassment if he watched her. Her hand massaged his
throat and shoulders, the relaxed muscles of his upper
arms.

Daevon basked in her gentle attentions, groaning softly

as she eased the tension from his shoulders and arms and then moved to caress the solidity of his chest.

"Must you be so damnably slow?" His voice was tinged with mischief.

"You are too impatient, my lord."

"Only when a beautiful young woman tempts me to lose control."

Kayte leaned toward him, lifting her head to press a kiss onto his lips. He returned it, restraining himself to allow her to retain control, though the waiting was burning to nothing the edges of his resistance. As she timidly, slowly, slipped her tongue into his mouth, her hand moved like satin over his throbbing hardness. Daevon's body stiffened; his arms enclosed her with no chance of escape. A pleasured, guttural sound came from his throat.

Kayte lost her timidity in the experience of his flesh, caressing the soft tip, encircling the steel shaft with her palm, her fingers gently teasing. She reveled in the obvious power she wielded, with Daevon's body coiled like a fierce cat beneath her hand, submitting.

"Daevon?"

"Yes, love?" He nuzzled her temple and ear with gentle kisses.

"I've changed my mind about marrying you."

He rolled her to her back, pinning her there with a steel grip on her wrists.

"Do you not think us compatible?" he asked.

"It isn't that, Daevon. It's . . . I don't want to wait until tomorrow."

He laughed, releasing her arms to finally return her caresses with his own.

Chapter 12

At the morning meal, only one figure was seated at the Merrick table. Tristan leaned both elbows on the smooth mahogany surface, giving no thought to the etiquette in which he had been schooled as a boy, cradling his head as if it were about to splinter into pieces in his hands. He cursed his stupidity, wondering what arrogant foolishness had caused him to drink the damned potion with liquor instead of water or tea, as Morley had instructed.

Arthur Morley knew only enough about medicine to pose a threat to the fair health of anyone upon whom he set his healing hands. He had been a promising student of medicine and had continued his education as long as his father's money supported the effort. Once the Morley assets had been swallowed up, the young man was forced out of his formal schooling and into the avenues of darker medicine—odd potions, remedies for destruction. He seemed to go a little mad with the knowledge of life and death, as though he had taken fruit of the Tree of Knowledge. Surely he thought himself crafty enough to find some way past the sword of fire that God Himself had set near the Tree to prevent such thievery.

And now Morley was a true master of medicine. As easily as others gave herbs to heal and incantations to soothe, Morley gave bitter remedies to kill, to bend the mind, or to draw the unborn babe from its mother's womb.

After enlisting Morley's aid in several acts of improper medicine, Tristan was suffering from the devilish effects of his first taste of the infamous doctor's handiwork.

It had been easy enough to convince Morley to prepare

one of his abortion-inducing mixtures when Monique had
become pregnant. Morley hated Monique's husband for
having taken over his father's business, thus ending his
legitimate medical schooling. Tristan used this knowledge
to its full advantage. Though the real reason for the Morley fall from wealth was their own corrupt dealings, and
the fact that their methods were no match for Clay's fairer
ones, Morley's mind had become twisted with hate. Believing Monique despised her husband for his cruelty,
Morley had been more than eager to help her rid her body
of what Morley believed was Clay's little vermin.

Convincing Morley to prepare enough of a sleeping
draught for Tristan's mother, the watchdogs, and Tristan
himself had been a little more difficult. Morley cared
nothing for his victims. If one of them was supposed to be
put to sleep for a few hours and became overdosed, falling
into an eternal slumber, it was of no consequence to him.
Tristan Merrick was another case, however, and Morley
had no intention of accidentally doing away with his best
client.

Still, Tristan felt as though the drug had almost killed
him. He poked at the food on his plate with sickening
detachment, finally pushing it away, opting for the glass of
cold water he had demanded. He drew only a sip onto his
tongue before realizing that that, too, would be a mistake.

He rose and moved unsteadily away from the table into
the hall. Daevon had been out all night and had not
returned, Tristan knew from the whispers echoing through
the corridors and the fact that Demon was still missing
from the stables. According to the stableboys, Dancer,
looking as though he had been through hell and high
water, had returned late in the night. Alone.

Tristan could only assume that Daevon's pretty Kayte
had fallen out of the saddle from exhaustion or been
dumped into the creek, which had probably become wild
in the storm. Either case served his purposes. Only one
twinge of regret tore at him. If she were already dead or
lost, he would not have the chance to sample her delicate
flesh himself. All through the heavy depths of induced
sleep he had seen her face in his dreams, her golden eyes
staring into his with tortured lust, her autumn hair enclos-

ing them like the curtains of a velvet-lined bed as he
entered her innocent body with his throbbing flesh. The
beauty had turned to blackness with her scream—of desire
or horror, he could not discern. He had come to his right
mind late in the morning with a shattering ache in his loins
as powerful as the one in his head.

Regardless of what had passed during the night, Tristan
fully intended to go to the hunter's cabin as soon as
Daevon returned, provided he returned empty-handed. Another possibility crossed the younger Merrick's mind, one
which pleased him mightily. Although unlikely, he knew it
was possible that Daevon himself had been injured or
killed in the storm. Tristan's mood lightened considerably
at the prospect.

Although the past days had been hard on her, body and
mind, Kaytlene could not sleep, not even in the comfortable circle of Daevon's arms. The steady sound of Demon's hooves sucking up mud with each step was soft,
slow, and constant, like a lullaby sung by nature. In spite
of the contentment that now spread through her limbs, she
was more interested in her conversation with the man who
kept a secure, protective hold on her as they rode.

Daevon led Demon upstream several miles to cross a
narrow bridge.

"Afraid you'll get wet again?" Kaytlene teased, tying
the end of one long braid with a strip of linen she had torn
from the hem of her chemise.

Daevon dismounted, leaving her to hold on to the saddle
as he led the mount across the rickety structure. Once
they were safely on the other side of the rain-gorged creek,
he reclaimed his place.

"No, my dear," he said in reply. "A man who has
faced worse does not fear a little water."

"Then perhaps you sought out this bridge simply to
lengthen our journey home."

Home. It would truly seem like a home now, he thought.

"You're much too clever for a female," Daevon replied, laughing. Then, as she reached up to return the kiss
he began, his face took on a more sober expression. As

their lips parted, he spoke gently. "Kaytlene, you said today we must talk. Now would be a good time, I think."

She nodded, slipping her left arm about Daevon's waist. Her free hand lay against his chest.

They discussed her meeting with Tristan the previous night, Tristan's concern for her safety and his professed fear of Daevon. When Kayte reached the place in her story where Tristan accused his brother of having hired the man who had tried to rape her the night at the inn, Daevon, who had been simply nodding now and then, pulled up Demon's reins, startling Kaytlene.

"God's blood!" he exclaimed, his brows knit deeply together. "How could he think—"

She placed a fingertip over his lips to silence the question. "You saved my life, Daevon. You saved my . . . innocence," she added shyly.

The anger cleared from his eyes. "As I recall"—a faint smile returned to his mouth—"I saved your innocence because I wanted it for myself."

"And for that, my lord, I am eternally grateful."

Daevon kissed her once more, a soft whispering of lips, and Kayte nearly shuddered from wanting him. Looking up into his face, she saw the same desire in his eyes.

"Daevon," she whispered, "why does Tristan hate you so much? And why is he trying to get rid of me?"

"I don't know, Kayte, but I don't think he'll stop trying to turn you against me. Will you do something for me?"

"Yes."

"When we get back, I want you to go through the kitchens. Find Darby and have her take you to your room by the servants' stairs. Stay there until I come for you."

"Why?"

"I want Tristan to think you're still at the cabin. I'll have him followed to find out what sort of help he intended to send you."

"You aren't . . . going after him yourself, are you, Daevon?"

"Worried about me, love?"

"Yes," she admitted. "If he wants to hurt you, he might . . ."

"Try to kill me? Tristan hasn't the heart to kill, even if

he is a little mad. He is devious and hotheaded, but not a killer. I'd stake my life on that."

Kayte nestled closer to him, and Daevon kissed her forehead. "Will you do one more thing for me, Kayte?"

"If I can."

"From now on, trust me. It almost killed me to see you running away."

She turned her face to his and slid her arms around his neck. "It hurt me, too."

His mouth covered hers quickly, before she could say more.

To Tristan's great joy and relief, Daevon entered the front foyer only a few moments after he himself stepped from the dining hall. His brother was most assuredly alone.

"How do you feel this afternoon?" Daevon asked as he saw Tristan's halting step and pale countenance.

"I feel as well as any man who has just been struck down with a good clubbing to the head, I suppose."

"This too, shall pass," Daevon replied pleasantly.

"I certainly hope so. If I had wanted to feel so miserable, I could just as well have emptied every liquor decanter in the house. At least it would have been more enjoyable."

"Have you seen Kayte yet?" Daevon's question stunned Tristan. "I rushed out so quickly last night that I neglected to see about her."

"Where . . . where in God's name have you been all night?"

Daevon gave the younger man a baffled glance. "What would you have me do? Let the thieves get away without a chase?"

"No. No, but . . . did you have any luck catching up with them?"

"Not yet, but it shouldn't be too difficult to track them once they try to sell the jewelry. Good Lord, Tristan, get to bed. You look as if you're about to collapse."

Daevon strode past his younger brother and up to his own room, demanding a bath on the way. When the tub had been filled and his long, angular body was relaxing in its steam, Lyle Miller appeared in the doorway.

"Mr. Todd has arrived, sir."

Daevon raised a brow. "Lyle, I think you've worked for me long enough to call me Daevon."

The young man forced a blond curl off his collar and smiled sheepishly. "Daevon."

"Better. Tell him to come up. And have cook send up a tray for Miss Newell."

"I just took the tray in myself, sir . . . Daevon. Yours will be ready as soon as you've finished."

The earl gave Lyle a warm smile. "I knew I made the right decision when I hired you, Lyle. Would you mind staying this afternoon? I'd like to discuss your taking on some additional responsibilities on the southern properties."

"Fine. I'll send Mr. Todd right up."

Henri Todd strode into the bedchamber as if it were his own. He threw off his hat and stretched his length into a comfortable chair near the window. Daevon was glad to see that he had shaved the rough stubble from his chin and trimmed his hair and mustache. His friend's brick-red hair was well complemented by a deep brown coat and pants, tan shirt, and reddish-brown waistcoat. His tall black boots had been freshly polished.

"Ah, I see you're quite the gentleman again, Henri. Glad to see it. Unfortunately, I am about to ask you to don your peasant garb once more."

Todd groaned. "Dear God, man, have pity on me. I've just met the loveliest little parlor maid. Don't send me back to Newbury before I have a chance to seduce the girl."

Daevon massaged a deep lather into his hair and leaned forward to rinse out the suds. When he emerged, rivulets of water coursing down his face, it was with a burst of jovial laughter.

"Don't be alarmed, Henri. I have no intention of sending you very far."

Todd sighed, leaning with relief against the chair.

"I have some tracking work for you to do this afternoon."

"Tracking, eh? Have you lost your bride-to-be so soon?"

Daevon cast an iron-hot glance at his closest friend.

"Sorry, Daevon. What did I say?"

Daevon grabbed a huge towel from the floor next to the

tub and held it limply for a moment, staring down into the
water. "Delamane was hired to kill Kayte."

"Dear God, man!" Henri leaned forward in the chair,
forearms resting on his knees. "Is she—?"

"She's fine, Henri. I found them before he . . . He tried
to rape her."

Todd ran a callused hand across his brow. "I would
expect as much from that bastard. I take it you did away
with the mongrel?"

"I only wish I had made it more painful for him. He
went too quickly for my taste."

"Just remember what a great service you've done for
the whole of civilized society."

Daevon stepped from the bath, dried, and pulled on the
fresh clothes that had been meticulously arranged for him
on the sitting room couch. As he smoothed down the dark
gray cravat, fastening it with a tiny pearl-headed pin, he
gave Henri instructions on the job he wanted done.

"I want you to watch Tristan."

"What?" Henri's expression registered his surprise.

"He went to Kayte last night. He told her about my
father's death."

"Did you think to keep it a secret forever?" Henri
asked with concern.

"No, I suppose not, but Tristan convinced her I was
mad. That I hired the man who tried to kill her. She ran. I
spent most of the night looking for her."

"And she's—?"

"In her room. Fortunately, I was able to convince her of
the truth."

"I see." Henri's remark and amused smile told Daevon
that he understood his methods of persuasion very well.

"Tristan thinks she's at the hunter's cabin where he told
her he would send help. I want to know what kind of
help."

Todd brushed a bit of dust from his sleeve.

"I'll—" A soft knock at the bedchamber door interrupted.

Daevon cast a wondering glance toward the door. Kayte
had been ordered to stay in her room until Tristan was
gone. Perhaps it was Lyle with Daevon's much-needed
meal.

"Come in," he invited in a businesslike tone.

The ornate handle turned and the door clicked open. Daevon noticed the manner in which Henri Todd leaped from his chair and turned as well.

Kaytlene slipped in quietly, snapping the door shut behind her.

"Kayte, I told you to stay put."

"Tristan's gone, Daevon. I saw him ride out two minutes ago."

"I'd better go then, Daevon," Henri said quickly, gathering up his hat. It was obvious to him that his continued presence would be intrusive.

"Miss Newell, please let me present my closest friend and confidant, Mr. Henri Todd," said Daevon.

"It's very nice to see you again, Mr. Todd. How are you?" Kayte warmly extended a hand, with a smile that sent a tremor of jealousy through Daevon. "It seems your mode of living has improved since last we met. Have you given up farming?"

Henri grinned sheepishly and shrugged his shoulders. "I met Miss Newell at the Newbury stables," he explained to Daevon. His attention returned to the lovely girl whose hand he still held in his own. "Miss Newell, please forgive me for my deception."

Kayte peered innocently into his face, then took in Daevon's guilty expression. "I see," she said finally. "So you were Lord Merrick's spy. And all that time you spent in my company was because you had been ordered to learn all about me and report back to your employer, is that it?"

Noting the sharpness of her comment and her cold glance at him, Daevon tried to explain. "Kayte—"

"Don't bother, my lord," she answered crossly. "I hope you understand my being upset when a man is *paid* to keep company with me." She patted Henri's hand, and the boyish grin returned to his face. "I forgive you, Henri. I realize you were only following orders. I hope we can ride together again soon."

"It would be my pleasure, Kaytlene," he whispered loudly enough for Daevon to hear.

"Would you please finish with your social niceties and get on with your business!" Daevon growled.

Henri gave Kayte a quick, knowing smile and took his leave.

"I hope I didn't interrupt you, my lord," Kayte said stiffly.

"No," he replied, "but had you come in a few moments earlier I would have asked you to scrub my back."

Kayte looked at the vacant bath and the wet towel thrown across the back of a nearby chair. "Perhaps Henri would have been willing to do it . . . for a price."

"Henri? How well do you know my friend, Kaytlene?"

"You paid him to watch me, Daevon. How well did you pay him?" As he stepped closer, Kayte glared up at him, trying to control her reaction to his newly handsome appearance. His dark gray jacket and pants looked as if they had been chiseled onto his tall, muscular frame. His waistcoat was black silk, the soft shirt pearl gray.

"No one would need pay a man to spend time in your company, Kayte." He reached for her, but she stepped back.

"Nevertheless, sir, I think it an insult."

"I think the lady doth protest too much." Daevon stood next to her, took a cinnamon curl onto his finger, and used the tress to pull her closer to him.

"Trying to make me jealous, are you, little girl?" His warm lips grazed her neck and she could not suppress a shiver.

"Did I succeed?" She tried to keep her voice level.

"You, my Kayte, have succeeded in a great many things where other women have tried and failed." He continued his passionate assault, his mouth leaving heat and desire wherever it touched. Still she forced herself not to respond. Finally he lifted his head.

"I'm sorry, Kayte. I'm sorry I had Henri keep an eye on you." He sighed, giving in to her pleading eyes. "And, yes, I was jealous."

She smiled, touching her finger to the slight indentation of his chin. "Good."

"Why, you rotten little vixen!" Daevon exclaimed as she began to laugh. He clamped his arms around her waist, lifting her off the ground until she was helplessly pressed against his chest and hips and legs. She was pleased and a little flushed to know that she had aroused him, the solid length of his desire pressed tightly against her abdomen.

Daevon's arm slid down to pull her buttocks fiercely toward him as his mouth explored hers with storm-ridden hunger. When she allowed her resolve against his obvious intentions to melt, her arms circled his neck and she moved against him, wanting his flesh on hers.

Daevon took his arms away and she slid breathlessly down until her own feet held her weight. He leaned to press a kiss to her temple.

"Do you want me, sweetheart?"

She grasped his jacket, praying he would continue. "Yes, Daevon. Yes," she whispered, and gasped in protest when he moved toward the door.

"Good." He smiled smugly. "Now remember, little girl, turnabout is fair play."

The dowager Lady Merrick sat upright in bed. The colors of the bedclothes reminded Kayte of the inside of a shell—cream, pink, and silver.

"Good afternoon, your ladyship." She curtsied.

"So nice of you to visit, my dear. Won't you come and sit beside me for a while?"

Kayte took a seat next to the bed, perching precariously on its edge as if she might bolt from the room at any moment.

"Goodness, child, you look about to die of fright." Lady Merrick waved a plump, middle-aged serving woman from the room and leaned over to pat Kaytlene's hand. "What has my overbearing son done to frighten you, my dear? I haven't forgotten how to give the boy a good thrashing when he misbehaves, you know."

The ludicrous idea produced a vivid image in Kaytlene's head, and she raised a hand to stifle a giggle.

Lady Merrick smiled. "That's much better, dear. Now, tell me—have you had an argument with my Daevon?"

"Oh, no. It's just that . . . he feared you were ill and told me not to disturb you. When I spoke to Darby, she said you were feeling well. I wanted to see for myself."

Lady Merrick's smile widened. "I see. You are not

going to be the sort of wife who follows her husband's orders without question.''

Kayte bowed her head, entwining her fingers over the plain, deep blue of her skirt. "I'm sorry, Lady Merrick. My father always said I was too wild for any man's tastes.''

The clear laughter that rang from the bed reminded Kayte of Daevon's and brought her head back up.

"My dear Kayte." Lady Merrick leaned back against the downy pillows, tucking the edges of a pink coverlet about her tiny waist. "You are the perfect young woman to suit my son's tastes. He's had enough of those fat-hipped milksops he calls women.''

"Mother, you never have appreciated my taste in women." Daevon's calm, deep voice made Kayte bite down hard on her lower lip to keep from laughing. She peered up at Lady Merrick, seeing no surprise in the older woman's face.

"Until now, my darling son," Lady Merrick teased him as Daevon strode into the bedchamber with its soft, feminine furnishings. His footsteps fell silent on the pale peach carpeting. When his hand slipped onto Kaytlene's shoulder, she stiffened, her flesh convulsing under that one easy touch. She knew that it was his body so close to hers that struck the tempestlike chord in her, and not any fear of his reprimands.

"I shall require my wife be a dutiful one," the earl of Merrick said quietly behind her.

"Don't tease the girl so, Daevon," his mother scolded. "We don't want Kaytlene to discover what his lordship is really like.''

Kayte turned her head slightly toward the man at her back. "Dutiful," she replied, "but not a milksop." As Daevon began to laugh, she continued, silencing him. "As for discovering his lordship's true colors"—both mother and son held their breath, waiting as she finished—"I believe Daevon has already made those clear to me and I have not changed my mind about becoming his wife.''

Lady Merrick's face took on a bright glow of pleasure. She had been told nothing of the night's events, left to think that she had had a long, deep sleep, a rare thing during her past months of illness.

"Mother," Daevon began again, "Kayte and I are to be married."

His mother smiled. "We have both known that for quite a long time, my son."

"Tomorrow."

His mother's eyes went from his face down to Kayte's, noting happiness in his, embarrassment in hers. As unbelievable as it was, Daevon Merrick was in love with his betrothed and she was beginning to feel the same emotion for him. That much was gleefully evident. But then perhaps it was not so incredible after all. Men had fallen irreversibly in love with the girl's mother at first glance, and Kaytlene was much more alluring than Patrice Newell had ever been.

"No," she said finally, folding frail white hands in her lap.

"No?" Daevon bellowed in the tone of a man who had never heard the word in his life.

"My darling," Lady Merrick continued, "you hardly give me enough time to prepare a proper wedding feast, not to mention arrange for guests, champagne, and flowers. And Kayte has had no time to choose a trousseau or a gown."

"We don't require a great deal of ceremony, Mother. Just a minister, thank you, and a honeymoon."

Kayte smiled into Daevon's face as he rounded her chair and sat almost reverently on the edge of his mother's bed. She told him with her eyes that in her heart she was already his.

"But, Daevon," Lady Merrick said, shattering Kayte's reflections, "we must arrange for the church."

"Oh, no!" Kayte gripped Daevon's hand, her clear eyes pleading with his. "We should have the wedding in the emerald hall."

"Emerald hall?" Daevon wrinkled his brow.

"Downstairs," she explained, "in the foyer. It would be lovely. Please, Daevon."

The earl's laughter enclosed her like a warm bath of

sound. "The emerald hall. Well, now that the foyer has an official title, we should initiate it. Don't you agree, Mother?"

"Are you certain this is what you want?" Lady Merrick looked to Kaytlene for a reply.

"Oh yes, Lady Merrick. The hall is lovely, and it will allow us to see to all the arrangements without leaving DenMerrick House."

Daevon smiled as the two women he most cared for discussed the intricate details of the wedding. He knew that Kayte meant to have the ceremony in DenMerrick House for his mother's ease. He would be certain to show his appreciation for her concern.

"Very well, Kayte," his mother finally announced, "I will prepare the house for your wedding party, but on one condition only."

"Which is?" Daevon cut in.

"That you agree to wait until Sunday morning. To give me enough time to arrange for a social coup."

"That's my mother, always at the pinnacle of the social scene. Now if you'll excuse us, Lady Merrick, I must suffer through an afternoon of shopping with Miss Newell."

As Kaytlene descended into the circular foyer which she had dubbed the emerald hall, a tall, roughly muscular figure with blond hair caught her eye. Daevon's hold on her arm loosened as they came to meet the young man at the base of the stairway.

"Lord Merrick, I'm sorry." He was breathless; one sun-bronzed hand swept a drop of sweat from his temple.

"What is it, Lyle?"

"It's . . . a private message, sir. May I speak to you alone? In the library, perhaps." The young man felt Kaytlene's burning speculation run over him and he shifted nervously, realizing that he had ignored her altogether in his haste. "I apologize, Miss Newell, for my interruption. I hope you're feeling better now."

"Do I know you, sir?" Somewhere in her memory there was a vague shadow of him, but she couldn't place it.

"Kayte," Daevon interceded, "this is Lyle Miller, my personal aide. He was at the inn. He helped search for you the night you were kidnapped."

To Daevon's shock and Lyle's utter joy and astonishment, Kayte threw her arms around the younger man's neck and kissed his forehead lightly. When she pulled away, a crimson flush stole over Miller's face.

"I owe you a debt of gratitude, Mr. Miller. I hope this means that I shall have the loyalty you obviously show my future husband."

Her mention of "husband" eased Daevon's jealousy and returned his sense of amusement. "Perhaps I should appoint Lyle your champion, my lady."

"I think that would be most fitting, my lord Merrick." Before Daevon could take back his jest, Kayte stretched out her hand to Miller. "Will you be my champion, sir knight?"

Lyle took the offered hand and slipped down on one knee. Daevon crossed his arms over his chest, impatient with the game that his lover and aide were obviously enjoying.

"By all that's holy, I swear to be your champion. To take up your cause in all battles, right or wrong, and sacrifice my life to spare yours until the hour of my death."

"Be thou my champion, Sir Lyle, and carry this as a token of our pact." Kayte slipped a white lace handkerchief into his palm as he rose, and the two grinned at each other.

Daevon listened to Lyle's flowery speech with jealous trepidation. Kayte was his, and his alone. Any man who stole her affections from him in truth, and not merely in jest, would face the consequences.

Chapter 13

Kaytlene Newell saw London for the first time in the company of her lady's maid. She and Darby sat stiffly in the back of Daevon's open carriage. To the keenest observer they were but two pretty young women riding in a carriage that proudly bore the Merrick crest of rose and silver. They might have been lower-class servants who had stolen their master's rig and masqueraded as ladies, their expressions were so grim.

Though Darby knew the sights of London and tried with all the enthusiasm she could muster to convey their names and importance to Kayte, her mistress seemed unaware of the knowledgeable chatter. After nearly a quarter of an hour of rattling off facts to an unresponsive audience, Darby consoled herself with a deep sigh.

"I'm sorry, my lady."

Kayte's eyes turned toward the other girl as if she were seeing her companion for the first time.

"Sorry? For what?"

"That I'm not his lordship."

Kayte finally allowed her expression to ease into a smile, drawing the attention of several well-dressed young men as their carriage slowed to a crawl.

"I should apologize for being such poor company," she answered pleasantly. She had been terribly disappointed when Daevon had emerged from the library with Lyle Miller, obviously distracted from the domestic duty which moments before he had looked forward to.

"Some very urgent business," he had said with an uncustomary hardness to his voice as she replaced Lyle in

the library. Then he had really looked at her, seeing the
deep amber, almost brown shade in her eyes. He tucked a
parcel of documents into the inner silk-lined pocket of his
waistcoat, then came to her as she waited quietly by the
door.

"I'm ashamed to say that I've sorely neglected my work
these past few days in favor of more . . . pleasant diver-
sions." He kissed her lightly. "And now my delinquency
catches up with me. I'm sorry, Kayte." He pressed her
firmly to his chest, tangling his fingers in the mass of
cinnamon curls that fell against the small of her back. "I'll
be at my office if you need me today. If you forgive me, I
shall make it up to you." The knuckles of his free hand
drew a soft course across her cheek.

Kayte brightened at the thought of what form his formal
apology would take. "We can go another time," she
murmured.

"No," he said sternly, "Darby will go with you. We
only have four days before the wedding and a great many
things to arrange."

He had kissed her brusquely, seeing Lyle Miller's tentative appearance in the doorway, and flashed her a smile
that sent a tingle up her spine even as he turned away and
the huge glass and oak doors closed behind him. Even
now, in the cool breeze of a June afternoon when he was
nowhere near, the memory of his smile sent a wave of hot
need through her.

She forced herself back to the present. "Darby, let's
enjoy the afternoon. I promise not to think too much about
Daevon."

"My lady, I doubt you mean to keep that promise, but I
agree. See there, that's Hyde Park. Stanhope Gate."

Kayte gave herself over to Darby's enthusiastic Irish lilt
and the stories of London she told, which transformed the
cold stone buildings and vacant storefronts into living
history.

The carriage came to a full stop in front of a bakery.
The building appeared to have been converted from an old
Georgian house, the street level stuffed with the confec-
tionery dreams of a child and the upper floor a simple
dwelling for the baker and his family. As the driver helped

both women down from the carriage, Darby inhaled the sweet fragrance of spices and fruity creams.

"We'll start here," Darby said. "Well, I mean, next door. At Lelanie's Dress Shop." But Darby's heavy brown curls tossed as she was distracted by the abundance of sugar-crusted turnover, cakes, and breads lining the plate glass display. She sighed ruefully.

"I think perhaps we should begin at this bakery, don't you, Darby?"

"Whatever you think, Kayte." The girls shared secret, naughty smiles and dashed inside, amid a flurry of silvery bells to announce their entrance. A well-rounded man in white apron and spectacles greeted Darby warmly by name.

"Mr. Kurtz," said Darby, "this is Miss Kaytlene Newell, his lordship's intended."

The flour-white hands, now pausing in their fastidious cleaning, reached over the glass cases of confections and grasped Kayte's with astounding warmth.

"So pleased to have you honor my humble establishment, Miss Newell. Won't you sit down and allow me to serve you a taste of my finest?"

Kayte was nudged gently toward a small corner table, her chair pulled out, then gently pushed back again once she had taken the offered seat. Darby was treated in a similar queenlike manner, and immediately a boy appeared with two tall glasses of icy lemonade.

Kurtz abandoned the two ladies for only an instant, returning to place an ornate silver tray of his delicacies on the table before them.

"Oh, Mr. Kurtz!" Darby exclaimed, popping a tiny lemon tart into her mouth, "you are the finest baker in all of London!"

The man bowed again, and his throaty laughter drew the attention of several other patrons. Kayte could find no grounds on which to disagree. She lifted a triangle puff of pastry to her lips, biting deeply into the lightest, sweetest vanilla cream one could imagine.

Having served his two pretty guests, Kurtz was off to discuss flavoring extracts with an elegant gentleman who sat alone at one of the other tables, leaving the women alone to sample each and every new delight. When they had finished, only a few pastries remained and those they looked upon longingly. They restrained themselves to keep their admirers from labeling them gluttons. When Kurtz returned to survey their progress, Kayte met him with a quick, sincere compliment.

"Your pastries are by far the best I have ever tasted, master baker," she said sweetly, drawing from him a wide, proud grin. "Especially these little cakes. What do you call them?"

Kayte pointed to the tiny, wheat-flour cake which lay alone at the far end of the platter, having been orphaned when she herself had snatched up its twin.

A mischievous smile lit the man's face. "Ah, the cinnamon cakes! They are his lordship's weakness, if it could be said he had any."

Darby had already told her mistress that the earl was a frequent and favored customer in the little shop, but she did not know which confections he preferred.

"He loves the cinnamon," Kurtz went on as if he were discussing a child with a notorious sweet tooth. "He likes the spice, but it must be sweet, too, and I see he has finally found the lady who suits his tastes as well."

Kayte warmed to this plump, friendly man whose perfect manners did little to conceal the hint of a German accent.

"Mr. Kurtz, do you have a boy to run parcels?" Kayte queried.

"For you, anything, my lady."

Kayte grinned, thinking how his words echoed Daevon's. *Anything you want,* he had murmured, delaying his own passion to allow her curious exploration. Reluctantly she dragged her thoughts back to the present, wondering what quality it was that she possessed which gave her such control over members of the opposite sex.

"My . . . his lordship has a great deal of work to do at his office today. Would you be so kind as to send half a dozen cinnamon cakes round to him?"

"Of course, my lady. With all haste."

"And, of course, you will come to our wedding. Sunday at ten o'clock. At DenMerrick House."

The man was as shocked by the invitation as he was flattered. "But my lady—"

"I shall expect you, sir. I am sure his lordship will be in a scolding mood if I should fail to invite you. Do you wish to count yourself responsible for my suffering his displeasure?" She smiled coyly, extending her hand.

"Thank you," was all he managed. Kayte slipped a coin into his hand, enough to pay for the confections she and Darby had consumed and those meant for Daevon as well.

"Good day then, Mr. Kurtz. It has been a pleasure."

With their bellies stuffed full, Kayte and Darby went next door into the cool, dark interior of Lelanie Hanlon's dress shop. They spent days there, or so it seemed to Kayte as she twirled about like a doll in the presence of the designer herself and a bevy of her seamstresses. She paraded about in an endless series of gowns of every color— palest pink, cream, emerald green, russet, and blue. A quickly growing pile of boxes were required to pack the garments she chose, Kayte constantly looking to her lady's maid for approval, having never had so many impossible choices to make. They agreed upon the ruby velvet cape with white satin lining and the pale turquoise gown that molded tightly against Kayte's breasts and waist, falling into a shimmer of sea-colored silk and silvery chiffon. There was a dark blue muslin for domestic wear, and another of rust. There were a sapphire brocade, a brown poplin with pretty accents of red ribbon and lace, and a green satin with golden overskirt and full sleeves.

The packages were dispatched to a waiting carriage, which followed their own as the trip continued and they bought lace, hats, scarves, gloves, shoes, and—finally—a full array of undergarments.

Kayte marveled at the feel of the silk chemises, the graceful sweep of starched petticoats, and whalebone-shaped corsets. The sheerest silk stockings were tucked lovingly into small paper-lined boxes of gray and red. Added to the pile were petticoats and nightgowns of materials Kayte thought would surely melt to nothing with the heat of Daevon's hands upon them. She blushed and said nothing, realizing that it was really for him she chose the garments.

Examining an assortment of rather plain corsets and tight-looking flaps of starched linen which she could imagine being viciously uncomfortable against the skin, she ran her finger along them until she touched a flash of silvery-gray satin. She pulled out the corset, concealing a gasp at its wanton yet beautiful adornment of pale lace and a trim of tiny seed pearls at the center of the low bodice. Despite the gasps and moans voiced loudly by the middle-aged clerk and her sallow-faced assistant, she purchased it. A pair of stockings which shimmered with the same grayish-silver light were also wrapped up, and Kayte and Darby, both with smiles on their faces, declared they were finished.

As they were stepping up to their coach, a tall glass pane on the opposite side of the street flared silver in the light of the setting sun and, before Darby could object, Kayte was darting toward it, through the busy evening traffic.

Baffled, Darby ran behind her. When they had dodged their way past quickly moving vehicles, ignoring the curses of several drivers, Kayte shoved her foot into the closing door of the newly discovered shop and demanded entrance. She was granted her request.

Daevon Merrick swung his darkly gleaming boots onto the edge of his desk, crossing them comfortably at the ankles. He leaned into the leather chair, its thick padding molded to the exact shape of its owner. He halfheartedly read a page of tightly scripted legal jargon regarding the requested permits for expansion of his already vast fleet of shipping vessels and warehouses. He had been refused, Henri Todd believed, simply because his business was growing too large too quickly. "You're just a man," he had joked with Daevon in his cool manner. "Nobody wants to help you make yourself a god!"

A god, Daevon now thought coldly as he gazed out the unshaded windows toward the ever-scuttling workers on the piers. The *Northstar Queen* had been moored expertly by his men, all of whom seemed pleased to be back among the civilized after months of sea travel.

The fleeting memory of a fawn-eyed daughter of an imperial prince wafted through Daevon's memory. She had been expertly trained, her hands running over his flesh as she washed him, sinking down onto the hardness of his sex in the steaming, perfumed tub. In his mind the pale jade eyes became golden, the hair a cascade of bright silk fanning his face. *Kayte*. In four days she would be his wife and he would be a god. Her god. One who would worship her instead of demanding homage for himself.

He tried to focus his thoughts on business once more, having been distracted over and over again by memories of Kayte.

The *Northstar Queen* would have to be relieved of its cargo from the Orient and reloaded quickly with illegal goods. It was easy enough to load his vessels with the materials he intended to smuggle. Once a ship was secured in port, it was filled with crates of food; barrels of rum, whiskey, and port; boxes of cloth, tea, and English china. These provisions were to be used as a basis for trade and received an official stamp of approval when the ship was full.

Then, on the last evening before a ship was to sail, Daevon threw one of his legendary bon voyage parties for his men. It amazed every other captain, owner, and crew in London's ports to see the wild revelry in which Merrick's men took part. It was not the boisterous drinking, nor the company of thirty or forty whores—ugly though they were— that brought the attention of others, but the fact that, after a night of dancing, drinking and wenching, Merrick's crews always sailed with the dawn as alert and bright-eyed as the freshest men in London.

Daevon had always known that it was simpler to work his secret rebellion in the open. Under the colorful guise of a party, complete with rows of paper lanterns strung from the ship's masts and a chain of wild dancers clapping and stomping on deck, he worked his wiles. The whores, who had developed a reputation on the docks as the ugliest women in England, were actually his own men, grudgingly dressed in wigs and gowns. The slightest of them was capable of carrying pounds of dried foods, tools, cutlery, or cloth beneath the folds of his skirts and in the flowing sleeves and ample bosoms. They were escorted below deck several at a time and the goods they carried stored in the captain's cabin, which was the largest available space.

Barrels of salted and dried meat, spice and tea were rolled onto the deck and marked RUM and WHISKEY, then moved to the hold. Tucked away in cloves and tea were documents and maps informing the Americans of English plans for new blockades, obtained from Daevon's own highly placed informants.

News of scarce commodities on American soil was relayed to Daevon's captains, who reported back to him. Tea was the most requested item, as well as spices, pottery, tools, and cutlery. Daevon, who had subsequently been dubbed the English Angel in his most frequented ports, supplied all of the needed items.

In addition to the heavy loads of common necessities carried by Merrick vessels, Daevon supplied the luxuries that were denied the Americans in their difficult struggle to survive—such riches as English chocolates, fine cloth, and even the latest designs from the best couturiers. Daevon had arranged for every possible item—everything from English china to Oriental silks and diamonds secured from Indian mines. He enjoyed the chance to aid the Americans by fulfilling both their needs and their desires. And, of course, he made a reasonable profit in the transaction.

Just as Daevon and Kayte had started out on their shopping spree, Lyle Miller had brought him several urgent messages, one of which had been delayed because of a newly positioned fleet of English vessels.

One of the requests was for winter supplies for an orphanage in New Orleans. They required food, medicine, wool for blankets, and cloth for the children's clothes. Sister Marie, the caretaker, had also asked if there might be a chance of having a hundred French Bibles, a case or two of wine for the taking of the sacraments, and—if it wasn't too sinful to ask—one milk cow and enough food to see it through the winter. Theirs, she had explained, had been slaughtered for food.

"Donations," she had written, "are deplorably low. With the southern landowners unable to export their tobacco and cotton, there is little extra money to give, and so we cannot find fault with the people's hearts, but with the conditions which are set about us. The poor boxes in the churches are all but empty, and so we have taken to feeding and sheltering those who come to our doors with such needs, as well as caring for the children. We beg your help."

Daevon had hastily written instructions on the back of the letter and handed it to Lyle. One hundred French Bibles, four cases of wine, two milk cows, and two steers. Enough hay and corn to feed the animals for six months. Woolen blankets, cloth. Salted hams for Christmas, fruit, and toys. And a pearl rosary for Sister Marie, with the English Angel's deepest regards.

Lyle read the list quickly and went off to fill the order with a grin.

"Excuse me, sir," interjected a rumbling voice from the door. Daevon's eyes shot up to find the captain of the *Queen*, a fair-sized crate slung over his muscled shoulder.

"Come in, Bayless. Good trip?" Daevon left his desk as the captain nodded and dropped the crate to the floor.

Daevon wrenched off the lid and drew out a red silk kimono. His fingers ran over its delicately embroidered flowers. Soft, satin soft. Like Kayte.

"I'm getting married on Sunday," Merrick said matter-of-factly.

"The old man's gone, then?"

"Yes."

"There's no breaking the contract?"

Daevon faced his friend squarely, his slight smile bringing a look of surprise to the captain's face. "I don't want to break it, James. I want to marry Kayte."

"Kayte?" The sea-blue eyes were clear beneath a wave of brown hair, its thickness tinged with the first signs of gray. "Lord a'mighty! I never thought I'd see this day!"

"She's a beauty, James."

"You bringin' her tonight?"

Daevon hadn't considered inviting Kayte to the shipboard party, and thought now how out of place she would feel with his sea-roughened crew. He enjoyed Kayte's company, but she was, after all, a woman. A woman whose place was in his home and in his arms. Would she ever belong— really belong—in his world?

A sharp rap on the door kept him from answering.
"Yes?"

Lyle Miller poked his head in the door.

"Come in, Lyle. You remember Captain Bayless?"

"Of course. Welcome home, captain. This just came for you, Daevon." He handed his employer a small white box.

Daevon took the box to his desk and sat with it in his lap. He slid open the top, and his nose wrinkled at the warm, familiar scent. Six cinnamon cakes were neatly arranged at the bottom of the box with a white card lying on their sugar-dusted tops. *Compliments of Miss Kaytlene Newell*, it stated simply, and Daevon wondered if the hasty scrawl was in Kayte's hand. It resembled more the handwritten bills which were made out by Mrs. Kurtz. To the amazement of the two men with him, he threw back his head and laughed.

Perhaps Kayte would fit into his world, after all.

Kayte paced the library floor, pausing only occasionally to pull back the curtains on the French doors. After half an hour she swung the doors open and ventured onto the stone terrace, allowing the late evening breeze to ease away the tiny lines furrowing her brow. She and Darby had returned an hour ago to find that neither Tristan nor Henri Todd had been heard from since they had left DenMerrick House earlier in the day.

Darby had gone directly upstairs to unpack the bounty gleaned from their day of shopping and Kayte had gone to the dining room to quiet her empty stomach, then bathed quickly and changed to meet Daevon. She'd chosen a simple gown of gold cotton. Darby had insisted upon it because of its smartly cut waist and bodice, and the nut-brown lace and ribbons that adorned it. It was the perfect foil for her freshly brushed hair, a lighter gleam of gold against the soft dress.

A clatter of hooves startled Kaytlene, and she looked hopefully across the well-kept lawn, her search rewarded at the sight of Daevon on Demon pounding up the wide drive. Daevon, still dressed in gray, seemed an extension of the animal moving beneath him, and Kayte leaned against the stone pillar at the front corner of the terrace, thrilled to watch the two of them. She straightened in surprise when, with no warning or hesitation, horse and rider veered toward her. They crossed the lawn in a thundering gallop, and Kayte came to the edge to lean a little over the stone railing. Daevon's gray eyes were less than a foot from her own.

"Welcome home, Daevon." Her voice was like a soft breeze in the night.

"I've missed being home," he returned. "I've missed you." His hand brushed the soft curve of her cheek.

"I . . . missed you," was all that came from her throat as it constricted with the painful need his touch called up in her.

"Thank you for the gift, Kayte. Who told you about my weakness for pastry?"

"Mr. Kurtz said you like cakes and . . . women who are spicy but sweet." Kayte gasped as Daevon's hands clasped her waist. Demon moved sideways toward the terrace and in a moment a second, lighter rider—Kayte—was settled on his back.

"You are far sweeter than any of Kurtz's confections, my dear. And more delicious."

Kayte's arms slipped around his neck, clutching at the fabric of his collar before his lips touched hers. As soon as his mouth fell with its steel tenderness, his tongue delving for the core of her passion, she moaned and wanted him.

"Daevon, love me," she pleaded as he pressed hot kisses along her throat.

He took her face between his palms as she shook with a sob, pushing away the silver tears that ran from her eyes along her cheeks.

"Kayte," he murmured, his voice deep with concern. "Why are you crying? Have I upset you, little girl?"

"I'm not a girl. I'm a woman!"

He smiled at her tearful defiance. "I have no doubt about that, my dear. Tell me what troubles you so."

"Daevon, I . . . I love you."

She felt his body stiffen. The arms that wound around her waist became a sweet trap. She buried her face in his shoulder, knowing it was the wrong thing to say . . . the wrong time. He would never believe such a declaration so soon.

"I'm sorry," she whispered. "You don't believe me."

Daevon let the words melt over him in a delicious wave. Since he had first seen her, he had known she belonged to him, and not because of some contract. If he was truly a descendant of Richard the Lion-Hearted and Ellen Merrick, then he had to believe it was possible to love a woman on sight. He had always been sparing in his faith in that particular miracle, but now he *must* believe it. Love had struck him with a force of inescapable reality.

Kayte grasped his coat as he urged Demon forward, into a gallop. When they stopped she slid to the ground, falling into the grass with a cry of disappointment. She stared out at the glassy water of a pond, hardly noticing Daevon kneeling beside her.

"Kayte?" He took her into his arms, turning up her tearstained face for his kisses. His tongue tasted of heat and salt.

"You're not angry with me, Daevon?" Kayte's eyes widened when he smiled, a slow, sensuous curving of the soft lips that drove her mad.

"I once thought I loved a woman, Kayte, but now I know it couldn't have truly been love. She wasn't you." He bent his head to taste of her mouth, a soft shadow of a kiss that left his hands trembling.

He pushed her back onto the luxury of soft, early summer grass, smelling its freshness, tasting hers. Their kisses spun out into long moments, the moments into a kaleidoscope of wonder.

"Kayte, Kayte . . ." He spoke her name into her mouth, the soft flesh beneath her ear.

"I believe you. I love you." His lips kept hers from answering with anything but a deep groan of contentment. She was charmed into a web of silence beneath his lips and tongue and the fingers that now traced the soft lines of her body. His hand slid beneath the gold skirt of her gown toward the full swell of her hip. She whimpered, wriggled closer, grasping his partially opened shirt as tenderness gave way to yearning.

"Daevon, I . . . I need you." Kayte could think of no

other words to express the heat that grew between her thighs, a desire she knew his body could fulfill.

Daevon could not repress a groan as his palm caressed the bare flesh of her calf and thigh. He had pushed her skirts to her waist, and she kicked away her soft doeskin slippers, leaving the bared ivory skin an offering to his own need.

They were far enough from the house not to be seen, well hidden by trees and a thick wall of honeysuckle. Daevon knew that this spot was secluded enough to conceal their lovemaking, but the evening was rapidly slipping away, and there was much to do to prepare the *Northstar Queen* for her predawn launching. He could not bear to refuse Kayte the physical closeness and passion she begged for, yet he did not want to rush her pleasure or take the time to make love to her as she deserved.

A tender smile touched his mouth. He would give her the pleasure she craved, then take her to the *Queen*. He looked forward to watching her dance with the flush of lovemaking on her cheeks.

Kayte sucked in her breath as Daevon slid down the length of her, his hands teasing the peaks of her breasts into hardness, his mouth gliding across her navel to the curve of her waist, his fingers removing the cloth barriers to his intimate touch.

His hands slid beneath her hips, drawing her up toward his mouth as he sank down onto her, pleased by the moan that came from her, the tensing of her body that pushed her eagerly to him.

"Daevon," she gasped between shuddering breaths, "what are you . . . doing to me?"

He replied by sliding his tongue along the sweet, wet satin folds, stopping to caress the tiny, hard center of her passion with his kiss.

Kayte took handfuls of her skirt into her fists, clenching and unclenching, moaning, wanting. Her body writhed on the cool grassy bed, held steady by Daevon's loving hands. She whimpered his name, a delicate and ferocious plea for the culmination of her need. And he brought it, the hard, velvet invasion of his tongue into her body shattering her once and again, for what seemed an eternity of intense pleasure.

Daevon stretched out along Kaytlene's heaving side, smoothing the skirt of her dress down over her passion-flushed legs. He kissed her temple reverently.

"We must go now, my love," he said gently, then whispered again, "my love," as if to make it real.

"Must we, Daevon?"

"Yes."

She turned to him, her fingertips playing a game of their own along his jaw and throat. "You've given me so much pleasure," she murmured against his lips, "and taken none for yourself."

Daevon hadn't even thought of his own desire. He had been fully aroused when Kayte first lay on the grass, accepting his kisses eagerly. Now he felt as though her shuddering climax, experienced through his hands and mouth, had been his own. Her pleasure had satisfied him. No other woman had ever had such power over him.

"Then perhaps," he said as he leaned on one palm above her, "you have taught a coldhearted man the true essence of loving."

The *Northstar Queen* was ablaze with multicolored lanterns. Music and laughter floated from its deck, and men and women danced and reeled as if they had no promise of the morrow.

Kaytlene Newell approached the vessel on Daevon's arm, feeling a little apprehensive. Her steps faltered as they neared the creaking gangway leading to the upper deck.

"Are you frightened, Kayte? Have you never seen a sailing ship before?"

"I've seen them," she answered, "far out to sea from the cliffs. I never realized how large they really are. So long and sleek . . . But Darby says they can give you quite the *mal de mer*."

Merrick laughed in reply, recalling Darby's stubborn refusal to board any sea-bound ship. "You can trust me, my love. This one is quite safe, you see." He pointed out the secure lines that held the *Queen* in port. "Darby neglected to tell you that the *mal de mer* usually occurs out to sea, did she not?''

Kayte nodded, allowing Daevon to coax her up and onto the boat, one of the newest and most prized of his fleet.

"Well, then. You can relax and enjoy our little bon voyage party. Will you wait here for me?'' He had noticed a potentially serious scuffle between two of his biggest— and dumbest—men and stepped into the circle of well-wishers to sort out the disagreement.

Kayte stood at the shadowy side of the *Queen*, folding her arms across her chest beneath her red velvet cloak. She had gone back to the house with Daevon to retrieve it and found that Henri Todd had just arrived. He and Daevon spoke in the library while she went upstairs. Daevon told her when she returned that Tristan had left the hunter's cabin and gone into London, but she had gleaned no further information from him and they had started off at once for the *Northstar Queen*.

"All right now, step lively there, darlin'!'' A rough hand attached itself to Kayte's arm and pulled her toward the entrance to the lower decks.

"Let go of me, you idiot!'' she exclaimed.

The man did not even look back at her as he jerked her roughly down the black stairwell and shoved her through a door marked CAPTAIN. His push landed her squarely in the midst of a velvet draped bed, throwing the hood of her cape over her face and hair.

"What in God's name do you think you're doing, you ignorant pig?'' she cried, her voice strained with fear and anger.

The man laughed in the near darkness around them. Only one lamp burned in the closed room and it was partly shaded. Several other men stood in the darkness, but made no move to help her.

"Come on, Buckey,'' said the steely, gruff voice with an edge of irritation. "I've got no time to be playin' your daft games. Now get those skirts off or you'll have some hell to pay!''

Kayte would have screamed had it not been for the fear caught in her chest. Why, this was Daevon's own ship. He'd have the bastard drawn and quartered for speaking to her like that! Her eyes fixed on the door, which was no longer blocked as the man moved about the cabin. The room seemed to be partially filled with crates. She lunged for the door, only to find herself being dragged back by her skirts.

"All right, Buck. Looks like I'll have to ravage ya after all, don't it?"

In a flash her feet were pulled up, forcing her head to the floor with a painful thump. The skirts fell away from her legs. And just as quickly the callused hands that held her ankles slipped away.

"Sweet Jesus," the man murmured as if in a trance.

Kayte regained her balance and sat up, throwing back the cloak's hood. The tall, dark-haired man in a captain's uniform took in a harsh breath as if it were his last. It probably would be, Kayte swore silently, as soon as Daevon heard of this outrage.

"Who the bloody hell are you?" the sailor demanded softly.

Before she could reply, the door to the cabin swung open and Kayte wheeled around, expecting another assault.

"What the hell?"

"Daevon, help me!" Kayte cried.

Before she could draw another breath he was lifting her, settling her beside him. His arm secured her frame to his. She was trembling so badly that she feared she could not stand on her own.

"What is the meaning of this, Bayless?"

The captain, still looking stunned, said only, "I didn't see her face. I thought it was Buckey, for God's sake! I'm sorry, Daevon."

And then, to Kayte's horror, Daevon laughed. He laughed! She had been abused and thrown about in the dark on his own ship and he thought it was funny!

"I'm afraid, my dear, that my friend here mistook you for . . . someone else." He brushed several strands of golden hair from her face. "And to ensure that it does not happen in the future," he continued, "Captain Bayless, meet Kaytlene Newell, the future Lady Merrick."

James Bayless had already guessed the woman's identity. As soon as he really looked at the golden eyes wide with fear and the tumble of long curls about her shoulders, he nearly fell in love with her himself. She was more than the beauty Daevon had described. She was a goddess, a sea siren, an angel come down to earth.

"How do you do, Miss Newell?" He bowed slightly.

"I am quite well, thank you, except for the lump you've given me." She rubbed the back of her head. "And being humiliated and bruised and nearly undressed!" she snapped.

Daevon stiffened, his weight shifting. "Mr. Bayless," he said sternly, "in the future, please do me the courtesy of asking my permission before you go about undressing my wife."

"Yes, sir."

Then they both broke into laughter. Kayte pushed herself away from Daevon's embrace.

"You . . . bastard!" she exclaimed and received only a kiss on her forehead in reply. She threw up her hands and groaned in frustration.

She was escaping onto the lower steps leading up to the deck when Daevon caught her by the waist, spinning her around to him. "Kayte," he whispered in the gently rocking darkness, "I'm sorry."

"Next time I shall remember to get your permission when a man tells me to undress for him!"

The thought sent a spurt of hot, protective jealousy through Daevon.

"Kayte," he said, the sound itself an apology. His lips closed on hers, holding her body and soul with a fierce possessiveness.

"Forgive me," he pleaded. "Please forgive me, love."

Kayte wished he would take his mouth away from her throat. She had no hope of thinking clearly when he kissed her so fervently. He could make her forget her sorrow, and now her anger. His kisses slowed her brain and let her body think for her instead.

"I love you, Kayte."

His words broke her remaining resistance. She slumped forward against his hardness.

"Daevon, why?"

He pressed his lips to her temple. "I'll explain later," he promised.

For now, she found it was enough.

Kayte had never seen so much activity. The deck was crowded with men, and a few rather odd-looking women, who drank, sang, and danced to their hearts' content. Barrels of what she assumed was rum were brought on deck and pried open. She noticed with some dismay that even the women on board were dipping tin cups into the liquid and drinking liberally.

When Daevon approached her with a cup of the dark brown stuff she adamantly refused to drink it, even to the point of pursing her lips tightly together when he held the cup to her lips. He laughed and finished off the drink himself, and although he plied her all evening, she continued to refuse him. Finally, as he stood with her at the railing after a particularly tiring dance, he took a cup again, playing carelessly along its rim with his finger.

"Daevon," Kayte said softly, "I'm about to die of thirst." She turned to find him smiling sensually down at her. He dipped one finger into the amber liquid and touched it to her lips. Forgetting how much she hated the taste of liquor, Kayte parted them. She could refuse the cup, but she was so desperately lost in his erotic smile that she could refuse nothing from his hand. Her tongue moved over his finger, sucking the liquid into her throat and drawing a soft, masculine sound of pleasure from him.

He bent over her so that his lips grazed her ear, sending a warm shiver down her spine. "My love," he breathed heavily, "I want you."

He swept her gently into his arms and, as he murmured of his love and of all the lovely and erotic thoughts she had kindled in his heart, she was hardly aware that they were again dancing together. When he paused in his hot, wistful description of what would pass between them when he had her to himself again, Kayte was glad for the silence, thinking she might beg him to take her away and love her right then and there. Then she noticed with interest that she had no burning taste of whiskey or brandy on her tongue.

"Daevon," she whispered, "what was—"

"Tea," he said softly. "Cold, sugared tea. You should learn to trust me, little girl."

He noted with a pleased expression that she did trust him. Her eyes told him she did. As she turned her face into his shoulder, he watched the hurried loading going on under the disguise of the party. As the music continued, Kayte's expression turned thoughtful. She moved with him as if her thoughts were a hundred miles away.

She slowed, unconsciously refusing to follow Daevon's lead, and became dead weight in his arms. Her face was pale and her hands trembled where they touched him. Daevon pulled her back to the ship's rail.

"Too much dancing?" he asked quietly. "I'd forgotten you spent your day shopping. You must be exhausted."

"The captain . . ." she said haltingly, spotting the man's figure across the deck through the dancers.

Daevon glanced in the direction Kayte's eyes were staring. "Yes?"

"He thought I was . . . one of them!" She grimaced as James Bayless took one of the women who had just arrived on board down to the cabin, where Kayte herself had been so roughly treated. "He thought I was a common whore."

In that instant Daevon understood that the lovely golden-eyed woman who melted so passionately in his arms believed that her natural desires were somehow wrong.

"Kayte, what you feel for me is honest, human passion. You love me, don't you?"

"Yes, Daevon."

"Do you feel this way when you're with any other man?"

Her eyes snapped up to his. "No!" she exclaimed, and then her voice softened as she stared into his face. "No. Of course not."

"Those women are not here to sell their favors to my men, Kayte. They're . . . helping us."

"Helping you?"

Daevon could not find the proper words to make her understand. Never in his life had he considered revealing his secrets to a woman who would have nothing to do with his covert operations.

"You must promise me that whatever you see or hear

tonight you will never tell to anyone. Friend, foe, or even family. Do you understand?''

She nodded her head, and Daevon took in a deep breath.

''I am going to show you one of the secrets in my life, Kaytlene. The most dangerous secret. If any of it becomes known to the wrong parties, I would most likely be shot. Or at the very least sent to Newgate Prison for the rest of my life. I am trusting you, and you must not fail me. My life is now in your hands.'' He took her palms and turned them up, placing a kiss in each one. ''Will you keep my secret, Kayte?''

''I'll die with it,'' she said solemnly. ''I swear it.''

As Daevon led her back toward the captain's cabin, Kayte felt the first cold fingers of apprehension crawl across her heart. If Daevon's secret was serious enough to have him thrown into prison, or even put to death, then he must be breaking the law. And if he used his ships to do it, then he was smuggling!

She paused at the bottom of the dark stairway and tried to discern Daevon's features. He couldn't be a smuggler. Oh, he had the dark, mysterious eyes of a ship's captain, the hard-muscled, tall frame and aura of fierce passion that she was sure pirates possessed. But her love for Daevon Merrick allowed no place for doubt. None. Or at least she tried to believe so.

They entered the cabin, which by now had been nearly filled with crates. A long empty space in the right corner was lit by an unshaded lamp, and Captain Bayless sat at the desk, comparing his tally with the figures on an invoice prepared by American contacts.

''We're almost loaded, Daevon.'' Turning to reveal more of his hard features, Bayless caught a glimpse of brown hair shimmering like a cloud just behind his friend and employer. ''Jesus, Daevon! What's gotten into your head, man?''

The earl pulled Kayte to his side. ''I believe we owe Kayte an explanation for your actions, James. She's to be told everything.''

''Lordy, Daevon, she's a female! We've never—''

''I am well aware of Miss Newell's sex. And of the danger involved.''

"Well," Bayless replied, scratching his brown-gray beard, "it's your decision."

"I'm glad you remembered that."

"Miss Newell, please accept my apology for my . . . ungentlemanly behavior earlier," the captain said stiffly, as though he had never apologized to anyone in his life.

"Don't let him fool you, Kayte," interjected Daevon. "He wouldn't use gentlemanly behavior even if he knew what it was." Daevon grinned knowingly at Bayless, and after a short moment, the captain smiled as well. The tension dropped away from them, and Kayte felt a wave of relief. The last thing she wanted was to be an unwanted interloper.

The cabin door opened again and one of the overly large women who had been on deck shuffled into the cramped space. As the intruder turned to face the three people already present, Kayte sucked in a hiss of breath.

"Dear God!" she whispered.

Chapter 14

Tristan Merrick tossed a heavy silver coin to the woman who lay moaning on the bed where they had just made love. She ignored the money and Merrick's pleasant "Good day," pulling the coverings over her bruised white body.

Tristan whistled as he left the inn, pleased for the moment. When he had returned to the hunter's cabin early that day, Kayte had been gone. But not dead. Somehow he knew that. Daevon was playing the prowling cat to his crafty mouse, baiting him. Tristan knew he had probably been followed, though anyone Daevon would have set to the task would be much too quick and clever to make himself known. Kayte must be back at DenMerrick House, convinced by now that Daevon's brother was a lying viper. That would have to be remedied at once. And now that she and Daevon were suspicious of him, he must be extremely cautious in regaining their trust.

Part of his disappointment at finding Kaytlene gone was that he had missed the chance to cradle that delicious body beneath his own. Since the first moment when he had seen her beautiful amber eyes he had known such a lust as had never befallen him before.

The women he had bedded in his lifetime knew him as an insatiable tyrant, attempting to find complete fulfillment by any possible means. Hard, forceful sexuality was his forte, and he found it quite satisfying.

The girl he had just tussled could attest to that. She was the daughter of a prominent member of Parliament, a well-situated English lord. She had teased and flirted with him for so long that, when he met her in London this afternoon, his desire for Kayte unrelieved, he had spoken sweetly to her. She had gone to his room willingly, under the pretense of having tea and a private conversation, then refused to perform as he wished. He had taken her by force. She had enjoyed it, he told himself, and should count herself fortunate that he had shown her any attention at all.

"Bitch," he said to himself. "Cold little bitch!"

Now that his pent-up desire had been temporarily spent, he must think how to deal with Daevon and Kayte. Now that Kayte would be wary of him, he would have to give up his attempts to do away with her and concentrate on making use of her in his larger plan. Monique would be opposed to that, but she had been easy enough to dupe all these months. She actually believed that he intended to let Daevon live. She actually thought that, once Forrest Clay had been eliminated, Tristan would persuade his brother to marry the French bitch he had once sworn to love for eternity. Instead Tristan had planned all along to be rid of both men, to marry Monique himself and become owner of the Clay holdings, to live as a wealthy lord for the rest of his days.

Kaytlene's arrival hardly changed his grand scheme at all. It would remain exactly the same, except for one small detail. He would rid himself of Monique as well and would have Kaytlene for his lady. The idea was quite stimulating, he decided as he mounted his stallion and turned it toward home.

The *Northstar Queen* sailed well before dawn. Daevon watched its departure from Demon's back on the pier and silently wished it godspeed. He looked down at Kayte who slept soundly, her head nestled in the crook of his right arm, while Demon paced nervously beneath them.

"All right, boy, let's go home." The horse moved toward DenMerrick House without a single touch of the reins.

Minutes later, Daevon entered the house with Kayte still in his arms and climbed the stairs to her bedchamber. Darby was sitting there, rocking gently in a comfortable old willow chair, her hands holding a thin volume that threatened to topple to the floor at any moment. She leaped from the chair at the sound of Daevon's heavy footfalls.

"Good evening, Lord Merrick," she whispered as he carried Kayte to her bed and laid her down gently.

"Good morning, Darby." He grinned. "Let her sleep as late as she wishes," he said, pulling a long, curling tendril of hair from the mouth he had so often kissed. He smiled, forgetting that anyone else existed but his lovely Kayte.

"Shall I . . . leave, your lordship?"

"No, Darby. I'll just say good night." He leaned over to press a kiss to Kayte's temple and rose. "Chaste enough for you?"

Darby grinned and nodded.

As he turned to leave, Daevon noticed a huge white box lying on top of a rosewood dresser. "What's this?" he asked as his hand went toward the lid.

"Don't!" Darby whispered anxiously, stopping him in midmotion. "You . . . she didn't want you to see that. It's a surprise."

"I see." He drew back his hand and went to the wardrobe. "May I?" he asked.

"Yes, of course. They're all on your accounts."

Daevon opened the wardrobe doors and was pleased with Kayte's choices. The colors and styles of the gowns would be flattering to her, and she would be the envy of London society.

"You both have excellent taste," he said with approval.

"Thank you, sir. Now if you don't mind, I'd rather not undress Miss Newell in front of a man without her permission." Darby's tone was wry.

Daevon smiled, pretending he hadn't heard. "This is lovely," he said, fingering a white gown of rose-sprinkled lawn. "I would very much like her to wear this one."

"Fine, your lordship, but you will never do so until I can remove the one she's wearing. Now get out!"

Daevon retreated to his own empty bed.

He woke sometime later with an annoying band of sunlight in his eyes and flung one arm over his face to shield it.

"Damnation." He groaned and started to stretch, finding that his feet were stopped abruptly by the arm of the couch on which he lay. He vaguely recalled having slept a few hours in his own bed then rising, dressing, and coming to the library to work. He had fallen asleep while reading a deed entailing the boundaries of his southern properties. He had no desire to return to it, or to stir from the warmth his body had created in the supple leather beneath him.

"Hellfire," he muttered, "I'm the master of this house and I'll damned well sleep until nightfall if I want to!"

"Yes, my lord," a gentle voice answered him, "but the master of the house would be missed by his guests."

Daevon kept his eyes closed as the soft rustle of a gown came nearer and the cloth-concealed curve of a hip slid down onto the couch at his waist.

"Good morning, Kayte."

"Good afternoon, lazy," she replied.

Dacvon's arm slipped from his eyes and crooked about her waist. "Lovely dress." He smiled, running a finger along the white lawn he had admired in her wardrobe.

"Darby said you ordered me to wear it today."

Daevon laughed, beginning to shake off the drowsiness that lay like lead in his muscles. "Do you always follow orders so willingly, my lady?"

"Only those that will please you, my lord."

"Then I have one you cannot disobey."

"I am yours to command, sir."

"Come here and kiss me, pretty Kayte. I can't think of a better way to begin my day."

She leaned forward, palms flat against the fresh white linen of his shirt.

Her kiss was liquid heat on his mouth. His arms kept her still as their tongues played, mouths teased. Daevon felt the shadows of his early morning dreams becoming reality.

Kayte thought of the trust he had shown her the night before by sharing the secret of his illegal activities. She had been shocked at first, thinking that his schemes were for profit. When Daevon assured her that he was investing any profit back into the operation, only one question re-mained. Why?

"For freedom," he had explained, leaning over the rail of the *Queen* and staring far out to sea. "I love England, and I would fight to my death if my freedom—her freedom—were threatened. A man must be free to survive, Kayte. He must be able to work his own land, to support his chosen government, to sell his goods and profit from his endeavors."

In that short and eloquent speech he had justified his treason, and she had thrown herself at him, her arms around his neck.

"I love you, Daevon Merrick," she had whispered to his groan of pleasure.

"I love you, Daevon." Her quiet adoration now echoed the sentiment she had expressed aboard the *Northstar Queen*.

"And I love you, Kayte. But before you seduce me here on my couch, perhaps I'd better have something to eat to restore my strength."

They went to the dining hall hand in hand and found the sideboard laden with the bounty of a late morning brunch. There were no other diners.

"You go ahead, Kayte. I'm going to check on Mother."

"Say good morning for me."

Kayte had not realized how hungry she was until the warm aromas of tea, pastry, eggs, ham, and several other delicacies assaulted her senses. She filled a plate and took a seat at the empty table as one of the kitchen maids appeared to present her with a tray of coffee, chocolate, sugar, and clotted cream. She chose tea and cream, nearly choking on the first swallow when a voice interrupted her.

"Well, good morning, Miss Newell. I shall have to reprimand my brother for having kept you out all night. Though you look perfectly lovely, even without sleep."

Kayte's eyes went at once to Tristan, who stood in the doorway wearing mud-spattered boots, light breeches, and a white shirt. He absently slapped a riding crop against his thigh.

"Tristan," she barely managed.

"Tristan!" came a deeper voice from the hall, and

Daevon strode in. "I have a great deal to discuss with you. Perhaps you will make some time for me today."

"Let's discuss it now, shall we?" Tristan began filling a plate for himself and sat opposite Kayte with a smile.

"Very well." Daevon sat at the head of the table.

"Before you give me the berating I deserve, Daevon, will you allow me an apology?"

Daevon said nothing. His jaw clenched. He waited.

"Kayte." Tristan turned his attention to her, attempting a serious, woeful apology to the woman he secretly wanted to throw to the floor and ravish. "I regret my actions since you've come into this house. I was drunk," he continued, "which is, of course, no excuse for the nonsense I told you. I've made no secret of the fact that Daevon and I haven't gotten along as well as brothers should. Still, I had no right to frighten you with that stack of skeletons piled in the Merrick closets."

There was a long silence.

"I lied to you, Kayte," Tristan continued. "About Daevon and . . . our father. You see, there was no proof that Daevon killed him and his whore. And even if he did, they certainly deserved it." As though struck with a sudden urge to do some violence himself, Tristan weighed the handle of a knife in his palm, then flung it across the room, shattering a pane of glass in the lower half of one terrace door.

Kayte nearly jumped from her seat.

"I'm sorry, Daevon." Tristan stood, pacing the room and speaking to his brother as if Kayte had ceased to exist. "It wasn't you I wanted to get her away from, it was this place. This name. These damnable secrets! You were so vehement about not wanting to marry. I—" He sat down. He appeared to be about to burst into tears.

Kayte saw in Tristan's expression something that she could only describe as madness. So that was why Daevon was so inhumanly patient with his brother. Tristan was unbalanced.

"She's too young, too innocent, to be dragged into all our shadows!" His voice softened, and his eyes turned up to Daevon's. "She loves you, I can see that now. And for the first time since . . . Monique . . . you're happy. I thank God for that. I think it might mean a fresh start for the Merricks. I want you to be happy. And I'm sorry."

"You will never approach Kayte again or try to frighten her. Do I make myself clear?" Daevon demanded.

Tristan nodded.

"And if you ever attempt to give Mother some drug that Dr. Ashton hasn't prescribed, I'll have you put away permanently. As for the jewels—"

"I've put them back already, Daevon."

Kayte watched their confrontation, absorbed in Daevon's transformation into an authoritarian figure. He not only carried the burdens of the Merrick businesses on his shoulders, but also a paternal responsibility for his family, and especially for Tristan.

Though Tristan was a few years older than Kayte, he seemed childish standing before Daevon, accepting a reprimand for his actions. And she guessed that that childlike quality kept Daevon from meting out the severe punishment Tristan deserved.

Tristan went to his brother, hand extended. "Forgive me."

Daevon rose as though his decision had already been made. He clasped Tristan's hand, then used the grip to pull his brother to him. Once more Kayte experienced an odd twinge of emotion at this display of mixed love and hate.

The incident, she soon learned, followed the usual pattern between the brothers. Once the episode was over, it was not spoken of again.

Tristan was, unofficially, second in command of the Merrick holdings, but Daevon explained to Kayte that his brother had never had a penchant for being second at anything, and the holdings were legally owned by Anna Merrick, who refused to give her younger, more irresponsible son any real power. Daevon respected her wishes, but he provided Tristan with a generous allowance and, after having seen Henri Todd cheated of his rightful inheritance, he had no intention of allowing Tristan to experience a similar shame.

Late that afternoon, after conferring for hours with Lady Merrick over wedding arrangements and dispatching servants with handwritten letters to florists, musicians, bakers, and clergy, Kayte was stretched out on the grass in the very spot Daevon had loved her the night before, her bare toes dangling in the cool pond water.

"I understand my mother has been battering away at you all afternoon," Daevon said behind her.

Kayte scrambled up from the grass and went into his arms, his lips covering her face and neck with kisses.

"I've missed you," she said invitingly. "Come lie in the grass with me, Daevon."

"I have been thinking of doing just that all day," he replied. "Between battles with my brother and disputes over lumber contracts at the office." His hands slid up both sides of her rib cage, thumbs caressing the soft outer curves of her breasts. "I have a gift for you, love."

"A gift? It could never be as lovely as the one you gave me here last night."

Daevon laughed and pulled away. "Dear Lord, you tempt me so! But this is important, Kayte."

"So is this," she answered, lossening the buttons of his shirt.

"Kayte, please." He groaned, then, left with no alternative, he threw her over his shoulder and started toward the stables while she let loose a string of oaths and clawed at his back.

"Daevon, you scoundrel!" she screeched, pounding his back with her fists. "You'll pay for this!"

"For what?" Daevon answered innocently. "Doesn't every lady-to-be go about in public being carried like a sack of grain?"

"Daevon, this in embarrassing!"

"Oh, no, my dear," he replied. "*This* is embarrassing." And he slid one hand beneath her skirts.

"Daevon! Oh, Lord!"

While Kayte squirmed, Daevon's hand slid to her thigh and tickled her mercilessly.

"Oh . . . Daevon!" she squealed. Kicking her feet wildly to free herself of his hand, she sent them both toppling to the grass and found herself lying beneath his hard body, her skirts dragged up to her knees.

"Do you call for quarter, love, or should I drag you the rest of the way by your ankles?"

Kayte's eyes widened in shock. "You wouldn't dare!"
But she felt the heat of his hand on her bare thigh again.

"Wouldn't I?"

"Yes." She sighed in defeat. "You would."

"Then you'll come willingly?"

"No." She giggled. "It's more fun to fight."

"You witch!"

Kayte screamed as he dragged her off the ground and
threw her over his shoulder again, but she had given up
fighting him.

He dropped her at the stable entrance and, ignoring her
moans of protest, turned her away from him, his hands
clamped on her shoulders. Her neck and face were assaulted at once by a large, gray-white blur. A velvet nose,
its gentle snorts as familiar as her own voice, nuzzled up
to her as she tangled her fingers in the shaggy mane.

"Circe!" she cried, hugging the animal's neck with a
fierceness that came from loving. A voice—male, but not
Daevon's—interrupted her joy.

"That's a fine thing," the voice said a little too loudly.
"Ignores me as if I were a fly on the behind of that silly
creature."

Kayte pulled her head from the sweet smell of horse and
saddle soap. "Justin!" she whispered gruffly, her voice
low under the pressure of emotion. She left Circe to throw
her arms around the boy. After a few moments of kissing,
which turned Justin red to the roots of his hair, Kayte
finally looked about for Daevon. He was standing at the
far end of the stables, feeding Dancer and a large roan
pieces of an apple, seemingly oblivious to what was going
on around him.

As Justin led Circe out to the pond, Kayte went to her
fiancé. "Daevon, why did you do this? You must have made
the arrangements while we were in Newbury. Before . . ."

"Before I loved you?" he asked thoughtfully. "I don't
think there ever was such a time."

"Daevon . . ." Kayte found her thanks choked off by
emotion.

"I had already arranged for the horse, but I couldn't
very well give you such a fine animal without someone to
care for it as well, could I?"

Kayte slid her arms around his neck. "Thank you," she murmured. "For everything."

"You are most welcome," he replied.

"Lord Merrick!"

Daevon pulled back from Kayte just far enough to see one of the houseboys running breathlessly into the stables. "Yes, Peter?"

"It's—Come quick, sir! They're fighting—in the sitting room! Master Tristan and—" The boy leaned against a stall to catch his breath.

Without a word Daevon ran past Kaytlene and up the gently sloping lawn to the house. Kayte joined Justin outside.

"What's all the excitement?" he asked, his charge nipping at the grass near the pond's edge.

"I don't know. It seems Tristan has gotten himself into yet another scrape. At least this time it's not with Daevon."

"Daevon, is it?" Justin teased with a familiar lilt.

Kayte smiled and ruffled the boy's hair. "He's wonderful, Justin. We're to be married on Sunday."

"I'm glad for you, Kayte."

"And I'm glad you've come to work for us," she replied. "I miss home so badly. Your being here will help. Now I'd best go see about cleaning up the destruction in the sitting room."

As Kaytlene came around the corner of DenMerrick House, she caught sight of an unfamiliar carriage in the drive, its doors embossed with a shield of pale blue. The silhouette of a falcon, its wings spread upward, was black on the face of the shield. Before she had ascended the front steps, the sound of angry male voices came from the room just left of the front door.

Hurriedly, Kayte entered, scattering half a dozen maids and houseboys clustered in the hallway, straining to see the argument. She took a place in the open doorway.

The first person who caught her attention was a slight, brown-haired young woman who sat near her, looking as though she had cried for hours and wished to bolt from the room. An angry young man with the same coloring and slimness as the girl paced stiffly behind her. Tristan sat in a chair near the fireplace, absolutely no emotion on his face.

Daevon was the only one of the four who noted Kaytlene's arrival. It was impossible not to, he thought, when her presence created such a sweet calmness about him. He did not move from his place before the windows, but his smile reassured her that, whatever the dispute, it would be settled with his evenhanded terms.

"I want to know," the young man shouted at Tristan, "if you are denying the charges that my sister has made against you."

"I most certainly do deny them," Tristan replied calmly. "Your sister, Mr. Mallery, is a liar. She probably allowed some young man liberties and fears she may be pregnant. She's trying for a wealthy husband by accusing me of rape."

The woman sitting next to Mallery paled. "Jamie, I—"

Her brother's hand came to rest protectively on her shoulder. "It's all right, Francie. The bastard won't get away with it."

"I've done nothing to get away with," Tristan replied. "It seems to me that your sister says she was molested in a public place in broad daylight. A man could hardly drag her through the halls of a respectable establishment without drawing some attention to himself. You, of course, have witnesses to prove that I did so? Witnesses who will stand with you in trial?"

Jamie Mallery stopped his pacing. He had tried—dear God, he had tried—but no one who had seen Tristan Merrick in that hotel was bold enough to say so. It was not so much a fear of the man's revenge, though that was reason enough, but fear of his brother, the earl. He glanced hatefully at Daevon.

"No," he said finally.

"Then I believe we can conclude that your sister went with her so-called rapist. Willingly," Tristan said.

That one word set a deathly pallor over both the woman and her brother.

"I think," Mallery said with a painful grasp on the back of his sister's chair, "that you leave me no choice but to make you a formal challenge."

Tristan worked his jaw to refrain from smiling. He looked forward to killing this pale little puppy. "I accept," he said calmly.

"No!" Francine Mallery jumped from her chair. "He is a pig, Jamie. He isn't worth dying for!" She headed for the door, nearly collapsing as she ran blindly into Kayte.

Jamie seemed to notice Kayte's presence for the first time. "What's this?" he asked. "Another of the Merrick whores?"

Daevon's eyes snapped up as if a shot had rung out. He saw the confusion and hurt in Kayte's face and wanted to separate her from the whole ugly scene.

"Watch your tongue where my fiancée is concerned, Mallery, or I'll cut it out myself."

"If she lives under the Merrick roof, she hasn't the decency of a common brothel bitch!" Mallery retorted, satisfied by the murderous anger his words created in Daevon Merrick. If he died for his impudence, so be it. At least he would have had the temporary satisfaction of having caused some pain himself.

"If you're hiring her out, I'd pay you handsomely for a night in her bed," he concluded.

Daevon moved toward Mallery, but as soon as he had taken the first step, Jamie's valor drained away, as did the color from his face. As the younger man backed into a corner, Daevon strode to the doorway where Kayte had been shocked into immobility.

"Darling," Daevon said evenly, "take Miss Mallery to the library and get her a cold drink and a compress."

"Daevon, you're not going to—"

"Kayte, do as I've asked. Please."

The doors closed on her with a snap.

Kayte settled Francine Mallery in one of the overstuffed library chairs, grateful to see Darby's clear green eyes peeking into the room. Once Darby had been sent for lemonade and a cold cloth, Francine calmed herself enough to speak.

"I'm so sorry about all of this, Miss—"

"My name is Kayte."

Francine's eyes flashed open wide and silvery brown. Tears came again. "Oh, my God," she wept. "My God!"

"Please, Miss Mallery. What is it?"

"You're Kayte," she gasped, pointing an accusing finger.

"Yes," Kayte replied, unsure of what to say.

"He . . . said your name . . ."

"What?" Kayte fell to her knees in front of the chair. "What are you saying?"

"While he was . . . Oh, dear God!"

Kayte dabbed at the girl's flushed face with a handkerchief. She was obviously distraught. Her face was blotched where her tears had smeared her powder, and her eyes were swollen and red. There was a faint bruise on her left cheek, an imprint that might have been made by a man's hand.

Francine touched the bruise lightly with her fingertips. She was trembling. "He did this to me."

"Tristan?"

"Yes."

"Why, Miss Mallery? Why would he do such a thing?"

"Because of you," Francine sobbed.

"Me?"

"While he was . . . when he raped me . . . he kept saying your name. Kayte . . ." With an anguished sob, Francine bolted from her chair and ran for the corridor.

Kayte heard the entry doors slam, but made no attempt to stop Francine. When Darby appeared in the doorway with a tray of lemonade and a cold cloth, Kayte rose numbly and went past her without a word. As she entered the corridor, the doors of the sitting room swung open and Daevon stepped out.

"Kayte?" he said softly.

She heard Daevon's voice, but looked past him at Jamie Mallery and then at Tristan. When Tristan smiled at her, she turned and ran blindly toward the stairs, tears stinging her eyes.

Daevon watched his betrothed run, sobbing, up the stairway and started after her. Jamie's voice stopped him.

"A bit early in the day to be chasing women to their bedchambers," he said coldly.

Daevon's jaw clenched. "Darby," he said quietly, "please see to Miss Newell. I'll come directly."

Darby set aside her tray and went off to find Kayte,

leaving the men to their business. Daevon, turning to Mallery, attempted to keep his anger in check.

"Tomorrow, Mallery," he ground out.

Daevon watched the young man leave and then focused his attention on his brother. He went to the door of the library.

"Tristan," he ordered, "I think we'd better continue in here. I need a drink."

After securing the doors behind them, Daevon went for a decanter of brandy and a glass. He watched Tristan take a glass of Darby's lemonade, overdose it with sugar, and settle comfortably into one end of the long leather couch.

"Did you do it, Tristan?" Daevon's voice was harsh.

Tristan stretched out his long legs and took a swallow of tangy-sweet lemonade. He sighed. "Do you believe her, Daevon?"

"Damn it, Tristan, don't play games with me!" Daevon shouted, his patience at an end. "I want to know if you raped Francine Mallery."

The men stared at each other—Daevon furious, Tristan deceptively calm. It was the younger Merrick who finally spoke.

"You know I would never do such a thing."

Daevon took a deep, steadying breath and poured himself a second glass of brandy, swallowing it quickly. He enjoy the burning sensation of the liquor and hoped it would dull the painful ache in his heart.

"God help me, Tristan," he said hoarsely, "I don't believe you." He sat down heavily in the leather chair behind his desk.

Tristan's eyes widened in shock. The glass he held slipped from his hand, but he took no notice of the dull thump as it fell or of the puddle of liquid which seeped into the carpet.

"You don't—"

"I don't believe you, Tristan. I think you lied to Mallery and to me."

Tristan relaxed again in his seat. While Daevon took another swallow of brandy, Tristan quickly considered his options. The truth was ugly, though guilt was something he had never felt and he did not feel it now. He had looked into Francine Mallery's eyes in the sitting room, and the confrontation had sparked no remorse in him. If he could face her, he could convince his brother that he was innocent. It would not aid him in his quest to take over the Merrick holdings if Daevon thought he had raped Francine Mallery.

"Daevon, I had assumed you would act as my second."

The only reply was a short, angry glance as Daevon finished his third brandy and set the glass and decanter aside.

Tristan, only slightly put out by Daevon's silence, went on. "The bastard called our Kayte a whore, Daevon. He deserves to die for that."

Daevon tore his eyes from the window. He had been staring out at the lawns without really seeing them. He couldn't erase the memory of Francine Mallery's face from his mind. He could still see the blackening mark of a man's hand on her face . . .

With a long, heavy sigh, Daevon stood, arms folded across his chest. He leaned against the massive mahogany bookcase next to the windows.

"A lot of men have insulted me in my lifetime," he said calmly, "and I've never believed that a few words are worth a man's life."

"But he insulted Kayte."

"And what of that?" Daevon replied angrily. "Kayte's honor is mine. If I decide to take offense at what Mallery said, then it's no business of yours. The man spoke out of pain, Tristan. He was a wounded animal backed into a corner. If Kayte had been raped, I would lash out as well. Can you kill a man because he's in pain?"

Tristan worked his jaw in frustration. If he could get Daevon to act as his second, it might prove advantageous. He could arrange a misfire, or if the dueling field was clouded in fog as it had been known to be, shoot Daevon himself. Kaytlene would be so emotionally distraught that she would be vulnerable—his for the taking . . .

"You're my brother, Daevon," Tristan said softly. If appealing to Daevon's sense of honor wouldn't convince him, then perhaps reminding him of his familial ties would.

"I won't be a part of this travesty, Tristan," Daevon said. "For the last time, did you rape Francine Mallery?"

Suddenly Tristan lost his patience, and his restraint. "She was willing enough!" he spat.

Daevon's eyes fixed on his brother and glittered with anger. "What did you say?"

Immediately, Tristan regretted his outburst. How could he sweeten the ugly truth and make himself appear innocent? He leaned forward, forearms resting on his knees. "I slept with her, Daevon."

"Ah, finally—the truth. Go on."

"She was hardly a virgin," Tristan insisted. "So you can't blame me for ruining the girl."

"And was it necessary to slap her so hard that she bruised?" Daevon demanded. He straightened, thrust his hands into the pockets of his trousers, and began pacing the room. "Was it?" he shouted after a moment's silence.

"Do you really want the truth, Daevon?" Tristan answered harshly. "Very well. That weeping little innocent you feel so sorry for is nothing but a whore. She took my money readily enough. And as for the bruise, well . . ." He paused to meet Daevon's eyes. "Let's just say that Miss Mallery likes her men heavy-handed. You've had a great many women, dear brother. Do you expect me to believe you never served a woman a little pain to heighten her passion?"

Daevon was across the room in an instant and had Tristan up by the front of his coat. "You raped her!" Before his hands could wrap tightly around Tristan's neck, as he wanted them to do, Daevon dropped his brother back onto the couch and strode away.

"I could kill you myself," he rasped, trying to control the white-hot urge to do just that.

"Let's get on with it, then," Tristan replied. "Dole out my punishment, Lord Merrick. What's it to be? Throw me into the streets to beg for my bread? Disown me? Tell Mother?"

"You know this would destroy her, Tristan."

"I doubt that."

Daevon glared back at his younger brother. "If she is told anything, Tristan—and I mean *anything* about this—I will have you thrown into the street."

"And what of me?"

Daevon stopped pacing. What of Tristan? He had tried to love his brother. He had given him a home, clothed him, fed him, given him as much money as he thought was prudent and then a bit more. And though Tristan had spent time and money foolishly, though he resented his older brother for having control, though he drank and gambled and argued constantly—still, Daevon had refused to have him watched or shut away like a criminal, for he had never seriously hurt anyone but himself.

Until now.

Daevon could no longer deny what he had failed to face for so long. Tristan had inherited their father's madness as surely as Daevon had inherited control of the Merrick holdings. Tristan could not be trusted or controlled.

"Well, brother?" Tristan interrupted. "What's it to be? Hanging? Newgate Prison? Or perhaps you'll expect me to marry the girl."

Daevon could not imagine forcing the poor young woman into such bondage.

"Jamie Mallery," he said calmly, making his decision.

"I beg your pardon?"

"Jamie Mallery will decide your fate, Tristan, not I. The young man has an excellent reputation as a marksman. I'd say he has a right to kill you tomorrow morning. Every right."

Tristan stood. "So you're leaving me to his mercy."

"I doubt he'll have any for you."

"You want me dead."

The statement was hard and, God help him, Daevon realized there was some truth to it.

"You agreed to the duel, Tristan. I'm willing to accept the outcome."

"But you won't stand with me?"

"No."

"How noble of you, Daevon. How very noble." With that, Tristan left the room.

Slumping down into a chair, Daevon wondered belatedly if he should have disowned Tristan or thrown him out. That was how their father would have settled the matter. But he couldn't treat Tristan with open hate and distrust as their father had.

Perhaps that was the root of Tristan's unsettled mind. The former earl of Merrick had been mercilessly cruel to the younger of his sons, constantly comparing him to his namesake and heir and finding Tristan sadly lacking. It was as if he believed Daevon was endowed with every Merrick virtue and Tristan with all the sins. Tristan was the black sheep, a whipping boy, and though Daevon himself had been punished severely for trying to protect and defend his brother, he still felt guilt and shame because he carried the name of the man who had treated a young boy so unforgivably.

Daevon had spent years trying to make up for his father's abuse, but it seemed to have done very little good.

Though Tristan had only been a child when their father was killed, those years he had spent with him could not be erased.

And now there seemed to be little more Daevon could do. There was one option of which he hadn't yet made use, and now it was necessary.

He would have to set someone on Tristan's heels—constantly tagging behind, watching. Someone to keep his brother from harm and from doing harm. It was a terrible thing to have to resort to, but the alternatives—prison or an asylum—were worse.

Returning to his desk, Daevon picked up the brandy decanter, poured himself another drink, and brought the glass to his lips. Without drinking, he set down the glass. It wasn't the bitter, numbing comfort of alcohol that he needed. It was the sweetness of understanding. He needed Kayte.

He knocked softly.

"Kayte?" he said against her door. He knew his voice was rough with need, and he made no attempt to conceal it. He knocked once more, then stepped back, relieved, as the door opened.

"I'm sorry," Darby whispered in the half-opened doorway. "She's asked to be left alone, your lordship."

Through the space over Darby's shoulder, Daevon saw the bed, and on it, Kayte's figure in a white nightdress. Her back was turned to him, but he could see that her body was curled protectively around a pillow and her shoulders were trembling as if she were sobbing into it. He wanted to go to her.

"Darby, please . . ."

The Irish girl put her hand on Daevon's chest and gently pushed until he stepped back. She closed the door after joining him in the hall.

"I've just gotten her to calm down," Darby explained. "She's going to try to sleep now."

"What happened?" he asked, still wanting to throw open the door and pull Kayte into his arms.

"She won't say, Lord Merrick. Perhaps you should wait until after she's rested to speak with her."

"Yes." He sighed wearily. "But if she asks for me—"

"Of course, sir. Right away."

With one more longing glance at Kaytlene's door, Daevon went to his own room and mechanically went through the task of dressing for dinner.

Twenty minutes later, he sat at the Merrick dining table. He stood when his mother entered, helped her with her chair, and made apologies for Kayte, who, he explained, was finding the wedding plans tiring. Lady Merrick only smiled, patted her son's hand, and assured him that it would not be so tiring for her after the ceremony.

"She'll have plenty of time for you then, my dear," she said. "You must not be so impatient."

"I'll try, Mother," Daevon replied. But in truth, it was all he could do not to run upstairs and rip Kayte's door from its hinges to gain admittance.

Tristan did not appear for the evening meal, but he must have told the servants not to spread news about the duel, for Lady Merrick would have mentioned it if she had known, and he discussed only wedding preparations throughout dinner. As she happily chatted about music, champagne, and flowers, Daevon ate little. He loved his mother, but this evening he found her endless pleasantries annoying.

Once dinner was finished and Lady Merrick retired to bed, Daevon excused the remaining household staff and attempted to find some activity to keep his mind from Kayte and his confrontation with Tristan. He paced the library, read a few lines of Aristotle, and found that philosophy, though satisfying to the mind, did little to ease the physical ravages that desire wracked upon the body. He stepped out the rear entrance of the house, seeking some solace in the night, wandering across the damp lawn to the edge of the rippling pond.

At the water's edge Daevon bent and picked up a smooth stone and threw it with all his pent-up force. It landed with a neat kerplop near the center of the pond, an insignificant blow, easily absorbed.

When out of the darkness he heard the rustle of satin skirts and a woman's arms circled his waist from behind, Daevon's hands closed over hers and his head rolled back as he smiled up toward the sky. "Thank God," he said passionately. "I've needed you. I've been worried."

But something about the feel of her hands, the soft stroke of her cheek against his back, chased his relief away. He pulled back and turned.

"I am so pleased you worry for me, *mon cher*."

"Monique." The word was full of disappointment.

"You are not happy to see me? I can remember a time when you were eager to hold me in your arms, my Daevon." She stepped closer to him, her black hair gleaming in a soft cloud about her shoulders.

"I'm not yours any longer, Lady Clay," he said stiffly.

She reached up suddenly, pressing her lips to his. Her mouth felt warm and familiar, but instead of the tenderness and passion it had once inspired, there was now only the emptiness of wanting another—of wanting Kayte.

As Daevon's hands pushed Monique roughly away, a flash of white in an upper window caught his attention, and he swore under his breath.

"Go home, Monique," he said brutally as he headed back toward the house. "There's nothing for you here."

Kayte pulled away from the window and collapsed on the pale carpeting. She knew without being told that the woman Daevon had kissed was Monique. She wept openly, fiercely, like a child, the tears subsiding only when the door of her bedchamber swung open. Daevon stood in the yellow candlelight like a vengeful god, a ring of keys in his right hand.

"How dare you!" Kayte cried, her hands turning to fists and clawing at the carpeting. "This is my room!"

The door closed behind him. The keys dropped to the floor.

"This is my house," he returned.

"Get out! Go back to Monique and leave me!" She rose up to her knees, grasping a bedpost for support.

"How did you know who she was?"

"I'm not entirely witless. Perhaps you thought I was."

"No, Kayte. No." His voice was laden with desire as he bent to drag her off the ground and up into his arms. The naked yearning in his eyes frightened her and sent a hot pulse of erotic sensation through her body.

"Let go of me!" She struggled, only to find herself entangled more securely in his arms, pulled fiercely to his chest. When he dropped her onto her bed, still keeping her immobile with his own body, she cried out softly.

"You wouldn't dare!" she gasped, partly from surprise and partly from desire. "I hate you. Leave me alone!"

"I didn't know she was coming here, Kayte. I sent her away." Daevon was forced to hold tightly to her as she fought him, but he refused to let her go.

"You don't hate me, Kayte. You love me." His hands were moving down her body, pulling the white nightdress from her shoulders. The hot kisses he left there made her quiver.

"I need your love." His tongue was burning her flesh.

"Liar," she said with less determination. "You said she meant nothing to you, but you kissed her . . ."

But he was kissing Kayte now, his teeth nipping at a soft earlobe. She noted with dismay that her body had stopped fighting him.

"She kissed *me*," he whispered, nearly lost in the experience of making love to the woman he truly wanted, needed. "I pushed her away. I wanted so desperately for you to come to me."

The nightgown came unfastened under Daevon's agile fingers, and he pushed it back to reveal the soft, pale curves of her shoulders and the fullness of her breasts. Sensing her reluctant surrender, he groaned with pleasure when his mouth fell hungrily over the tip of one breast.

When he looked up after long, delicious minutes of adoring her breasts, she was panting, waiting, the tears drying on her cheeks.

"I need you tonight, Kaytlene. I love you." He kissed her forehead, then her eyes. "Believe me," he whispered.

"Daevon," she said quickly, "there's so much here that frightens me."

"I know." He smoothed back her hair, and his mouth reached for hers over and over again in the stillness.

"The secrets . . . I'm afraid, Daevon." She began to cry again, the tears soaking into his silken hair. Her hands clutched at his shoulders.

"Love me, Kayte, and I'll keep you safe," he vowed. "Love me."

"Yes, Daevon," she breathed.

"Say it." His hands were pulling the nightdress from her body, sliding up the curve of her leg, finding the soft heat that burned between her thighs.

"Tell me, Kayte."

She was blindly grasping at the buttons of his shirt and, with a laugh that was half desperate desire, he moved away and undressed slowly, tearing down her resistance and heating her blood to something hot and delicious.

"I love you, Daevon. I love you," she chanted as he returned to her, pulling her body atop his and entering her with a fierce cry against her throat.

"Tell me again, Kayte. I need you so much tonight." His body was lost in pure sensation.

"I . . . love you, Daevon." She whispered it, groaned it, screamed it in her mind when they came together. Daevon's body took away her doubts and fears and gave her only pleasure. With it, she knew, he would reassure, devote, adore. And it was more than enough.

Chapter 15

Jamie Mallery and Edward Spears, his second, arrived at the dueling field only minutes after Tristan, who had come alone. Merrick's decision to appear without a second was unusual, but Mallery did not question it. He was gratified to see that Daevon Merrick had not come in support of his brother. It was a good indication that even Tristan's brother believed him guilty.

The duel was to take place on Mallery property in a rectangular field less than a mile from the Thames. It lay behind the long, two-story brick building which housed the Mallery Carriage Works, a business that Jamie's grandfather had built from a six-stall barn.

Dr. Ashton, the Merricks' physician, arrived on horseback, dismounted, and set his black leather bag on the ground. "Remember, boys," he said gruffly, "clean wounds. No goddamned kneecaps and no head shots."

"Had a rough night, doc?" Spears asked.

"Damned right. Lost the patient, so I'm not in the mood for another one. Got that, Mallery?"

"Of course," Jamie answered solemnly.

"You, Merrick?"

Tristan gave the doctor a smile and discarded his cloak. The black breeches and rough white shirt he wore offered little protection from the cold, but the whiskey he had consumed for breakfast warmed him a little.

Dr. Ashton humphed at Tristan's attitude. As he and Edward Spears checked the dueling pistols, the principal characters in this death's charade were locked in a silent, long-range confrontation of bitter glances. Holding the pistol case so that both men could chose their weapon, Ashton noted the clear, dangerous glitter in Jamie Mallery's eyes. The young man was dressed all in black and had the look of the devil about him.

Tristan, conversely, smelled of liquor, and his eyes gave away the fact that he had been awake much of the previous night. Wenching, more than likely. Ashton only hoped Merrick had enough of his wits about him to avoid taking a ball in the heart or lungs.

Weapons chosen, the two men took their places back to back in the field and Ashton, acting as mediator, counted off.

Three steps. Four. Five.

The sounds of early morning in the city filtered through to the field and were ignored. The only important things in the world now were honor, a beloved sister's violation, and the need to exact retribution.

Six. Seven. Eight. Nine.

On ten, the men turned, took an instant to raise and aim their pistols, and fired two shots simultaneously.

Ashton saw Tristan take a step backward. Though Merrick's shot had missed its mark, Jamie Mallery's hadn't. A bright red stain spread on Tristan's arm, and he dropped his pistol.

Jamie Mallery walked across the field and watched dispassionately as Dr. Ashton opened Tristan's shirt and examined the wound. It was a clean hole, an inch above the elbow, and Ashton with a shake of his head began working to staunch the flow of blood.

Mallery glanced at the wound and then into Tristan's face. "I should have killed you," he said coldly. "If you ever come near my sister again, I will." And he turned on his heel and strode off.

Tristan moaned and crumpled to the ground.

Kayte sat before her dressing table mirror, hands twisted nervously in her lap. She stared thoughtfully at her reflection and swore.

"Darby," she grumbled unpleasantly, "cut it off."

Surprise registered in Darby's face as she met Kayte's eyes in the mirror. She was in the midst of combing the tangles from her mistress's freshly dried curls. The comment stopped her only for an instant.

"Do you think his lordship would appreciate a bride with her hair all bobbed like a boy's?"

"No." Kayte sighed. "I suppose not."

"It's all right, you know."

"What is?"

"Being nervous. All women feel this way on their wedding day."

"Do they?"

"Of course."

That reassurance seemed to help. Kayte relaxed in her chair as Darby finished combing and began to arrange her hair.

"Darby?" Kayte whispered.

"Yes, ma'am?"

"Do you . . . do you think I'll trip on the way downstairs? I mean, the train on my gown is so long and—" Kayte stopped as Darby broke into laughter. "What's the matter?" she demanded.

"Oh, I'm sorry. It's just that . . . you'll not trip, Kayte. You'll be very careful, I'm sure."

"Yes, I'll be careful," she murmured. Then, more softly, she added, "Darby, I'm afraid I'll do something wrong. Or say the wrong thing. I'm not really a lady. I'm not sure I know how to act like one."

"He loves you."

Kayte closed her eyes and enjoyed the sound of that. He loves me. He wants me. All her anxiety melted away. In a few minutes she would be walking toward Daevon, saying "I do," and committing herself to loving him all her life.

Thank you, Papa, she thought. I never dreamed . . .

"Time to get dressed now, Kayte," Darby said.

As Darby took her wedding gown from its box at top of the wardrobe, Kayte slipped off her robe and stood before a cheval glass. Smiling, she decided that Daevon would hardly care if she made some innocent faux pas. When he found his wife dressed in such wicked sensuality, he would forgive her anything.

She was wearing the gray satin corset, with its revealing lace and tiny seed pearls, and shimmering silk stockings with a pair of white satin slippers. It was the night's lovemaking that she was anticipating. The thought of Daevon's hands undressing her lovingly and his kisses on her skin made her wish for the evening to come quickly.

"Well now, that's better," Darby noted. "You look more like a bride with that smile on your face."

Kayte nodded, knowing that the thoughts running through her mind would turn the girl crimson.

It was several minutes later when Darby left the bed-chamber. Kayte's dress of ivory satin had been arranged just so, its layers of airy French lace moving about her like an angel's robes. The bodice was snug and revealing, adorned with rows of tiny diamondlike beads, the sleeves baring her shoulders and ending in a cluster of ribbons just above her elbows. A pale pink satin sash was tied at her waist and fell in a long trail from the small of her back; tiny bows of the same color adorned the flounces at the bottom of the skirt. She wore short pink gloves to accent the dress, and a tiny crown of rosebuds held her veil, a sheer panel of silvery netting. She grasped the bouquet of pink and white roses as though it would calm her, its cascade of flowers and glossy greenery falling over the front of her gown.

She was startled when Darby appeared in her doorway to bring her to the staircase.

Daevon paced in the small side parlor off the sitting room. The foyer, library, and drawing room were full of guests who were not nearly as impatient as he.

"Calm down, Daevon," Henri Todd said pleasantly. He put a hand on Daevon's shoulder to stop his friend's pacing and pinned a white rose to Daevon's black lapel.

"She's only half an hour late. Women are supposed to be late, aren't they?"

"Your knowledge of the fairer sex overwhelms me," the earl replied dryly.

The first strains of an Irish ballad coming from the foyer reached them. Daevon straightened his jacket and went toward the door, wondering why his hands were a little unsteady.

Kayte appeared at the head of the stairway like an angel.

Daevon's expression of longing intensified as he watched her, not believing that from this day forward she would truly be his, heart and body and soul.

As if in a dream, Kayte moved down the stairs, her eyes fixed on the tall figure in black who waited for her. His face radiated a joy and passion that kept her from tumbling headlong down the staircase. Her Daevon.

Their vows sounded softly in the hushed calm, as though Daevon and Kayte stood alone in a great, empty chapel. And then it was finished and blessed, sealed as Daevon lifted the veil from his wife's face and kissed her tenderly, his hand caressing the bare softness of her shoulders.

"I love you," he murmured against her lips. "Kayte . . ." With a gentle pressure he took her arm. They were husband and wife.

Kayte's sense of reality returned as the day wore on, her duties as mistress of the household drawing her frequently away from Daevon. It was important to her to be sure that Daevon's guests—her guests—were well cared for.

Musicians played in a cool spot beneath a white awning near the pond, and the guests danced on the terraces, in the house, in the huge outdoor pavilion.

Kaytlene was introduced to so many people she could not possibly remember them all. She smiled sweetly and suffered through a full day of hand kissing and polite conversation.

When Daevon found his new bride assisting the servants for the third time in as many hours, he swept her into his arms and kissed a smudge of icing from her cheek.

"You are the lady of the house now, madam," he murmured. "You shouldn't neglect your husband so often."

"But there's so much to do, Daevon," she answered wearily. The last two nights had been restless ones, and her days a rush of activities to prepare for the wedding, leaving her exhausted.

With an oath Daevon swept her off her feet and strode through the thick crowd, shamelessly grinning in response to the cheers that went up.

"Daevon," Kayte murmured into his shoulder, "they think we're—"

"Going to bed? We are, my love."

In a few short steps, he was opening a door and carrying his wife up a long flight of steps that curved to the left. Another door opened, and Kayte slid to the floor.

"Daevon, this is your—"

"Our bedroom," he corrected. "From this day forward, you must honor and obey me and sleep in my bed."

Kayte took in the huge, elaborate bedchamber that lay beyond the sitting room where they stood. The master's bed was draped in midnight-blue satin, a canopy of the same color covering it. Kayte caught only a quick glimpse of paler blue carpeting, dark wood, and greenery before Daevon pulled her to his chest and kissed her with aching tenderness.

"It needs a woman's touch," he said. "I should have had it redecorated for you, but there wasn't time."

"I love it all, Daevon. Just as it is."

"Do you, Lady Merrick?" he asked softly. When Kayte looked up at him in surprise, he laughed. "Not accustomed to your new name yet, I see. You will be soon. I have a gift for you." He went to the wardrobe near his bed and came back with a long dressing gown of embroidered red silk.

"Oh, Daevon . . ."

"It came with the *Northstar Queen* from China," he explained. "I thought you would like it."

"It's lovely," Kayte replied, unable to suppress a yawn.

"Try it on and take a nap, Kayte. You're exhausted."

"But our guests, Daevon—"

"They won't miss you for an hour or so. Though I will." He gathered her up again, carried her to the bed, and kissed her once more. "If I don't go now, sweet, I'll never get out of this room. Rest as long as you like."

"Daevon?" she murmured, already comfortably sleepy.

"Yes, love?"

"I want . . . to make you happy."

"You will," he whispered. "You do." Straightening, he gave his wife a grin. "Get accustomed to your new bed, Lady Merrick. You'll be spending a great deal of time there from now until death do us part."

"Will I?" She smiled. "And what about you?"

He laughed. "I'll be waiting on you hand and foot, I suppose. Lazy wench."

"Um-hmmm."

"Good night, sweetheart."

"Um-hmmm."

Daevon left her reluctantly. Only the thought of having her to himself later in the evening allowed him to abandon her now.

As he returned to his guests, Daevon found himself forgetting business, and even his problems with Tristan. Kayte was his! The reality of that fact filled his mind, and the desire for her filled his heart. There was no room for anything else.

When he entered the library, he was greeted by a serving maid with a cold glass of champagne. Making his way through the room, he was stopped by a firm hand on his shoulder.

"Well," said a male voice behind him, "I never thought to see the day. Devil take me, the earl is married."

Daevon turned, smiled broadly, and shook Forrest Clay's hand.

"You saw Kayte," he replied. "She's reason enough to change any man's mind about marriage."

"Oh, yes. Quite a beauty. And by God, if that isn't love I see in your eyes when you look at her, then I don't know love."

Daevon smiled. "Is it that obvious?"

"Yes," Clay replied. "I'm pleased for you, old man. You're going to be very happy with her."

"Forrest, I owe you an apol—"

"No, Daevon. It's not necessary." Clay held up a hand to stop whatever words of apology Daevon had wanted to say.

Daevon nodded. He had wanted to tell Forrest how much he regretted his past affair with Monique. Forrest and he had been friends for nine years, and although Monique had not destroyed the two men's friendship, Daevon knew that the love she still claimed to have for him kept her from loving her husband as he deserved. Daevon felt responsible for that, though Forrest had what he wanted— Monique was his wife. He loved, pampered, and provided for her, and though she was well known for her numerous affairs, he looked the other way and pretended not to know about them. Forrest was certain that someday she would come to him after finding no real happiness in the arms of her lovers. He was not a dull, cuckolded husband. He was simply patient. And in love with his wife.

"Don't worry about me, Daevon," Forrest finished. "Monique will come around. After all, she married me, didn't she?"

"And you take pleasure in reminding me of it," Daevon joked.

"It's not good business to be nice to your competitors."

"So I've learned. Have you eaten?"

"No, as a matter of fact, I was waiting for Monique to appear. It looks as if she won't."

"Well, since we've both been deserted by our wives, let's enjoy ourselves. I'll meet you in the pavilion after I find my mother."

"If you're in here for more than fifteen minutes, I'll come to rescue you. Mothers love to give lectures on your wedding day about how soon they expect you to provide them with grandchildren."

"If I know my mother, her deadline is nine months from today."

Daevon found Lady Merrick chatting with several young ladies, enchanting them with a much exaggerated story of how Daevon had found his beautiful young bride in a poor farming village and swept her away.

"Mother," he chided, grinning at the young women, "you forgot that awful black knight who nearly killed me in a sword fight. And the dragon. Don't forget that hot-tempered dragon."

"Well," she replied saucily, "it's mostly the truth, my dear."

"All right, mother, I concede. It was mostly the truth."

"If you ever decide to reveal the whole truth about how you discovered your little jewel," a male voice said softly behind Daevon, "I'd like to hear it." Tristan, dressed elegantly in gray, stepped forward.

"Excuse me, Mother," said Daevon. "I'll let you get back to your fairy tale. Ladies." Daevon gave the young women a disarming smile, causing several of them to giggle and blush, and turned to lead his brother to a private corner.

"Lovely affair," Tristan commented dryly. "And has your bride left you already?"

"She's exhausted."

"Ah, abed already then?"

"Tristan, I'm in no mood to exchange sarcasms with you."

"That's fine. I have no wish to be anything but pleasant."

"Then make your point." Daevon glared at his brother. He had heard rumors that Tristan had been injured by Jamie Mallery, but he saw no evidence of it. Tristan had stayed away from DenMerrick House since the duel and Dacvon had made no attempt to find him.

"I've decided to leave DenMerrick House, Daevon."

The idea was unexpected, but not unwelcome.

"Where are you going, Tristan?"

"I thought since you're settling here with your wife, I might make good use of your town house."

Daevon carefully considered the idea. The town house was in Hounslow, a fair distance across London. It would keep him away from Kayte and yet . . .

"Afraid you won't be able to watch me closely enough?" Tristan asked.

"The town house is yours."

"Good. I'll—"

"There are two conditions."

Tristan's expression hardened. "Of course. How could I expect otherwise? And they are?"

"First, that you return to DenMerrick House only when invited."

"I see. Protecting your precious Kayte?"

"Protecting Kayte, Mother, and this house. You've misused them all, Tristan. I'm thoroughly justified in this demand."

"And the second condition?" Tristan asked.

"I won't continue to provide the kind of money you've grown accustomed to," Daevon said plainly. "I can't with a clear conscience. You'll begin work at the shipping offices a week from tomorrow. You'll be paid only if you earn it and not because I feel obligated to provide for you. You will provide for yourself, Tristan.''

"I'll remove my belongings tomorrow," Tristan answered, showing no emotion. "Oh, and by the way, congratulations." Turning abruptly, Tristan made his way through the crowded room and disappeared.

Daevon looked around the room and went toward a stately, gray-haired servant. "Ashe," he said quietly.

"Yes, sir?" the gentleman replied. Ashe had been in the Merricks' employ for over six years and was solely responsible for the house and grounds staff. Daevon spoke softly to him, but with steel in his voice.

"Ashe, in the morning Tristan will return to remove his belongings from this house. Please speak to the staff in the morning and inform them that after tomorrow Tristan is not to be permitted in the house or on the grounds without prior notice from me. Is that understood?"

Ashe nodded.

"There are to be no exceptions. If anyone admits him to the house or onto the grounds, they will lose their position with me."

"Yes, of course, sir." Ashe replied. "Yes, sir, I'll take care of it."

Daevon could not help but feel a wave of relief.

As Kaytlene slipped out of her wedding gown, she decided against wearing the Chinese robe Daevon had given her. She smoothed both garments over the sitting room couch and slipped almost fearfully into her husband's bed, sighing at the coolness of the satin coverlets. She slept almost immediately, leaving her gentle reality for a world of disturbing dreams.

Tristan's face hovered over hers, his mouth stifling her scream with a brutal kiss. He repeated her name as his hands slid over her breasts.

"Kayte . . . Kayte . . .''

Then another voice was splitting them apart, a soft hand and then a face. A strangely familiar woman tore Tristan away from her. A pain ripped through Kayte's body as she and Tristan were separated. The woman's face was clear now, a childhood memory.

"Mother!"

Kayte bolted upright in bed. The bedchamber was empty, but her head rang with the sound of her own cry of fear. She had known her mother only as a baby. How could she remember her face? Perhaps she was only imagining what her mother might have looked like. An icy shiver ran down her spine, and she knew she must find Daevon.

She dressed hurriedly in her wedding clothes, struggling with the cumbersome fastenings, and slipped from the room and down the stairs.

She found Daevon seated at one of the tables in the pavilion, sharing a crystal decanter of brandy with another gentleman while a kitchen maid cleared away the china from the meal they had just finished.

Daevon's profile was ruggedly dark and handsome against the gold light of the late afternoon sun, and Kayte stood still for a moment, delighting in the beauty of him—in his strength, his laughter, his voice as he discussed some matter of business with the man sitting cross from him.

"Daevon?"

At the sound of her voice he twisted in the chair, smiling. "Feeling better, my love?" He rose to meet her, and the light kiss that touched her lips soothed away the lingering sensations of nightmare. She nodded, taking his hand as he led her to the table.

"Forrest, this is my wife, Lady Kaytlene Merrick."

The gentleman stood, kissing her hand and executing a well-practiced bow. "I am so pleased to meet you, Lady Merrick."

"Kayte, this is Forrest Clay," said Daevon.

"Forrest Clay . . ." She knew she had heard the name.

"Monique's husband," Forrest explained, and at once Kaytlene remembered. "But don't hold it against me," he added with a disarming smile.

Kayte found herself quite taken with him. He was attractive, tall and light-haired with pale blue eyes deep set against tanned skin. He was an expert storyteller who delighted Kayte with his tales of sirens and sea beasts for nearly an hour before a pretty black-haired little girl ran up to him and crawled into his lap with a shy smile.

"What, no kiss for me, pretty Lisle?" To Kayte's sur-

prise and the little girl's sheer delight, Daevon leaned
across the table, feigning unhappiness.

"Mama says you have a new lady now and you don't
need me anymore."

"Come here, Lisle," he commanded.

The girl scrambled off her father's lap and ran giggling
into Daevon's arms.

"I will always have enough love for you, Lisle. You
promise you'll remember that?"

"I promise."

"And this is Lady Merrick. My wife."

The girl smiled up with eyes of silvery blue. "How do
you do?" she said shyly.

"I see you've met my Lisle," said a soft, feminine
voice from a few feet away. Kayte raised her lashes.
Monique. Both Forrest and Daevon rose as the lovely
raven-haired woman came to the table. She smiled sweetly,
her bright blue eyes drinking in Daevon before moving
quickly to Kayte.

"Lady Merrick, I hope you will forgive our tardiness.
We only just arrived from another engagement."

Kayte tried unsuccessfully to hide the glimmer of anger
in her expression and said nothing in reply.

"Monique . . ." Daevon said reproachfully, and Kayte
looked up once more.

"And I am . . . sorry for my behavior the other evening. I wish you every happiness, Lady Merrick."

As Daevon sat beside Kayte again, his arm encircled her
shoulders.

"Thank you, Lady Clay," she said. "Perhaps you will
have tea with me one afternoon."

Shock registered on the three faces, but Kayte smiled,
knowing that she would need to find out whether Monique
was a threat to her. If she was, it would be best to keep the
enemy within constant sight.

As the afternoon melted into soft evening, Kayte found
that she and Monique enjoyed a great deal in common.
She actually began to feel comfortable with the lovely
French woman, to Daevon's amazement.

Kayte and Monique were close in age and Kayte could
speak a little French, which Monique found charming.

They were both fond of the Greek legends and French poetry, and neither could abide being ordered about by overbearing husbands or restricted by social obligations.

"Sounds as if you're going to have some trouble with this one," Forrest said to Daevon, laughing.

"No more than you've had, *mon coeur*," Monique said softly to her husband, leaning over to kiss him on the mouth.

Kayte watched Forrest's eyes turn dusky blue and his hand left the back of Monique's chair to curl around her waist. It was obvious to Kayte that he loved her deeply. Kayte was more than a little relieved. Daevon's taking a wife had evidently convinced Monique that she had no chance to reconcile with her former lover, and that would make all of their relationships less strained. Though Forrest Clay was one of Daevon's business rivals, it was obvious that the two men were also good friends. Kayte guessed that the Clays would be frequent guests at DenMerrick House, and she wouldn't enjoy playing hostess to a woman who was lusting after her husband. If Monique's friendly manner was sincere, Kayte hoped they could become friends.

The celebration went on well into the night, though Daevon wished his guests would have their fill of joy and be gone. As he watched Kayte dancing with Forrest, a relentless desire for her consumed him. He had watched her all day, unable to stop thinking about her even when she had napped in his bed. And now, after hours of fantasizing about their night to come, his skin was hot under its stylish coverings. He wished to be rid of everyone but Kayte, to feel her flesh against his. As one dance ended and another began, he left the shadowy corner where he stood and took his wife away from Clay and into his arms. As he pulled her body to his, she looked up into his face, smiling.

"Kayte," he whispered, his voice floating on the liquid strains of music, "I want you."

"I'm yours," she replied. "Until death. Didn't you hear my vows?"

His lips grazed hers hotly. "In our bed," he explained, his voice hoarse with desire.

Her erotic smile streaked through him like fire. "Did you think I would let you have me here in the middle of the pavilion?"

"You're teasing, little girl."

"I like having some control over you."

"Do you? Perhaps you would care to prove it to me later this evening." He took the velvet curve of her earlobe between his teeth and lapped the flesh with his tongue.

The dancers still moving gracefully around them, Kayte came to a sudden stop. "Daevon," she murmured, the tone of her own sweet voice heavily laden with yearning, "I'll wait for you."

As her husband stood alone at the edge of the pavilion, a pleased smile on his lips, she went into the house.

By the time he entered the foyer, sometime later, the house was barren of its guests who were all outside dancing, drinking, and laughing. The halls had not been lit, but Daevon ignored the blue-gray darkness. In the center of the foyer he crushed something small and soft beneath his foot and bent to retrieve it. He caressed the tiny white rosebud and dropped it. A path of roses—pink and white— led up the stairs and along the hallway to the door of his own chambers. The door stood ajar, as if in invitation, though he hardly needed one.

He entered silently and locked the heavy door behind him. He wondered if anyone would miss the bride and groom if they stayed locked up here together for a week or so, at least.

"Daevon?" Kayte appeared in the arched doorway of the sitting room.

"Kayte."

"Do you like it, Daevon?" She turned slowly as he surveyed the red embroidered silk that swirled around her.

"It comes alive when it touches you," he said as he neared her. "As do I." He bent to take her into his arms and she went silently, spreading hot kisses along his throat as he carried her like a glass treasure, precious and easily broken.

"Kayte," he breathed as he lay beside her in the bed where he had known so much loneliness. "My love. My wife . . ." Their mouths touched lightly and refused to be released.

"Lord, Kayte," he said with a moan as his kisses ground against her lips. "I love you, my pretty witch." There were a thousand things he wanted to say to her—how he had feared this day, how he wished he had met her sooner—but every word crumbled beneath the weight of his love, his desire.

"Daevon, I love you." Kayte pushed the black coat from his wide shoulders and he shook it off, dropping it to the floor. He reached for the sash at her waist.

"No." She put her hand over his. "Not yet." She smiled, pushing him out of the bed and, as he stood beside it, she knelt on the edge of the bed, slowly releasing the buttons of his waistcoat.

"Controlling me again?" His hands tangled in her hair.

"Don't say no, Daevon," she pleaded, beginning on the buttons of his shirt. As she helped him remove the garments to bare his chest, she peered up through half-lowered lashes to see the desire in his eyes. She wanted this night to last forever.

"I could never say no to you, Kayte."

Her hands and mouth and tongue heated the hard angles of his broad chest and shoulders. Playing like a child with a magnificent gift, she felt a pleasure of her own at each soft, need-laden groan that rose from his throat. When she pulled away to drop her hands to the fastenings at his waist, Daevon took her face into his hands and bent to kiss her with a gentleness that drowned her in need.

"I want to be sure it isn't a dream," he whispered.

"It is a dream," she replied. "The most beautiful dream I've ever had, and I never want to wake up. Stay in the dream with me, Daevon, always."

He could not have denied her anything, even if it meant riding into Hades itself and back again.

Kayte's hands trembled with an exhilaration that warmed her flesh as she removed the remainder of his clothing, Daevon kicking off his boots to help free his body from the hindering cloth. Her hands skimmed warmly up his calves to the outside of his granite thighs to his waist.

"Daevon . . ." His mouth came down on hers again before

she could speak, and as his hands gently persuaded her to lie back, she reached down to caress the hard flesh between his thighs. She knew it was wanton and brazen of her, but the obvious pleasure it gave Daevon encouraged her to explore every inch of him.

Daevon groaned her name and kissed her throat, holding his weight back as he raised over her to allow her exploring hands full access to his body. He reveled in the feel of her hands moving softly along the hardness of his sex, her touch becoming firmer at his murmured encouragements. Finally he brushed her hands away, kissing her fully on the mouth for long moments.

Kayte was disappointed. "Did I displease you, my lord?" she asked demurely.

"Oh my love." He sighed in her ear. "I would like you to go on, but I fear your touch would satisfy me too quickly and I want us to take our pleasure slowly tonight. I want to love you until dawn."

Kayte resigned herself to his plans with a little sigh. "Very well, my lord."

Daevon laid his wife comfortably back on the pillows. "My turn," he said, smiling erotically as he untied the sash of her silk robe. The rich garment fell away from her shoulders and Daevon's brows rose.

"Your wedding gift, Daevon." Kayte smiled as she shrugged off the robe, enjoying his pleased expression.

"You are full of surprises, little girl," he murmured. "It's lovely." He touched the shimmering gray satin of her corset, one finger skimming over the jewellike crystals that gleamed temptingly between her breasts. "Lovely," he repeated, his voice lowering as his hand traced the upper curve of her breasts.

"Daevon?"

"Mmm?"

"I want you, too," she whispered.

He grinned down at her, lightly brushing her forehead with his lips. "I know," he said smugly.

Daevon made love to Kayte with a passion that had never been known to him before. He knelt, pulling one of her feet up to rest against his chest as his fingers rolled one stocking down and off her slim leg. His palms moved down her skin like fire and massaged her soft inner thigh, teasing as she whimpered encouragement.

With the stockings left in a silky heap on the floor he moved his hands to the delicate corset, caressing the curve of her waist through the fabric. His hands covered her breasts and moved in playful circles over the jewel-hard tips.

"Now you're teasing," she whispered, running her hands along his powerful arms.

"Kayte," he said quietly and a little sadly, "I know I cannot give you a life of perfect happiness as you deserve. You've married a man with a dark past. But here I can give you everything. Every pleasure you could desire."

"You do make me happy, Daevon. Just be with me."

He kissed her mercilessly, tearing at the closings of her corset as she panted harsh, loving endearments. Free of the gray satin, she clutched his flesh, wanting to pull all of him into her—his hardness, his gentleness, his white-hot gaze. She was pressed back, her body fully his and willing to be so. His mouth suckled currents of light, hot and throbbing, through the tip of one breast as his hand went to the center of her need between her thighs.

His first touch drew a rough gasp from her throat. She arched her back, tightening the velvety thighs about his hand as his fingers dipped into the sweet liquid of her arousal. His thumb caressed in quick, soft circles as his fingers explored the depths of her and she grasped at his nape, his shoulders, on the delicious, violent brink of ultimate pleasure.

"No, Daevon . . . not yet. Not without you."

He went on, gently pushing, soaking in the raw lust of her moans and the feel of her body writhing beneath his hands and mouth.

She could not elude the explosion as it reached her, tearing her with colored claws and growling with a fierceness that both frightened and thrilled her.

Daevon felt it devour her, whispering to her as it dragged her down beneath its force.

"I will make love to you forever. Forever, Kayte. I love you."

Before she returned to reality, his body was over hers,

entering her with a single stroke of flesh into flesh, adding to the pulsing heat that had begun to ebb from her womb.

"Kayte, come with me," he murmured as his movements took her upward toward pleasure once more. "Come into my dream and stay forever."

"Yes, Daevon." She groaned, moving her hips against his, reaching the plateaus and pinnacles as he did, curling her hands in his hair and pulling his mouth to hers. She splintered against him and he into her with a kiss that entangled their moans and froze them in an instant of time.

Chapter 16

The next days passed with a joy and peace that was new to the Merrick household. Servants no longer fled at the sound of their master's footsteps, nor did they worry that their best efforts were not enough to please him. They knew that the presence of his new wife, even the mention of her name, would soften and dissolve his anger, leaving them all well satisfied with their lot in life. They began to whistle as they went about their duties.

Kayte spent her days with Lady Merrick, whom she now referred to as Mother after the older woman's insistence upon it. Though some days Anna was kept in her bed because of the pains in her heart, the dowager Lady Merrick was pleasant company and taught Kaytlene a great many of the social duties of a lady.

And Kayte spent long afternoons riding Circe. She was finally able to convince Justin that he could ride one of the stable mounts along with her without fear that her husband might punish them both for disobeying orders. Daevon had told her never to ride into London without a proper escort, but since they could not agree on what a "proper" escort was, she decided that Justin was sufficient.

They rode out into the countryside, or occasionally into town to see the ever-doting Mr. Kurtz. One particularly adventurous afternoon nearly two weeks after the wedding, Kayte rode into London with Justin tagging along at her side on a shaggy brown mare. They went to the pier to see Daevon's *Sea Lady* return home. Kayte led Circe to the water's edge, ever fascinated by the way the vessel was led into port like a pony on its picket rope.

"Kayte, I think we're in trouble," Justin said quickly.

Smiling, Kayte turned Circe and saw Daevon's figure appear in the freshly washed windows of his office. She waved, knowing how angry he was even without seeing his face very clearly. He didn't like her riding without a proper escort, and he was constantly reminding her that Justin would not be strong enough to defend her should someone decide to take advantage of her vulnerability.

"I know very well," she had replied, "that only two burly escorts would be enough to satisfy your demands. You will be busy with work, so that rules you out. And the English forces are distracted. Minor difficulties with Napoleon, I believe." She knew her teasing drove him mad at times, but she found the situation amusing. Besides, after that particular outburst he had carried her to bed and ravished her, with the late afternoon sun streaming over their entwined bodies. For that sort of punishment she would disobey him at every turn.

The captain of the *Sea Lady* stepped onto the pier, wishing Kayte and her companion a good day. Before he could say more, Kayte thrust a box of Mr. Kurtz's confections into his hands and said, "For Lord Merrick, compliments of his disobedient wife," and rode away, Justin and his dark little horse close behind her.

Captain Michael Stephenson stood numbly watching the dark beauty, the pale pink skirts of her gown snapping in the breeze. He looked down at the box in his hands and then up again as Daevon reached the pier.

"Damnation!" Daevon exclaimed.

Stephenson had dreaded this moment since his departure four months ago. He had brought a woman aboard to share his cabin the night before launching, and Daevon had found out about it. Though the girl had been too drunk to remember even having been on the ship, Stephenson had suffered Merrick's wrath for having brought a woman aboard.

"What the hell was that woman doing here?" Daevon demanded.

Stephenson groaned. "Daevon I swear, I didn't even know her!" The last thing he wanted was to be blamed for having a woman anywhere near Merrick's ships.

Daevon studied him for a moment and then laughed, to the captain's amazed confusion.

"I . . . she gave me this." Stephenson held out the box to his employer, watching with interest as Merrick opened it.

"Excuse me, my lord, but who was that?"

"That, my friend, was my wife."

"Your—"

"Wife," Daevon finished for him. His features softened, and a smile curved his lips.

The captain was amazed at the obvious change in the man who had been solid steel a few months ago. Now he could swear the man was . . . human!

"What's she doing in London with that slip of an escort?" Stephenson asked as the owner of his vessel turned away.

"Oh, I don't know. Probably buying silk corsets."

"What's that?"

"Nothing, Michael." Daevon slapped the man's back in a friendly gesture as they headed toward the office. Daevon held the open box out to the captain.

"Want a cinnamon cake, Michael?"

Kayte sat curled up in a chair in the drawing room, giggling and sharing a pot of chocolate with Darby, when a discreet knock on the closed doors disturbed them. She was the first to leap from her seat, anxious for Daevon to be home.

When Lyle Miller was announced and entered the room, Kayte could not hide her sigh of disappointment.

"I'm sorry," Lyle said softly, "that I am not who you were expecting."

"He'll be late, won't he, Lyle? Oh, Darby, this is Daevon's aide, Lyle Miller."

"Yes, we've met," Darby said sweetly. "At the wedding."

"Of course." Lyle bowed and Kayte saw a glance and smile pass between them.

"I shall retire, then," she said. "Don't get up, Darby. I hope you'll come and have some chocolate and keep Darby company, Lyle. I suppose I have grown quite dull for her after all this time.''

"I would be honored.'' Lyle grinned. "Oh, he sent this for you, Miss—I mean, Lady Merrick.''

"Thank you.'' Kayte took the envelope from his hand. "Good night,'' she said, but the two were already absorbed in each other. She closed the drawing room doors as she went out.

Kayte changed into a plain white nightdress and curled up in bed to read Daevon's note.

"My disobedient wife,'' it read. "Since your actions this afternoon require a strict reprimand, I regret that I shall be delayed in returning home this evening. However, if you will await me, I will see to your punishment as soon as I arrive. Daevon.''

She folded the note carefully and dropped it onto her night table, giggling with growing anticipation as she curled up in the center of the bed. She tried valiantly to stay awake but finally gave in to drowsiness, knowing that Daevon would rouse her as soon as he returned home.

To her dismay, Kayte woke late that night, feeling cold and quite alone. She pulled up the heavier quilt from the bottom of the bed, snuggling into the warm nest her body had created. A sound from the sitting room nearly sent her burrowing beneath the coverlets. A door opened and closed.

"Daevon?'' she called, her voice low. At the sound of his voice she smiled into the darkness.

"It's all right, love. Go back to sleep.''

"I can't,'' she protested gently. "I'm cold. Come and make me warm, Daevon.''

He chuckled softly at her invitation, sitting on the edge of the bed to pull off his boots. When he fell back against the pillows, he was wearing only his dark breeches.

"Daevon, what have you been doing to be coming home half dressed?'' She sat up, her voice accusing.

He smiled again, tiredly. "No, Kayte, I was not with another woman. I haven't the strength for that right now.'' He paused. "There was a fire on the pier. Not any of my cargo, but we stayed to help put it out. I'm sorry I'm so late.'' He yawned and stretched, folding his hands behind

his head as Kayte pulled off his breeches and covered him
with the blankets, pressing her body to his side.

"I washed in the kitchen," he explained, "because I
knew you wouldn't want to sleep with a man who smelled
of smoke and dirtied your bed with soot."

He sighed, closing his eyes, welcoming sleep. His left
arm curled around Kayte and he pressed a kiss to the
crown of her head as she snuggled closer to him.

When her hand moved along his chest to his thigh he
made a sleepy sound of pleasure. Her touch was like a
potion, taking away all the ills of life outside their own
chambers.

When she began to kiss his chest and shoulders and
neck he groaned in protest but made no attempt to stop her
warming affections. His body was unable to resist re-
sponding to her gentleness, her exploring hands. When her
fingers boldly moved down to burrow in the soft black hair
between his thighs, she found the flesh nestled there already hardening with life. She caressed it to its full, thick
length, grinning wickedly when she peered up at Daevon's
closed eyes and expressionless face. She would teach him
to play dead.

She stroked with a firm touch until the physical arousal
in her hand throbbed with a desire for release. At the
sound of the first soft moan from Daevon, she rolled away
from him, settling on the opposite side of the bed.

It took only an instant for Daevon to react. He rolled to
his side, grabbing her as she giggled and pulling her back
to him with a playful shake.

"You rotten little witch!" he exclaimed, feigning anger
as he pulled her body atop his. The length and hardness of
him lay against her abdomen like an invitation.

"You started this," he reminded her, "and now you
finish it."

"I thought you said you didn't have the strength."

"I said I didn't have the strength for another woman.
Enjoying a tryst with my enchanting wife is quite another
matter."

Daevon leaned back, again taking on the appearance of
sleep.

Kayte stayed still. In all of their lovemaking in the past

weeks Daevon had taken control of her body. Now he was insisting she take the initiative.

"Well?" He opened his eyes halfway and grinned.

"I . . . don't—"

"You were doing quite well a moment ago. Relax, Kayte. Do whatever feels comfortable and natural. I love you."

She returned his smile and he closed his eyes again, somehow knowing that she preferred it that way.

Natural. Comfortable. As Kayte discarded her night-dress, the feel of Daevon's skin against hers returned the fire to its high point, searing away her shyness. She pressed her body to his, kissing his jaw, his mouth, the softer bronze of his neck. The friction of their bodies caressed her breasts and she groaned against him. Without thinking of proper behavior or timidity, she reached for his hands, drawing them toward her breasts as she straddled his hips.

Daevon could hardly pretend to be unaffected by her passionate seduction. It was clear she had already learned a great deal about the pleasures of the flesh, and his eyes flew open when he felt the pulsing heat of his shaft slide against the wet silk between her thighs. His hands answered her need for his touch, and when his mouth closed with a soft groan over the hard pink tip of one breast, she sank down onto him, filling the aching emptiness in her womb with a fire that raged throughout her body.

"Daevon." She moaned as he rocked his hips against hers, his hands at her waist to secure her as he thrust upward.

"Ah, Kayte!" He groaned, pulling her down against his chest, caressing her hair, rolling her onto her back to bring her to the same unearthly crescendo toward which his own body was moving inexorably.

"You're heaven," he whispered over her soft cries. "My heaven."

And he took her there and back again before they slept.

Since Daevon spent his early hours riding or at his offices, Kayte had grown accustomed to rising alone. Waking in his arms was an unusual pleasure. She stretched against his length, wrapping her leg over his and hugging herself to his chest in a shy attempt to rouse him.

When she peered up to judge her success, she found him already awake.

"Trying to strangle me in my sleep?" He smiled as she continued to hold tightly to him.

"I have no desire to become a widow just yet." She slid up to nestle against his shoulder. "But when I do, I'll think of something a bit more original."

"Of course."

"Poisoned lip rouge, perhaps. I'll let you kiss me to death," she teased, one hand outlining the hard shape of his chest.

"What a pleasant way to die," he murmured against her hair.

"Or perhaps," she said shyly, "I shall make love to you until your poor heart stops from sheer exhaustion."

"Even better. Let's start now, shall we?" He pulled her up to him with one lithe sweep, kissing her until she nearly fainted from pleasure. When he released her, she fell back against the pillows, her body tingling, eyes half closed. He leaned on one elbow to consider her.

"It seems, my lady, that your heart would give out long before mine."

"Mmm. I don't mind, Daevon. Kiss me again."

He obliged her with a fatherly peck on the forehead.

"Hardly a kiss," she grumbled as he pulled away, grinning.

"Sorry, my love. I thought perhaps you might like to have the gift I bought for you."

"Yes, please, Daevon!" She sat up eagerly, keeping one thin sheet wrapped around her. Daevon had been showering her with surprises over the past two weeks, everything from hand-picked bouquets of flowers to exquisite jewelry, emeralds and pearls and one spectacular ruby. With a sudden flush in her cheeks she thought how delicious it was to make love dressed only in emeralds, as Daevon could not resist doing whenever she tried them on for him in bed. He returned to the bed, handing her a flat, rectangular red box.

"What is it?" she asked, not waiting for his reply.

His hand covered hers as she began to untie the white ribbon. "First the sheet," he bargained, tugging at the satin that she had tucked snugly under her arms.

"Daevon, I'll freeze!" she lied.

"I'll keep you warm, little girl." He slid beside her, taking the sheet away and pulling Kayte back to his chest. She shivered, even with the warmth of his body against hers, and he tucked a coverlet about them both.

"All right, my bashful angel, open your gift."

She tore away the ribbon and pulled off the lid. "Daevon, chocolates! I haven't had chocolates since I was a little girl." She squirmed in the bed until she faced him, the scent of rich chocolate surrounding them.

"Thank you, Daevon. You're much too good to me."

"A man could never be too good to you, Kayte. You deserve the best of everything."

"I'll never ask for anything but you, Daevon. That you love me."

"And I do. I never believed I could be so happy, love. Especially with the woman I was forced to marry."

"Forced?"

He nuzzled her temple with warm kisses. "I had no choice. I couldn't live without you."

He bent to take a kiss from her lips and found a piece of chocolate blocking his path. She grinned mischievously.

"Would you like a taste, my lord?"

"First the candy," he whispered in reply, "and then you." He bit off half the dark covering with its soft, faintly orange-flavored center, and she laid aside the box, finishing the single piece. She ate it slowly, her teeth and tongue moving over it with erotic enjoyment. When she finished, he took her sweetly smeared fingers into his mouth, then claimed her lips, searching the recesses of her mouth with his tongue, savoring the sweetness of the lingering taste of chocolate and his love.

They left their room well after midmorning, hand in hand, and ate a satisfying late breakfast alone on the dining hall terrace. Their solitude was interrupted by Darby, who appeared as Kayte bit into a hot roll that Daevon had lavishly spread with butter and offered with a sensual smile.

"Good morning, Darby." Kayte wiped a smudge of butter from the corner of her mouth and noted with a pleased smile that her Irish maid had a pretty glow about her that morning. "Enjoy your evening?"

"Yes, Lady Merrick. Thank you."

Daevon's brows rose as the two women shared a smile he did not understand, and he thought it best not to ask.

"Your lordship, Lady Merrick sends her apologies. She is feeling poorly this morning and had me send for Dr. Ashton."

Daevon looked up quickly. He knew that the doctor was never summoned unless the heart pains his mother suffered became severe, and he immediately assumed the worst. As he rose, Darby's hand on his shoulder stopped him.

"She's sleeping now, your lordship. The pains were severe this morning, but they lessened after she took her medication."

"You should have called me," Daevon said without a hint of anger in his voice.

"She wouldn't let me," Darby explained softly. "She said . . . she said you would not want to get out of bed until you were good and ready."

She blushed and he laughed, pleased that his mother's spirits had been so high since Kaytlene's arrival. As had his own.

Darby threw her mistress a startled glance as the master of the house stood and pulled the maid into his arms, kissing her softly on the forehead.

"I owe you a great deal, Darby. You've been a fine nurse, a skilled housekeeper, and a good friend. I don't know what I would do without you."

"Your debt is nothing compared to mine," she replied, pulling away in bashful haste.

"If you insist upon grabbing my friends and kissing them at any opportunity, I may resort to becoming a shrewish and jealous wife," Kayte commented dryly as she rose from the table.

"You'd better go, Darby. I think my wife is about to give me a sound thrashing."

Once the girl had gone, Kaytlene found herself in her husband's arms once more.

"Don't be jealous, Kayte. I'm very fond of Darby. Her father was a close friend."

"I'm not jealous. Not after last night."

"And this morning," he breathed in her ear. "And this afternoon."

"This afternoon?"

His smile was full of sultry warmth. "Planning ahead," he said.

"Just like a businessman," she taunted, frowning a little when he groaned.

"Damn," he said softly.

"What's wrong, Daevon?"

"I have to meet with Stephenson today. I should have gone this morning."

"I'm glad you didn't." She rose up on tiptoe to kiss him gently. "Don't worry. I'll take care of Mother."

"You'll send for me if she gets worse?"

"Of course I will. Don't worry."

"I love you."

"Hurry home, Daevon."

Chapter 17

Lady Anna Merrick slept through most of the afternoon. She awoke just before Dr. Ashton arrived at a little past two o'clock. The doctor was hopping like a rabbit who fears it's being chased by a fox.

"Sorry to be in such a rush," he apologized as he hurried into Anna Merrick's bedchamber, his leather case large and well worn. "But I've got babies on the way. They're premature, I think. Twins, you understand. I don't wish to seem unfeeling, Lady Merrick, but a doctor's hands reach only so far." He gave Kayte a quick, bright smile as he took note of her mother-in-law's condition.

"And congratulations on your recent marriage."

"Thank you, doctor," said Kayte.

"And you appear to be feeling better, Lady Merrick," he told Anna. "Resting well, I see. That's the thing for you. The medication"—he indicated a bottle on a bureau across the room—"keeps you relaxed so that your heart won't beat too quickly. Just sleep now, and Darby will see to the dosage." In a low aside to Kayte he added, "It must be exact, you see, or the medicine will stop her heart altogether."

"I understand," said Kayte. "I'll leave it to Darby, then." In a louder voice she added, "Doctor, would it be all right for Lady Merrick to eat chocolate while taking the medication?" She smiled at her mother-in-law. "My husband gave me a box of the most delicious assorted chocolates, and I can't possibly eat them all myself."

Anna's eyes lit up with pleasure. "Oh, chocolate! My

favorite. Are there by any chance chocolate-covered cherries . . . ?''

"There most certainly are," said Kayte. "Doctor?"

He scowled and gruffly cleared his throat, then smiled. "I don't see why not, my dear. But save them for later this afternoon, after she's more thoroughly rested."

"And you'll save the cherries especially for me?" asked Anna.

"I will," Kayte promised.

"And now I must get back to my babies," said Dr. Ashton.

"Your babies?" Kayte thought perhaps it was a way of his to refer to babes he brought into the world as his own.

"Oh, yes." He beamed. "Our third and fourth. Twins, you see. Hope for girls this time! Good day, Lady Merrick." He grinned. Kayte thanked him and escorted him downstairs.

The doctor's open buggy rolled away with a steady clip-clop-clip as another carriage entered the stone archway at a more stately pace, a green and gold banner emblazoned on the door. The driver wore a coat of the same colors, and the black geldings who pulled the vehicle looked a bit silly, Kayte thought, with their gold tassels and green mane ribbons.

The driver tipped his tall black hat to Kayte, who stood waiting on the stairs to see whose taste in animal apparel was so ostentatious. When Monique Clay stepped from the carriage, Kayte wasn't sure whether to be shocked or pleased.

"Good afternoon, Lady Clay. If you've come to see my husband, he isn't at home."

"Oh, *petit*!" Monique said quickly, "you are still angry with me, no? I shall go, then. But it wasn't Lord Merrick I came to see. It was you, *chèrie*."

"Oh?"

"Please forgive me, Lady Merrick. I wanted to explain to you my bad behavior. When I came to see Daevon before you were married, it was only because I worried for him, you see? He was so upset before he left, you know. I was so glad when he told me of his feelings for you. We have been friends for a very long time and he mistook my show of relief for passion, I think."

"The two are hardly interchangeable."

"*Oui*, but he forgets we French are great advocates of showing affection. I am so sorry it has caused you to hate me."

Kayte's heart softened one small measure. "I don't hate you, Monique."

"*C'est magnifique!* I was hoping so much we might be friends, *chèrie*. My baby, we lost him not long ago, you see. I have been a little sad because of it. And our husbands—they are away so much. It would be lovely to have someone to share the time with."

In half an hour, the two women drew a bevy of open-mouthed stares and servants' gossip as they took tea together in the drawing room. They became well acquainted with each other's childhoods and were chattering away about the latest styles of dress, sharing the box of chocolates that Kayte explained was a gift from Daevon.

"Oh," Kayte said suddenly as Monique reached for a chocolate-covered cherry, "I don't eat those. Lady Merrick—Mother, I mean—loves them. I'm saving them for her."

"Ah, the cherries," Monique replied, carefully returning the piece to its separate section in the box and choosing from the others. "I was never fond of them myself."

"Excuse me, Lady Merrick," Ashe interrupted from the doorway.

Remembering her mother-in-law's condition, Kayte rose at once. "Is she—?"

"Lady Merrick is eating a little broth and tea," Ashe reassured her, throwing a questioning glance toward Monique, "but there is a gentleman here to see you. His card." He presented Kayte with a dull white card embossed in black.

MR. RONALD DARRELL, SOLICITOR
LONDON

Kayte glanced up at her guest. "Will you excuse me, Lady Clay?"

"Of course." Monique watched Kayte step into the corridor and then the library. Ashe, excused by his mistress, closed the double library doors and glanced once more into the sitting room.

"Can I get you anything else, Lady Clay?"

"No," she replied. "Thank you, Ashe."

Monique nearly giggled as he walked away. He was obviously reluctant to leave her alone, but could hardly stay without insulting Lady Merrick's guest. When he had been gone for a few moments, Monique walked to the doors of the sitting room and, after assuring herself that the hallway was empty and the house quiet, closed them. She went back to her seat, opened her beaded reticule, and took out a small vial.

With a smug smile on her mouth, she pulled the half-empty box of chocolates onto her lap and popped a piece into her mouth. Then she opened the vial and poured a little of the clear, sticky fluid over each of the chocolate-covered cherries. She recapped the vial, slipping it into the tissue paper that lined the box, and replaced the box on the table between herself and the couch. The mixture dried to a clear, hard coating that would add only the faintest bitter aftertaste.

The mixture had cost her a great deal of money and a great deal of trouble as well. Contacting Arthur Morley without Tristan's knowledge had been difficult, but once she had located him, his silence had been as easy to buy as his poison. Monique had suspected some time ago that Tristan was not willing to go through with his original plans and, therefore, she thought it best to take some action of her own.

When Tristan became her lover several years before, Monique knew he did so only because she wanted his brother. Tristan had been excellent company in bed, however, and he had offered her a way back into Daevon's life. It was what held them together. He wanted a mistress, and she wanted his help in getting Daevon back.

Tristan's original idea had been simple. He would have Kaytlene Newell killed and, once Monique had worked her way back into Daevon's heart, Forrest Clay would die as well. Monique would marry Daevon and provide Tristan with as much money as he could want. Somewhere, how-

ever, the plans had gone awry. Tristan was taken with
Kaytlene himself, and that made him reluctant to kill her.

Monique tapped four long, tapered fingernails on the
arm of her chair. Daevon's little wife was causing her a
great deal of discomfort. Monique had come today hoping
to find some opportunity to poison Kaytlene herself, but
had decided on an alternate plan.

It would be more satisfying, Monique thought, to see
the little farm wench suffer a bit before she died. Tristan
had told her it would take some time to decide how to
work out their plans now that he was not permitted at
DenMerrick House. In the meanwhile, she would enjoy
playing cat and mouse with Miss Kayte.

If her little potion worked, Kayte would soon find herself accountable for murder. And Daevon would not be
able to blame Tristan this time.

"Poor little Kayte," Monique murmured, smiling. She
rose and went out to the hall, where she found Ashe
speaking to a houseboy.

"Ashe," she said pleasantly, "would you be so good as
to give my regrets to Lady Merrick? I must get home."

"Of course, Lady Clay. Good day," he replied, stepping forward to open the front door.

"Good day, Ashe," she said cheerfully.

"Good afternoon, Lady Merrick. Please forgive my
coming unannounced." A balding, paunch-bellied man
rose from the couch to greet Kayte. Deep, leathery lines
wedged his face and his hands had a slight tremor.

"I'm sorry, Mr. Darrell. You may have to call on my
husband again. He is working at his offices today."

The man seemed nervous standing, a well-worn hat
clenched in front of him. Kayte motioned for him to
resume his seat as she took a chair across from him.

"My business is with you, Lady Merrick."

"You're my husband's lawyer. What sort of business
would you have which doesn't concern him?"

"I never claimed to be in his employ."

"Then perhaps you would enlighten me as to your exact
purpose, sir."

"Of course, Lady Merrick. Forgive me. I am your

London representative. Or I should say, I was your father's. After his death, I was to represent his wishes to you and see to the assignment of deeds to his property.''

"I was not aware of that, Mr. Darrell. I had assumed that my husband's solicitors would handle all the pending legal details.''

"Yes, I understand. But your father wished to protect all your interests by securing a personal representative.''

"And did my father provide a trust to pay your fees?''

"It was his intention that the property in Newbury be sold to pay our fees, Lady Merrick.''

Kayte's stricken expression displayed her dislike of that idea. "I don't want to sell the cottage. It was my home.''

"If you care to make alternative arrangements, we'll hold the deed.''

"I'll see what can be done. Is there anything else?''

"Yes. This is a copy of the final will.'' He handed her a sheet, tightly handwritten. "It is the formal document which is filed with the proper agencies.''

"I wish to keep this document.''

"Yes, of course. There is another parcel, your ladyship.'' He placed a long, heavy envelope in her hands. "It was your mother's,'' he explained. "Left with us at the time of her death. James never made mention of it again, but with them both gone, it falls to you.''

"Thank you.''

When Mr. Darrell had departed, Kayte opened the envelope and pulled out a soft, leather-bound book that appeared to be a diary. Without reading it, she put it back into its package, wondering whether she should burn it.

Daevon returned home for a late meal, relieved to be told that his mother had spent a restful day and was now complaining about the tray of food which had been sent up to her at Dr. Ashton's orders. Daevon was exhausted, having spent the entire day hauling cargo, and his body ached for rest.

Kayte greeted her husband at the door of their bedchamber with a warm smile.

"Welcome home, my love,'' she said, reaching up to press a kiss to his mouth. He smelled of sweat and salt water. "Come with me,'' she ordered and took his hand to lead him into the sitting room. Inside he was surprised to find a low fire warming the room against a chill night.

When Kayte's hands moved over him, loosening buttons and tugging to remove his clothes, he found enough strength to laugh. "I'm sorry, my insatiable little witch," he said, "but all I have the strength to do right now is fall into bed and sleep."

Kayte grinned and continued her gentle disrobing until he stood naked before her, his hardness softened by pale firelight.

"Perhaps you intend to ravish me," he murmured, laughing, as she pulled his hand again, leading him closer to the fire. When he saw what she intended, he was unable to hide his pleasure at his wife's thoughtfulness.

A large tub of steaming water stood before the fire, and he gladly eased his body into it, leaning back with a sigh. When Kayte disappeared he closed his eyes, only to open them again when her soft hand glided up his throat, a soapy cloth washing the sweat and grime from his flesh.

"I can do that," he muttered gruffly. He was certainly not going to allow his wife to treat him like a helpless baby.

"I know your lordship can do a great many things well," she said with a sensual murmur, "but sometimes it can be pleasurable to let me help."

He could hardly disagree as her hands glided over his skin, washing, massaging. After she had coaxed him into allowing her to lather and rinse his hair, she concentrated on kneading his hard shoulders, easing away the tension there until the muscles were pliable beneath her fingers. It was difficult to coax him out of the tub, but once he was dry, Kayte led him to their bed. He fell onto his belly with a contented sigh, one arm hanging comfortably over the edge of the mattress. Kayte continued her loving massage from his arms down his back and then to the rigid muscles of his thighs and calves. When, after nearly an hour of her silent touch on his body, she slid the coverlet to his waist, he gave her a pleasured little groan.

She pressed her lips to the center of his back. "I missed you today," she whispered, unwilling to take her mouth from his warm, soap-scented flesh.

"Kayte, you're a wonder," he said sleepily. "I adore you." And he collapsed into sleep.

Once she was certain he was sleeping soundly, Kayte pulled the coverlets to Daevon's shoulders and sat up against a wall of soft cushions. She picked up the envelope that Ronald Darrell had presented her, once more dropping the diary into her lap. All afternoon she had been unable to stifle her terrible curiosity and knew well she would succumb to it now. The yellowed pages crinkled beneath her touch as she pulled open the cover, a pale red leather worn soft by her mother's hands. Looking closely at it in the dim light of her single lamp, she found the word JOURNAL barely discernible. A light, flowery script sprawled out in line after line across the pages.

My mother's hand, Kayte thought as she touched the words. She hung balanced between pain and anger for a long while, wondering whether there was anything she cared to know about the woman who had abandoned her as a babe and broken the gentle heart of a loving man.

In the end she wanted to know everything.

Kayte found most of the first half of the thin book filled with unimportant notations. Receipts, poor attempts at poetry, copies of lines from famous works. A single flower pressed into the center of the book broke into several pieces as Kayte tried to lift it out. A silk ribbon dropped out several pages later.

The last third of the volume was completely unreadable, its pages stuck together as if they had been glued. Kayte guessed that the book had been damaged by water that sealed the pages together as they dried.

The disappointment—or was it relief?—sent her leaning against the pillows with a sigh. Daevon stirred beneath the coverlets, turning toward her. The length of his hard body molded against hers, his cheek nestled warmly against her hip. He threw one arm over her thighs, the faintest of smiles on his lips as he slept.

Kayte pushed a wisp of hair from his forehead, letting her fingers trail down his neck under the coverlets to rest on his back. He moved again with a sleepy groan, tightening his hold.

"Kayte," he murmured, and she wondered if the name

had come from his conscious mind or from his dreams.
Regardless of its source, it was reassuring, reminding her
that, no matter what her past, her future was secure.
Whatever she might read in her mother's journal would
never change Daevon's love for her, or mar their happiness.

She flipped quickly through the legible pages, eager to
satisfy her curiosity. And then her eyes fell upon a different page, one headed with a date, and she began to read
with renewed interest.

14 June 1783

It has come to this. What can a mere woman do when
her father forces her to do something she abhors?

I have married him not out of love, but for duty's
sake. A duty I will resent until I die. I cannot even
retain my own name any longer. I am Mrs. James
Newell.

7 September 1783

I feel I have been bearing this damnable weight of
wifery for an eternity. There is absolutely no enjoyment
in this drudgery. The daily rounds of tasks are endless
and have already begun to suck away the color from my
face. I am ugly now because of him, that soft-mouthed
imbecile whom I married. He dotes on me, the poor
dear, says he loves me when he couldn't possibly. How
could a man love a woman and condemn her to a life she
hates? A life of cooking and scrubbing and running like
a slave to please every one of her master's whims?
Surely I am no better than a servant girl and paid nothing
for my trouble. I cannot abide his hands on me at night.
God save me from this horror!

16 September 1783

God delivers me! Thankfully, salvation has come before
my body and soul were destroyed completely. I took a
lover this past night—a man on business from London
who met us as we left a coach in Cornwall. He followed
us to the inn where we were keeping a room for our
delayed honeymoon trip. James came into our room
after his business was completed and began to kiss me.

A few days before, I had been stupid enough to accept his inexperienced fumblings. He was encouraged by that, I suppose. He thought I would submit to him again gladly. Idiot. We fought and he went to the tavern to drink his sorrow away. I stepped out into the corridor and found the man staring at me from his open doorway. I went to him.

Kayte wiped tears from her cheeks. She cried not for her mother's obvious unhappiness, but for her father's pain. Kayte had known that her mother had taken a lover, but she was surprised to learn it had happened so early in the marriage. And she was disgusted that any woman could behave so callously toward someone who cherished her. She thought, too, of the man who was her mother's lover. How could he destroy sacred vows so easily for his own pleasure?

Only a few paragraphs remained before the page ended. The rest of the pages were stuck fast.

20 September 1783

He visits me nearly every day and we make love as it was meant to be, with a passion that makes it difficult to breathe. He adores me, showers me with gifts. I no longer share James Newell's bed. He spends his time with the O'Connell cousins, a ridiculous pair who fill their time and bellies with drink.

Kayte smiled at the reference to the people she knew and loved so well. Her mind flitted back to memories of Newbury, then again to the journal's final readable entry.

18 October 1783

He must return to his home soon. His wife, Anna— God, how I envy her place at his side—grows weary of his excuses. What a fool she must be! His son was six this past week and he failed to send the brat some token, so the lady is angry and he says he should go and smooth her feathers. He had promised to come soon or send for me.

Kayte gasped. Anna? His son . . . How old would Daevon
have been? His birthday was early October . . . What year?
Oh, yes. The year after American independence, his mother
had told her—1777. He would have been six!

Had Patrice Newell and Daevon Merrick, the former
earl, been lovers? Kayte's eyes returned to the page.

> Oh, my darling, what shall I do without you? Without
> your hungry kisses and your hands to warm me? My
> beautiful Daevon, what shall I—

The page ended there, to its reader's shocked gasp.

"Oh, my God," Kayte managed to choke out. The
book fell to the floor and a fearful, childlike sob rose from
Kaytlene's chest. Afraid she would wake Daevon, she
slipped from bed but found her legs too weak to carry her
even a short distance. She collapsed in the doorway to the
sitting room, her hands grasping vainly for the door frame.

"Kayte?"

Daevon rose to his elbows, waiting for his eyes to adjust
to the darkness. When he recognized the pale, shaking
figure several yards away, his sleep-muddled mind cleared
quickly and he went to her, dropping to his knees to pull
her into his arms.

She sobbed relentlessly against him.

"Kayte, love, what's frightened you? Have you had a
bad dream?" His hands and voice caressed her but were
unable to calm the torrents of pain that assaulted her.

She pushed away, a maneuver that sent her reeling onto
her back on the thick carpet. A gray-black void crawled up
over her as she looked into the eyes of her husband—eyes
filled with love and confusion.

"I didn't know, Daevon," she cried as the void sucked
her more deeply into it. "I swear I didn't know. I love
you, Daevon." Her voice faded into a pleading whimper.

He bent to her gently, lifting her into his arms as she
lost consciousness.

When she woke, dawn was slipping, rosy gold, into the
bedchamber, lighting the muted blues and grays of Daevon's
furnishings.

"Good morning, Kayte," he greeted her as she sat up, yawning.

She stared incredulously at him. He had dressed in a pair of black riding breeches and black boots. His pale blue silk shirt hung free over the waist of the breeches and revealed most of the upper half of his hard brown chest. He had evidently just entered the room, for he carried a breakfast tray, its bounty fresh and still steaming. He was smiling!

Kayte burst into tears.

The tray laid aside, Daevon was sitting next to her at once, gathering her into his arms and whispering words of love until she quieted.

"I'm sorry, Daevon," she whimpered pitifully against his throat, her hands full of his shirt. "I'm truly sorry. I didn't know."

He gently rocked her in his arms. A warm, reassuring chuckle rumbled in his chest. "If we had been married longer," he said softly, "I would suspect you carried my child. I'm told that a woman expecting a baby sometimes experiences vacillating moods."

She pulled away only far enough to see his face. He hadn't read the journal, of that much she was certain. If he had, he would never suggest such a possibility.

Daevon misread her searching gaze. "Kayte," he said slowly, "are you pregnant?"

Oh God, yesterday the thought of being pregnant with Daevon's child would have sent her into raptures of happiness. Today, it brought her to the depths of despair. Because suddenly a possibility existed that she could not state, could barely even think. For if her mother had made love with Daevon's father, then she herself might be Daevon's half-sister . . . their marriage a sacrilege . . . their child a product of sin!

But she could not bring herself to destroy the look of expectant joy in her husband's eyes. "I . . . don't know enough about these matters to be certain if I am pregnant," she murmured, her heart breaking.

He kissed her lovingly. "We shall see, my pretty wife.

And if you should prove not to be with child, I shall try all the harder to become a father." His suggestive tone and smile were ineffective against the melancholy that had taken hold of her.

Daevon laid her back against the pillows, carefully nudging the stray wisps of hair from her face. "Do you not want to have children, sweetheart?"

"Yes, Daevon," she assured him. "I wish I could give you sons and daughters. Children of our love," she said sadly.

"But I do love you, Kayte. And you love me, don't you?"

"Yes, yes." She began to sob again. "But you won't love me after . . ."

"After what, Kayte? You taught a very angry, lonely man that it was possible to be human and to love. What would make me stop loving you after all that?"

"The truth, Daevon."

"What are you talking about?" His voice took on a harder edge.

Kayte explained that her mother's journal had been delivered to her by a solicitor's office in London. She handed it to him, certain that her being the daughter of his father's mistress would damn her in his eyes for all time.

"I didn't know, Daevon. I can only hope you love me enough to believe me."

Deep lines began to furrow Daevon's brow as he took the volume. His thumb ran purposefully over the word embossed in gold on the cover—JOURNAL. He battled for several moments, only his heavy sighs giving testament to the inner war he waged.

He looked into Kayte's amber eyes, now seeing fear where so often these past weeks there had been only joy. And love.

"Part of the truth about us is in that book," she whispered. "Isn't that what you've always wanted?"

Yes, his mind screamed, *the truth!* But his heart wanted to hear nothing that would revive the past. Not now, when he had Kayte. He wanted to hide his doubts and fears and not face them.

"Read it," she prompted.

"No," he said finally, softly.

"You're afraid!" she accused, knowing that the shock of the truth still prevented her from thinking as clearly as she ought to. "You think I'm a whore, like she was, lying and deceiving and false. I'm not, Daevon! I'm not!" She closed her eyes, vacillating between anger, fear, and pain. As Daevon took the journal to a chair near their bed and began silently to thumb through the pages, she became lost in her own thoughts.

After several silent moments, Daevon's reason won out over his heart and he began to read. He glanced frequently at his wife, curled into a tight little ball in the middle of their bed. He wanted to know what had done this to her. How awful could it be?

When he finished, his breath caught in his throat. He slammed the book shut and his head rolled to the chair's back. He made a deep, rumbling sound, a groan of anger and final comprehension that came from his heart and soul. He straightened, finding Kayte even paler, trembling violently, her eyes fastened to his, muscles tensed like those of a cat preparing to flee.

"Now you see," she whispered. "I'm tainted, like her. You don't want a whore's child. She was my mother. My blood."

Daevon knew from the icy rivulets of sweat that ran down her bloodless features that she was in a severe state of shock. Without speaking he rose and leaned over the bed to touch her face lightly. And then he left her.

Darby was in the chamber an instant later, with a large basin of cold water and a cloth. She bathed Kayte's neck and face, crooning softly to soothe her. Lord Merrick had appeared in the kitchen from the back stairway, shouting orders to her and the cook and then to a houseboy, who was dispatched at once for Dr. Ashton. No explanation was given, except that her ladyship was taken ill, and everyone had attended his orders with no further inquiry or hesitation.

In the library, Daevon was too upset even to pace. He stood at the corner of his desk, gripping a crystal decanter of whiskey in one hand. He drank several glasses in quick succession. Sweet Jesus! He knew his father had indulged in affairs, but with Patrice Newell?

He took a long, thirsty swallow to help dull the pain of the truth as it formed a clear picture in his mind. He had married the daughter of his father's mistress, God help him. He had discovered an answer to one of the questions that had haunted him. But was it a truth he could bear to live with? For, as it must have occurred to Kayte, he realized the full implication of his discovery. He and Kayte might be half-brother and sister! In which case, their love was an abomination!

A young servant entered the open library doors. Daevon swung around to see him.

"Sir," said the boy, Dickson, "this gentleman has come to see Lady Merrick in Dr. Ashton's place."

Daevon's eyes swept over the man as he extended his hand.

"How do you do, your lordship?" he said with oily smoothness. "I'm Dr. Morley."

Chapter 18

Daevon stepped into his mother's bedchamber, the diary of Patrice Newell grasped in one hand. The doctor had declared Kayte violently distraught and sedated her.

"Yes, darling?" His mother's voice came from the bed. "What is it? Darby tells me that Kayte—"

"She'll be fine, Mother. She's sleeping."

"She's had a shock, has she?"

"Yes. How are you feeling, Mother?"

"Oh, well enough. A little tired."

Daevon felt the worn cover of the book between his fingers as he paused.

"What is it, Daevon?" Anna asked quietly. "You look as if you've got the whole world on your shoulders this morning."

He sat down heavily on the side of her bed, a privilege allowed to no one else, and took her hand.

"I want to ask you something, Mother."

"Yes, dear?"

"I'm afraid there isn't any way to put this delicately," he murmured.

"Very well. I'm a tough bird, aren't I, dear?"

Daevon couldn't find it in himself to smile. "Yes, Mother, you are. I want to know," he began stiffly, "if Kayte's mother was . . . was she one of father's mistresses?"

Lady Merrick's hands clenched on the coverlets, and her face drained of color. "Well, you know then, do you?"

"She was."

"Yes. But she was not just one of his mistresses. She was the one he loved."

Daevon felt his mouth go dry and his breathing quicken.
"Do you mean—"

"She was the woman your father was so obsessed by.
Patrice Newell was the lover your father brought to
DenMerrick."

"Oh, God—" The diary dropped to the floor and Daevon
buried his face in his hands. His father had destroyed
Kayte's family and Patrice had destroyed his. Kayte had
been given a gift to ease her family's wounds, and he was
the gift. How could he live with that knowledge?

"Why didn't you tell me?" he whispered.

"Would you have gone to her, Daevon? Would you
have married her?"

"No. No, I never would have married her."

"But you love her, Daevon."

"Yes. She's brought me . . ."

"Joy?"

"Yes."

"You must not blame her for this, Daevon. She knew
no more of it than you did."

"But how can I live with her, always reminded of my
past? My father's—Sweet Jesus, she could be my—"

"Half sister? No, my dear. You are the son of Daevon
and Anna Merrick. She is the daughter of James and
Patrice Newell. That is something you must not doubt."

Daevon rose from the bed.

"It does not make this any easier to bear," he whispered before leaving.

Daevon informed Ashe and Darby that he would be
leaving DenMerrick House for an indefinite period of time.
He ordered a coach and driver to take him to the Merrick
shipping offices.

Adjacent to his own office on the third floor was a sitting
room where he was accustomed to discussing business
with bankers, lawyers, and important clients. It was comfortably furnished with a settee and chairs, a dining table,
and a fully stocked liquor cabinet. Beyond this room was a
small bedchamber and adjacent water closet.

Ignoring his first impulse—to empty every bottle of

whiskey in the liquor cabinet—Daevon fell heavily onto one of the green velvet chairs and stared out at the docks.

One fact was already settled in his mind—he loved Kayte. It was not because of her that he had left the house. He had left because an anger, bitterness, and hatred toward his father that he had no desire to vent on others was eating him up. Here, alone, he could come to terms with them.

As a child, Daevon had been forced by his father to act like a man. Tears were not allowed, or anger, or any other emotion that did not befit an heir of Merrick. When his father was killed, he was forced into the roles of father to Tristan and caretaker to his mother. He had accepted these responsibilities without question or complaint, meeting and overcoming every challenge and reconstructing his life from the broken disorder his father had left. Daevon Merrick, the new earl of Merrick, had survived his father's death, cared for his family, and strengthened and expanded his businesses. But there was one thing he had never fully faced—his vicious hatred for his father.

He realized now that he had forced his hatred deep down inside himself—to a place where it ate at him, turning him into the kind of man his father had been. Hard. Relentless. Unfeeling.

Kayte had changed all that, but she could not erase the years of rage, bitterness, and resentment that had become so much a part of him. All because of a man who had been laid to rest two decades ago.

Patrice Newell's journal had brought it all back to the present.

The only good thing that his father had done for Daevon was to give him a sense of pride. He'd taught his elder son that, as the heir of Merrick, he would have strength, cunning, and respect. And Daevon had held on to that one positive belief—that his father thought him worthy of the title and wealth he would one day inherit.

And now there was Patrice Newell, his father's mistress, to consider. Daevon decided to break open a decanter of whiskey after all, and went to the cabinet to pour a generous glassful.

He had spent years thinking that his father had believed in him—even loved him, perhaps. It was what every young man sought. A father's approval and love, even if the father was as hard and violent as his had been. And yet the truth was far less appealing. His father had sold him in marriage to his whore's daughter. He'd been a pawn paid to a woman for her services in bed. His father had signed his life over to Kaytlene to make Patrice happy, with no thought of his son and heir.

He had not cared.

Daevon realized suddenly that his father had used him as badly as he had used Tristan. He had felt nothing, even for the son he had groomed to take his place as the earl of Merrick. The pain of that brought a fresh rush of anger and bitterness into Daevon's heart.

He could not go back to Kayte now, or to his mother. He was too vulnerable, his feelings too raw. If he returned, he would only lash out at them. He could not bear doing any harm to the two women he loved. They would be safe enough without Tristan in the house. He would stay here, immerse himself in his work, and exorcise his pain and hatred. He would unbury it all, dig it all out of his heart.

And when he returned to Kayte, he would be whole. With a heart free of anything but love for her.

Kaytlene paced the house in a sleepy haze. Dr. Morley was constantly in attendance, ordering a special diet and checking her pulse and color and temperament with annoying frequency. The shock of her mother's involvement with Daevon's father had diminished, leaving a sharper, fiercer pain. Daevon had left her. She had called his name in the blackness where she had spent most of the past two days, but he had not come to her, and only this morning Darby had explained that he had gone late Sunday morning, after being assured that she was sedated and would be well. He had told only Ashe where he would be staying.

Now, with Daevon's absence like a void, the world seemed not worth venturing into and she walked the house like a restless phantom.

She was in the sitting room in the middle of the afternoon, the box of chocolates Daevon had given her open in her lap. Unable to eat, she sat looking at the sugary lumps

as they began to melt in the glare of sunlight falling
through the tall front windows.

"Good afternoon, my dear."

Kayte's head tilted to one side as Lady Merrick entered
the room, as graceful as ever.

"Hello, Mother."

"My dear Kayte, you look so pale." Lady Merrick
settled herself in a chair beside Perdie and began feeding
the bird small bits of bread. "Daevon hasn't contacted
you, has he, dear?"

Kayte's amber eyes flew up to meet silvery blue ones.
"No," she said stiffly.

"Don't be so upset, Kayte. He won't be away from you
for long. He's a different man since meeting you."

Kayte glanced questioningly at her mother-in-law. "You
know why he left, don't you?" she whispered.

"Yes. He knows about your mother."

Kayte nodded, explaining in a rush the events that had
brought her mother's journal to them.

"My mother was the woman whose presence in DenMerrick
forced you out of your own home, wasn't she? She was
the woman who was shot to death with your husband, the
woman Daevon was accused of murdering!"

"Yes, my dear," said Lady Merrick sadly, "I'm afraid
that's all true. I'm sorry it has come to light so abruptly,
but perhaps it will be better this way."

"Better?" Kayte said sharply. "He hates me for it. He
married the daughter of a whore. The whore who destroyed his family."

"He loves you, Kayte. Your mother's sins are not your
own."

"Then why? Why did he leave me?" Kayte's voice
quieted. "Mother, why didn't you tell him?"

"My son was disillusioned. He believed for so long that
women were not worth his respect or love that he didn't
want to love for fear he would be hurt."

Kayte's hard shell of defensiveness softened as she listened to Anna Merrick's unfolding story.

"I met your father shortly after you were born, Kayte.
He was a very gentle man. Hurt, of course, but he loved
you deeply. I knew that in his care you would grow to be a

lovely young woman. The betrothal was signed to prove
that you were not my husband's bastard. I'm sorry, my
dear. I know that sounds cruel.''

"My father . . . wanted me to marry Daevon because of
his money."

"No, Kayte. It's true that a parent who betroths a child
at such an early age usually does it for that reason. And
perhaps it was that way at first with your father. But he
loved Patrice. He needed to know that you were a part of
himself and of her. You were the only part of her that
could not be taken away. The betrothal was really to
affirm that you were truly his."

"At first?"

"After much heartache and prayer, your father and I
believed that the match between you and my son would be
a good one. You were a beautiful child and I knew you
would have James's gentle, loving spirit as well as your
mother's beauty. As the years passed, my son Daevon
became more and more hardened. He hated women and
didn't trust them. True, your mother was the start of it, but
Monique and others helped it along as well."

"Why didn't you allow Daevon to marry Monique if he
loved her?" Kayte asked finally.

Lady Merrick laughed. "I am a better judge of character
than my son believes," she answered, "and your father and
I swore to uphold the contracts. If, once you and Daevon had
met and had had a chance to fall in love, you still didn't
wish to wed, we would not have forced you. But until that
time I wouldn't break the contract. If I had, Daevon might
have married Monique, who would have been disastrous for
him, or not married at all, in which case Tristan's children,
should he have any, would have inherited everything."

"Tristan," Kayte murmured. "Why does he hate Daevon
so much?"

Lady Merrick paled. "They . . . are only half brothers,
Kayte. Tristan is not my son."

"He isn't—"

"Let me tell you the whole story, dear. You should
know the truth. Your parents were married in June of
1783. They were in Cornwall in September, taking a
belated honeymoon, when my husband met your mother."

"That was when the affair began."

"Yes. Patrice became pregnant. She gave birth to my husband's son the following summer."

"Tristan."

"Yes."

Kayte took a long, slow breath. "Then why wasn't Tristan raised as my brother?"

"Your father knew the child could not be his. He knew that Patrice had a lover. She taunted him with the fact that another man was . . . fulfilling her needs, while she denied her husband."

Kayte paled visibly. "How could you know such things?" she whispered.

"James and I met soon after Patrice and Daevon's deaths. He wanted to be certain that I intended to keep the betrothal contracts. He told me what his life had been like . . ." Anna's voice trailed off when she saw the pain in Kayte's expression. "I am sorry, my dear. Let me continue. After James learned that Patrice was pregnant, he demanded to know her lover's name. She told him and he sent her to DenMerrick—alone. He told her that if she returned with the child he would throw her out into the gutter. She lived at DenMerrick for most of her pregnancy, during which time she begged my husband to take the child as his own. He agreed, but sent me and Daevon away while she lived there. When we returned, my husband put Tristan into my arms, told me that I would claim the child was my own, born while I was away, and sent Patrice back to James."

"Why didn't Merrick simply keep her for a plaything?" Kayte asked bitterly. "I think she would have been happy enough as his mistress. She would have been paid well, at least."

"Yes," Anna agreed. "But she was much too greedy. When she gave birth to a son, she was overjoyed. She thought that since Tristan was a child of love, he should be named as Daevon's heir. She tried to convince him, and they fought. Though he agreed to take Tristan in, he refused to treat him as anything but a bastard. Patrice left in a rage."

"She stayed with my father only because she had nowhere else to go," Kayte guessed.

"Yes, and when Daevon made no attempt to come to her, she finally gave herself to James. She became pregnant again in the winter of 1785. You were born the following October."

"And Father thought that I might be illegitimate as well."

"After being hurt so badly by Patrice's first pregnancy, he was afraid to trust. But he did, until Daevon came back to find Patrice again, just before your first birthday. He begged her to return with him, promising her whatever she wanted, short of marriage. She came to DenMerrick with him."

"And my father began to doubt that I was really his," Kayte mused. "So he demanded that I be betrothed to your son. It would be illegal to betroth me to my own half brother."

"Yes, and Patrice liked the idea as well. She was happy to know that her daughter would share the wealth of the Merricks, as a legitimate wife, something that she had been denied. The contracts were signed. And then Daevon and Patrice were killed."

Lady Merrick's voice dropped off.

"My dear, I am afraid all of this has been quite painful for me. Will you call Darby and ask her to bring something cool to drink to my room? I'm afraid I am not feeling well."

"Yes, Mother. Of course." Kayte did as she was bid, then went out to the pond behind the house in search of solitude, her thoughts inescapably tied to Daevon.

She slipped off her shoes and pulled up her skirts to wade into the cool water. The smell of honeysuckle was faint and pleasant, as was the feel of mud between her toes. The sky was growing dark with the promise of rain. And for the first time in several days, Kayte felt content.

Daevon would return, she was certain. He was disturbed by the past and the fact that her mother's diary had stirred up memories and truths that were painful to him. He only needed time alone, and she was willing to give him that time. Even if the waiting was painful.

Daevon surveyed the pale glow of his home as it lay beneath the full moon. He had loved DenMerrick House since the first time he had walked across its crisp green lawns and through its spacious halls. And with Kayte's presence, it had become a true home, a keep in which to secure his greatest treasure.

He had been away for too long, torturing himself with memories of the past. But, finally, he had put his past behind him and was eager to build a future. A future with his wife. He nudged Demon forward with an even touch of his heels.

Kayte rolled from one side of the bed to the other, more restless than she had been at any time since Daevon's departure. Her green silk dressing gown clung to her skin, not even the breezes from the open windows easing the heat. A pale V of lace began at her shoulders, curved down low over her breasts, and ended in a point at her waist. It was damp with sweat, and Kayte slipped her fingers beneath it, lifting it to cool her skin. A touch on the deprived flesh of one breast caused a ravenous hunger to blossom in her belly.

Daevon had been gone for five days, an eternity during which her arms and lips and heart had been starved for him. She kicked away the satin sheets and dragged her gown up until her legs were almost completely exposed to the breeze, one knee raised slightly.

Daevon nearly choked on a breath as he slipped into the sitting room from the back staircase. The windows had all been thrown open, as had the doors separating the two rooms of the master bedroom suite, and he could see Kayte clearly, lying in the center of their bed, bathed in moonlight. He had wanted her—needed her—so desperately these past days that the sight of her doubled his heartbeat, and desire surged hotly through his blood. He went to the bedchamber door.

"Angel," he whispered hoarsely. "Beautiful angel."

Kayte opened her eyes slowly, afraid the voice she had heard would prove to be another dream.

"Daevon . . ." Her own word tore into a sob as she saw his face, his lean, hard figure standing there.

He came to the bed.

"Daevon?" Kayte touched his shoulder with sweet apprehension. "I don't care if you hate me. Just love me tonight. Make love to me. Please." She pulled him toward her, her mouth heating his bare neck and shoulders with kisses.

"Please," she murmured, "I need you. Hate me tomorrow, Daevon. Tomorrow . . ." She pressed her body to his, the soft pressure of her breasts forcing a groan from him.

He pushed her back, holding her wrists above her head and raking her body with his eyes. "I cannot hate you, angel," he whispered. "I love you too much." His mouth was pressing down on hers, his hands releasing hers to hold her to him.

"Forgive me, love," he went on. "I only left because . . ."

"Because you needed time. I know. It doesn't matter, Daevon. You've come back."

He moved away. "I want you to know why, Kayte." Taking her hand in his, he kissed it gently. "I didn't leave until I knew you were going to be all right," he began apologetically.

"I know, darling."

He smiled at the endearment. "I was sleeping at the offices, Kayte. I don't want you to think—"

"That you were sleeping with another woman?" Kayte slid one palm to his knee and along his thigh. The snug tan breeches he wore left no doubt about his desire for her. "I know," she murmured.

He caught her free hand with his own. "I've been thinking about the past," he said softly. "Finding out about your mother was very hard for me. And I know now that my father used me. It makes me feel . . . well, I once believed my father may have loved me. I know now that couldn't be true."

Kayte's heart twisted painfully for him. A father's love was so important to a young man, and Daevon's one hope that he had had his father's love had been destroyed.

"I'm sorry," she whispered. "It's my fault."

"No," he said firmly. "They were at fault. You are no more responsible for his actions than I am." Daevon pulled her tight against his chest. It was so good just to hold her. Then he eased her back against the pillows. For long minutes of silence he held her there, his eyes drinking in her flesh. Then his hand moved down her jaw, across her lips, and along her throat. She moaned as it closed over the softness of one breast, hard and possessive. His thumb teased its center to stiffness.

"Kayte, I've buried the past," he murmured. "I want a future with you."

She cried out softly in pleasure as his mouth bent to the swollen breast, licking and tugging through the sheer veil of her gown. He tore the thin material away, freeing her body for his fierce caresses.

Kayte accepted his violent pleasure, his haste only feeding her own until she thought she must die from the wanting.

"Daevon," she pleaded, "please, I need you."

His body covered hers and there was a pause in the midst of their heat. Daevon's eyes, as silver as the light falling from heaven, met hers with a passion that burned through her.

"You're mine . . . forever," he said roughly, sealing her flesh with his own.

A scream roused Kayte, who woke to find herself alone once again. She nearly cried out at the realization, fearing that Daevon's lovemaking had been a dream. The smell of him lingering on the sheets and his clothes still strewn about the floor reassured her, but a second scream pierced her senses.

It was Darby.

Kayte pulled on a heavy dressing gown and hurried into the hallway toward the now sobbing voice. A light burned in Lady Merrick's bedchamber.

With a fearful, hasty prayer, Katye entered the room.

"Dear God," she muttered. "Mother!"

Daevon was on his knees beside Anna's bed, her frail hand in his. She was pale, her breathing labored and uneven. "Darby," Daevon said quickly, "have you sent for Dr. Ashton?"

"Yes," she said. "Ashe has gone. Oh, dear God, let her be well." She moaned, sinking into a chair.

Kayte, recovering from the first shock of having been awakened to such turmoil, spoke softly to Darby. "Bring up a pan of hot water in case Dr. Ashton should need it for his instruments," she directed. "And prepare some coffee for Daevon and Ashe and the doctor. Go on, Darby. And get hold of yourself."

"Yes, ma'am," she answered softly, brushing away her tears.

Kayte held a corner bedpost for support. Lady Merrick's heart was weak. Perhaps too weak now to keep her alive. Daevon was smoothing the older woman's hair, murmuring softly. Kayte did not want to disturb them if these were their last moments together, and so she stood nearby and wept and prayed.

When Dr. Ashton appeared in the doorway, Daevon did not move. The room was silent as the physician checked his patient's condition. Scowling, he repeated the motions, taking Lady Merrick's pulse, listening to her heart, his expression one of growing consternation and despair. Darby returned with an earthenware bowl filled with steaming water.

"We won't be needing that, dear," Dr. Ashton said softly. With a harsh sob, Darby ran from the room.

Kayte pressed her forehead against the bedpost as tears washed down her cheeks. Daevon had just dealt with so much pain. How could he stand more? She looked up again when Dr. Ashton spoke.

"I'm sorry, Daevon, she has very little time left." The doctor continued, "There is nothing I can do."

Kayte saw Daevon's shoulders tense. He nodded. "I want to be alone with her."

Riley Ashton rose from the bed, and slipped a comforting arm around Kayte's waist. "Let me take you downstairs, Lady Merrick," he said softly.

Kayte looked at him, then at Anna's closed eyes and still, barely breathing form. "Yes," she said, and allowed him to lead her downstairs to the sitting room.

Darby and Kayte sat together, taking sips of warm, frothy chocolate between bouts of crying. Comforting each other was futile, they knew, and so they sat in silence. With uncharacteristic anxiety Dr. Ashton paced the room, seemingly deep in thought, then hurried out when he was called back to Lady Merrick's chamber. He was there now with Daevon.

Kayte nervously tapped her foot against the floor as she waited, wanting to be with Daevon, to comfort him in his pain.

When he appeared at the doorway, Kayte stood, wringing her hands.

"She's gone," he whispered hoarsely.

Kayte ran to him, sobbing, and he enfolded her in his arms, pressing her head close to his heart for a long moment. Then he stepped back from her, and Kayte thought she saw more anger than pain in his expression.

"Daevon," she asked softly, "what is it?"

He glanced at her, one hand clenched into a fist at his side. "Darby, leave us," he said sternly, then added a softer "please."

"Of course," she answered, trembling with quiet sobs as she replaced her small china cup on its tray.

Daevon closed the doors once she had gone. He took Kayte to the couch and sat with her there, keeping enough space between them to make her feel that he was a world away.

"Daevon," she started, faltering. She reached out to touch him, but his eyes told her to withdraw her hand, which she did.

"When did you last see Mother?" he asked coldly.

"What?"

"When?" he demanded.

"Last night after she went to bed. I was reading to her."

"Did you take her anything to eat or drink?"

"No. I don't understand, Daevon." She forced herself to look into his eyes. He was furious—more so than he had ever been—and she knew there was very little self-control holding back the violence that he was keeping in. A shiver of fear ran through her like an icy knife.

"What's wrong, Daevon?"

"Did you take the chocolates to her room?"

The question surprised her. "She was fond of the cher-

ries,'' she said calmly. "We finished the box last night.
Dr. Ashton said it was all right."

"Did anyone else have access to the box?"

Kayte stood, finally comprehending. "She was poisoned!"

He nodded. "Dr. Ashton says that she didn't die of
a heart attack. She ingested a substance that killed her."

"The chocolates were poisoned?"

Again a silent, painful nod.

"You think I did it! You bastard!" She went past him,
out of the room.

"No, Kayte," he whispered after she was gone, his face
in his hands. "I know you couldn't have. I won't believe
it."

Daevon would not allow himself to weep, even now.
Someone had murdered his mother and he had lashed out
at the person he loved most—Kayte. Tristan would have
been his first suspect, but he had not been allowed at
DenMerrick House since the wedding, and the chocolates
had been purchased after that. For the moment Daevon
was at a loss for an explanation.

Straightening, he went to find his wife, to beg her
forgiveness for his doubts about her. He knew he would
not be able to survive this loss without her.

Kayte went to her bedside table and pulled open the
drawer where she kept the gifts Daevon had given her.
Dried flowers. Jewelry. The empty box of chocolates. She
tore the contents from the drawer, dumping them onto the
bed. As she cried, her fingers ran lovingly over the deep
green velvet of a small box—her favorite gift, the emeralds. Then she placed them all aside and opened the candy
box. The scent of rich chocolate still clung to it. She
turned it upside down and shook it.

She picked up the vial that fell out, a tiny glass con-
tainer holding the last drops of a clear liquid. She knew
immediately what it was.

The chocolates *had* been poisoned!

"Kayte?" Daevon's voice frightened her and she made
a harsh, choking sound.

"Daevon!"

"I'm—" He started to say that he was sorry for making

her believe that he blamed her, that he needed her love as
never before. Then he, too, saw the medicinal-looking
vial.

"What is that?" he said almost under his breath.

"I . . . found it. In the chocolate box," Kayte sobbed,
knowing what Daevon must be thinking.

She said nothing to defend herself. There was nothing
she could say.

"What have you done?" he said harshly.

She looked up at him, tear-darkened lashes shadowing
her golden eyes. "I won't defend myself to you, Daevon.
To anyone else I might, but not to you. Do you believe
that I had nothing to do with your mother's death or not?"

The silence was like a pain drumming between them.
Daevon's mind rushed through every possible explanation
for Kayte's having the poison. Someone had placed it
there. Who? Ashe? Darby? Neither of them had any reason
to kill his mother. Even Tristan, who could not possibly
have gotten into the house, knew that Daevon would inherit everything. And how had Kayte known exactly where
the vial was? She had only been a moment ahead of him
coming up the stairs, yet she had gone directly to it. Was
she trying to throw it out before anyone began searching
for clues? And how was it that Kayte herself had not been
poisoned? She had eaten the chocolates as well. The cherries . . . Hadn't she said she saved the cherries for his
mother? Not even he had known about his mother's fondness for that particular sweet. But Kayte had known. And
she was the only person who would benefit from his
mother's death. She would be the only Lady Merrick now.
She would run the house and have the authority that her
mother, Patrice, had always wanted . . .

Daevon finally turned to leave the room and stormed
through the house until he found Ashe in the servants'
wing. "Ashe," he demanded, "has Tristan been allowed
in the house?"

"No, sir. I arranged for full-time security about the
house at all times. The men have tried to be inconspicu-
ous, sir. I hope they haven't caused a problem?"

"No, Ashe. I wasn't even aware that you had done so."

"I will let them go if you wish, your lordship, but with your concern over Master Tristan, I felt—"

"You did the right thing, Ashe. Have there been any visitors to the house during the past few weeks?"

"Visitors, my lord? Well, Dr. Ashton, of course. Dr. Morley. Lady Clay. Mrs. Kurtz's delivery boy, and—"

"No, Ashe. What I meant was, have there been any uninvited guests?"

"No. Wait . . . yes, sir. A gentleman. He was here to see Lady Merrick."

"My mother?"

"No, my lord. Your wife."

"Who was he?"

"I don't know, sir. He presented a card, of course, but handed it to me facedown and told me that his business with Lady Merrick was private. I am not in the habit of peeking, sir."

"No, Ashe, of course not." Daevon wished that, for just that moment, the man could have dropped his stiff, proper decorum and peeked. He thanked Ashe and turned away. Kayte normally related everything about her time away from him during the day. Her hobbies, her visitors, the new places she discovered in London on her outlawed rides. Why had she never told him about her gentleman caller? Had he supplied her with the poison? If not, she could easily have arranged for it in London.

Was she like her mother? How far would she go to have the authority, the jewels, the house to herself? Could she have killed because her own mother had been denied those very things? Daevon stopped halfway to the library. His mind froze on one thought.

She has been playing me false all along!

Forcing himself to go on, he closed himself in the library and sat in the darkness. It was all a lie. Her love, her companionship . . . all a ruse to get his name and his money.

Just like her mother.

A quiet family burial was held on Saturday at dawn. Kayte rode back to DenMerrick House in an open carriage with her husband, the black gown she had worn at her father's funeral now adorned with a veil that had been pulled back from her face. Only the occasional rustle of her skirts disturbed the silence.

She removed her lace gloves and adjusted the tiny black hat that held her veil in place, anything to avoid contact with Daevon's eyes.

"Are you ill, Lady Merrick?" he asked.

"I beg your pardon?" she said abruptly, looking straight ahead.

"You seem agitated this morning."

"I'm sorry, your lordship."

"Guilty conscience, perhaps?"

She turned toward him, anger flashing in her eyes. "You are the only one who seems to feel I'm guilty."

"That's because I was gracious enough not to share the evidence with anyone else."

"How considerate of you, Lord Merrick," she ground out harshly. She gasped when he took her face in his hands, bringing it close to his.

"Even I don't hate you enough to see your beauty rot in prison," he said softly. "I have better ideas."

"Do you intend to keep me until you find another whore to take my place? You might use your evidence to chain me to you."

"Quite possibly," he remarked with a menacing smile.

"I don't want to be with you," she lied. "Not if you don't love or trust me."

"But aren't you the girl who begged me to make love to her? Who didn't care if I hated her? You don't want my trust, pretty Kayte. You want my touch." His mouth came down like molten steel on hers, one arm sliding to her waist to pull her against him. She moaned softly as he caressed her breast through the silky crepe of her gown. Her mind could not possibly focus clearly when he wreaked such havoc on her senses.

"You see," he said mockingly when he finished the assault, "I think you a liar and a cheat and still you give yourself to me."

"You think me a murderess as well," she returned, shaken, "and I only give myself to you because I love you, Daevon."

He laughed. "Then you are more a fool than I am, my lady."

"Perhaps I am," she admitted softly, returning to the opposite side of the coach.

Daevon watched her move away, a stab of disappointment and frustration cutting through him. In his heart he wanted desperately to believe her, but his mind recalled how love had betrayed him in the past. Monique's eyes had regarded him with the same tenderness. Her lips had vowed her eternal love only a few hours before accepting another man's hand in marriage. And Kayte was, after all, the daughter of the woman who had destroyed his family. The daughter of the woman he himself may have killed! Kayte had cunningly convinced her father to keep the betrothal contracts to ensure her position as Lady Merrick. And even if she hadn't poisoned his mother, her death certainly aided Kayte in her quest for the Merrick titles and wealth. Daevon smiled cruelly, unaware that Kayte was watching him from the corner of her eye.

"I believe we can come to a mutually satisfying arrangement," he said finally.

She glared at him. "What on earth are you talking about?"

"I intend to give you exactly what you want."

"You bastard," she said calmly. "I'll run away from you before I let you use me. If you want a mistress, hire one!"

He clasped her hand much too tightly, and her teeth scraped her lower lip as she fought the urge to resist him.

"As much as I've enjoyed your affections in bed, my dear, I won't require you in that capacity any longer. I will be more than happy to take my business elsewhere."

"Business?" She returned scathingly.

"Don't worry. You can keep your emeralds, my sweet. And your pretty clothes and your pearls. You've earned them."

"Earned them . . ." she repeated numbly, the color draining from her face. "I don't want them, Daevon."

"But you'll need them, my dear. As the lady of DenMerrick you shall have to keep up appearances."

"You intend to let me stay at DenMerrick House?"

"I didn't say that, Kaytlene. I think it appropriate that you take up residence at DenMerrick. Your mother wasn't able to take possession of it. I'm sure she would have been pleased to know that her daughter will.''

"You're sending me away?'' She turned her face up to his, and his grip and expression softened simultaneously.

"Yes," he replied, though the pain in her eyes and her whispered plea nearly broke his resolve.

"Daevon, please don't. I've done nothing to hurt you or deceive you. Hate me for the rest of your life if it pleases you, but don't make me leave you.'' She leaned toward him, afraid. He was confused and hateful, but if he sent her away now there would be no chance for her to win him back. She must stay at any cost.

Her free hand closed on his arm. ''You don't want to send me away, Daevon. You want me. Please don't do this.'' Her hand slipped up the black silk of his lapel.

"Don't!'' he forced out, pushing her away. ''Don't play your pretty whore's games with me, Kaytlene. When I want one, I shall pay for her.''

"Very well, then. Send me back to Newbury, but divorce me first.''

"No.'' The word came suddenly and unbidden to his lips. Abruptly his tone softened. ''Not yet, at least.'' He had no desire to keep her with him, to remind him that he had been wrong about her. Kaytlene Newell was a woman like other women. But he did not want to sever his ties to her altogether. He could easily comprehend how his father had become entangled in her mother's web. Wrong as it was, he was obsessed by Kaytlene, as his father had been obsessed with her mother. He couldn't let her go just yet. Not yet.

"We leave this afternoon.''

DenMerrick was a day's journey south. Daevon gave his wife a few hours to pack and looked surprised when she appeared on the front lawn with only a small bag and the worn trunk she had brought from Newbury. Later, after returning to the bedchamber to pack his own things, he found all of her new garments still hanging in her tall oak wardrobe. Across the bed her jewels were strewn carelessly, as if she had tossed them there in an angry tantrum. And across his pillow lay a shimmer of gray satin—the corset she had chosen for their wedding night.

While Daevon rode to the Merrick estate on Demon, his
skin bronzing even darker beneath the midsummer sun,
Kayte and Darby sat stiff and uncomfortable in his coach.
The young Irish girl had insisted upon accompanying her
mistress, remaining impervious to Lord Merrick's ranting
as she packed her belongings for the journey.

Justin had also made his opinion perfectly clear to the
master, determined to be a part of the entourage and
preparing Circe for the trip as well. Daevon had agreed,
adding grudgingly that two other mounts from his stable
should also be taken.

"The DenMerrick stables are empty," he had mumbled
angrily. "You'll need something to keep you busy."

And so the black and roan geldings Daevon had chosen
pulled the coach while Justin drove a small open buggy
with Circe tied behind on a long lead rope. Daevon had
decided that Justin would need his small cart to run errands
and carry parcels to and from the estate to the village
below it. If Kaytlene's faithful followers were to be im-
prisoned with her at DenMerrick, they would at least have
the basic necessities.

After a few hours of suffering the heat of a closed
carriage, Kaytlene kicked the front of the coach until the
driver stopped. She jumped down immediately, latching
on to Darby's arm and pulling the girl out behind her.

Daevon swerved Demon toward the coach doors with an
angry curse. "If you intend to run away now, Lady Merrick,
you have quite a long way to go."

"Lord Merrick," she replied, one hand shading her
eyes as she looked up at him, "if you intend to make me a
prisoner, then you should do your best to keep me alive
until we reach the prison. I shall die in that carriage. Or
perhaps that is what you intend."

Kayte pushed Darby toward the open buggy and, though
the girl protested, she appeared grateful for the fresh air
and Justin's company. Kayte went to take Circe's saddle
from the back of the buggy and found Daevon's stronger
arms doing the work for her.

"If you must ride," he said sourly, "at least save your
strength so that you can keep yourself in the saddle all
afternoon."

"You underestimate me, my lord."

"I'm sure," he replied, taking her by the waist to lift her onto Circe's back.

She placed her hands over his when he hesitated in taking them away. He looked up at her, and she could tell it was torture for him not to pull her down into his arms. Suddenly he wrenched himself away. Her thumbs traced soft arcs over his wrists.

"And you underestimate me as well, my lady."

They rode until Kayte's backside was sore and she could not stand another moment of Daevon's cold glances. For the last hour before dusk, he rode ahead of her, and she was forced to stare at his back. Better that, she supposed, than having to speak to him.

They stopped for the night at a small wayside inn, where they all sat together in the common room to have supper. All except Daevon, who preferred brandy at the crude wooden bar to roast lamb and red wine at the table. He stared purposefully at Kayte, and she stared at her plate. When one of the maids who had finished serving the food approached Daevon with an enticing sway of her trim hips, Kayte choked on a swallow of wine. Daevon looked over the redhead's shoulder to smile at his wife and slipped both arms about the wench to kiss her soundly. Kayte ran for the comfort of the sleeping quarters upstairs.

But she couldn't sleep. Her only thoughts were of Daevon and the pretty little maid in his arms . . .

Damn him to everlasting hell! She was his wife, and she had every right to sleep in his bed, whether he loved her or not. No whoring little slut was going to take her place! With steely determination, Kayte stripped off her modest gown and replaced it with another of filmy pink gauze. She brushed out her hair, slipped into a silk wrapper, and threw open her door. The hallway was dark and silent. She realized suddenly how impulsively foolish she was being. She couldn't possibly explain to anyone what she was doing prowling about the halls in the dead of night, dressed as she was. She went barefoot to the door next to hers and put her hand on the knob. A crash from the common room downstairs and the cursing that followed it had her bolting into Daevon's room, making enough noise of her own to wake the dead.

Daevon turned from the window where he had been staring into the darkness. He wore only a pair of soft breeches. His hair was wet and drops from his bath still glistened on his chest. Kayte shut the door and leaned against it to keep herself from melting at the sight of him.

"What the hell are you doing?" he demanded, coming forward.

"I thought . . ." Looking slowly about the room, she saw no evidence of the redhead, and the bed had not been disturbed. She looked back at Daevon, feeling suddenly sick.

"You thought I was entertaining a lady," Daevon said and smiled wickedly.

Kayte's anger returned, full-blown. "She's hardly a *lady*!"

Daevon, close enough now to touch her, refrained from doing so. He came closer until Kayte was pressed back flat against the door. "Jealous, are you?" he teased coldly. "Or perhaps protecting your investment from other whores?"

"I'm not a—"

"Aren't you, Kayte?" he said, grabbing her by the shoulders and forcing her body against his. "Aren't you here to sell that luscious body for a ticket back to London?"

"No! You bastard!" She struggled, only to find herself being dragged back into the room and divested of her robe.

The moonlight from the window made Kayte's pink gown transparent, and Daevon took long, hungry moments to enjoy the body that was all but exposed to his eyes.

"Where shall I have you?" he murmured sensually.

"W-what?"

He forced her against the wall near the open window.

"Where shall I have you?" he repeated, his hands pushing the gown from her shoulders. "On the floor? The bed? The chair?"

Kayte gasped. He was seriously considering making love to her now, when he hated her! But isn't that what you came for? her mind whispered to her. Isn't this what you wanted all along?

"No, Daevon . . . please . . ." she said hoarsely. But his mouth was trailing fiercely across her exposed throat, and the burning between her thighs confirmed that this was, indeed, what she had wanted. One last time . . .

His hands tore the gown from neck to hip with one smooth pull on the cloth. His fingers dipped inside the gaping pink gauze for her breasts. She felt herself sliding down . . . down . . .

Daevon pulled her up into the hard cradle of his arms. God, he wanted her! Christine, the inn's redhead, had tried to arouse him, but he had felt nothing for her. He wanted only Kayte. Desperately. She was staring at him with passion-glazed eyes, her breasts full and tempting between the edges of the gown. He carried her to the chair next to the bed and let her feet slide to the floor. The gown fell, and he tore off his breeches, watching her eyes move down his body with slow deliberation.

Groaning, he pulled her against him and kissed her viciously, hungrily. The breeze from the window cooled their heating bodies.

He tried not to show any tenderness toward her, but it was there, in the way he drew his fingers through her hair, the way his lips and teeth played at her earlobe, the gentle caresses he used to adore her breasts. They said nothing, but allowed passion to draw them together. Daevon sat in the chair and pulled her down onto his lap, her back to him. She understood the position, was excited by it. Her hand touched the hard shaft that pulsed between her thighs. She caressed him, sliding him teasingly into the wet heat there. He moaned, jerking her torso back to lean against him, his hands on her breasts. She lifted her hips for him and guided him into her, throwing back her head in abandonment. While he took her with long, slow strokes, his right hand covered hers and, with his fingers guiding hers, he brought her to quick, successive climaxes. He joined her finally, groaning his pleasure against her throat as they shared the final release.

Daevon took in a hard breath, then lifted Kayte and stood her on her feet. He rose, pulled on his breeches, and threw her robe at her. His brusque manner was chilling. He waited until she had secured the cloth around her waist before speaking.

"Now get out," he said gratingly. "I haven't changed my mind."

Kayte peered up at him and bit her lip to keep herself from screaming. She wouldn't throw herself at his feet and beg him to love her. She knew he did—she saw it in his eyes. It would only take time.

"Get out!" he shouted, and watched as she ran for the door like a startled rabbit.

All night he could hear the sound of her sobbing through the damnably thin walls of their rooms. All night he tried to tell himself he didn't care.

Kaytlene's first glimpse of her new home came just after midmorning the following day. She noted with interest Daevon's sharp sigh. She thought better of asking what the reaction meant, but he offered the information anyway.

"I haven't seen DenMerrick in twenty years," he said in a tone that made her think he might change his mind and stay with her after all. Then, after bellowing a single, sharp command, he raced Demon down the knoll and across the overgrown tangle that comprised most of the grounds.

They approached from the rear. Even choked in years' worth of overgrowth and strangled by ivy clinging to its outer walls, DenMerrick was obviously a palatial home. Or it had been, at one time. As Daevon had explained, it had been constructed in the days of gallant knights, built from massive blocks of hewn stone. The rear wall of the estate was relatively plain, but many of the upper windows were arches of colored glass. From the others the original shutters had been removed and the colored windows replaced with panes of clear glass. The chimneys seemed to have been rebuilt fairly recently, though birds flew freely in and out of them, not an unusual sight even for a new home but a problem when the estate had been deserted for so long.

A semicircular wall of newer brick cradled what Kaytlene guessed had once been a flower garden to the right of the rear yard. On the left was a series of grape arbors, collapsing and rotting under the weight of their tangled vines. Farther left was a small pond and then the flatland rolled down a slight angle to the village, a tiny place surrounded by acres of working fields. It seemed odd to Kayte that there was so much activity not a mile from the deserted estate.

The stables, if one could honor them with that title, were located on the north side of the pond. Most of the acreage beyond the overgrown flower garden to the right was, to Kayte's delight, well kept and cultivated, now thriving with a summer crop of wheat.

But more exciting to Kayte was the familiar scent of sea air. The sight of gray-white cliffs and ocean beyond the village somehow lessened the pain of her arrival.

Their coming was met with great interest as they rode along the narrow path between the working fields. Laborers stopped their activities, pointing and speculating. To Kayte's amusement, they even crossed themselves furiously.

"You really are the devil, aren't you, my lord?" she said.

Daevon cast her a sidelong glance, already having seen the gestures. "I can be," he said simply. "When provoked to it."

The front of the estate was nothing less than magnificent, though years of decay had taken their toll. Two four-story towers stood like sentries on either side of the facade, and the front entrance was a square door of hand-carved hard wood. The old window openings had been enlarged and filled with hundreds of small glass squares.

Kayte was unaware that Circe had stopped moving until Daevon's thigh brushed her own and his hand took her reins.

"Daevon, it's lovely," she said.

"On the outside, perhaps," he said as he dismounted. Once she was on the massive granite steps he pushed open the door. "Behold your castle, my queen." He bowed mockingly as she entered.

Her castle. The house where her mother had been killed in the master's bed. The house where Daevon's youth had been destroyed. Where she was now a prisoner.

The interior of the house was still furnished, though musty cloths covered most of the pieces. As Kayte surveyed the lower floor, rats scurried across her path, drawing no reaction from her.

Daevon followed behind her with sure strides, his hands clasped lightly behind his back. They examined the kitchens, pantry, dining hall, library, and finally the guest chambers on the lower floor. When they returned to the entry, Kayte declared cheerfully, "I shall be quite comfortable here, my lord."

Daevon smiled ruefully, pretending to be more interested in the others, who were piling luggage inside the doorway. "Will you?" he asked absentmindedly.

"Why, yes. Did you wish me to tell you how miserable I would be? I won't give you that satisfaction."

"Of course," he murmured. "Come, I want to show you something." He took her hand and went down the wide corridor toward a staircase. "Let me show you where the ghosts walk in DenMerrick," he said coolly. She hesitated at the top of the staircase and again when they stopped before a door at the north end of the house.

"My father's chambers," he explained brusquely.

"I don't . . . want to see it," she said, suddenly frightened. "Please, Daevon."

"But you are now mistress of DenMerrick," he said.

"Mistress of DenMerrick," she repeated, "but not your mistress. I am your wife and I won't be treated with so little consideration!"

His hand went to the door handle, one arm winding around her waist when she began to move away. "Don't run, little girl," he said harshly.

"I won't go in there," she answered, clawing at his chest. "You cannot treat me this way."

Daevon forgot about the door. With both arms he pulled Kayte to him until she was forced to stop struggling and peered fearfully up at him. She groaned when his mouth fell hard over hers, drawing out a kiss that punished and inflamed. His hands tangled in her hair, forcing her head back, his mouth consuming hers.

"Make me believe in you, Kayte," he whispered hoarsely. "Prove me wrong." And he broke abruptly away from her, going down the hall to the stairway and descending, leaving Kaytlene Newell Merrick alone and trembling. A few minutes later, she heard a horse gallop out of the yard, away from the estate. She ran to the window, but she was already too late. She was to have no last glimpse of her departing husband to savor in the days to come.

With effort Kayte pulled herself together and went down-stairs to begin the work of turning DenMerrick into a home. Hands on her hips, she surveyed the kitchen, grimacing at the piles of ancient dust and rats' nests. Turning to the two people who stood waiting behind her, she began issuing orders.

Justin was to make their animals comfortable and return to the house with as many buckets and pitchforks as he could find. Kayte and Darby, delighted that the kitchen pump brought up fresh water after a considerable amount of wheezing, washed away the grime that had accumulated during their trip and changed their clothes.

Kayte chose a brown muslin dress, one of the few she had brought. Then she and Darby sat side by side in the buggy and drove to the village. Their first errand led them into a dry goods store that smelled of plain soap and pickles.

When Kayte entered, her slow, delicate step and the shower of brown hair falling about her face drew immediate attention from several other customers. She was quickly sought out by a young woman in her mid-twenties with a rather plain, milky-white face. She wiped her hands on the apron tied around her waist and approached Kayte timidly.

"Good afternoon, I am Lady Kaytlene Merrick."

"Pleased to meet you, your ladyship," the woman replied. "I'm Pattie Hanley. My husband owns the store. Inherited it from his father a few years back."

"I'm very happy to meet you, Mrs. Hanley."

"Is there anything I can do for you, your ladyship? This silk is lovely, don't you think?"

"Oh, yes." Kayte admired the deep violet fabric. "But I'm afraid I don't have much need for such luxuries at the moment. I'm more interested in some cleaning supplies. Brooms, mops, scrubbing brushes, soap. That sort of thing. Oh, and vinegar. And food."

"Oh," the woman said excitedly, "Lord Merrick is coming back to DenMerrick?"

Kayte tried to regain her composure. "Not at present," she replied. "But once I return DenMerrick to its former beauty, I am certain he will. In the interim I shall be in charge of the estate."

"It will be lovely, I'm sure of it. I'll collect your supplies."

"Mrs. Hanley." Kayte stopped her with a hushed tone and one hand on the woman's arm. "I'm afraid his lordship did not discuss . . . financial matters with me. Regarding accounts and such."

"Your account is in good standing here, your ladyship. Paid every Thursday afternoon. That's true all through the village."

"And who pays them?"

"His lordship's overseer, Mr. Miller."

"Lyle Miller?"

"The very same. He lives in one of the tenant cottages and takes care of his lordship's properties here."

"I see," Kayte replied as Mrs. Hanley scurried off to fill her requests. Darby would not regret having come to DenMerrick after all, Kayte thought.

Kayte found an equally warm reception wherever she visited that afternoon. She not only managed to secure her supplies, but also arranged for the seamstress and carpenter's apprentices to arrive at DenMerrick the next day, hiring them out for a fair wage. The stonecutter was also engaged to repair the front steps and several of the stones in the outer walkways.

At the edge of the village, Kayte led the horses past a small cottage that had been gutted and blackened by fire and was now the site of a vigorous game of tag.

"Good afternoon," Darby called to one of the little girls at the front of the house. She got a soft "Hallo" in reply and a little curtsy.

"See our school?" the girl said, pointing to the cottage. "All burned up, it did."

"Yes, I do see," Darby replied.

Kayte pulled in the reins and stopped the buggy. "And where do you go to school now?" she asked the yellow-haired child.

"We don't," said a second, older girl, about twelve. "Teacher got married. Moved away after the fire."

By now several of the other children had become interested in the conversation and gathered around the buggy.

"I'm sorry. Would you like to go to school?" Kayte asked.

There was a mixed reaction to the question. "There's no one here qualified to teach school, my lady," Mrs. Bain, the seamstress, replied from the porch of her nearby shop.

"I will," Kayte said quickly.

"You, my lady?"

"I taught for several years in Newbury. French, arithmetic, geography, Latin. Oh, and history."

The woman seemed to consider the offer as her son scampered around the corner of the shop. "It would be good to have him taking class again," she said finally. "But we have little money with which to pay your ladyship."

"Perhaps a trade would be in order," Kayte said, thinking of her own advantage in the swap.

"A trade?"

"The children will take class all morning at DenMerrick," she explained, "then stay to work for me for three hours in the afternoons. We shall start tomorrow."

DenMerrick was undergoing revolutionary changes. The days passed quickly as Kayte tried to lose herself in the cleaning and clearing and mending. She polished furniture and scrubbed windows until she was sure the stench of vinegar would follow her to the grave, and mercilessly beat rugs hung on lines in the side yard. The work on the stables began unsteadily, but Justin had a keen, watchful eye, and he and the carpenter's apprentice soon became fast friends, which made the work easier for them both.

Within two weeks, the overgrown fields had been cleared, and Kayte took inventory of the grounds. The young men who sat in her classes each morning she set to repairing the grape arbors and scrubbing clean the three Italian statuettes that had been hidden beneath the weeds in the old rose garden.

She needed a gardener, she realized.

On the morning that heralded her first month at DenMerrick, she found the answer to her unspoken prayer. He appeared just after breakfast. Kayte went to greet her students at the front entryway and threw open the huge door to find an old, rather gaunt gray-haired gentleman surveying her land with interest.

"May I help you, sir?"

The man gave her a suspicious glance as she stood on the top step. "Your boys ain't so good," he said. "Too rough. If you don't take care with those grapevines, they'll snap. You've got a lot of years of growth there. Be a real shame to waste it."

Kayte sighed. "I know. If you can recommend a gardener, I'd hire him today."

"I wouldn't work for his lordship that devil again," he spat.

"Well, Mr—?"

"Walker. Hermann Walker."

"Well, Mr. Walker, you won't be working for his lordship, you'll be working for me." She stepped down to the freshly mortared walkway. "And if ever I hear you speak of my husband that way again, I shall cut your tongue out myself."

Kayte soon found that her threats were unnecessary. For a kind word and a fair wage, the man touched bare earth and made living things grow. Under Walker's control, the DenMerrick gardens took on a stately beauty.

With her own supervision, the house did equally well. But hard work and the satisfaction of refurbishing DenMerrick were not enough to keep Kayte from lying awake at night, praying for the return of her husband . . . and of his love.

Chapter 19

Daevon had returned to London in mid-July. He departed with the *Sea Lady* two days later, unwilling to delay the launching for even one day. The crewmen complained and crossed themselves. Launching on the thirteenth, as Daevon ordered them to do, would mean ill luck for them all. But they were accustomed to Daevon Merrick's temper and had no desire to test it. When he came aboard and demanded they sail, they sailed.

A hasty message had been conveyed by Daevon's last courier from New Orleans. Darby's sister Evelyn and her husband Luke were settled there, and along with his other requests, Luke had written for stores for the winter months. Evelyn sent her love, inviting Daevon to come to America with the shipment. They longed for a visit and hoped he would honor them.

It was a good enough excuse. Daevon needed to escape to the sea, forgetting what he left behind him on the shore. He closed up DenMerrick House, dismissed all the servants to other family estates, and left.

At that moment he wondered what Kayte was doing. Was she making the best of her situation?

The emotional glaze clouding his reason cleared quickly and Daevon knew she would not be thinking of him like some lovestruck puppy.

"Damn her to hell where her mother lies," he muttered, steering the *Sea Lady* into a lunging wave. "I've had enough of women."

Lyle Miller made his first appearance at DenMerrick late in August, sweltering beneath the properly stiff cloth-

ing of a gentleman caller. He was surprised when his hasty
knock was answered by a slim, silver-haired woman in a
black gown and immaculately white apron. She introduced
herself as Mrs. Graves, the housekeeper.

Upon introducing himself, Miller was ushered along the
wide entry corridor and through a door to the left. At first
he was certain he must have knocked on the wrong door.

DenMerrick was a polished gemstone, gleaming in the
light of late afternoon. Its windows glinted shafts of multicolored light onto the polished hardwood floors and walls
of dark cherry paneling. Most of the original furniture
remained, but it had been rubbed to a glossy finish
that made it seem new. Bright new fabrics covered the
couches and chairs and a small rose-colored settee had
been added.

Bowls of roses adorned every table, and even the curtains and huge Oriental carpets had been revived. Kaytlene
Merrick seemed determined to banish the old, dark shadows of DenMerrick and replace them with a freshness that
hinted of happiness and the joy of everyday living. He was
anxious to see the rest of the refurbished estate.

Upstairs, Darby reacted to the news of Lyle Miller's
arrival with a squeal of unabashed pleasure.

"Darby, please!" Kayte groaned. She had fallen into an
exhausted sleep an hour before, only to rise with a fierce
headache and a queasy thrumming that seemed to reach
from her throat down into her belly.

"You'll have to see him, Kayte," Darby replied more
softly. "He's here on business, I'm sure. Besides that, you
can't hide your pregnancy forever." She moved to help her
mistress out of bed.

"I don't want to hide it, Darby. I want it to disappear
altogether." With a bite of warm bread and a helping
hand, Kayte was able to dress. Darby brushed out her long
hair.

"All right, Darby. Let us see what sort of business Mr.
Miller has with us today."

Moments later, Kayte entered the front parlor and gratefully collapsed onto the flowered cambric sofa, fanning
herself with a handkerchief. She seemed not to notice Lyle
Miller's immediate look of concern.

"Can I help you, Lady Merrick? A drink perhaps?" He sat near her, taking over the fanning with a stiff sheet of paper.

"Thank you, no, Lyle. It's just this damnable heat."

Lyle seemed a bit confused by Kayte's transformation into a pale, trembling female.

"Don't be upset, Lyle." Kayte managed a smile. "I understand women have babies every day."

"Do you mean to say," he began harshly, rising, "that you're—"

"Going to have a baby, Mr. Miller." Almost inaudibly she added, "The heir of Merrick." She bit her lip hard to keep the familiar tears in check.

"Good God," he muttered. "Do you have any brandy here?"

Once Darby had shown him to the store of liquor, Lyle helped himself to a glass and sat down again, this time near the green-eyed Irish girl.

"Something's happened . . . to Daevon?" Kayte asked, trying to ignore her fear of what his answer might be.

"No. No, but if . . . if he had known he wouldn't have gone, Kayte. I swear it."

"Gone?" she repeated sadly. "Gone."

Lyle repeated the facts as he knew them, that Lord Merrick had received urgent pleas from several Americans, including Darby's family, for help in supplying them with necessities for the winter. "Daevon could hardly refuse. He wanted to see to the shipment personally."

"I see," Kayte said softly, staring through the massive front windows.

"Yes," Miller replied. He was surprised by the smile, the look of sudden strength and pride that came over Kaytlene's face.

"My traitor of a husband," she murmured absentmindedly. "I would expect no less." Then she turned to her guest with renewed vigor. "Come, Lyle. Let me show you the new DenMerrick."

Unlike the completed work that Miller had witnessed in the drawing room, much of the rest of the house was a mad bustle of activity. In the room directly across from the front parlor, two young women were sewing a ruffle at the

base of a long, overstuffed couch. Another was arranging
a vase of freshly cut flowers atop an ivory-inlaid desk.
Here, the walls had been paneled in the same dark
cherrywood, masking the cold gray stone beneath them.
The damaged fireplace had been repaired with new red
brick and its original green-veined marble mantel scrubbed
to a brilliant sheen. The furniture in this room had been
re-covered in a dark green silk delicately edged in a red
and gold ivy pattern. The curtains were of the same fabric,
as were the fat cushions that lined a window seat.

"You've done miracles here, Lady Merrick," was all
Lyle could say.

"I was hoping you would think so," she replied slyly,
"because I'll need a great deal more money to complete
the house."

By supper, Lyle Miller had been coaxed into becoming
DenMerrick's unofficial banker. As well as paying the
accounts for supplies and labor, he agreed to cover the
wages for the small staff Kayte had hired—a cook, Mr.
Walker the gardener, Justin, Darby, and Mrs. Graves the
housekeeper who had greeted Miller at the door. All of the
expenses would come from income from the estate.

"The students I teach in the mornings work for their
lessons in the afternoon, so most of the labor is free,"
Kayte explained over the roast chicken and new potatoes
Darby had prepared. "And I'll make do with as small a
staff as possible. I have no desire to drain his lordship's
coffers dry, but I also don't want this house to be an
embarrassment to him when he returns."

She went on to discuss her plans for improving the
house. The master suite on the upper level was being used
as storage space, and she would take up residence in the
refurbished guest chambers on the ground floor. Guests
would be housed in the tower bedrooms, servants upstairs
in a secluded wing. The chimneys were being cleared and
wood and coal bins filled with fuel for the long winter
ahead.

Kayte leaned back in her chair, rubbing a gnawing
cramp in her still-flat abdomen. "Do you think he'll return
by Christmas?" she asked, musing over the idea of how
lonely her past weeks had been. She could not bear the

thought of spending the winter without Daevon. Would he
be pleased that she was carrying his child? The child of a
whore . . .

"I couldn't say with much certainty," Miller stated
hesitantly. "I don't see why not. Would you . . . like me
to send a message? About the baby?"

"He probably won't care to know," she said sadly as
she rose. "He probably won't believe the child is his."

Darby and Lyle shared sad glances as the mistress hurried from the room.

Kaytlene Merrick spent her days waiting for news; hoping for the sound of Demon's hooves along the cobble-
stone walkways of DenMerrick. Days passed, hot and dry,
and nights, cool and even drier. October came with crisp
colors and spectacular grandeur. In less than three days
Kayte would celebrate her twenty-second birthday.

Without Daevon.

The work at DenMerrick had been completed a week
before, and with much better results than Kayte had ever
expected. That much was due to Lyle Miller's help. He
had been providing large amounts of money from the
accounts Daevon had left in his charge, paying wages and
buying materials required for the restoration. Lyle knew
that the earl would tear his heart out if he returned to find
his pregnant wife living like an impoverished widow. Lyle
did all he could to make her comfortable.

Kayte asked for nothing for herself. No clothes, no
jewelry. Not even a pair of new leather slippers to replace
those she had worn thin working in the rose garden,
though Lyle provided those as well. She continued to wear
her old, loose gowns, even though they were beginning to
show the marks of gardening, scrubbing, candle dipping,
jam making.

A great portion of the crops and livestock that were
normally sent to DenMerrick House were now diverted to
the estate. The lands to the west of DenMerrick were used
freely by the townspeople, and they gave their portions
gladly. Even those who were wary of his lordship had
grown to love his wife. She taught their children, nursed

their ill, and brought beauty and life to the place that had been standing empty for the past twenty years.

Kayte hired many of the village men to work on the grounds and in the growing DenMerrick stables, paying fair wages for good work. She was an honest taskmaster and much more pleasant to look upon than most.

The lady herself sat in the thickly padded window seat of the master bedroom, pleased with the home she had created. Three rooms comprised the suite, two large bedchambers and a smaller one, all of which lay connected on the ground floor facing east.

The smallest room had been transformed into an elegant bath. The bedchamber was swathed in lavender and gray with thick carpeting of darkest violet. A set of shelves lined one wall, along with a drop-leaf writing table. The huge bed was a hand-carved masterpiece. Made of highly polished mahogany with a scalloped headboard adorned with large flowers of mother-of-pearl and jade, it was draped with a canopy of violet silk and gray netting that fell into cascades of violet and gray ribbons at the corner posts.

The second bedchamber had been converted into a sitting room, much like the arrangement at DenMerrick House, and was decorated in darker grays and black. The fireplaces in both rooms retained their original stonework, the white marble mantels adorned with the small ivory statues Daevon favored, which Lyle had ordered brought from London.

Kaytlene wondered if her husband would ever occupy the rooms. If he would even see them. She turned her attention back to the scene beyond her windows.

From her vantage point, she had a fine view of the thriving grape arbors, the stables, and the pond where a group of ducks had taken up residence.

"Kayte?" Darby's brown curls bobbed as she poked her head into an open bedchamber door.

"Yes, Darby?"

"Are you feeling well? Enough to receive visitors, I mean?"

"Is it—?" she began hopefully.

"No," Darby said quietly, "it isn't his lordship. But they've come from London to see you."

Kayte went along eagerly, glad to have some new diversion to ease her loneliness. In the entry hall she stopped short.

"Kayte!" Tristan came forward from the doorway, arms outstretched to enclose her in a boisterous hug.

"Tristan!" Kayte pulled away quickly.

"Surprised to see me? I'm sorry it took so long to get here, but Daevon left me a load of work to finish before he shipped out. I've brought you some company."

As he stepped out of Kayte's way, a familiar figure appeared in his place. "Monique," Kayte murmured, unsure whether she was pleased or disappointed in the face of such company.

"How nice to see you, *chèrie!*" Monique came into the hall, her royal-blue satin coat making Kayte uncomfortably aware of her own stained beige muslin dress.

"Please forgive our intrusion, Lady Merrick," Monique said softly. "We won't impose on your hospitality. You don't seem quite prepared for guests." There was a hint of sarcasm in her voice that made Kayte's spine stiffen.

"We'll take a room in the village, then," a voice behind Monique said cheerfully. It was that familiar tone which made Kayte decide she would enjoy this company after all.

"Forrest!" She exclaimed.

He strode forward and gave her a pleased smile and a gentle hug.

"Darby, see that Geoffrey takes the bags to the tower. Tristan will have the east room and Lord and Lady Clay the west."

"Yes, Lady Merrick." Darby smiled craftily as she followed orders, anxious to see the reactions of their guests when they were confronted with the new DenMerrick.

"And please ask the cook to prepare us some tea. We'll take it in the library."

"Yes, my lady."

Kayte smiled warmly, taking Tristan's arm. "Let me show you my home," she said graciously.

By the time they reached the library, the largest room on the lower floor, only Kayte was unaffected by the tour. Monique lowered herself into a deep blue velvet setee. To

Kayte's delight and pride, Lady Clay could not find her tongue for several minutes.

While the men praised Kayte on her excellent taste in color and furniture, Monique studied her with odd disdain. When she finally spoke, it was with sticky-sweet venom.

"Forgive me, *chèrie*," she said, "but I was given to believe his lordship had left you without . . ."

"I don't know what you were told," Kayte replied pleasantly. She had no intention of feeding the hope evident in Monique's eyes. "His lordship left me with instructions to refurbish the estate and provided enough assets to accomplish it. I think he'll be pleased, don't you?"

"Of course," Monique answered, becoming a little more pleasant. "It's just that he seemed angry when I saw him the evening before he sailed."

Kayte flashed her eyes up to a lovely portrait of Lady Anna Merrick holding a black-haired baby in her arms—Daevon. What was Monique hinting at? That Daevon had spent his last night in London with her? A determined smile formed on Kayte's lips as she realized that the child she carried would altogether destroy Monique's ideas of having Daevon.

"He *was* very angry," Kayte said plainly.

"Oh?" Monique's brows rose in surprise.

"Yes. I'm a little ashamed to say why. You see, before Daevon left I told him I suspected I was with child."

A shocked gasp came from Monique and the men paused in their own conversation.

"He wanted to stay, but it was too late to change his plans. When I assured him that women do very nicely without their husbands in constant attendance, he was angry that I didn't seem to need him here. I suppose I hurt his pride, but I won't be keeping him housebound like a little boy."

"And are we expecting a Merrick heir?" Tristan asked pleasantly.

"Yes. In early April, I think."

"Congratulations, my dear," Forrest added more enthusiastically.

"Well, I'm certain Daevon will be returning home soon,

since he is so concerned for you and the child," Monique said coldly.

"Yes." Kayte smiled a little stiffly. "I'm certain he will." Her eyes were on the picture again as she prayed it would be so.

Three days later, the *Sea Lady* was moving at incredible speed back to England. The near-empty holds had been filled with just enough food and fresh water to keep the crew fed.

Captain Stephenson had never seen the earl in such a black humor. He was far too quiet, spending his days repairing the rails, tending to the injured men, even sitting on deck with the crew mending sails and cleaning muskets.

On the last day of October, the captain found his friend standing at the bow, the late evening wind snapping the edges of his black cloak. His work-callused hands grasped the new section of railing, his storm-gray eyes staring out to sea as if the intensity of his gaze could pull him nearer to the shores of England. Stephenson had seen that look of loneliness and longing on the faces of many men on his ship, but never before had Daevon Merrick allowed such emotion to show.

"Good evening, Daevon." Stephenson joined the man at the rail. "Brooding about something?"

Daevon shot him a searing glance but said nothing.

"I'm sorry, Daevon. It's just that you haven't been yourself since we left Baltimore."

Merrick's expression softened. "Today is my wife's birthday," he said sadly, again turning his gaze out to sea.

The first official celebration to take place at DenMerrick occurred with little pomp. A simple dinner had been prepared, to please Kayte's uneasy stomach, with a white-frosted cake for dessert. The cook placed the confection at the head of the table, its candles glowing softly against Kayte's hair as she bent to blow out the flames.

"Make your wish," the cook said in her German accent, and Kayte closed her eyes to obey.

Please, she whispered to herself, *please come home to me, Daevon. And love me again.*

An enthusiastic cheer went up as all the candles were extinguished and the cake was cut slice by slice. Gifts were presented and Kayte opened them in the drawing room.

There were two hand-carved hair combs from Darby, delicate pieces made of pink shell and set in a box of black velvet. An engraved silver hairbrush and comb from Lord and Lady Clay, and a gown of deep green velvet from Tristan.

"I thought you would like something to greet your husband in when he returns," he said boyishly as she thanked him with a soft kiss.

Her guests departed a few days later, after promising to return for Christmas. Kayte refused to return to London with them, despite Tristan's repeated attempts to persuade her. She wanted to be at DenMerrick when Daevon came home.

As her visitors' coach drove away, Kayte stood in the doorway watching the first silver-gray clouds of November race across the sky. Winter set itself down around the estate with a cold, quiet foreboding.

Suddenly there was very little to do. Kayte was grateful to have lost the sickness that had plagued her early pregnancy, and gradually she regained her color and appetite. She and Darby sat reading or embroidering in the evenings. Kayte wrote long, cheerful letters to Elizabeth and Sean O'Connell, continued teaching the village children, and spent her nights longing for the arms of her husband. She knelt every day gazing out of the huge windows of her bedchamber, praying for his safe return. And frequently her thoughts turned to Anna Merrick and her untimely, still-unexplained death. Who could have poisoned her and why? And had the murderer deliberately manipulated events to make it look as though Kayte had killed her mother-in-law?

Haunted by unanswered questions, and longing for her husband, Kayte fought to hide her underlying unhappiness.

On the afternoon of the first snowfall, Kayte, Darby, the cook, and Mrs. Graves were seated around the dining room table having tea and cakes and discussing the arrangements and menus for Christmas. A blast of wind and scouring snow shook the windows, rattling the inside shutters. Reluctantly, Kayte closed them and pulled the heavy drapes. She hated to lose the light but supposed that would be better than freezing to death.

Several minutes later the rattling resumed and Kayte realized it was not the windows.

"The door," she exclaimed, and ran toward it, her hopes rising. She pulled the huge front door open to a gust of snow and two figures shivering on the step.

"Come in," she said against the sound of the wind. They obeyed silently. When the door closed, Kayte found the bundled figures unwrapping themselves. One was Kitty, a girl who sat classes with her each morning. The other was a bent old woman with hair as white as the snow that smothered her shoulders, and piercing eyes as blue as the sea.

"Good afternoon, Lady Merrick," Kitty said, a smile on her cold-reddened face. "This is my grandmother. She asked if I would bring her here to see you."

"Oh?" Kayte looked up as the old woman disappeared into the sitting room.

"My grandmother is a seer," Kitty explained.

"A what?"

"She sees the future, the past. She wanted to speak to you alone. I hope we haven't disturbed you."

"No, Kitty. Don't be silly." Kayte was more than a little intrigued. "I'll see her. You run along and see if Darby can find you some hot chocolate."

The grandmother was seated in a wingback chair, her back as stiff as the seat's, as Kayte closed the doors of the room to secure their privacy.

"You wanted to see me?" Kayte sat on the couch several feet away and waited for a reply. She felt oddly uncomfortable as the old woman's eyes scanned her, resting for a long moment on her swelling abdomen.

"A male child," the seer said dryly. "You must be careful for his safety."

"I will," Kayte replied, now eager to hear what this woman knew of her.

"No," the older woman said sharply, as if she read Kayte's thoughts, "I do not mean be careful to eat prop-

erly or not to strain yourself. I mean be careful to keep
him safe from others.''

"Others?"

"Others who wish your child harm. Who wish for you
to be out of their way."

Kayte sucked in a long breath, trying to understand.
"Kitty says you see the future. And the past."

"You want to know when he returns."

"Yes." Her voice was a sorrowful plea. "Please."

"Soon he returns. From the sea, yes?"

Kayte nodded.

"He is sorry to miss your celebration."

"My birthday." Kayte smiled. "Does he—"

"Love you?"

Kayte held her breath, annoyed by the woman's calm,
even tone of voice.

"Do you not already know in your own heart?"

"I don't. I'm . . . not certain."

"Then none other may know, either. You don't enjoy
my riddles, eh? Then we will speak of the past. And of
present dangers."

"I don't understand."

"We will speak of the past. Your past. This house.
Your mother, the whore who sold herself for a few jewels
and died in the room upstairs."

"How do you know about her?"

The blue eyes swept over Kayte again, this time meeting
her wavering amber gaze. "Ah." The woman nodded, as
if pleased. "You know other truths as well, I see. About
your brother."

"Yes. Tristan."

"Half brother. Blood of your mother and of Merrick."

"What do you know of it?"

The woman pulled a long black scarf from around her
neck, revealing a scar that nearly circled her throat. Kayte
gasped.

"I saw your husband into the world," she said, ignoring
Kayte's shock at her deformity.

"You were Lady Merrick's midwife."

"Yes. And when your mother came to this house, I
assisted her as well. Merrick gave me this scar. As soon as

I delivered Patrice of her bastard son, he saw to it that I would be silenced. I was left for dead.''

"Why are you here?" Kayte whispered, not entirely certain she wanted to know.

"To warn you. Tristan wants what your mother wanted—control. He will do anything to have it.''

Kayte sighed, resting one hand protectively on her stomach. She knew that if Daevon was with her, she would not be afraid, but facing Tristan alone was another matter. Just how far would he go to get control? Would he try to rid her of Daevon's heir? Kayte's chest felt constricted and she found it hard to breathe. There was still one thing she wanted to ask the woman.

"Who killed them? Who killed Merrick and my mother?" It brought an almost physical pain to refer to the woman with such a gentle title.

"His lordship your husband holds that secret in his heart. And in his fear.'' With that, the woman rose. "I will go now. You may send for me if you have need.''

"Thank you,'' Kayte replied.

They left the room together and found Kitty already bundling up in her shawl and coat in the entryway.

"How did you know we were finished?" Kayte asked the girl.

"She has a bit of me in her, I venture," the old woman answered, obviously pleased by the notion.

Kayte helped them into their wraps and watched as they disappeared into the white blur of snow outside.

The first two weeks of November passed with a light powdering of snow, though Mrs. Graves insisted that before another week was gone they would have the season's first major storm.

Kayte considered canceling her invitation to Tristan and the Clays to come for Christmas, wondering whether Daevon would return by then. But she knew Tristan might arrive at DenMerrick at any time, and canceling their scheduled visit would not keep him away if he was intent on coming alone. She preferred to have other people at DenMerrick when Tristan was there—Forrest, Monique, and their children—and she would keep Lyle or Darby with her at all times. Her bedchamber doors could be securely locked from the inside. She would be safe enough, she decided.

Even Daevon, who had kept Tristan out of DenMerrick House because his trust in his brother had been destroyed, had assured her that Tristan could never kill. If Daevon had thought Tristan meant her harm, he would have forbidden him to come to DenMerrick as well. She waited for her guests to arrive from London and prayed that Daevon would return by Christmas.

The London entourage arrived four days before Christmas, bundled in furs against the cold and bearing gifts to celebrate the season.

Monique seemed to be in a more pleasant mood, chattering away about domestic difficulties and the latest London gossip. Tristan brought several more gowns, designed by a London couturier, to accommodate Kayte's pregnancy while allowing her to stay fashionable. She had not yet worn the green velvet gown, but now she put it on for the first dinner of their visit. She brushed her hair and secured it with the delicate pink shell combs, leaving two wisps of curls falling over her ears.

She went to the dining hall to join her guests for dinner and was met in the doorway by Forrest Clay.

"You're even more lovely than the first time I saw you, Lady Merrick." Forrest offered his arm, leading her to the head of the table. She sat stiffly, grateful for a man's strength to lean on, but skittish because of Tristan's presence and the memory of the old woman's warnings. As Kayte smiled up into Forrest's appreciative eyes, he whispered softly to her, "He'll be home soon, I'm certain. No man could stay away from you for long, Kayte."

The evening progressed well, with dinner followed by drinks in the sitting room. Kayte avoided Tristan and was constantly attended by either Darby or Lyle, who had also come for dinner, as he often did these days. Tristan hardly seemed to notice Kayte, and she began to relax. He did not seek her out or try to lure her away from her other guests. He read, discussed business with Forrest Clay, and made every attempt to be pleasant.

Still, his presence made her uncomfortable. By the time she had decided to retire, the men were involved in a game of cards, so it was easy to slip away to her chambers and secure the doors before changing into a warm nightgown and climbing into bed.

She wondered if her husband would ever sleep here, by her side, and sighed. She had spent so many tears over Daevon's absence that now she had no desire to weep. Instead, she closed her eyes and remembered the soft, deep sound of his voice against her ear, the way her body had fit so perfectly against his hard length.

She thought of the day he had carried her over his shoulder to the stables and their laughter when she caused them both to fall. She relived the memories a hundred times over. Every word he had said, every gentle brush of his lips over hers, every caress of his hand, she savored.

Where was he tonight?

Was he with some experienced whore, taking his pleasure as he had with Kaytlene on their last night together at the inn? A tear slid down her cheek, disappearing into the tangled mass of dark curls. Her mood had been unpredictable of late, but now her torment raged anew like the winter storm that had begun to whirl outside the walls of DenMerrick. The wind howled against the windows, shaking them mercilessly, and Kayte shuddered as if the storm were assaulting her. The roaring fire in the bedchamber and the heavy layers of quilts piled over her did little to ease the chills that plagued her.

Finally she succumbed to sleep. Snow-reflected moonlight bathed the room while Kayte surrendered to Daevon's dream lovemaking, climbing the heights of pleasure in his imagined arms. Forgotten were the threats of the past and of the guests who slept in DenMerrick, with their plans of desire and revenge.

Dawn crept over the snow-laden estate, barely warming the chill winter air. It found Lady Clay and Tristan Merrick sharing tense whispers in the sitting room.

"You promised we'd be rid of her by now, my darling," Monique said as she paced before the windows, making a poor attempt to conceal the apprehension and anger in her tone.

"All in good time, my dear." Tristan yawned, stretching his long, muscular legs and rolling his eyes in an impatient gesture that raised Monique's ire all the more.

"By Christmas!" the raven-haired woman demanded. "You shall do away with her by Christmas or I'll do it myself."

"You idiot of a female!" Tristan stood finally, attempting to keep his angry tone low. "Don't you know where my honorable brother is right now?" His voice was coldly menacing, sending a chill up Monique's spine.

She shook her head.

"In America," he replied. "Smuggling illegal goods to the Americans under the noses of the bloody English. How about that!" He grinned at his lover's shocked expression. "Yes, sweet Monique, your beloved Daevon is a traitor. And he may soon be a dead traitor."

"Dead?" she whispered harshly.

"Yes," Tristan answered. "All to our advantage. You see, if he doesn't return, I shall have to marry the poor widow myself. For the sake of the child, of course."

Monique recognized only too well the devious gleam in Tristan's eyes. "Don't tease me, Tristan. I'm not in the mood."

"Are you so certain I'm teasing, my dear?"

"You bastard!"

The door snapped open, silencing the laugh that threatened to spill from Tristan's lips. He nearly coughed instead at the sight of Kaytlene standing in the open doorway. She had thrown on her plain brown robe of homespun wool, and even its rustic lack of fashion made her as appealing as she had ever been. She had not brushed the long cinnamon-colored hair that curled in wild disarray down her shoulders and back.

"I'm terribly sorry," she mumbled uneasily, surprised to find her guests awake so early. "I . . . just came to retrieve my book," she added.

Tristan picked up a volume bound in dark blue and brought it to her. "Here you are, my dear. But you must forgive us for waking you at such an hour."

Kaytlene clutched the book to her breast, stepping back into the corridor. "You didn't . . . wake me, Tristan. Thank you." She hurried away.

Once she had gone and the sitting room doors were closed, Tristan went back to the settee.

"You'll stay," he said finally.

"What?"

"Once Forrest and I have gone, I want you to offer to stay behind."

"Have you another plan, *mon cher*?"

"Yes."

Monique's eyes narrowed. It was obvious that Tristan had no intention of telling her the details, but she had a right to know, and a way of finding out. She sat close to him on the settee and began to caress his thigh.

"Do you not trust me, my love?" she purred into his ear, nibbling his earlobe. Her hand slid up to the juncture of his thighs and she heard him moan softly.

"It has been too long, Tristan," she breathed. She knew he was ready to take her, there on the couch. She rose, locked the doors, and came to stand before him. He dragged her down to straddle his lap, and she pulled her skirts out of the way as he unfastened his breeches and filled her with his hardness. She groaned, grinding her hips against his.

Tristan took her quickly, pumping himself into her until he brought them both to climax. When they had both straightened their clothing afterward, he smiled.

"Very well, my pet," he said. "You've paid the price. Now what do you want for it?" He knew her sudden passionate mood was only a ploy to get what she really wanted.

"Your plan."

"You stay here and keep Kayte from leaving DenMerrick. Make certain she has no contact with anyone outside the household. I expect Daevon back soon, and I don't want her to know it."

"But why?"

"Because, my dear girl, I am going to tell Daevon that his poor little wife died in the act of miscarrying his child."

"But why would you want him to think—"

"Because it will make him weak. It will keep him drunk for at least a week."

"And then?"

"And then, my sweet, I may be able to get Daevon to sign half of the Merrick holdings over to me. Without his ladylove to give him heirs, what reason will he have to keep it all? In the state he'll be in, he'll have very little care for anything but his guilt. After all, he left her here—alone—without the proper medical care that she might have received in London. She was so distressed by his desertion that she miscarried and then bled to death."

Monique smiled. "And then we will kill her?"

"No. I'll convert my assets into cash and come here to take Kayte with me. France, perhaps. Or Ireland. You can have Morley fix you up a little potion to get rid of Forrest, and then you can nurse my brother out of his depression. He'll be so indebted to you that he'll marry you, and we'll all get what we want."

"You are too clever, darling," Monique cooed.

Tristan smiled in answer. Yes, he was far too clever—for her, at least. He intended to see his brother commit suicide in his grief—with his own help, of course. Tristan himself would then marry the grieving widow to give her child a father, and Monique be damned. If she caused problems, she could be easily eliminated.

Monique, too, was thinking about Tristan's new plot. She liked it, but it left something to be desired . . .

Kaytlene Newell Merrick deserved to suffer for having taken Daevon away from her.

And Monique knew just what sort of pain to inflict . . .

Christmas passed without Daevon. Kayte tried desperately to believe that he would return to her, and it was only that hope that kept her from succumbing to depression. Hope, and the fact that she carried his child. No matter what happened, she would always have a child born of their love.

As the New Year arrived, Tristan and Forrest returned to London, along with the children and their nanny. Monique asked Kayte if she might stay, and Kayte was glad to agree. Darby had been keeping her company in the evenings, but she knew the girl was only doing so out of selfless duty and would much rather pass her time with

Lyle Miller. Kayte had been feeling guilty about keeping them apart and had tried to convince Darby that she would be well enough if left alone, but Darby insisted on caring for her like a mother hen. With another woman in the house, it would be easy to convince Darby to see her beau.

Unfortunately, however, that very day Lyle was called to London on business and didn't even have a chance to say goodbye. He sent a note instead, saying he expected to return within a fortnight.

On the second day of January, Kayte sat in a splash of sunlight in the library, absently studying the details of the room. As Darby made a final, cheerful attempt at interesting her in a particularly intricate piece of needlework, the doors burst open and Monique appeared, her eyes wild with emotion.

"Kayte!" she gasped breathlessly. "Dear God!" She stumbled into the room, falling at Kayte's feet and grasping her hands.

Kayte's eyes went to Monique, then strayed to a figure lingering in the doorway.

"For goodness sakes, Lady Clay," Darby said sharply as she, too, noted the man in the entryway, "get hold of yourself! What's happened?"

"He's . . . dead!" Monique cried.

Kayte stiffened and came to life once more. "Daevon?" she murmured.

"Yes! Oh, dear Lord, Kayte, I'm sorry."

"No!" Kayte threw herself out of the chair with unholy strength. "No, it isn't true. He's coming back to me!" Kayte's head jerked around at the sound of Darby's sobs. "No!" she told her. "Don't cry! He isn't dead. He isn't." She turned to Monique. "Monique . . ." She choked on her tears. "Please . . . it isn't true. It isn't true."

"You must be still, Kayte. Think of the baby," Monique replied softly.

Kayte started pacing the room. Her mind was numb, her heart screaming that it must be a lie. It must!

"How do you know this?" Kayte turned on Monique, her tone accusing. "You're lying! You want him for yourself. You'd say anything to be rid of me!"

Monique shook her head. "I know why he was in

America, Kayte. Smuggling goods to them for the winter.
They were found out, Kayte. On their return voyage, they
were stopped by an English blockade and boarded. I received the message from Forrest only a moment ago.''

Kayte froze in the middle of the room. Monique could
not have known of Daevon's secret life unless she was
somehow part of it. Could she have been? Or perhaps
Forrest was helping Daevon and they both knew. Her
thoughts were swimming. Was her beloved husband, the
father of her child, dead? Oh, God, was he dead?

"No," she moaned, sinking to her knees. "Daevon
loves me. He loves me. He's coming back to me . . ."
And, weeping, she fell to the floor.

Vaguely, Kayte was aware of being carried a short
distance and laid down on her own bed. Voices spoke
soothingly, offering hope and explanation.

"That damnable crusade of his," Monique was saying
between tears. "He was working to help them to the very
last."

And Kayte heard another voice, oddly familiar. A dose
of bitter medicine was poured into her mouth and trickled
down her throat. A gentle hand soothed away her pain. A
doctor. Thank God, Darby must have sent for a doctor.

Kayte sank gratefully into a sleep that consumed her like
death.

Chapter 20

Tristan pulled a heavy wool cloak around his shoulders and braced himself to face the harsh snow as he stepped from his carriage. He was out of the coach and through the tall, elaborately carved doors of the Merrick offices on the pier before the cold could penetrate his outer clothing. As soon as he was inside, he shed the snow-covered cloak and tossed it over a brass hook on a coat rack. Ignoring the pleasant "Good mornings" of the clerks in their well-lit cubicles, Tristan Merrick made his way to his brother's office.

Two hours before, he had been rudely roused from a pleasant sleep, only to be informed that the *Sea Lady* had docked and Daevon Merrick was expecting him in his offices promptly at ten o'clock. There had been scarcely enough time to dispatch a message for Monique. Knowing that Kayte was the source of Monique's vile jealousy, Tristan had sent his regards attached to a spectacular ruby bracelet. He hoped the silly French bitch would have enough sense to faithfully follow the details of his plan. One simple mistake could cost him everything now.

The door embossed with Daevon's name and title loomed before him, and Tristan set his intricate plans into motion. He entered to find his brother furiously sorting through a pile of documents on his desk.

Daevon grumbled as he finished the last of the paperwork that had piled up in his absence. He was still dressed in coarse black breeches and a loose white shirt, a week's worth of stubble on his jaw. His hair was mussed, curling up at his nape, and he was tired.

The one thought that consumed him was a desire to see Kayte again. God, but he had wanted her so badly the past weeks that it had become a physical ache. She was an obsession that he couldn't cleanse from his blood. Perhaps a few nights in her bed would ease . . .

He looked up to find Tristan standing before his desk.

"Hello, Tristan."

"Welcome home, Daevon." There was an edge to Tristan's voice that caused Daevon's eyes to narrow.

"What's wrong, Tristan?"

"I'm sorry, Daevon. You're taking it well, I see. As one would expect from a Merrick."

"What are you talking about?"

Tristan went to the rear of the desk where his brother sat, staring out at the chopping waves beyond the pier.

"Tristan," Daevon said wearily, "if you've come to discuss mother's will, I've already told you that I would not try to cheat you of your rightful part of the holdings."

"It hardly matters now, Daevon." Tristan turned to face his brother. "I can hardly grieve for a loss of money when you have lost so much more."

The strange, soft quality had returned to Tristan's voice, and Daevon noticed that he seemed to be holding back tears. Tears were something Tristan Merrick had never given in to.

"If it's Kayte you're worried about," Daevon said, "I'm leaving as soon as I get a change of clothes. I don't know if we can work this all out, Tristan. I still don't know who could have put that poison in—"

"Dear God, Daevon, has no one told you?" Tristan's eyes were wide with shock.

"Told me what, for heaven's sake?"

Daevon's throat constricted with fear as his brother sank into a chair, head in his hands.

"What's happened to Kayte?" He said the words slowly, as if wanting to delay the answer he feared was forthcoming.

"My God, Daevon! My God," Tristan choked, "she's dead!"

A book fell from the desk, but Daevon hardly heard it strike the floor.

"Dead?"

"Barely a fortnight ago," his brother whispered. "I sent a message. I thought you knew. They were to tell you as soon as you came into port."

Daevon's heart twisted within his chest as a terrible pain assaulted him. His hand shook.

"Dead?" he murmured. He thought of the golden eyes that had tormented him for the past months, the sweetness of her body beneath his, the voice that he had tried so desperately to catch as it floated through his dreams. Never again. Never again to touch the perfect, fragrant skin. Never again to win back her love.

"How did it happen, Tristan?" Daevon's voice was miraculously free of the pain that ripped at his soul.

"Daevon," he replied reluctantly.

"I have a right to know! I . . . loved her, Tristan."

"You should never have left her alone." Tristan was beginning to enjoy his lie, torturing his brother with guilt until he delivered the final, devastating blow.

"I know." Daevon groaned into his hands. "I was a fool. But I couldn't bear to think that she might have . . . Besides, she was so strong. So determined. I thought she would make DenMerrick a home again. Dear God, I was such a fool."

"She refused to leave, Daevon. She wanted to be there when you came back for her. And, yes, she did turn DenMerrick into a showplace."

Daevon smiled faintly. He had come home hoping he could love her again, but now she was gone. Dead!

"Was she ill?"

"She was pregnant, Daevon." The final blow struck, Tristan could not have been more pleased by the earl's horrified reaction. "Didn't you know? It was all too much for her. She taught the village children in the mornings, slaved all afternoon to make the place something you would be proud of. She lost the child, and the miscarriage took her as well. Bled to death."

Daevon stared straight ahead, his heart turning colder than the gray morning beyond the windows. Disbelief washed over him.

"I want to see . . . the grave," he whispered softly. "Now."

"Of course." Tristan nodded.

Daevon slipped on a thick overcoat and followed his brother to the street, where they entered the waiting Merrick coach and headed back toward DenMerrick House and the little cemetery where Anna Merrick had been buried.

Tristan smiled inwardly as the coach lumbered through the muddy roads and came to a jarring stop. Daevon followed him as he stepped out into the snowy field that served as the family burial ground.

After leaving DenMerrick, Tristan had begun to fit the pieces of his plan together, and this was but one of them. He pointed toward a spot beneath a huge tree whose stripped branches creaked under a weight of snow.

Daevon knelt, his gloved hand brushing the snow from a small headstone.

KAYTLENE NEWELL MERRICK

BELOVED WIFE

1786–1808

Daevon's hands clenched into fists.

I won't let anyone hurt you. Or take you away from me ever again, he had told her when he'd rescued her from the hired killer. And now it was he who stood guilty of both.

His eyes fell upon the tiny headstone on his right. He reached out to clear its face as well, his breath frozen with fear and longing. To his horror he read,

DAEVON ADAM MERRICK IV

DECEMBER 1808

Tristan thrust his head into the master bedchamber. Daevon had been sitting before the fire for several hours, silently consuming brandy, and Tristan was sure that his brother was completely intoxicated. He went to remove the glass decanter from Daevon's right hand and pulled a crumpled document from his left.

He had seen to it that Kayte's death certificate was conveniently placed where his brother would be certain to find it. The forgery had had the desired effect. He had also been careful to hire a few new house servants who knew nothing of past family matters. With DenMerrick House open to him, he had made good use of the time during Daevon's drunken stupor, searching through his brother's desk and personal belongings for more proof of his illegal trading. He found only one thing of value—an old, worn book. Patrice Newell's journal.

Daevon mumbled incoherently as Tristan helped him to his bed, where Daevon fell heavily onto the soft mattress.

"She was carrying my son," he said with a groan, the words slurred with brandy. "I loved her, Tristan."

"I know, Daevon. I know." Tristan loosened the buttons at Daevon's throat and smiled as his brother fell into unconsciousness.

"You're playing beautifully into my hands, Daevon," he whispered. "And now for the final steps of my plan."

Daevon's head had never throbbed so painfully, even after the vast quantities of liquor he had consumed on his last birthday. He groaned, throwing up one hand to shade his eyes from the white light of morning. His tongue tasted like wet flannel; his bare flesh was hot beneath the bed coverings. He closed his eyes, wanting only to escape reality.

His breath stopped sharply when a soft, white arm was thrown across his chest and a familiar scent of lilac seemed to clear his head. He opened his eyes in astonishment to see a head nestling against his shoulder, its brown hair splayed across pale shoulders.

"Kayte?" he breathed.

He held his breath as the woman stirred with a long sigh. Had it all been a dream?

He found himself staring into dark brown eyes and an unfamiliar smile.

"I told you last night my name isn't Kayte, darlin', but after your performance you can call me whatever you want."

Ignoring the pain in his head, Daevon sat up. "Who in the bloody hell are you?"

"Forgotten already, have you, love? That's not much of a compliment, is it now?"

"Get out of my bed!"

"Well!" the girl replied with affront as she stumbled off
the bed and began to dress. "If your father was as bad as
you say, then you certainly were right."

"What are you talking about?"

"Sweet Christ, you really don't remember, do you? All
last night while you were gettin' drunk and makin' love to
me, you said you were just like your father. If you hadn't
been so luscious in bed, darlin', I would have left you for
a madman. Mumblin' about killin' women in bed. Really!"

The woman felt the thick bundle of pound notes Tristan
Merrick had given her several hours before, and knew he
would be satisfied with the performance she had given.
She smiled seductively at Daevon, thinking it was a shame
she hadn't gotten a real taste of him.

Daevon's eyes closed again. "Get out," he said roughly.
"Get out of my house."

Arthur Morley was enjoying the comforts of DenMerrick.
He had arrived the day before after being summoned by
Monique, and her promise of payment had been generous.

In the kitchens, he checked the precise color and odor of
the concoction he had prepared. The snowstorm had prevented him from finding enough of a particular root for his
needs and he grumbled at the faint reddish color of the
mixture.

"Good enough!" he snapped, heading for the patient's
bedchamber. The house was unusually quiet, its staff having been dismissed. No visitors were permitted, and Morley himself kept a close watch on Darby, the only person
who was allowed to roam the house freely. The girl was
needed to cook and clean—tasks which Monique would
never have resorted to doing—and Morley found Darby
amusing.

Entering the master bedchambers, Morley saw Darby
kneeling by her lady's bed to collect the bed linens she had
just replaced. The girl straightened, frowned, and eyed
with suspicion the mixture Morley held.

"What are you giving her now?" she demanded. Her
voice startled Kayte, who groaned in an uneasy sleep.

"Quiet, girl," Morley murmured as he took a seat at

Kaytlene's side. "It's an herbal remedy. Quite potent."
With a practiced hand he felt the weak pulse at Kaytlene's
throat. He felt an unfamiliar twinge of remorse at the
girl's condition. She had become deathly pale and lethar-
gic, not altogether from the medications he had been ad-
ministering. Morley had seen similar cases before and
knew her distraught state of mind would aid his cause
greatly. Her spirit, her will to live, had been crushed to
nothing.

The once gleaming amber eyes were dark, hollow, and
dull. Her exquisite hair lay in tangles against her pillow.
Her soft pink mouth had lost its lush color, and she
constantly murmured her husband's name in her sleep.

Morley waited until Darby had gone off with the soiled
linens before he roused his patient as best he could. She
drank the potion from the glass he held, not bothering to
object to its bitter taste and smell. Then she returned to
sleep.

Morley touched her hand where it lay protectively over
her abdomen and noted the immediate flush of color on her
skin. Her breath quickened at once and she unconsciously
reached up with her free hand to pull the coverlets from
her chest. The thick gown she wore clung to her body as
she began to sweat. Even in her illness the soft curves of
her breasts were enticing beneath the open neckline.

When Morley felt the first violent contraction beneath
his hand, he got up from the bed. It would work, he was
certain. He left the chamber, not wanting to take part in
the bloody scene that would follow. Monique had hired
him to administer the concoction; whatever happened afterward was God's doing.

"Where in the hell are you going?" Morley snapped at
Darby as she fled past the bedchamber door wearing her
heaviest boots, cloak, and gloves.

"I . . . Justin was going into the village for some
supplies for Lady Clay, and I thought it would be nice to
get some fresh air."

Morley's hand clamped down hard on her arm. "Liar!"
he spat. "Did you think to bring back some help for your
poor mistress?"

"You bastard!" she returned, her voice full of fury.

"You're no doctor. I don't know what you're doing to her, but it has to stop!" She attempted to wrench away from his hand but found him more of an adversary than she had at first thought. He pulled her toward him, one arm pinning her to his chest.

"If you love your mistress," he said threateningly, "you'll stay in this house and keep silent. Do you understand me?"

Darby was about to reply when a scream of violent pain came from Kaytlene's room.

"It seems your mistress has need of you, Darby." Morley smiled sweetly and pushed her toward the door.

Three days later, Kaytlene woke to late afternoon sunlight gleaming onto her face, feeling as though her limbs would never move again. Her hair was matted and tangled, her gown and linens dotted with blood.

Her hand went to the flat, soft flesh of her abdomen, and a fresh wave of pain tore at her. Through a nightmare-blurred memory she recalled her own screams—cries of pain and terror that did little to ease the loss of her child. Daevon's child.

A weak sob escaped her. How could God be so cruel as to take her husband, only to cheat her of their son as well? Daevon had brought meaning to her life. Their love had surpassed the most fantastic dream of any passion-starved girl.

Now he was gone, killed fighting for an ideal he held precious, and the child he had given life had joined him in death. With an incredible strain of numb limbs and aching muscle, Kayte sat up and brought her feet to the floor. Daevon would not have wanted her to lie around forever in a self-pitying heap. She must act the mistress of DenMerrick, in a manner that would have made him proud.

When she emerged from her bath in a cloud of steam, she felt as though the hot water had evaporated most of the lingering illness from her body. She was still a bit sore and stiff, but the rituals of dressing and combing out her clean, wet hair seemed to return her to some semblance of normality.

When Darby quietly entered Kayte's bedchamber, it was to find her mistress fastening the buttons of her gown.

"Kayte!" The women shared a tearful hug. "How are you feeling?"

"Sore. Thank you, Darby, for helping me through this ordeal. I'm afraid I'll have to lean on you during these next few weeks."

"I . . . I did the best I could, Kayte. I pray it was enough."

"I know, Darby. Perhaps if this damnable village had a decent physician . . ."

"But we had a . . . doctor. Dr. Morley's still here. Kayte, I think he gave you something to make you lose the child."

A wave of realization swept over Kayte. In her dream-like memories of the past days, she recalled Monique's face.

"Darby, is Lady Clay still here?"

"Yes. She dismissed the cook and Mrs. Graves."

"Dismissed? How dare she!" Kayte's fists clenched. "I want to see Lady Clay and Dr. Morley in the library, Darby. Now!"

Darby smiled, pleased to see that Lady Merrick's spirit was intact. "Of course, Kayte. Right away."

Kayte settled herself in a deeply cushioned chair of blue velvet, the folds of her pale gold skirts fanned out over it. She waited in tense silence for the library doors to open, her hands folded regally in her lap, her lips set in a tight line.

Monique entered first, a smug smile on her scarlet lips. Morley followed, absentmindedly checking the silver watch at the end of a chain dangling from his waistcoat. Lady Clay seated herself in the couch opposite Kaytlene.

"I see you've been enjoying my hospitality," said Kaytlene.

Monique smiled—a little too viciously, Kayte thought—and turned to Morley, speaking as though the angry golden-eyed girl across from her did not exist. "I see your little potion didn't quite do its job."

"I did far more than I should have," he replied with an

equally evil grin, "and only because you provided so generous an incentive."

Kayte couldn't stifle her horrified gasp. "You . . . paid him? To kill my baby?"

"No, my dear," Lady Clay replied. "I hired him to kill *both* you and your baby. Since you're still alive, I should have paid him only half the amount we agreed upon."

"You bitch!" Kayte's hands clenched in her lap. "You hated me because Daevon chose me over you, didn't you? He never loved you, Monique."

From the expression on Monique's face, Kayte knew she had struck a nerve.

"You're wrong, *chèrie*. About a great many things. Daevon married you only because the contracts dictated it. He would have done away with you himself one day."

"Liar!" Kayte threw back. Such a thing could not be true. "He loved me," was all she could say in her own defense.

"What a sweet, innocent little dolt you are, *chèrie*!" Monique laughed. "You were a nice distraction for him in bed, my dear, but Daevon and I had no intention of cooling our affair to suit you."

Kayte wanted desperately to hide the pain that tortured her heart. "It hardly matters now," she said hoarsely. "He's dead."

"Ah, just so, *petit*. And you are no longer of any use to us here."

"You caused the miscarriage because you knew Daevon's child would inherit everything."

"Such a clever girl! You see, the will makes no specific mention of who inherits once Daevon and his heirs are dead. So Tristan is now lord and master."

"And now I suppose you have your sights set on him as well."

"And with you out of the way, it is accomplished so much more easily."

"Me?"

"I see your innocence has kept you from realizing how he lusts after you."

"I would never marry Tristan."

"All the better. Now, if you would be so good as to

pack your things, we have a coach coming for you in the morning.''

"And where do you propose I go?"

"Back to Newbury.''

"And if I refuse? I was Daevon's wife. Surely if I decided to fight for a portion of the Merrick holdings, no court would deny me.''

"You won't fight,'' Morley finally broke in, striding across the room and bending menacingly over Kayte, a hand on either side of the plush chair. "As a matter of fact, you will never speak of this to anyone. Nor will you return to DenMerrick or to London. And you will never call yourself Kaytlene Merrick. You are Kayte Newell. If you try to turn on us, you'll find yourself traveling with all haste to heaven or Hades, along with your friends Darby and Justin. And perhaps your friends in Newbury as well.''

"You wouldn't dare kill me!''

"And who will stop me? Your beloved Daevon?'' His cold, bitter laughter cut through Kayte like a dagger's point slowly drawn across her throat.

Kayte twisted her fingers in her lap. She hadn't wanted the Merrick money or the position of lady. She had only wanted to be happy, to be loved. Daevon had given her the love she craved, and that was something Monique and Morley could never destroy. But now Daevon was gone . . .

If the son they had conceived had still been alive, she would have fought for his place in the Merrick lineage and for his rightful inheritance. Daevon would have wanted that. But Monique had taken that away from her. It was not worth fighting for her own place with the Merricks if it would mean constantly struggling with Monique and Tristan, and jeopardizing the lives of her friends. She wanted nothing for herself except the gifts that Daevon had given her. She had a thousand beautiful memories to hold and cherish. That would be enough.

"I'll go,'' she whispered.

"Don't go, please Kayte,'' Darby pleaded as she watched her friend packing the last of her gowns in a worn trunk. Its old leather straps threatened to snap at any instant as the two women struggled to tighten them.

"I have no choice, Darby," Kayte replied wearily. "There are other people involved now. People I love."

"I know, but that Morley gives me cold shivers. And Tristan is due tomorrow. I'd rather not—"

"Tristan? Are you certain?" Kayte's eyes glowed with the beginnings of a plan.

"Well, yes. I overheard Lady Clay talking about it with her courier."

"Darby, you must help me."

"I'll do whatever I can, Kayte."

"Good. Now then, Darby, you must listen carefully to everything I'm going to say."

The next morning, Kayte peered out into the corridor from her room and quickly shut the door and bolted it.

"It's all right," she whispered. "How do you feel?"

"Terrified," Darby replied, pulling on a pair of black lace gloves.

"Oh, wait!" Kayte took her wedding ring from her left hand and slipped it onto Darby's. "Now you look like me."

Darby peered at herself in the mirror. She was wearing Kayte's black crepe mourning gown and black veil, which effectively covered her hair and face. The heels of her slippers were stuffed with rags to make her a few inches taller. And now, with Kayte's wedding ring and gloves and the gown padded to resemble Kayte's more generous curves, she actually believed Kayte's plan might work.

"Now remember," Kayte instructed softly, "You're proud and angry. Hold your head up—there!"

A knock at the door caused both women to jump. They waited, silent, until four sharp raps sounded. Then a pause and two more knocks. Kayte opened the door to admit Justin.

"Ready?" he asked.

"Yes," Kayte replied. "Darby?"

The Irish girl nodded. "Is all this really necessary, Kayte? Why don't we all just sneak out?"

"Because if Tristan knew I had disappeared, he'd look for me. I need him to believe I've gone to Newbury so I can really go to DenMerrick House and get my things, the gifts from Daevon. Besides, I've already told him you and Justin ran away as soon as he ordered us all back to Newbury and that I don't know where you went. So only one of us can get in that coach and go to Newbury. And, Darby, it's got to be you."

"But he might have the house in London watched, too," Justin added. "Let's forget it, Kayte, and just you go to Newbury."

"I can't, Justin. All I want are the things Daevon gave me. They're all I have left of him. If there's a guard, then you'll just have to help me create a diversion, won't you?"

"Let's go then," he grumbled.

Kayte kissed Darby's cheek and wished her luck, then she and Justin slipped out the window of the ground floor chambers and mounted the horses waiting for them below.

Darby took a deep breath, then stepped into the corridor and down the stairway to where a carriage waited outside, loaded with Kayte's trunks and ready to take her to Newbury in Kayte's stead. Darby prayed their plan worked—for both of them.

Chapter 21

Daevon paced the house for hours after nightfall, not bothering to light the lamps. Some time after midnight he stretched out on the long leather couch in the library and fell into a restless sleep.

But his sleep was awash in dreams and memories—memories he had buried long ago, deep and well, because the torment of remembering was too great. Now, his thoughts consumed by that dark past, those hidden secrets, the dream he dreamed had the power of the resurrected past.

He was a boy again, at DenMerrick. It was night, and he was walking the upper hallway, groggy with sleep. Raised voices were coming from somewhere. He was following them, trying to find them. He paused in the corridor and his hand went toward a door. Behind it, the voices were clear and angry, and he was inexplicably drawn toward them. He peered inside as the door swung inward and gasped at the scene being enacted before him. His father, dressed only in dark trousers, stood at the corner of the bed.

A woman was in the bed—his whore. Her nudity was only partially concealed by thin coverlets. She was shouting at someone Daevon could not see, her brown hair and deep brown eyes flashing in the firelight.

"Well," she said haughtily, "here is your heir, my darling. Anna's little brat."

His father turned, saw him there, and grabbed him by the shoulder, bringing him into the room. "Will you do it in front of him?" he roared.

"Mother?" Daevon whispered, finally seeing the object of his father's bitter words.

She was standing in the corner, her eyes wild and face streaked with tears. She held a dueling pistol in her hands and was pointing it directly at her husband. The matching pistol lay in its velvet-lined box on the table beside her.

"I've had enough, Anna!" his father bellowed, pushing Daevon away.

He fell on the bed at the whore's feet, watching numbly as his parents struggled with the gun. A shot reverberated and his father fell, a hand on his chest, blood spreading quickly over his bare torso.

His lover sat up, gasping. "Daevon!"

A second shot rang out . . . and the whore fell back, bleeding from the neck.

With a cry of terror, Daevon bolted upright in bed, his heart pounding, his body damp with cold sweat. He gasped for breath and stared into the darkness, trying to orient himself as the events he had just half dreamed, half remembered consumed his mind.

Gradually he realized where he was and, with trembling hands, he lit a lamp, finding the warm light reassuring.

Oh, God, he had remembered. After all these years he had remembered the horrible events of that bloody night.

Why had his mother never told him? All these years she had never so much as hinted that she had been in the room with them. Never once had Daevon suspected that she had been responsible for his father's death, and the death of his father's mistress. How had Anna kept the secret after all these years? Or had she, too, blocked out memories too inconceivably terrible to bear?

For the first time since Daevon had learned of Kayte's death, and the death of his unborn child, he allowed himself to weep. After years of guilt, he knew he had not killed Daevon Merrick and Patrice Newell. But he *had* killed Kayte—with his petty anger, his abandonment, his lack of trust—and that sin would haunt him forever.

Hours passed while Daevon grieved, his heart and soul wrenched with pain. Kayte's loss had robbed his life of any good it had once contained. His desire for her remained so fresh and strong, it seemed powerful enough to reach beyond the grave to touch her. If only he knew how to perform such a miracle . . .

Kayte pulled up the black hood of her cloak and tucked her wayward curls beneath it. She and Justin had arrived in London late that day, after having ridden almost without rest. She didn't intend to waste any time in accomplishing her task.

"Be careful Kayte," Justin whispered in the livery's faint light. "You shouldn't be doing this alone."

She swung up onto Circe's back with a tight smile that revealed her anxiety. "It's all right. If I can get in alone, don't expect me for a few hours. If the house is being guarded, I'll come back for you. Besides, Tristan could return at any minute. It's dangerous, I know, but I must do this."

"If you aren't back in a few hours, I'm coming after you."

"Yes, do." Kayte nudged Circe gently with her heels.

The night was cold but clear, and only a little powdery snow still lay on the ground. Kayte had hoped for a flurry to help mask her direction, but that was not to be. She kept to alleys and deserted streets, easy enough around the shabby hotel where she and Justin had taken up temporary residence.

As she rode, Kayte wondered fleetingly how Darby was faring. If their charade succeeded, she would be safe in Newbury by now, thus giving Kayte plenty of time to retrieve her belongings from DenMerrick House.

She and Justin had made good time from DenMerrick, stopping for only several hours to sleep in the shelter of an abandoned shack. Kayte had decided to sell her mother's emerald ring to keep them housed and fed. They had taken a room at one of the less respectable hotels and bought hard cheese, bread, and dried beef to slake their hunger. Kayte knew her father could never have afforded the ring, meaning it must have been a gift from Daevon's father. Because of that, Kayte felt no remorse at parting with it.

There were, however, several things that she did want. Though she didn't care about losing her portion of the Merrick riches, there was a treasure hidden in DenMerrick

House that was hers alone, and she'd be damned if she would let Monique touch any of it. She was determined to have it before she returned home to Newbury.

Approaching DenMerrick House from the rear, she tethered Circe to a low bush near the pond and crept in through the cellar doors, then entered the kitchen. The house was completely dark and silent, all to her advantage. She crept up the back staircase and, trembling uncontrollably, opened the door that led to the sitting room of the master bedchamber. It was empty. With a sigh of relief, she tiptoed across the sitting room and opened the door to the bedroom in the same careful manner. The sight of the room brought back memories that she had to push from her mind to keep herself about her task. Kneeling in the darkness beside her small bedside table, she slid the bottom drawer noiselessly open and began removing her treasures.

"You let her go! You stupid French whore!" Tristan paced the length of the main corridor, still dressed in his traveling clothes.

"You can fetch her as easily there as here," Monique said flippantly. "She lost the child, didn't she, so you don't need to marry her for the brat."

"I have no doubt you and Morley had something to do with that," he bellowed, his brown eyes full of fire. "Now you and your petty need for vengeance may have caused me to lose her forever. Do you think she'll let us find her again? You might have cost me a fortune, Monique. If my brother dies of grief, she inherits everything. Everything! Do you understand?"

Monique blanched.

"Where is Kayte?" Tristan demanded, shaking her ruthlessly.

"Newbury," she whispered, dazed. "Oh, God . . . Daevon . . ."

"Then we leave for Newbury at first light." Tristan allowed her to fall to the floor in a faint. "Stupid bitch."

Daevon wandered aimlessly through the shadows of DenMerrick House. His heart ached to be awakened from

the nightmare of torture he had been living through. He
went toward the master bedchamber with trepidation. Since
the morning he had awakened to find the whore who
looked so much like Kayte in his bed—Kayte's bed—he
had not gone near it because of the way he had dishonored
his wife's memory. He was not guilty of the death of
Patrice Newell, but the sins of his father had been passed
on to him. With that knowledge and with Kayte's bright-
ness and love absent from his life, he wondered whether
he could bear to go on at all.

Silently, and with an unconscious sigh, he took the door
handle into his palm and clenched his fingers around it. He
wanted somehow to be closer to Kayte, to touch the
delicate silks that had caressed her skin, to smell the faint
lilac perfumes with which he had once anointed her.

He smiled ruefully into the darkness, recalling the morning that he had returned early from his ride to find Kayte
in her bath. She had smiled seductively as he closed the
door behind him and crossed to where the brass tub gleamed
before the fire. As he stood, slowly removing his doeskin
gloves, she came out of the herb-scented tub like Venus
from the sea, drawing the pins from her hair. It shone like
autumn fire, falling over her back and breasts in a sheath
of curls.

He dropped his gloves carelessly, going to her, and she
held out a delicate glass vial of perfume. When he showed
his reluctance to take it, she pressed it into his hand and
taught him how to apply it to her skin.

"It's better to warm the skin first," she murmured, and
as he pushed aside her long tresses to touch a clear drop to
her temple, he found her flesh hot with desire. The scent
surrounded them, sped the pounding of his heart and the
rush of his blood.

"Here," she said, leading his fingers to her throat, her
wrist. "Where a pulse can keep the scent warm. And here,
where my heart can heat it." She moved his hand to the
silken space between her breasts and he massaged the
scent there, his fingers lingering, brushing the wet tip of
one breast, his mouth following.

"God," he now moaned quietly, remembering, leaning

his head against the door, "Kayte, I miss you. I don't want to live without you."

When he opened the door, the pain and desire he felt were washed away in shock and anger. A figure was kneeling before Kayte's bedside table. The black cape and hood hid all but the dark-gloved hands that were holding Kayte's emerald necklace.

"What in God's name do you think you're doing?"

Kayte froze, unable even to release the necklace she held so lovingly. There had been no light, no sounds, and she had assumed the house was empty. Now she found herself completely paralyzed, the fear even managing to still the trembling in her fingers and freeze the tears that had soaked the hair about her face.

Quickly, she took account of her position. The sitting room doors were still ajar. She could probably outrun the man with some sort of distraction.

Daevon stood in the silence, wanting to move forward and crush the bastard's skull, waiting for him to attempt an escape.

When the figure moved, it was with a lithe grace and speed that allowed him to nearly beat Daevon to the sitting room doors. Daevon cursed, blaming his lack of agility on a lack of sleep over the past days, but he managed to tackle the thief by grasping a corner of his cloak and yanking him roughly to the ground in a wild tangle of legs and cloth.

Daevon grabbed at what he thought was the intruder's waist and found his hands attached to a petticoat and silk-covered buttocks. When a scream, quite definitely female, came from the intruder, he nearly choked in surprise but did not let go.

A flash of green caught his eye in the faint light, and he realized that whoever the thieving bitch was, she was still holding on to the necklace as if for life itself. One of the house girls, perhaps? Whoever she was, he was not about to let her escape. He hauled her up roughly and dragged her back into the room, finally throwing her across the bed.

Kayte landed roughly on one side, in no mood to give up meekly. The bastard was in for a good old-fashioned fight. As she rolled to her back to face him, she heard his steps nearing and knew he was only a few feet away. She looked up to seek his face in the darkness which encased them both, her hood falling back. Abruptly her anger melted into shock and she screamed.

Daevon watched as the woman twisted to face him, revealing her hair . . . and eyes. When she screamed, he fell heavily to his knees, gasping for breath.

"My God," he whispered, unable to release his eyes from the familiar golden stare, "you've taken her from me. Must you reduce me to raving madness as well?"

Amid the broken pieces of reality and dreams which Kayte tried to fit together into some reasonable form, she recovered her voice, low and melodic and haunting.

"Daevon," was all she whispered, and the softness of her voice brought them both to tears.

She reached out to touch his living flesh, to latch on to it and never break free, but he moved slightly away.

"You're dead," he whispered harshly. "If I touch you, you'll disappear. Just let me look at you. Let me see your face one last time before you slip back to the grave."

All at once the monstrous deception that had been practiced on them both became clear to Kayte in all its venomous glory. She had not thought it possible to feel such hatred for the deceivers while loving Daevon so passionately.

"Daevon," she replied, "I'm here. I'm real."

"Kayte," he murmured, the word filled with awe and desire and disbelief. "Alive," he whispered, the word half question, and his fingertips reached up to touch hers where they had lingered in midair, an inch from his face.

"Alive." The word came again as he realized the solidity of her flesh, the warmth and softness and beauty of it. "Alive!" he cried, and the word became a shout of breathless joy as his large hand enclosed hers.

"Kayte!" His free hand went to cup her delicate jaw and she sighed, calming every raw and battered nerve in his body. Both of his callused hands went to her face, his thumbs tracing the fine arches of her cheekbones, the softness of her lips. He moved his palms down her throat to feel the soft vibration of her moan, low and sweet and sensuous. He drew off her cloak.

Kayte's disbelief was transformed to joy and once again to desire. When Daevon's hands fell to her shoulders, freeing her of her cloak, and then to her waist to pull her down to the floor with him, she cried out his name in relief and passion and threw back her head as his mouth came down onto her throat. His hands tangled gently in her hair, pulling her to him, into him. She was like an unquenchable fire against him, her lips welcoming his brutal kiss, wanting the exquisite pain, for in that she knew they were both truly alive.

"Daevon," she whispered against his ear.

"Yes, my love?" He paused long enough to hear words from the lips he had thought cold beneath the winter snows.

"They said you were dead. Why have they done this to us?"

Again he slipped his hands up to cradle her face between them, stormy darkness in his gray eyes. He said nothing after a long moment of studying her features, though Kayte knew fully well that the emotion he harbored was hatred, as pure and true as her own.

Then the darker emotion vanished as if it had not existed and he bent to pull her into his arms, taking her to the bed. She reached up like a child desiring its last evening kiss and pulled him down with her. With the heat of his hard, muscled length against her, she sighed.

"For now," he whispered into her hair, "for this moment, does it matter so much?"

"Nothing matters," she answered with no hesitation, "except you, Daevon. Just love me. Make love to me now, or I shall die." She grasped the front of his open shirt so desperately that she feared the force of her own desire.

Daevon smiled and his soft rumble of laughter melted her to him. "It seems, my lady, that you have brought laughter back to me again."

"Oh, Daevon, I want to give you so much more than that. I want to give you a home and love and children." The last word came out on a choking sob, and she buried her face against his shoulder.

"Children," he repeated, gently stroking her firm abdomen. "Was it true that you were pregnant and lost the baby?" he whispered.

She nodded, unable to say more.

"Don't cry, my love," he reassured her. "We shall have scores of children if you like." With a gently persuasive finger he caught her chin and turned her face up to his.

"And if not"—he smiled—"then I shall love you no less."

She began to sob, her tears hot against his skin.

"My love," he said like a man who has at last been beaten down, "if you wish, I shall adopt all of London's orphans and street urchins, if only you won't torture me with your tears."

She peered up at him as he leaned above her on one elbow and could only smile at the loving warmth in his eyes. "I've missed you so much," she said weakly as his hand went to the smooth pearl buttons of her bodice.

"And I've missed you," he whispered with a gentle brushing of his lips over hers. "I decided just before I opened that door that I could not live without you."

The bodice of her dress parted to give him access. He drew one finger along the delicate lace of her chemise, watching it rise and fall with her straining breaths.

"No silk corsets this time?" he said teasingly as he drew his tongue along her neck.

Kayte shivered beneath his caress. "I shall wear one every day from now on, if you like," she murmured.

"I would like," he continued as his mouth moved down to the swell of her breasts beneath the thin chemise. "I would like it even better if you wore nothing at all."

She giggled. "My lord, you are wicked."

He groaned, rising over her, holding back his weight so that the hardened tips of her breasts barely touched his chest.

"Wicked." He smiled wolfishly. "And burning with hunger." His mouth fell on hers with insatiable lust. He kissed her until she could neither breathe nor see.

"And I'm lusting to devour you," he finished. He pulled away, kneeling between her legs, and removed his shirt so slowly that Kayte nearly fainted from the pulse of wet heat that grew between her thighs.

"I shouldn't have gone," he said. "I should not have left you alone."

"Had you done any less, you wouldn't have made me so proud to be the wife of a noble traitor," she whispered, and he pulled her hand up to kiss it passionately.

"I love you," he said impatiently. Her hand slipped purposefully from his to release one of the buttons of his breeches.

"Take them off, Daevon," she ordered sweetly. "Please."

She sat up as he left the bed to obey, letting her gown fall from her shoulders.

"Come here." She pulled him toward her. He knelt beside her and his fingers burrowed into her silken hair as hers went to caress him.

Kayte moved with unabashed fervor as she took his rigid shaft into her hands, reveling in its smooth, veined hardness, the softer flesh of its tip. She did not care that he watched her. All that mattered was pleasing him, fulfilling him, and obeying an irresistible urge, she bent her head to him, cradling the length of him in her palms, and pressed a hot, wet kiss to the sensitive tip. She felt him take in a surprised breath and groan, but his spine stiffened and arched as hers did when his mouth gave her so much pleasure. She lapped at the flesh with her tongue, thinking how pleasant he tasted.

Her tongue played along the length of him as he ground out her name and when, finally, she took the satin tip of him into her mouth, lavishing it with the caresses of her tongue, his head fell back and the sound of pleasure that rose freely from his throat threatened to shatter the tension building in her own body. He pushed her back onto the bed.

With a half-savage growl he buried his face between her breasts, his palms holding their silkiness, thumbs arcing over them, teasing. When he sucked one delicate tip into his mouth, Kaytlene thought the sweet ache would kill her. His mouth explored the curve of her waist, the smoothness of her hip, and then traveled to her thigh, drawing pathways with his tongue as though he were navigating a labyrinth. When he found her center, she gasped and moved beneath him, her voice creating its own melodic pleas.

Daevon parted the satiny folds of flesh and his tongue delved inside for the hard center of her sensation, as if trying to extract one single drop of dew from the hidden core of a flower. He caressed with long, warm strokes until Kaytlene shuddered and tensed, whimpering for release.

"Not this time, my angel," he whispered as he rose over her once more. "Not without me." His taut muscles relaxed and he smiled down into her face with calculating fierceness.

"You are so sweet, my Kayte," he breathed against her temple. "So sweet and hot and wet. Only for me."

"Yes, Daevon." She sighed in an equally breathless voice, gasping as he thrust into her without warning, then pulled back until he drew himself almost entirely from her. Taking her wrists, he held them on either side of her head and silenced her pleading whimpers with kisses.

"The thought of this has tortured me for so long," he said with a groan. "Of your body beneath mine. Of your wanting me. Tell me, Kaytlene. Say what I've waited to hear for so long."

She was silent, wanting only to be lost in the sensations of his flesh in hers, but he pressed only a little further into her and she cried out in frustration.

"Tell me," he demanded. "Say it!"

"Daevon," she cried hoarsely, "how can you doubt it? I have been dead without you! I lie awake every night wanting your kisses and your touch. Wanting you to come back and make love to me forever as you promised. I need you, Daevon. Beside me, around me. Inside me." She groaned. "Daevon, please!"

"Yes, yes," he murmured, coming into her with long, smooth, caressing strokes. Kayte's fingers curled to clench his.

"Harder, Daevon," she whispered. "Make me a part of you."

Their hands locked together, he complied, the thrusts fierce and deep and breathtaking. He said her name once and clenched her wrists until she thought they would snap.

His body shuddered and stiffened as she cried out her own release. Their mouths sought hungrily for breath and kisses.

With every fiber of his love and strength Daevon wished he could resist the dawn, hold it back with the arms that now cradled his wife. In the past days he had spent so much time in drunken sleep that now, after having made love to Kayte and experiencing the pleasure so long denied them, he was unable to sleep. Through the hours of the night he had kept silent vigil over her—as she yawned, curled against his chest in the warm afterglow of their passion; when she fell with a little smile into sleep; and now, as she lay nestled in his arms, the pale, sweet swell of her breasts moving against him.

"Precious," he murmured. "My precious girl." His lips brushed her forehead. "My precious wife."

She sighed and stretched, eager to rid her limbs of their sleepy weight.

"Daevon, you're still here," she whispered, smiling as one hand moved up to touch the rough stubble covering his chin.

"You've neglected a great deal in my absence, I see." She smiled.

He dragged her tightly to his chest and kissed her relentlessly. "Kayte," he groaned against her eager kiss, "I had no reason to live without you."

"Do you think I was any less miserable?" she replied with love trembling in her voice. "There could never have been another man to take your place, Daevon." Nervously, recalling the pain that had been real only a day before, she giggled. "You nearly made me an old widow."

"My love," he answered in a tone that showed his returning sense of humor, "even in mourning dress you would have had scores of young men begging for your hand."

"No other man could ever make me feel so alive. Or so wanton." She grinned, taking his hand beneath the coverlets and sliding it over the softness of her breast. Daevon groaned with pleasure and frustration at her invitation.

"Wife, we must rise and face the day," he murmured

as she kissed his neck, drawing her tongue downward, across his collarbone.

"Must we?" she returned, pushing him onto his back. As her mouth continued its hot, wet path down his chest, his long fingers tangled in her hair.

"We must return to DenMerrick," he insisted as her hand encircled his hard manhood, gently teasing its length with her fingers.

"Must we?" she whispered once more, her tongue sliding up the length of his hard flesh.

"Kayte," was all he could manage in reply.

Her lips parted, shimmering pink warmth, and she took the tip of him into her mouth.

"Dear God, Kaytlene," he said with a groan and then, more softly, "Kayte . . ."

"Mmm," she murmured. "I thought not."

It was nearly dawn when she served him breakfast, simple fare composed of what she scavenged from the neglected kitchens. It was well past dawn when she rode with him over the icy gravel of the estate's drive. They discussed what had happened to each of them, but Kayte couldn't talk about the miscarriage in detail yet. She felt as if the frigid air cut straight through her heavy clothes and the strong arms that held her steady on Demon's back to chill her soul.

She peered up into her husband's eyes, as cold and gray as the slate sky above him, and the anger she saw there sent a tremor down her spine.

"Too cold for you, love?" he asked.

Her muscles relaxed as his gaze changed to melting heat. "I . . . you seemed so angry just now."

"I was," he replied, though his voice was tinged with sadness.

She reached up to touch his smoothly shaven jaw with the soft doeskin glove that covered her slim fingers. "Can't we forgive them, Daevon? I just want to go on with my life. Our life."

"Oh, that I had your kind heart, my love." He smiled gently.

"You do, Daevon. You're the most gentle man I've ever known. Aside from my father," she added quietly.

As he bent to warm her lips with his own, a sudden realization swept over him, cold and bitter.

"And to think," he said as Demon plodded through the snow, "that I nearly fell over myself trying to give him half of the Merrick holdings."

"Who?"

"Tristan, the bastard. I can't forgive him—not after all of this. Not after what he did to you."

"Daevon!" Kayte stiffened and sat up abruptly, throwing her weight and sending Demon into a sidelong prance necessary to keep his riders out of the snow. "Did Tristan inherit nothing from your mother?"

"Not a farthing. Not even DenMerrick, which he coveted, which I suppose is quite a palace by now."

"You're too kind." Kayte smiled beneath his proud and loving eyes. "And you're right. But Daevon, I'm sure . . . I mean I . . . he wants to kill you. I think he planned that all along. Monique convinced me that you were dead and after I . . . lost the baby, she and Morley arranged for me to go back to Newbury."

"But why? They couldn't gain a thing while I was still alive."

"They knew that you were too strong . . . we were too strong. They had to weaken us before they could get what they wanted. They chose to weaken us by separating us."

"Tristan understood me better than I understood myself. Losing you . . . losing our child . . . Was it—?"

"A son," Kayte whispered, her head bowing to a gust of frigid air and the weight of her pain.

Daevon pulled her face up to his, cradling it between his warm, gloved palms. With his gray eyes fixed upon hers, Kayte didn't notice that they had stopped in the midst of a busy London street.

"A son," he repeated softly. "Tristan knew how I wanted a child. Our child. When he told me you were both dead, he knew it would be more than I could stand. He was waiting for me to kill myself out of despair." He caressed the silky reddened cheeks beneath his fingers. "I would have, Kayte, if you hadn't come to DenMerrick House last night."

"And Tristan really would have inherited it all," Kayte mused angrily.

Daevon took up the reins with a laugh. "Not quite. If I had died, my dear, you would now be the wealthiest and most beautiful widow in London."

"Wealthy?" she breathed in disbelief.

"Of course. I supposed you already knew. Mother was always taking you into her confidence."

"Daevon, what are you talking about?"

"All right, little girl, listen carefully. I am not quite as stupid as Tristan thinks. I have had a will prepared since I took over the Merrick holdings. Of course, I amended my will once I fell helplessly in love with you. That, by the way, was entirely your fault," he teased.

Kayte grinned up at him. "You shall have to reprimand me severely, my lord."

"Of course," Daevon replied, his mind suddenly filling with memories of the delicious punishments he had dealt her in the past. "At any length, my will passes all of my holdings to you. And since I inherited everything, that's exactly what you would have received. Everything."

"Everything," she whispered in a hollow voice.

"That's right, my love. And the only way Tristan could ever hope to gain title to the Merrick holdings would be to marry you. What's wrong, Kayte? You're as pale as a ghost."

In a flurry of sensation, images passed through Kayte's mind. Francine Mallery's horrified voice saying, *He kept saying your name.* . . . Even Monique had admitted that Tristan had wanted her. *He lusts after you,* she'd said.

"My God, Daevon—he'll go to Newbury. To Darby!"

Chapter 22

Daevon's first priority was seeing that his wife was safe. He insisted she stay at a room in one of the large, comfortable hotels in London while he went out to find Henri Todd and Lyle Miller. He sent Henri directly to Newbury, ordered Lyle to follow as soon as he could, and returned to the hotel well after midnight.

Daevon slipped soundlessly into Kayte's room, kneeling at her bedside to pray for God's protection on them both, then kissed his wife as she slept and left once again.

Demon and Dancer, their coats steaming in the cold, were once again straining toward Newbury under the harness of the Merrick coach. As Daevon fingered the smooth, freshly oiled pistol in his lap, he hoped this trip would end as much to his satisfaction as his last journey to Newbury. Settling into a more comfortable position, his boots propped up on the opposite side of the carriage, he pulled his thick cloak more tightly around him and closed his eyes in an attempt to sleep. It was well past four, but his attempts to rest only ended in his conjuring up images of Kaytlene. Even now, exhausted as he was, the thought of her came fresh and seductive and vibrant. With a heavy sigh, Daevon succumbed to a fitful sleep. His last conscious thought was that Kayte would be fit for Bedlam when she woke to find him gone.

When Kayte woke, roused by the fleeting remembrance of Daevon's kiss, she looked around the rich bedchamber and saw only Justin, sleeping in a nearby chair. Daevon was gone.

"He's gone to Newbury!" Kayte cried, sitting up at once and throwing off the blankets. "Justin!" she screeched, scrambling out of bed. "Daevon's gone! He left without me! Justin, wake up!"

"Kayte?" The boy yawned sleepily. He caught a glance of his friend scuttling around the room in a rage and realized that she was behind a dressing screen, tearing off her nightdress.

"We've got to go, Justin," she called over the top of the shoulder-high barrier. "Get me a pair of breeches and one of those heavy shirts of Daevon's there. And my dark cloak, with the hood."

Justin groaned and got out of the chair. No matter what sort of fool's scheme was taking hold of Kayte, he knew her well enough to realize it was useless to object.

Darby sat up stiffly in the wingback chair near the fire, her body stiff with fear and the exhaustion of having been awake most of the night. Even now, the light of dawn was just filtering into the cottage.

"Are you certain Tristan is coming tonight?" she asked with a fearful glance at Elizabeth O'Connell in the chair opposite her.

"Late tonight, most likely," Sean said. "Daniel rode out to look for him. Tristan's going to have a hard ride in a coach, the roads are so clogged with snow. Besides, he had stopped to spend the night and was drinking heavily when Daniel found him. Assuming he gets a late start this morning, it'll be well past dark when he arrives."

"We'll just tell Tristan the truth," Elizabeth said quietly. "If it's Kayte he wants and he can't find her here, he'll have no reason to stay and bother us. If she's hiding in London, he'll never find her. She'll make her way back here, don't worry."

"But we must make him think she's here," Darby insisted. "We must give her as much time as we can. Sean—" Darby's nerves had been stretched so thin over the past weeks that she screamed when a firm knock at the O'Connells' door surprised her.

"It's all right, Darby," Sean assured her as he went to the door.

Darby nearly fainted when she saw the familiar figure who stood outside in the dawn shadows. By the time he had stepped to the fire to take the chill from his limbs, she had fallen to his feet, sobbing.

"Thank the Lord," she rasped. "I thought you were . . ." Looking up into his face, she said softly, "I thought you were dead."

The O'Connells, who had been told all of Darby's harrowing story, were just as shocked to see Daevon Merrick return from the dead.

Daevon bent to ease Darby up into his arms, where she unleashed all the fear and pain that had been mounting for so long, her tears mingling with melted snow on his cloak.

"Kayte?" she asked fearfully, her eyes widening.

"Darby, it's fine now. She's safe." His voice was low, soothing, and weary.

When Darby's tears had all been spent, Daevon allowed her to slip back into the chair. As he bent to press a tender kiss to her forehead he whispered, "Lyle is fit to be tied worrying about you. He sends his . . . highest regards, and he'll be arriving shortly."

Her clear green eyes peered up with a grateful light.

"My lord," Sean interrupted, "your brother will be here by midnight."

Daevon nodded grimly. "I need a man who can be trusted," he said.

Sean supplied the name of someone who, in his words, was as good as any and better than most. Stefan Lindsay was a ruddy, blond farmer, son and grandson of farmers, and unremarkable in every aspect save his eyes, which were an exceptionally pale blue.

Late that morning, Stefan sat with Daevon in the kitchen of his farmhouse, located several miles outside of Newbury. They cupped huge mugs of mulled cider between their palms. As the hours passed, Daevon explained with cool calculation what he expected of each man. And while the afternoon progressed quickly into cold, crisp winter night, Daevon carefully refined his plans into a trap that would catch even the most cunning mouse.

It was well after full dark when Tristan's carriage barreled down the single road leading to Newbury and pulled to a halt in front of the White Doe inn. He strode inside with a brash arrogance that turned heads and stopped busy hands and tongues. The innkeeper spoke to him in a tone that belied his own anxious fear.

"A mug of warm cider, your lordship?" The man prayed that the stranger would not ask for lodging. He looked as if he had hell's own temper, and Newbury had no use for a troublemaker.

"My name is Merrick," he said coldly. "I've—"

"Merrick! Merrick!" A thundering voice caught Tristan unawares as a huge, rough hand slapped his shoulder in welcome. He swung about, dagger poised. The overly friendly giant stepped back, surprised but not alarmed by the action.

"Now I ask you, is that any way to treat a fellow sufferer? Eh, Merrick?"

"What in God's name are you talking about?"

"You said you're Merrick, eh?" The giant's voice slurred with liquor.

"Yes?"

"Then you must be a-lookin for your purty wench, eh?"

Tristan was suddenly interested. He replaced the dagger in its hiding place and led the man quietly to a secluded table, then ordered the inn's best wine from a barmaid who looked at him strangely, as if they had met before. It was possible, he supposed, for he had bedded a hundred nameless wenches in any number of such poor villages.

"Now, friend," Tristan said, "tell me about this wench."

The man laughed, crashing his fist onto the table with drunken joviality. "Why, I've the same trouble myself, Merrick," he said pleasantly. "Got a wife what never stops aching at me until one of us walks out. It's a curse, it is. A curse to love the bitches, ain't it?"

"Yes, indeed." Tristan smiled. The bumbling idiot farmer thought him a lover separated from his lady by an argument! "I've been nearly a week on the road, held up by snow, the roads almost impassable. I feared she'd be long gone by now."

"You've got a beauty there, Merrick, though it's those who do the most fussin', God save us. She don't come

down here, but spends her time up at the O'Connells'."
The giant leaned over the table, adding quietly, "They say
she's got her heart broke, what with her cryin' and all."

"Crying?"

"Spends her nights just sittin' on the shore up there,
cryin' for her lover, they say. I've a mind to see her
myself. They say she be quite a sight in the moonlight
with her long hair and golden eyes. Imagine that! Golden
eyes! You're the lucky man, Merrick. Probably up there
now, a-waitin'."

Tristan's wine was delivered and with a deep draught,
he watched the barmaid's enticing sway as she left him.

"Yes, sir, Merrick, if'n I had a girl like that I sure
wouldn't mind a little cold up there on them cliffs! She'd
warm you quick enough!" He laughed again as Tristan
poured them both more wine.

"Yes, sir, if'n she was mine for the takin' . . ." He
winked at Tristan, a bawdy gesture full of meaning.

"Mine for the taking," Tristan repeated, smiling as he
rose to leave. "Thank you, my friend." He tossed several
gold pieces before the giant, who appeared too absorbed in
his drink to pay any mind to his benefactor's departure.

Once Merrick had disappeared, the giant scooped up the
coins, tossing them to the barmaid as he went to lean
against it.

"Them's yours, Meg," he said, his voice as sober as
hers when she thanked him. He smiled down at the girl,
his warm, pale blue eyes glittering with joy at the success
of their conspiracy.

Demon's hooves seemed to throw sparks off the iron-
hard earth and melt a path in the snow as he thundered
across the fields several miles inland, leaving Stefan Lindsay's farmhouse behind and heading back to Newbury.
Henri Todd on Dancer tried gamely to match Daevon
length for length as he maneuvered along the snowy fur-
rows, but he finally abandoned the race.

"Daevon!" he shouted above the sound of hooves, "I
forfeit! Let up, will you?"

Daevon pulled back on Demon's reins so sharply that
the animal reared, scattering clumps of muddy snow. He

turned in the saddle to face Henri, cold hatred sparkling in his eyes.

For the first time in their long friendship, Henri was afraid of the man and pulled his own mount back a few steps.

"Daevon," he said shakily, attempting a smile, "I'm sorry. I . . . you know my expertise with horses doesn't match my skill with women."

Daevon apologized for his haste. "I've never been a coward, Henri," he said thoughtfully, "and I've never turned my back on my duty, but I'd like this matter dealt with as soon as possible." He sighed deeply, as if the cold air gave him barely enough breath to stay alive, and shrugged, unable to voice the reluctance he was feeling about facing Tristan.

"Daevon, you're no coward. Good Lord, man, he's your brother!"

"Yes," Daevon answered solemnly. "My brother, God forgive me."

"You're going to kill him." It was a simple confirmation of what Henri saw in his friend's eyes.

"I think he would prefer death to spending the rest of his life in Newgate Prison," Daevon said, staring toward the distant glow of the moon as if in a trance. "His plots have nearly ruined me, ruined my marriage. Even a god would grow weary of forgiving, and I'm no god."

They pressed on, a little more slowly this time to accommodate Henri's unfamiliarity with his wild-tempered mount, and kept well hidden despite the bright silver glow of the full moon. When they reached the crossroads that marked Newbury's eastern boundary, they stopped altogether. The village below them was clearly illuminated, and Merrick scrutinized its every detail as the church tower rang out eleven bells.

Henri pulled his cloak tightly about his shoulders and shuddered. "They'll be here soon."

"They're here already."

Henri followed the direction of his friend's gaze and saw the gleam of a rose and silver coat of arms emblazoned on a coach pulled up in front of the White Doe inn.

"Tristan," Daevon whispered.

A rustle of frost-crisp leaves and breaking twigs had Henri wheeling his mount to face an intruder, but it was only Lyle Miller, who had been keeping watch since early evening.

"Daevon," Lyle gasped breathlessly. "He's arrived!"

Daevon nodded. Lyle pulled a pistol from his inner pocket.

"Can you use it?" Daevon asked.

Lyle smiled. There was no need to answer the question.

"Is he convinced that Kayte is here?" Daevon added.

"Meg says he swallowed the story whole. He seemed in good spirits when he ordered a room. He called for a saddled horse to be brought to him within the hour."

"Keep your eyes on my back, but keep away from Tristan." The silent message in Daevon's eyes was plain. Tristan was his alone to deal with.

The three men rode silently through the icy woods skirting the cemetery to reach the base of the knoll where the O'Connells' home was located. There they separated to await Tristan's arrival.

In the glen below Sean O'Connell's house, on the edge of the sea, they would play their game. Daevon took his place behind a wall of sheer rock, surveying his gameboard appreciatively. On the edge of the field overlooking the small white beach where Kayte had accepted his proposal sat a young woman. She was slightly hunched over, her face in her hands as though she were sobbing. She wore a gown of deep green velvet under a long black cloak, its hood only partially covering her pale face and golden-brown hair. Daevon smiled. Even he was nearly convinced that the dressing dummy, clothed in Kaytlene's garments, was his wife, living and breathing. For authenticity, Sean had even saddled Cyclops, who gnawed patiently on nearby tufts of grass, his reins dragging on the snow.

After waiting a quarter of an hour, Daevon was rewarded by the sight of a single horse and rider coming across the field on the village path.

At the sight of Kaytlene, Tristan urged on his mount more quickly. She was kneeling at the edge of the field, weeping. He thanked the fates that none of the curious locals had chosen this night to investigate the beauty's tears. He was riding close enough to see the tremors of cold and despair that shook her slumping shoulders. He dismounted a few yards from her.

"Kaytlene," he said softly, "I've come to take you home, my dear."

Daevon hardly knew whether to laugh or kill the bastard. The fact that Tristan was speaking to a lifeless figure was comical, but his gentle, lying tongue infuriated Daevon as nothing ever had. He pushed the heavy folds of his cloak back over his shoulders and cocked the pistol hammer, his mouth suddenly dry, his heart numb at the realization that he was about to kill his own flesh and blood.

"Kayte," Tristan repeated. "Come with me, love."

Daevon's heels paused an instant before digging into Demon's sides, an instant in which he thought he must have lost his mind.

She had moved!

"Sweet Jesu!" Daevon groaned under his breath. The inanimate doll moved, straightened, turned. Her eyes were more alive than they had ever been. Traces of real tears stained her reddened cheeks.

"You dare come here," Kayte ground out harshly, "after all you've done? Go back to your money and your whores, Tristan. I've no use for you here."

The smile on Tristan's face was serpentlike, but Kaytlene noted gladly that the corners trembled with anxiety.

"I'm sorry, Kaytlene, for—"

"Don't you dare to apologize to me, Tristan. I know your hand was just as deeply into this scheme as Monique's and Morley's."

"Ah, I see. Very well, pretty Kayte. Let's have the truth out, shall we?"

"The truth, Tristan? I would wager my life you couldn't spell the word, much less know its meaning."

Tristan strode to the field's edge to stare out to the sea, keeping a margin of space between himself and his brother's wife to stop her from bolting. His laughter was void of humor.

"The truth is, dear Kayte, that I would have preferred

the child remained alive. It would have made it all so much easier.''

"Your marrying me?''

Tristan's eyes glinted with surprise and humor. "So Monique told you everything, did she?''

"Monique," Kayte said bitterly, "and Francine Mallery. She said you . . . called her by my name when you . . . raped her.''

"I see," Tristan said, his voice a little harder. "And does it surprise you to learn that I am as hot for you as your beloved Daevon was? Innocent child!''

Daevon's hands trembled with rage, his knuckles ashen as he clenched Demon's reins. He knew Tristan too well to think that his brother was unarmed, and if he attempted to rush in as he had planned, Kayte's life would be threatened.

She would suffer a sound thrashing at his own hand when this was finished, Daevon decided. He could understand her wanting to come to Newbury, but how had she known about his plan to trap Tristan? And why had she thrown herself so recklessly into the middle of it? Daevon waited in silence, hoping there was some good reason for her rashness.

"God help me, Tristan," Kayte said slowly, icily, "but I despise you. I never knew how vile a man's greed could make him.''

"A man's greed?" He laughed mockingly. "And what of a woman's greed?''

"I've asked for nothing!''

"Oh, no, my lovely." Tristan came nearer, his eyes freezing her to the place where she stood. He touched her face, smiling as she flinched. "But what of your mother?''

"Sweet Jesu," Kayte whispered. "How did you—?''

"How did I know? You were careless enough to leave your whoring mother's journal at DenMerrick House.''

"Very well, Tristan. You know." Kayte strode away, moving unknowingly toward Daevon as she fled his brother's touch.

"Yes, I know. And because I know, you'll marry me.''

Tristan went to her suddenly, as if unable to keep himself away. He gripped her shoulders until she bit down on her lip to keep from crying out. Daevon must be nearby, watching from somewhere in the darkness. Darby had told her all the details of Daevon's plan. Wait, my darling, she prayed. Wait until I've had my own revenge, Daevon.

"If you've given me a choice, Tristan, I'll die first," she said.

"Little fool," he whispered harshly against her ear. His hands moved caressingly down her arms, then up again to shift the curls from one side of her neck. "I won't treat you as I did the Mallery bitch," he whispered. "You're deserving of so much more, lovely Kayte. I'll be gentle with you. I'll teach you to love my touch and forget his."

As Tristan's mouth pressed hard against her throat and his hands slid to cover her breasts, Kayte screamed and struggled. Instantly she found herself thrown to the ground.

"Bitch!" Tristan spat as he towered over her. "I'll kill you if I must, but if you die, it will be slowly and after I've had you under me!"

"No!" Kayte screamed, throwing up her arms to shield her face when he raised a hand to strike her.

"Tristan!" Daevon shouted.

Tristan wheeled about, his eyes wild with fear and disbelief as the gray horse and its rider materialized from the swirling snow. Step by step Demon advanced, steadily and inexorably, then, mere inches from Tristan, he reared, his glistening hooves flashing in the moonlight. As he came down hard, his feet struck Tristan in the temple, then the side, throwing him violently to the ground.

"Get up!" Daevon ordered angrily. Tristan wiped a stream of blood from the side of his head.

"I said get up, Tristan. You've worn out my patience, so don't keep me waiting."

Tristan rose with a smile, holding out his hands to show his brother he carried no weapons. "Just helping the lady, dear brother."

Though Daevon's pistol was aimed directly at Tristan's heart, Daevon knew—as his brother did—that it would be nearly impossible to pull the trigger. Tristan stood too close to Kayte for Daevon to get an accurate shot with Demon prancing nervously beneath him.

"Kayte?" Tristan bowed with a mocking smile and held out his hand to help her up.

She hesitated for an instant. But as she peered up into Tristan's face, the clear figure of her husband's gun aimed at Tristan's chest gave her courage.

"Don't touch me!" she threatened, rising to her feet, but Tristan was already close enough to make Daevon's aim uncertain, and Tristan caught her by the waist as she stumbled. In another instant she was jerked against his chest, a dagger teasing the cloth at her ribs.

"Daevon," she whispered fearfully. He was all in black like Satan riding a gleaming silver destrier, his eyes full of hate.

"And now, dear brother," Tristan said pleasantly, "I believe we each have something the other wants."

"Take your hands off my wife," Daevon returned coldly. "I have enough reason to kill you."

"Ah no, Daevon. I underestimated you once when I hired Delamane to kill Kayte and you saved her. But I won't underestimate you again. I'll keep my pretty hostage until I get what I want."

Kayte gasped from shock. "Don't give him anything, Daevon!" she cried.

"What are your terms, Tristan?" Daevon asked unemotionally, his eyes on Kayte.

"Just this, brother. I want a legal document signing over all Merrick assets to me. Everything."

Daevon said nothing.

"It's my birthright," Tristan went on angrily. "And all these years I've been deprived of it while you controlled me like a child."

"Birthright!" Kayte broke in suddenly. "Daevon, he has no rights! He's your father's bastard!"

"Lying bitch!" Tristan dragged her back, pressing the dagger point through the thick velvet of her gown. Kayte cried out as he withdrew it, holding it up for Daevon's eyes, its point dripping with her blood. The side of her gown showed a small wet spot of red.

Daevon's eyes were hot and angry. He moved suddenly to dismount, but Kaytlene's voice stopped him as he rose in the stirrups.

"Daevon," she whispered, her head swimming with pain, "he'd kill us both and not regret it." Her eyes, though shining with tears, pleaded with him not to come to her.

"Tristan," she went on in a soothing voice, "even if I wished it, we could never marry. Patrice Newell was your mother."

"You lie," he denied, holding her more tightly.

"You're Daevon's half brother," she added quietly, "and mine as well."

Tristan's mind went all to black. The vile revelation passed through his consciousness, burning thought until all that remained was sensation. Surf pounding, ice cracking. He breathed. He heard the wind blowing. He faced the death of all he had strived to accomplish. He knew now why his father had hated him.

"No!" he cried, dragging Kaytlene back. "She lies! I am a Merrick!" He grabbed for Cyclops's reins and shoved Kayte up onto the saddle, holding the dagger snug against her abdomen as soon as he was mounted behind her.

"I want the documents." He spat the words like venom, as if they might have the power to kill where he could not.

"You will give the Merrick fortune to me, Daevon. And every day you deny my inheritance, I'll have my beautiful half sister in my bed, and I won't bother to be gentle! Perhaps if you wait long enough, she'll carry my bastard to take the place of the brat you lost."

Kaytlene slumped forward over Cyclops's pale neck as if she had fainted. Perhaps she could save herself if she could get the horse to throw them off . . . Though Tristan held the reins, it was her hushed command to which the animal responded.

"Go, Cyclops!" she whispered, and the beast lunged toward the sea.

As Cyclops's huge body moved unerringly into the force of a wave, both riders were violently unseated. Tristan lost his hold on both Kayte and the reins and tumbled into the icy, churning water.

Kayte heard her own screams as she fell into the sea, the heavy weight of her wet clothing dragging her down, the waves sucking her back. The dagger wound at her side stung with salt, and her body stiffened with shock.

The roaring in her head grew stronger. The waves rose and crashed upon the shore with no mercy, like the sound of a thousand horses thundering down upon their enemy. Blackness threatened to engulf her . . .

Then she was being pulled upward. Cold wind slapped her face with an icy blast, and her chest ached as she breathed in sharply and began to cough. She glimpsed moon-sparkled white sand as strong arms carried her, as cold hands pressed her chest to force bitter liquid from her lungs.

"Daevon," she rasped between laboring breaths, "please God—"

Chapter 23

Kayte's body jerked into awareness. It was night. The moon drenched everything in bright silver light . . . and she was being held in powerful arms. A cape was wrapped tightly around her, and she felt the slow, easy gait of a horse beneath her.

"Awake, sweetheart?"

She closed her eyes and wept.

"Daevon," she said, the name muffled against his chest, his voice sounding achingly sweet in her ears.

Daevon reined Demon to a standstill and held his wife, combing the wet strands of her hair with his fingers, murmuring softly to her. He allowed her to cry until her body was weak from the effort.

Finally, Kayte looked up at him. "Tristan?" she asked.

Daevon's eyes lifted to some point far off on the horizon before shifting back to hers. "He never came up."

Kayte sighed and relaxed in Daevon's embrace as he took up the reins again and nudged Demon with his heels. The lazy sound of plodding hooves lulled her into silence.

Daevon was not pleased that Tristan's life had ended so abruptly. Nor did he take any pleasure in the way his brother had met his end. But, rightfully, a man could only reap what he sowed, and Tristan had never sowed anything kind or beautiful in his life.

"Daevon?"

Nudged from his thoughts, he gazed down into Kayte's face. Wet and sandy and thoroughly mussed, she had never looked more beautiful to him.

"I'm sorry about Tristan. About the way he died, I mean. But please don't feel guilty. It wasn't your fault."

"I've felt enough guilt for one lifetime," he answered. "I wasn't responsible for the way my father treated Tristan, and I'm not responsible for Tristan's death." He sighed and shifted his weight in the saddle. "You, however, have a great deal to feel guilty for," he added.

Kayte's eyes widened. "What?"

"How in God's name did you get yourself in the middle of all this? You were supposed to stay in London with Justin. Who told you about the trap we had planned for Tristan?"

"In the first place," she replied angrily, "you never actually told me to stay in London."

Daevon smiled. "You have me on that point," he conceded. "Next time I'll leave my orders in writing. But how did you know about our little scheme to catch Tristan?"

"When Justin and I got to Newbury, we went directly to Sean and Elizabeth's. Darby was there. She was so nervous, she couldn't stop prattling on and on about your idea."

"I never should have told her."

"She meant well, Daevon."

He nodded. Now that Kayte was out of danger, there were a hundred questions he needed to ask.

"There are still a few loose ends," he murmured. "Kayte, there's one piece in the whole puzzle that doesn't fit. Mother's death."

Kayte sat up suddenly and her body stiffened. "You don't think—"

"Hush, sweetheart," he reassured her, brushing his lips over hers. "No, I don't think you did it. But I want to know everything you did and everyone you were with before she died. Someone put the vial in that box of chocolates and I want to know who it was. You can start by telling me about the gentleman who paid you a visit at DenMerrick House."

"But, Daevon, I don't . . . oh, you mean Mr. Darrell."

"Mr. Darrell?"

"He's a solicitor from London. He brought me mother's

diary. Remember, I told you. With Father dead, they weren't sure what to do with it.''

"You told me the diary had been sent to you. I assumed it was delivered to the house by courier."

"Well, it was sent to me by the solicitor's firm. He delivered it. I didn't go into town those last few days, Daevon, and no one else visited. Well, Monique came by for tea. It was the same day Mr. Darrell called. I had to leave her alone in the sitting room while I . . . oh, God—''

"What?''

Kayte stared up into Daevon's questioning glance. "I left her alone in there. With the box of chocolates.''

Daevon's body shuddered with anger. "Monique,'' he whispered. "But you were eating the chocolates with Mother the night she died. You told me you finished off the box.''

"Yes.''

"Then why weren't you poisoned as well?''

Kayte recalled her afternoon with Monique and their conversation, then frowned. "Because I told Monique not to eat the cherries. I told her that Mother loved them, so I saved them for her. Oh, Daevon, it's all my fault!''

Daevon hugged his wife tightly and stroked her hair. "No, darling. You couldn't have known.''

He reined in again, stopping in the yard of Kayte's little cottage.

"Here we are,'' he said softly as he dismounted. "You go in and I'll see to the horses." He took Kayte by the waist and set her on the ground. Several minutes later, he entered the kitchen door at the back of the cottage. Kayte sat at the wooden table and smiled at him. Daevon stopped in the doorway.

"What the—?''

"It looks to me like Elizabeth paid us a visit,'' Kayte said.

Daevon joined her at the table and carefully looked over the array of foods that had been left for them. Cold sliced beef, bread, a generous chunk of yellow cheese, a pitcher of cold milk, and a fruit pie.

"Hungry?'' she asked.

"I'm starving.''

It wasn't until they had finished eating that Daevon

spoke again. "Kayte," he said gently, "how did you know about Tristan? About his being your half brother?"

"Your mother explained it to me just before she died. Soon after Patrice and your father became lovers, Patrice realized she was pregnant. Since my father knew Patrice had a lover and the child couldn't be his, he sent her to DenMerrick. She lived there until she had the baby."

"That was the year my mother and I were sent away. And the child was Tristan."

"Yes. Patrice came back to my father because she had nowhere else to turn. Your father wouldn't marry her and my father refused to give her a divorce. The affair broke off until after I was born." Kayte paused to give Daevon time to absorb the truth before she went on.

"When your father decided he couldn't live without Patrice, he came to Newbury for her. It wasn't until she had gone that my father began to doubt that I was really his daughter. He demanded that I be betrothed to you to prove there was no common blood between us. If your father had been mine as well, it would have been illegal to betroth us. So the contracts were signed. My mother liked the idea of having me share the Merrick money. Though her son would not inherit, mine would. But I didn't want anything except you, Daevon. I swear it."

"The rest I know," Daevon said. "Enough of the past, now. Tell me what happened at DenMerrick while I was gone."

Kayte smiled sadly. "I refurbished the place," she murmured. "I think you'll like it."

Daevon took her hand. "I'm certain I will. But I want to know about the time you spent there. And about the baby," he added softly.

Kayte's eyes filled with tears. "When I knew I was carrying your baby . . . I wasn't certain you would want to know. I should have sent you a message."

"You wouldn't have known exactly where to find me," he replied. "I shouldn't have left you alone."

"Oh, it wasn't so awful. I had Justin and Darby and Lyle."

"And Tristan?"

"He came only twice. Both times he was with the

Clays. He was polite. He never tried to speak to me alone
or be with me except when we were with others.''

"I thought perhaps he had hurt you. That he had caused
the miscarriage.'' Daevon looked down at their entwined
hands.

Kayte bit her soft inner lip. "No, Daevon. It wasn't
Tristan.''

His head snapped up. "You mean someone did hurt
you? Who was it?''

"Monique.'' Kayte saw the pain and anger in her husband's eyes as soon as she had spoken the name. "When
she told me you were dead, Daevon, I was so upset . . .
She sent for Dr. Morley. He gave me something to drink
and I lost the baby.''

"Morley,'' Daevon said angrily. "I'll have the bastard
drawn and quartered.''

"And what about Monique?'' Kayte asked. "It will tear
Forrest apart.''

"I know.'' Daevon released his wife's hand and stood.
He walked to the two windows at the back of the cottage
and looked out silently at the night. Monique's deceit and
the crimes she had committed would break Forrest Clay's
heart.

"I have to tell him,'' Daevon said finally. "I don't want
him to find out from the authorities. He'll want to get the
children away from London to avoid all the scandal.''

"But what if he doesn't believe you?''

"Forrest loves Monique, but he's not an idiot. He's
looked the other way for a long time. Ignoring murder is
something he couldn't do.''

"And Morley?''

Daevon took a deep, slow breath as he considered the
cunning doctor. "If he was in on Tristan's plans, he knew
Tristan wanted me dead. And he doesn't know if Tristan's
succeeded or not, so I think he'll stay in London until he
knows for certain. He'll be easy enough to hunt down.''

"And if he isn't?''

"I'll find him, Kayte,'' Daevon promised roughly. "I'll
find him.'' And then, as Kayte turned away from him, a
shaft of pale candlelight lit her features, and Daevon realized that they had a future—a chance to make all the

wrongs right, to correct all the mistakes. He went back to her and knelt on one knee before her chair.

"Kayte," he said, "there's still one thing I want to explain. It's about my father's murder. And Patrice's, of course."

Kayte looked down into his face, seeing the deep lines of worry etched there. Her right hand held his, her left hand on his shoulder.

"You know who killed them," she said softly.

Daevon nodded. "When I got back from America and Tristan told me you had lost our child, that you had died, he knew how much it would hurt me. I closed myself away at DenMerrick House. I drank to try and forget. I got very little sleep and I spent all my time thinking about you and that journal . . . and the past. I was feeling so many things—anger, pain, guilt . . . I hurt so much thinking that you were gone. I wanted to die, Kayte, because living without you would have been impossible."

"It was the same for me, Daevon. I could not have lived without you. I didn't want to."

"Kayte, I don't know why, but when I finally slept that night I remembered everything that happened the night they were killed. I went to my father's room. There was an argument. I opened the door and went in. Patrice was in the bed. She said something about me . . . I don't recall what it was exactly. My father grabbed me and pulled me into the room. My mother was standing in a corner with a pistol in her hand and another next to her on a table. My father asked her if she intended to shoot him in front of me, then pushed me back. I landed on the bed, and they fought for the gun. When it went off, my father fell. My mother was crying . . ." His voice trailed off and Kayte stroked his hair, waiting for the pain to lessen.

"She picked up the second pistol from my father's dueling case and shot again. Patrice was bleeding from the neck. I fainted. I didn't kill them, Kayte. All this time I thought—"

"Daevon, don't dwell on it. It's over," Kayte whispered, wrapping her arms around him and pulling his head against her breast. They held each other tightly, letting the last vestiges of pain drain away.

When Daevon pulled back, his eyes were adoring. Wordlessly, for endless moments he touched her—her hair, her face, the soft sweep of her throat. When his mouth touched hers for the first light kiss, she sighed and her lips trembled beneath his.

He lifted her into his arms and carried her into the main room of the cottage. There he stopped, his deep, throaty laughter ringing in the small space.

"Well," he said, "I'm certainly glad your friends paid us a visit."

Kayte looked around the room. A fire had been lit several hours before, but it was nothing but red embers now. The area in front of the hearth had been swept clean and cleared of furniture. A makeshift bed lay in the center of the floor, made of two single mattresses placed side by side and every coverlet in the cottage.

Kayte grinned. "Elizabeth brought your food. She wouldn't want your other appetites to be denied."

Daevon kissed her and let her slide slowly to the floor. He said nothing, but the smile he gave her let her know how he felt. Leaving her to stock the fireplace with more wood, Daevon found himself feeling something new. Freedom. There was no anger now, no guilt or sorrow. He liked the sensation. But even more, he liked the way Kayte made him feel. He crouched on the hearth, feeding the growing flames, watching them grow red-orange and hot.

"Daevon?"

He twisted to look back, and his reply caught in his throat. Kayte stood next to the bed, her wet gown in one hand. She dropped it to the floor.

"Kayte," he whispered. She was dressed in a nearly transparent shift, her hair hanging in freshly dried ringlets about her face and shoulders, the small wound that Tristan had made on her side arousing in Daevon a protective yearning. She was bathed in firelight and incredibly beautiful.

"About your other appetites," she murmured softly.

"Yes?"

She smiled seductively. "Can I satisfy them now?" Her voice was soft and throaty. With her forefinger, she slipped the straps of the shift off her shoulders. The bodice drifted down, barely covering the stiff rosy tips of her breasts.

"Or perhaps you aren't hungry." She let the shift fall.

Daevon rose slowly and came to her.

"I'm starving," he whispered against her mouth. He kissed her thoroughly, deeply, and stepped away. "Lie down," he ordered gently.

She settled on her back in the middle of their bed and watched as he stripped off his clothes, teasing her desire as she had his.

At last he lay beside her. They loved slowly, silently, then slept without dreams.

When Kayte woke, it was nearly dawn, but her body protested at the thought of rising so early. She grinned sleepily as Daevon slipped into the freezing air of the cottage to feed the fire, his oath emphatic.

He moved back into the warmth of the bed, and Kayte shivered when he pulled her against his cold skin.

"Daevon, you're freezing!" She giggled.

He smiled seductively. "You shall have to warm me again, my love," he whispered, his tongue tracing hot, wet lines along her throat.

"I'm sleepy, Daevon," she murmured teasingly.

"Ah, then perhaps a bit of persuasion is in order."

"Perhaps." She grinned.

His hands slid down to pull her hips against his, passion firing in his eyes when she groaned at the feel of his hardened shaft.

"Mmm. We shall see who's sleepy," he breathed against her throat.

He disappeared beneath the covers, his hands and mouth covering her with more heat than layers of wool or down or satin could ever have provided. He teased with kisses, his mouth and teeth tugging gently at the tip of one breast as his hand slipped between her thighs.

"Daevon," Kayte whispered, her voice and body trembling in the heat of passion.

He parted her thighs, holding his weight back, only the pulsing tip of him sliding against her wet, melting heat.

"We've broken the curse Ellen Merrick placed on the Merrick family," he murmured. "Forever."

"Um-hmmm," was all she could manage.

"Still tired, my love?" His kiss was thorough and exquisitely tender.

"Daevon," she said, hardly able to think of sleep. "Love me . . . please."

He brought them together with a groan, her sigh of pleasure adding to his need.

"I will love you with all my heart, all my soul," he whispered solemnly. "All my life."

CHERYL SPENCER

CHERYL SPENCER, a native of Akron, Ohio, now lives in the small college town of Wilmore, Kentucky (near Lexington). She and her husband, Mark, began dating while portraying lovers in a college production and were married six months later. They have two children: Anna, 5, and Caitlyn, 2. They are expecting their third child in late May and are praying earnestly for a boy.

Cheryl's love for writing began in the seventh grade. She finds that overcoming her own procrastination is much more difficult than getting rejection slips and that the best inspiration usually strikes her after 1:00 A.M. Cheryl loves to hear from her readers.